D1528419

MISSION

A. M. CORMIER

For Kim
He knows all the reasons why.

ACKNOWLEDGMENTS

I want to thank:

My mother, Joan, whose forbearance in the face of repeated loss, has long fascinated and inspired me;

My father, James, too soon gone, for passing on to me the love of laughter and vivid memories of the farming life;

Rene´ Smit, CNM, for helping us bring two healthy sons into the world and twenty years later, helping in the delivery of this work as well;

Mark Sargeant, a great friend and a patient tutor on matters military;

J. Mark Evans, M.D., superb orthopedist and all-around nice guy;

Both the lay and religious educators of Sacred Heart School and Van Buren District High School, for laying a foundation that has served me well.

ONE

It was hump day.
Midweek.

A day at University Medical when operating room suites were usually packed with orthopedic cases, and stretchers lined up halfway out to the waiting room.

I slapped my alarm clock into silence and grabbed the underwear and scrubs laid on the nightstand. Before I could succumb to the temptation of a bed willing me back into the nest of its early morning warmth, I flung free of covers, stumbled into the bathroom, and showered awake under a high-pressure assault of the hottest water I could stand.

I soaped.

I shampooed.

I spun shut the controls and whipped open the shower door to the condo's morning chill. Toweling dry, I whispered irreverently, "Mother of God. Why's it so cold?" then remembered I was the one who'd set the thermostat to sixty-two.

Naked and shivering before an oval of antique dresser mirror, I slipped into black bra and panties, then somehow forced my damp legs into support hose. Older and wiser co-workers insisted they were a must, and no matter how uncomfortable they were, I'd decided it was never too early to start the battle against my profession's ugliest liability, ye olde varicose veins.

Still half asleep, I rubbed on deodorant and squirted a dollop of moisturizer into my palm. I massaged the softly scented lotion into cheeks, fore-head, and chin, added sheer lip gloss, and voila! My morning make-up regime was complete.

I thanked God for good skin and a delicate bone structure, then topped off my efforts with a smear of number ten styling gel to give the mass of my dark, curly hair the illusion of control.

Good to go.

Scurrying around the condo, getting things ready to go, I remembered again that it was Wednesday. A host of cases were on tap. Hip replacements, bilateral knees, and rotator cuff repairs. Sometime during the day, the ER would probably ship up a couple of surprises—a compound forearm fracture that some kid had gotten popping wheelies or a shattered hip resulting from elderly inattention—and then it would fall to me to scrounge up staff enough to cover both the new cases and the surgeries that'd been on the schedule for weeks.

I'm a p.a. for a busy orthopedic practice—a physician's assistant—and on bad days that's code for someone crazy enough to take on whatever grunt work the orthopods throw my way. Not unreasonably, they like to focus on research and publishing, *raison d'etre* in teaching hospitals, and often leave me to manage the nuts and bolts of the practice's routine work. As a result, I'm part workhorse, part social worker, at times part shrink to my bosses' extracurricular aspirations. No matter that I go through the motions of griping, I'm never happier than when I'm juggling my assorted responsibilities and moving through the day at warp speed.

On a day like this one, I conduct pre-surgical interviews, order meds, and examine patients to make sure there are no new developments in pain or mobility before we wheel them into pre-op. I check lab results, certifying that elderly bodies, in particular, can handle the rigors of surgery, and I make darn sure I'm available to meet with anesthesiologists, our "gas passers," before the scheduled start of each case.

In the OR itself, I function as scrub nurse or surgical tech, depending on the need or physician preference. I handle aspects of surgery that once would've been the exclusive province of first year residents, holding retractors and closing surgical incisions. In wrapping up cases, I apply dressings, administer antibiotics, and often I'm the one assigned to follow up in the recovery room, making sure that patients are breathing well and not feeling inordinate post-operative pain.

On non-surgical days, I see patients in the clinic and make rounds on the floors. I rotate call:

Monday, Wednesday, Friday nights one week; Tuesday and Thursday the next. Every third weekend I provide 24-hour coverage for the group, 7 a.m. Saturday through Monday, same time, and it's the intersection of weeks one and three that can be a killer, requiring call on both ends of a full Monday schedule.

Call weekends have other drawbacks. Stuck on site, I often wind up skipping meals and gorging on popcorn eaten out of never-used plastic bedpans, some warped nurse's idea of grossing out visitors, no doubt, and I spend at least one night of the two tossing and turning on a slab of worn and exceedingly hard twin mattress in the interns' quarters, too wiped to make the drive home.

Somehow I survive, and I thrive.

On this late October morning, I was feeling the energy pinch. My intention of getting an early start had been thwarted, the twenty-nine year-old bod not moving quite as fast as it had when I was blowing through college and p.a. training. Running eight minutes behind schedule according to the stove's digital readout, I splashed hot coffee into a travel mug and threw on my worn L.L. Bean barn coat against the week's unseasonable cold. As I rushed out the door with a slice of peanut butter toast clenched between my teeth, I glimpsed a blurred image of myself in the hall mirror and said with irony, "Glamour thy name is Parise."

The elevator descended smoothly from sixth floor to the subterranean parking garage, and it took only a minute for me to reach my car nestled in its corner spot. The small and sturdy four-wheel drive, in addition to a snow-free, ice-free, potentially rapist-free parking space, were essential to me doing my job, the extra cost of high rise living worth every penny—at least until it was time for me to write the mortgage and condo association checks every month. In those moments when I was hemorrhaging cash, I was consumed by the thought that the same money could've paid for a small bungalow with trees and a yard in southern Maine, a place where the sea, the charm and the chance to run and play with the half dozen children my siblings had collectively fathered, were worth considering. Alternately, I saw myself in a loft close to the historic downtown of Winston-Salem, North Carolina, the city that had won my heart in the two years I'd lived there and had become (secretly) my number one favorite place in the world.

Unfortunately, I was hundreds of miles removed from either idyll, mired in a metropolitan area of five million and swearing, as I inched along in traffic, that one day soon I was going to leave. There was no way Washington was going to be the place I lived out the rest of my natural life.

I started the engine, carefully exited from beneath the garage's rising steel door, and hit the still-quiet streets of northern Virginia. As I drove, I took a good, hard look at my life.

My move to UMC had been a smart one. I'd seen and done more at University Medical than I ever could have in a less progressive, less busy practice. I had stretched and grown and garnered the respect of my colleagues over the last four years, but the professional experience had come at a price. I had a long, tough commute back and forth to work—about forty-five minutes going in and anywhere between an hour and three hours getting home at night, hampered by accidents, rain storms, or unseen traffic demons that often slowed the trek to a measly five m.p.h.

Headed into another twelve-hour day, though, I had few regrets. I loved my job; I did it well; unless struck by lightening or mind-blowing love, I looked forward to doing it, full bore, into the foreseeable future.

In the pre-dawn gloom, I veered off the Toll Road and sped onto the Beltway. A few miles later, I took the exit marked "George Washington Parkway," and merged into eastbound lanes slowing already and crowded with the expensive, late model cars that were a hallmark of life in the affluent suburbs. While politicians bellyached about insufficient revenues and budget shortfalls, there seemed more than enough local liquidity to sustain the ambitious well-to-do. Regular diners at the public trough, they drove Audis and BMWs; they passed me in Humvees massive enough to have part of the Iraqi invasion.

For the record, I'm not talking about your average federal employee or medical professional here, people who live the way people everywhere do, balancing savings and reasonable debt and being as fiscally responsible as they've been taught to be. I'm really describing the fat cats who make up the consulting industry's upper management and their close friends, the uber-lobbyists, diehards who pass through the revolving door between government and the private sector, building cost overruns into already bloated contracts then hiding behind the gates of their luxury estates bemoaning the state of the economy—or of late, their shrinking investments. These were people for whom the status quo was never sufficient, the need for huge homes, huge cars, and huge debt never-ending as they, consciously or not, made those in lesser circumstances want the same.

Even though it was still early, I was in the thick of things today, vehicles streaming past me toward the District, an unbroken chain of their winking taillights stretching into traffic infinity. I kept my crossover glued to the curves of the road I considered the region's most picturesque, moving steadily past hillsides, towering trees, and twinkling city lights intermittently visible through barren branches. The pavement was dry, the dark sky clear, and on the eastern horizon, there appeared a golden tracing of dawn.

Another beautiful day on the banks of the Potomac that I would ride out in the windowless warren of sterile, tiled rooms that collectively made up University Medical's vast operating room complex. If things went as expected, I'd work until five or six o'clock that night and become ensnared in the city's nightly exodus. I'd stumble back into my condo sometime around 7:30 and settle for a dinner of salad and Lean Cuisine consumed on a bar stool, watching The News Hour and wondering how long it would be before experts' glum economic projections made themselves felt more powerfully in my life.

Tomorrow I'd get up and do pretty much the same thing over again.

In a sudden flash of introspection, I saw my life as family and old friends might. Thirty years old this coming Christmas eve, I was a woman who, until the country's recent economic debacle, had accumulated an enviable balance in her 401-K and together with the bank, owned a home. I worked upwards of sixty-five hours a week at a career that required me to wear a cell phone glued to my hip, and I dated only sporadically, usually not the same man for long.

"Who would willingly marry that kind of woman?" I imagined my mother asking.

Who, indeed.

While my mother was a child of the 60s, in the literal if not the figurative sense, I think she'd missed the memo on the whole women's lib thing. She'd married young and devoted herself to home and hearth—a decision that worked out well for my siblings and me because it meant homemade meals and cozy days in our parents' bed when we were sick. There wouldn't be any "death prevention centers" for the St. Amand children, I'd heard my parents when they thought I was out of earshot, the term capturing perfectly their shared cynicism toward the abomination known as day care.

Similarly, while they both believed that family, friends, and neighbors should encourage and support parents in guiding children through life, they also thought that ultimate responsibility for the welfare and moral development of kids fell to their parents. Period. The old Harry Truman adage of the buck stopping here was especially apt in their view. For most people, they thought day care constituted an abdication of parental roles and was increasingly seen as necessary in a culture that couldn't or wouldn't be satisfied with the basics.

Given my mother's early choices, she was hard-pressed to support her only daughter's career aspirations. Whether from true conviction or from a capable woman feeling frustrated at the things she hadn't done, Mom occasionally accused me of being obsessed—with school, with work, with being a woman for whom disease and gore and the details of injury were a normal and frankly unappetizing part of everyday conversation.

"What eligible man would find that appealing," she challenged. "Some of us don't need or want to know all the disgusting details, Parise.

"Must you share?"

Well, yes.

I was trained to get accurate information from my patients. Could I help it if curiosity and bluntness bled over into the rest of my life? If the need for tact struck me as awfully time-consuming?

In low and lonelier moments I did concede, though only to myself, that my mother had a point. I could be borderline obsessive. Since finishing school, I'd gone from having a student's rather predictable schedule to putting in ridiculously long work weeks. I'd retired my student debt in under two years and had qualified for a special first-time buyer mortgage a year later.

In that same time, I'd managed only a single real vacation, a beach getaway with friends in which I'd traveled the length of North Carolina's Outer Banks studiously documenting each stop with pictures and video and post cards as though I might never enjoy myself again.

Little wonder my parents and siblings complained.

Just last week, my brothers Al and Brad had called to tease me. "We can't actually remember what you look like," Al said.

"Yeah. We hear you're still alive, but we can't find any physical evidence that the rumor is true," Brad added.

"I'll come up for Christmas," I'd promised, treating myself—and them by association—to two glorious weeks of northern Maine R&R.

On telephone extensions they'd mocked me in unison, "Sure."

I heard Al taunting, "I'm penciling you in as we speak . . ." as I was hanging up.

I refocused on the traffic darting in and out around me, feeling torn. While I was proud of doing my job well, I missed the days when I'd taken the time to drive up to Maine from Boston or North Carolina to join my brothers, and later their families, descending on Mom and Dad's house. Filling it with our noise, our demands for favorite meals, and a litany of off-color jokes that made Mom blush and shoo us away to confession.

In my Washington life, I didn't have time for any of that. I rarely met friends for leisurely dinners downtown or went to the KenCen to see a play. I'd even stopped riding my XS hybrid on Bike Virginia excursions, my weekends simply too busy with work.

Added to the things I felt were lacking in my life, I had a more important concern—one with eternal implications. While Parise Marie St. Amand was and always had been a committed Catholic, there was little outward evidence of that in her life now. In truth, I was disappointed at my faithlessness. I couldn't live without God.

I prayed to Him. I ran to Him for solace. I was aware and thankful that, with Him in my corner, I could handle anything life threw my way. Had handled it. While many criticized belief as the opiate of the masses, I saw it as the foundation of my life.

It bothered me that I wasn't making it to Mass more than once or twice a month—and that, usually on Saturday afternoons. Sitting at the back of St. Joe's, one of several hundred worshipers, I was often too exhausted to pay close attention and too out of touch with parishioners to do more than nod to a few whose faces I recognized on my way out.

This dearth of a spiritual life disappointed me, as did my lack of service to the community beyond my parish. While I blessed the name of John XXIII for his foresight in allowing the Saturday Mass alternative, an option that kept me from becoming a complete apostate, I wondered how he could have intuited, in the early 1960s, that forty years later society would be consumed by work and never more than a customized ring tone from its beckoning.

In reality, my excuse of heavy work responsibility was irrelevant. My great-grandmother had borne a dozen children and together with her husband, had grown and preserved nearly all the food it took to keep the family fed, never mind clothing and educating the brood. There was no justifying my spiritual sloth in the face of how hard that woman had worked, squeezing an hour here or there from the relentlessness of farm chores to function as Our Lady of Mount Carmel's organist and choir director.

Alone in my car, considering Grand-me´mere's hard life, I paraphrased scripture in the way a Jewish God might have. "The sick you'll always have with you, Parise. Me, not so much."

Falling away was not my style, nor was it my family's. While neither the St. Amands on my father's side, nor the Cyrs on my mother's, were breast beaters or active proselytizers, we did tend to be strong in our beliefs and faithful to doctrine in the relatively tame and honorable ways we chose to live our lives—a recalcitrant bachelor uncle addicted to gambling, a possible exception.

It didn't matter whether things were going well or had turned to crap. My aunts, uncles, and their

parents before them universally acknowledged
the blessings of health, intelligence, and stamina
inherited from their Acadian forbearers. They also
admitted, from ample evidence, that in and of themselves, they were a regularly sinful lot and didn't
see a problem with saying they needed God's help
in defraying the effects of their all-too-human
failings.

I was cut from that same spiritual cloth.

Nearing the city, traffic on the Teddy Roosevelt
slowed. There was no apparent reason for the
change, no accident, car fire, or ambulance bullying
its way through. Still, from a speed of 50 m.p.h., my
fellow travelers and I were down to inching along
under ten, a phenomenon common on the major
arteries in and around Washington, and something
for which traffic engineers rarely offered a precise
explanation or cure.

I downshifted and let the car coast. Alone with
my ruminations, I vowed to get back to the life I
wanted.

The life I needed.

I'd make time for close friends. Somehow, I'd
travel to visit family, because realistically, they
almost never made their way south. I'd get to the
gym, making sure that the fifteen irksome pounds
I'd managed to whittle from my five foot, two inch-
frame after the starchy college years, didn't creep
back on.

Last, and most vital, I would show God some
sign of life.

He'd been patient, I had to hand it to the Guy. He hadn't turned me to a pillar of salt or sent a plague of locusts to remind me Who was in charge. He kept sending people into my life who, by dint of the way in which they lived, interacted with, and cared for me, were exemplars of the person I wanted to become.

It was time I take the next step.

I'd work up the nerve and approach my boss Geoff to set up a one-on-one. I'd suggest we re-negotiate my hours and responsibilities, maybe even delegate a few duties to the newest class of residents, an ambitious lot not all that committed to the current division of labor.

The doctors in my practice were good guys. People. There was a woman in the mix. They could be made to see reason. Using a little finesse, I'd point out it was time to let others shine. Mention that while I was splinting fractures, wrapping sprains, and slowly sacrificing my fitness to work, the partners in the practice regularly ventured into the world of play. Two were members of a local rugby league, a sport so rough most colleges could no longer afford the insurance needed to sponsor it. Geoff and Sam Phillips loved the thrills of white water rafting, and Thom Stephens rappelled down the face of sheer granite cliffs in the Blue Ridge on weekends off. Even Nell Saunders wielded a mean, formerly semi-pro, tennis racket.

While I didn't want to go as far as they did wresting excitement from the jaws of my limited time off, I needed to get back into shape—a benefit both to the practice and to me. Tugging on a dislocated shoulder as I reduced it, or hanging traction for a badly fractured femur wasn't enough to keep me healthy.

Or sane.

My body and I longed for therapeutic play, but I had to put it in terms of dollars and sense. It was the only way miserly Geoff Tate would ever see the wisdom of my rationale.

I screeched into the hospital parking lot, somehow only two minutes off my customary breakneck pace. I quickly parked and made up the rest of my time by hightailing it into the massive brick-and-steel fortress that was my second home.

In the lobby, I bypassed a clot of sleepy employees waiting for the elevator doors to open, and with new resolve, used the stairs. I climbed them two at a time all the way to the fourth floor and made it into the dressing room, a little breathlessly, by 0638.

I was in pre-op, talking to our first patient of the day four minutes later, barely breaking a sweat. I reached for the chart hanging off the end of Liana Williams' stretcher and asked, "How you doing, kid?"

Even in a nondescript gown and bouffant patient headgear, the thirteen year-old was a stunning child. She had large, expressive eyes the color of Maine blueberries and a complexion that readily bloomed a blush. Her eyebrows, exquisite twin arches, looked perfect enough to have been professionally waxed, which, given the area's overall affluence, was not out of the question.

"I'm all right," Liana lied, anxiety marring her open features.

"Really?" I challenged. "Then what are we doing here?"

I winked at her hovering parents, and they smiled back. A reflex, I was sure. They were strung so tightly I could've plucked them like banjos.

Liana winced when I checked the pulse in her injured arm. "Sorry. Just making sure the blood's pumping through there the way it should."

I launched into a short explanation of what Liana could expect to have happen in the next little bit. I glanced at her parents, including them in the discussion. All three were my patients, and while I was judicious in the amount of detail I provided, I knew it was smart to keep everyone as informed as was practical. Information and concern were the best antidote to nuisance law suits, and I'd long included liberal doses of both as part of my bedside technique. Conversely, pontification was the absolute enemy of trust, and I avoided it at all costs.

"You're going to hurt for a while after surgery," I confessed to Liana. "Even with the medicine we're going to give you. But," and it was an important distinction, "it'll be nothing compared to what you've been through the last couple of days."

An active teenager, Liana had taken a header off a borrowed skate board on Sunday afternoon. Having unwisely shed elbow and knee pads in an effort to look cool, she'd shattered the distal end of her humerus, the bone of her upper arm, and had a second hairline fracture in the larger of the two forearm bones as well. We'd given the swelling a couple of days to subside but even with meds, she'd been miserable.

I gingerly initialed the area where one of her parents, under a nurse's supervision, had already marked the skin YES. I added an arrow pointing more precisely to the joint. "So. We're all in agreement," I concluded.

Liana still seemed apprehensive.

I grinned and took her healthy hand in mine. "Sam Phillips is the most brilliant elbow man in these parts," I told her truthfully. "When he's done, you'll be pitching your softball team to a state championship."

"I don't play softball," she told me.

"Okay then. You'll be ready for the Olympic diving team."

"Afraid of heights." Hint of a smile.

I sensed she wanted me to keep guessing. "Give me some help here. Tennis?"

"A lousy backhand." Now she was giggling. "Polo?"

"Not rich enough."

There went my eyebrow theory.

"How about this?" I said. "I promise when all's said and done, you'll be the same wonderful kid you were before this crazy spill. You'll be able to play a game of street hockey or take up snow boarding.

"You might even be able to grab the video game controls away from your brother." A prediction that seemed more to her liking.

Liana's eyes teared unexpectedly, and she sniffed back a runny nose. "Okay," she said, sparkling with new bravery. "I think I'm good."

It was about the best I could hope for from a teenager.

"I have to run," I told her, "but I'll be back before they wheel you into the OR."

"Promise?" she asked with renewed concern.

"Promise."

I jumped feet first into the day.

TWO

By midday I was firing on all cylinders. Three of our docs had cases scheduled, and I'd already been called up to provide one service or another for each of them. In OR 7, Geoff had had a hip nailing threaten to go long. The patient, an eighty-five year-old woman with history of heart disease, needed to be out of there, p.d.q., so after helping get Liana settled with Sam in OR 8, I beat a path to 7, where I circulated, adjusted the portable fluoroscopy unit for a nervous and inexperienced radiography student whose supervising technologist had thoughtlessly abandoned her, and I put in the last few sutures so Geoff and the chief resident, Tyler Spence, could prep for their next case.

OR 11 called as I was helping clear the hip's detritus to tell me that a newly-pregnant nurse who'd scrubbed in on the lumbar laminectomy, Susannah something or other, had vomited twice already, both times contaminating her gown and an instrument tray. "Can you sub?" the scheduler asked.

"Sure."

I affected a quick change of scrubs since mine were spotted brown with iodine and dried blood; took a few gulps of o.j. for energy; and changed my shoe covers. Scrubbed, gloved, and gowned, I bumped open the door to OR 11 with my backside, and within moments, was slapping instruments into Nell Saunders' competent hands, five exhausting hours into non-stop Go, Go, Go.

By one thirty, I'd collapsed into a corner of the staff lounge and was tearing into predictable cafeteria fare—a chicken Cesar salad, garlic bread, and a bottle of chocolate Silk—the second half of my work day still ahead.

"I hear it's been quite the morning for you," a male voice declared.

I turned and saw Rand Szabo approaching the scarred and stained coffee table where I'd planted my Nikes, his expression, as usual, inscrutable.

When he asked, "Mind if I join you?" I resisted the urge to be truthful and said, "No, not at all."

He dropped into the worn sofa across from mine.

My reaction to Szabo might have seemed a little hostile to the uninitiated, but let me say by way of explanation that Randall Atticus Szabo, Chairman of UMC's Orthopedics Department, was the one exception to my orthopedists-are-the-best-guys-in-medicine rule.

He was brilliant, not especially handsome, and demanding beyond reason of OR staff, floor nurses, and the army of allied health professionals who saw him coming and spun on their heels. Accounts of Szabo pitching scalpels at operating room walls, or of blistering attacks turned on new residents before packed conference rooms were legend. Even the partners in our practice didn't like the man all that much, though they and other Szabo colleagues diplomatically went the, "If you can't say something nice, say nothing at all," route when reports of his (mis)behavior raced through the hospital rumor mill.

The reason for their collective reticence?

They knew, as did we all, that if they or someone they loved suffered a serious, unusual, or potentially debilitating orthopedic injury, Rand Szabo was the first person in the world they would call.

Hands down.

Szabo was genius. He had come to University Medical about seven years earlier, a prodigy who'd finished high school as a young teenager, earned an undergraduate degree in engineering by the time he turned eighteen, and graduated first in his medical school class at twenty-one. By thirty, the man had completed the country's most demanding orthopedic residency and was working as an attending physician at one of Boston's premier medical centers, in his spare time having designed a revolutionary knee prosthesis whose universal adoption had made him a millionaire.

That said, it was Rand's world class talent, certainly not his personality or his questionable professionalism, that administrators at University

Medical had aggressively wooed. It was his brilliance, similarly, that they used in promoting UMC's image both here and abroad. Challenging cases, famous patients, and money came to Rand from around the world, and there were those pressuring him to accept the job of Medical Director, a position that someone with his talent could master in his sleep.

To his credit, Rand resisted the move upstairs. He was first and foremost devoted to patient care, and as far as I knew, nothing that anyone had offered had come close to changing his mind on that score.

Despite my reservations, I admired the man.

Until times like this when, sitting across from me, Rand bit into a sloppy mess of steak sandwich, chewed, noisily swallowed, and cleared his throat like a longshoreman alone on a dock.

In those moments, I was just the tiniest bit grossed out.

"Got many cases left?" Rand asked, spewing crumbs.

No pleasantries.

Okay then.

I averted my gaze as he dabbed at his chin with a wad of paper napkins, wiping away meat juices and the strand of caramelized onion just hanging there.

"A tendon release and a closed ankle reduction," I answered. Two could play at word thrift.

"Mmmm." As he chomped, he flung one arm back against cushions imprinted with the exhaustion of a hundred overworked staff. A thousand. Then he leaned forward and reached for a 20-ounce Coke, high test from the looks of it, and took an unhealthy slug. An orthopedist, of all people, should have known better than to ingest such swill—unless, of course, he thought osteoporosis was a good thing.

Without preamble, Rand declared," I hear a lot of good things about you."

How to respond?

Thanks?

That's nice?

I'm sure all of it's true?

I settled for a noncommittal, "Oh?"

He took another gargantuan gnaw from the leaking sandwich and spent a minute grinding it to a pulp. After swallowing, he cleaned away a spot of bread stuck to his teeth with a couple quick swipes of his tongue.

While I could stand pretty much any unappetizing display related to my job, watching Rand masticate was among the more disturbing sights I'd recently witnessed. But, genius had its privileges; I waited him out.

"I know this is short notice, and I apologize," he said, finally approaching what I hoped was the point. "Something's come up that I need help with, and frankly, you're the best candidate . . .

"Take that back," he rescinded. "You're the only candidate."

Don't let this be a job offer, I prayed. One couldn't gracefully and rationally rebuff the opportunity of a lifetime. Szabo walked on water hereabouts, and while very few people liked him, saying no to him would be professional suicide.

"It's like this," he continued. "I'm scheduled to leave in a few days on a medical mission trip."

Hadn't seen that coming.

"I had a full complement of staff scheduled to go with me until a couple of days ago. Two nurses; two physical therapists; three engineer types to help service equipment." His delivery was like automatic weapons fire. Steady. Unrelenting. Accurate.

"Judd Henderson had committed to coming," he informed me.

Henderson was an orthopedist from Georgetown whom I knew only by reputation. A great reputation.

"He's had to back out," Rand revealed. "I'm not breaking any confidences telling you that his daughter was just diagnosed with leukemia. He's spending every minute scouring the country for the best treatment options. Sloan. Hopkins. You know the drill."

"Of course." We'd all do the same.

"So here's the deal," he said, as though I hadn't just spoken. "We've got a bunch of cases lined up over there. Patients who won't be able to get treatment for six, eight months, if we don't get over before winter hits.

"For some of them, a protracted delay in treatment could mean they'll be permanently crippled."

He didn't have to spell things out. I saw where this was headed, and I felt my extremities go cold at the prospect. Heard my gut churn.

Rand threw back another slug or two of soda, burped softly, and spoke again. "I hope you won't mind, but I took the liberty of talking to Geoff."

My boss, Geoff?

"He tells me you're more than overdue for time off." This last stated as fact, not a question.

When I didn't respond, he spoke again. "I mentioned to him the pickle I was in, we were in, and he volunteered you to the cause.

"Only if you're willing, of course."

That was something.

"You wouldn't need to use vacation time," he assured me. "And you'd get a little change of scenery . . ."

And then some.

He grinned at his own forced sales job, then sobered before delivering the last part of his pitch. "You'd be helping out a lot of needy folks, Parry. And a few of my long, lost relatives."

I vaguely recalled that Rand's parents had been forced to leave their homeland decades earlier. The Czech Republic, was it? Some other country nearby.

"Are you going to Hungary?" I ventured.

"A neighboring country that has a large community of Hungarian expats. Some Ukrainians. A few other nationalities. It's a mix."

"Leaving when?" I asked.

At my curiosity, his expression changed subtly, and I saw that he thought he had me. He had the tact not to appear overconfident. "Sunday. Early evening. From Dulles." He smiled, then elaborated, "The flight is non-stop to Munich. We take a second, short flight to Budapest. After that, it's another 150 kilometers by bus." About ninety, a hundred miles if memory of the metric system served.

Altogether a long trip for someone not especially fond of travel.

No. That was being too generous. I was literally the only person in my circle of acquaintances with the nerve to admit she hated traveling. Domestic. Foreign. It didn't much matter. Trains and boats and planes, Burt Bacharach's sixties' melody notwithstanding, simply weren't my thing. It wasn't being in a foreign culture that bothered me; it had to do with the rigors of getting there. I longed for the advent of the Star Trek transporter age but alas, waited in vain.

"Our first case is scheduled for Wednesday morning," he told me. "We're due back the fifteenth."

Almost two weeks out of country! My stomach clenched.

"Do you have a current passport?" he asked.

I did. I'd applied for the thing because documents were necessary now even for quick trips into Canada from my parents' home in northeastern Maine. They lived a stone's throw from the border, and like other locals, they often ate at restaurants or shopped on the other side of the St. John. Thanks to the virgin-seeking madmen of 9/11 and increasingly brazen drug traffickers, everyone had to pack papers when crossing over, otherwise they couldn't get back into the U.S. It didn't matter that Customs agents on both sides of the river knew three generations of residents and felt silly asking, "Anything to declare?" They had to do their jobs.

"I'm up to date," I assured him.

He polished off the last of his sandwich and pulled a toothpick from the pocket of his lab coat. "Good to hear."

Evidently the thought of having to strong-arm the State Department into an expedited passport when he had a hundred other things to do between now and the time of departure didn't sit all that well. Nonchalantly grooming his pearly whites, he asked, "So, what do you think?"

I considered saying I thought only zoo animals performed acts of tidying in public, but I resisted. In truth, I was imagining the explosion of roadside IED's and suicide bombers making mincemeat of a market, nails and C-4 shredding and burning innocent flesh. Myself in the midst of all that.

Aloud I admitted, "I'm not sure what to think. I don't know enough to make an informed decision."

"You have questions. Shoot."

Intemperate words, given my frame of mind, but I forged ahead anyway. "For starters, Rand, I'm not sure how my going on this trip will solve the problem of Judd Henderson's NOT being there. Wouldn't you do better getting another orthopedist on board?"

"Sure," he told me honestly. "And believe me, I tried. Everyone I talked to had 'commitments.'"

I read disappointment in his gaze, but his voice was enthusiastic as he confided, "While we may get one or two fewer cases done without a second doctor, I have confidence in you. In your ability to complement my skills.

"You can take over pre-op screening and order meds. Help in surgery and post-op. I predict you and I can get through the bulk of the cases scheduled, if we put our minds to it.

"At the very least, the most serious cases."

I'd heard stories about Rand's superhuman stamina in the OR and, frankly, I knew I was a mere mortal in comparison. Most people were. How effective was I going to be if, in trying to keep up with him, I was blind with exhaustion?

"Parry, everyone in the group has turned his or her life upside down to make this mission trip happen." He leaned forward with sudden intensity. "Twice.

"We were due to go in August," he explained. "But things over there were iffy. Now, winter's almost here; this is our last chance to go until spring."

"Which brings me to my next question," I interrupted. "Where precisely are we headed?"

He spoke the name of the country in question, and my eyebrows peaked. I knew very little about it other than its former role as a Soviet satellite. A place of secrecy and danger, I thought, even with its evolving democracy.

"Aren't things unstable over there?" I confronted.

Media had spoken of unrest during the spring and summer, of escalating tensions between the pro-

American regime and military authorities whose troops, in their role as newly-minted U.S. allies, had been pressed into service in Iraq.

"The prime minister has made concessions," Rand claimed. "Several units were withdrawn from Mosul recently, and things seem to have quieted.

"The unofficial word from State is that we should be safe."

Not comforting, given the questionable accuracy of intelligence from that part of the world—and not all that long ago. I backpedaled to Rand's earlier reference. "The 'unofficial word' from State?" I echoed.

"You know that diplomatic types have to cover themselves," he answered. "My contact privately gave the trip a thumbs up after our briefing yesterday."

"What about weather?" I asked. "Will we be traveling into the mountains?"

"Nothing higher than about fifteen hundred feet. Long-term predictions indicate this will be a mild winter. We should be able to get in and out without hitting anything more serious than rain or a little sleet."

I had kept the most significant of my reservations for last. "You know, Rand, we've never worked together before." I hesitated before admitting, "I'm not convinced our styles would 'mesh' all that well."

"Diplomatic. I like that," he complimented. "Look. I know the reputation I have around here. But you have to understand, time has greatly embellished my actions. One flying scalpel and suddenly I'm a beast."

Apologetic grin.

"You have my word I'll behave. You're doing me a favor of monumental proportions. I won't let my considerable 'enthusiasm for the well-done job,'" he said, mimicking quotation marks with his index and middle fingers, "get the better of me. Or the situation."

It was a start. And consistent with the more admirable aspects of his character.

"I've never been to that part of the world," I confessed. "I don't have the first clue what to take."

He broke into an all-out smile, an act that transformed his features from ordinary to strangely appealing. His dark eyes sparkled eagerness, and his customary sternness was softened by fleshy dimples etched into both cheeks. "Linda can fax you a list of recommended gear and supplies." An OR nurse on permanent assignment to Rand, Linda Wellington was supremely competent and friendly. "This is her third time over."

"Who else is going?" I asked, emboldened by his uncharacteristically relaxed manner.

He cracked another smirk, this one marginally more triumphant than the last. "Ken Fortin. Paul Minnelli." Physical therapists I knew through contact on the job. Both were nice guys. Great therapists. Ken was a bear of a man in his early fifties while Paul, his partner in a successful practice, was an athletic and fun 40ish. Solid family men.

"So far so good," I conceded.

"Linda you know,"' she who had been a nurse almost as long as I'd been alive. "And Beverly Duke."

Interesting.

Beverly had a reputation as something of a prima donna. Beautiful and aloof, public opinion was divided on the issue of her competence. Some doctors loved having her as part of a team, saying she anticipated their every need; others, many of whom were accomplished, quietly avoided her when they could.

She was a whiner, according to her worst detractors, ready to take a break or a day off whenever she felt the need. She was married to the head of neurosurgery, Mason Duke, and worked only part-time, neither trait boosting her image among co-workers.

Given her husband's standing in the medical community and the worsening nurse shortage, though, Beverly was indulged and tolerated, if barely.

"So what do you think?" Rand asked again.

"Of Beverly?"

"No. Of joining us on the trip."

I lowered my feet from the coffee table, stood, and stretched out the kinks. "You need an answer this minute?"

"I can float you twelve hours," he offered. "Then I've got to call it."

"Generous," I said, imbuing the single word with irony.

I polished off the last of my soy milk and threw the remains of my salad in the trash. The ankle reduction was due to begin in minutes. "I'm intrigued," I told him honestly, "but I have to say this is all a little fast."

"Granted." He paused. "But, I'm not asking frivolously. When Judd backed out and none of my colleagues could get away, you were my one and only choice as a replacement."

Strange. There were easily three or four equally qualified p.a.'s at UMC; probably another dozen at hospitals across the Metro area, any of whom might have actually wanted to go. Short term mission trips were the going, sexy thing. Fairfax Hospital. Georgetown. GW and the Hospital Center. Teams traveled to Central and South America, the Caribbean, and Africa on an almost continuous basis from one or another of those facilities.

"If you turn me down," Rand explained a second time, "I WILL cancel the trip."

Standing there, needing to decide, my conscience dinged me.

People I'd never met were hobbling on broken ankles, trying to work and feed their families through the winter. I envisioned others handicapped by misshapen hands and wrists; by fingers crippled with unhealed fractures or malfunctioning tendons; by a host of arthritic changes that would put pressure on the healthy joints, compensating for sick ones, making already arduous lives much harder than they needed to be.

I juxtaposed those difficulties with my little reverie in the car earlier; the way I'd told myself then that I needed time away; that I wanted to serve.

"Well, chickie poo," I imagined God saying, "here's your chance."

Why hesitate?

Several reasons came to mind.

First, the trip was to an unstable part of the world, and here I'd let my surface-to-air certification lapse! Second, I had virtually no time to prepare. Finally, there was the matter of my mother, sure to use everything in her maternal arsenal to get me not to go—the well-rehearsed weeping, wailing, and gnashing of teeth.

Could I handle the load of guilt she'd inflict once she got wind of this plan?

I looked at Rand's hopeful face and came within a whisper of declining. Of letting what were really only excuses keep me from a higher purpose.

Hand on the doorknob and turned to run, I heard a voice asking in a calm and reasonable way, "So, Dr. Szabo, where do I sign up?"

The voice was mine.

THREE

"WHAT?" my best friend Alana shrieked from her end of the line. "YOU'RE GOING WHERE?"

I switched my cell phone to "speaker," to preserve what little was left of my hearing. I repeated for her the details to which I was privy.

Alana did me the courtesy of listening, but when I finished, she accused, "You haven't driven the measly five hours to visit us in almost a year, and now you're going to the third world on a lark??

"What's up with that?"

"Second world," I corrected, "and this isn't pleasure travel." A contradiction in terms if ever there was one. "From the look of the schedule Szabo's nurse faxed me, we'll be working like fiends."

Alana understood the concept of timely intervention; I shouldn't have to explain it to her. She was a physician's assistant, too, and while she'd gone the cardiology route, handing out statins and coercing patients at Duke into healthier lifestyles,

I hoped there was more to her concern for patients' welfare than extolling the virtues of diet, exercise, and the routine flossing of teeth. On some level, she had to identify with my desire to help.

Okay. Realistically, she might not.

Alana and her work-addicted husband Trent were nicely established in their careers and together, if I had to guess, they brought in an easy $175,000 a year. They were building a life that reflected their dual incomes, living in a great neighborhood just outside Raleigh. They had a beautiful home with killer kitchen, assorted fitness toys, and high-end furnishings of every description: silk curtains (synthetics were so déclassé); a massive sectional sofa in the man room; and staid wing chairs in the living room primly angled toward a fireplace large enough to accommodate a man. All the bathrooms in the house featured handmade Mexican tiles and granite countertops (what else?) and on the bedroom walls there hung original works of art, a few so appealing I'd been tempted to cut canvases from their frames and spirit them home with me to beautify my too-neutral condo walls.

No matter the beauty of Alana and Trent's home, after a weekend luxuriating in their stuff, I became mildly depressed by the perfection of their settled suburban lives.

Yeah, I know. Pot calling the kettle black—an impolitic reference for which I apologize. I too lived in trendy and expensive digs, but there was a difference. I had bought my home on a short sale at way-below market price, and it was a living space

I considered more an investment than a home. One day I'd sell the thing and get to my real life, but in the interim it precisely fit the bill.

As far as my car was concerned, yes, it was relatively new and certainly pricier than any I'd had before. But in my defense, I drove my first car, a 1993 Geo Prism, into the ground. What else could a girl do with a hefty bonus than buy a more reliable ride?

Finally, while I complained as loudly about Washington, D.C.'s high crime rate as any middle-aged suburbanite who chose to work but not live in the District, the difference between them and me was that, in my heart, I was still the kid who'd grown up in edge-of-the-earth northern Maine, wearing the secondhand clothes of kids whose parents, while not rich by city standards, had a heck of a lot more in their bank accounts than my parents had in theirs.

And though I had a few nice things now, I knew I could be happy with less. Had been happy with less.

I knew I had too much stuff. I thought so every morning as I left for work and again every night when I unlocked the door to my sleekly modern condo. I was painfully aware, in my heart of hearts, that I was different from friends and acquaintances who were constantly looking and planning for the next big thing.

The next pay increase.

The next toy.

The next rung on the ladder of professional achievement.

Sadly, little about my external life set me apart from them, and it was that, more than anything, that had to change.

I looked down at the things I'd started accumulating for the trip and at the soft-sided luggage open on the floor to receive them. No more time for navel gazing, I thought. "Alana, hon, I've gotta go.

"See you soon."

"Heard that one before," she laughed as I clicked off.

I got busy. I compared the list of must-haves with what I'd collected so far. Five sets of scrubs and two pair of solid work shoes. "Be sure to take extras," Linda had advised. "We'll be working you hard."

I'd purchased the recommended over-the-counter meds—Tylenol, Pepto, and anti-diarrheals. Water purification tablets. For food I had tuna and salmon in sealed pouches. A small stash of beef jerky. The diet in our host country, while filling, didn't always provide adequate protein, I'd learned, hence the need for food.

I'd bought travel-sized toothpaste, deodorant, and hand lotion. I'd been to Stein Mart to buy two sets of bamboo underwear to keep me warm in what was reputedly the coldest OR I would ever experience.

"The hospital rarely turns on the heat before December," Linda explained. "Even when weather conditions get a little nasty. They run things strictly by the calendar." Long-sleeved underwear, thick tights, or merino wool turtlenecks were *de rigueur* under scrubs, and I was advised to bring all I had.

Check.

In the short time since I'd agreed to go, Rand had handled the transfer of Judd Henderson's e-ticket, climbing the Lufthansa pecking order until he found someone sympathetic to the cause, someone who'd written off extra charges. He'd also retrieved the sleeping bag good to ten degrees below zero and the camping cot that Judd had paid for out of his own pocket, both necessary given our limited accommodations overseas.

We'd be sleeping in the basement of an orphanage, Rand had finally divulged. The women of the group would be sharing bathrooms with girls ages five to fifteen, another bit of information left out of his initial courting.

Such a man!

My cell rang, and it was Alana again. Without a hello or a, "Hey, listen to this," she started reading—shouting—information to me gleaned from various websites. She rattled off a list of potential dangers at 120 decibels. "EARLY CASES OF INFLUENZA. SPOTTY WATER QUALITY. HERE'S AN INSTANCE OF MARTIAL LAW BEING DECLARED JUST LAST YEAR!!"

"Alana, hey. Hey. Quiet down.

"I prefer not to listen to speculation. Anyone with a computer can post anything."

Call me Pollyanna, but I thought there was something to the notion that expecting the worst sometimes attracted it. "I appreciate your concern. Really I do. But I've made the commitment. And I still have to do laundry and figure out how I'm going to get about a hundred pounds of stuff into two carry-ons.

"I'll talk to you when I get back . . ." I promised.

"Parry . . ." she interjected.

"What?"

"I can't talk you out of this, can I?"

"You really can't."

A few seconds passed then a more sincere Alana said, "All right, then. You be careful."

That was the old Alana, my buddy through thick-and-thin.

"I will. We'll be fine. I'm sure Rand's anticipated the pitfalls. He won't let anything bad happen to us."

I decided to throw her a bone. "There are a couple of engineering wonks coming along, I just found out. I hear one of them's a former Army Ranger."

"That sounds good."

"It could be. He's evidently 'concerned' about being trapped in-country, so he's taking freeze-dried rations and maps and who knows what else."

"Great."

I let myself get seduced into a few more minutes' excited chatter and promised to relay every exciting bit of my adventure to her when I got back.

I hung up on Alana a second time, cautiously confident I'd be all right.

Didn't I always land on my feet?

FOUR

Only weeks from my thirtieth birthday, a burst of familial concern, some subtle, some downright obnoxious, had erupted over the matter of my marital status.

This was nothing new. *Tante* Yvette regularly pinched my cheek at Christmas gatherings, telling me what a pretty girl I was, oh, and did I ever consider that carrying those few extra pounds might not be a good thing?

Me'mere St. Amand, a woman for whom food was life's panacea, had a different approach. She waved me over to the kitchen table the moment I walked through her kitchen door and served me homemade bread pudding slathered with whipped cream. "*Finis ça,*" she encouraged if I did anything less than lick my plate clean. Finish that. Then as a way of inspiring me, she turned the subject of her progeny, six great-grandchildren at last count.

For the decade of my twenties, I'd been able to ignore or tune out most of the curiosity or advice directed my way, but in the last year the comments had become a virtual cacophony.

Aunts. Cousins. Friends. Even my brothers, not usually given to interfering in their little sister's love life, weighed in. Did I hate men, the boldest of them, Tom, asked in a recent telephone conversation.

What???

"You do tend to talk a lot about the bad things that've happened to friends of yours, Parry, and sometimes it sounds like you're really down on the male of the species."

"I don't hate them, Tom. But I gotta say, sometimes I hate what they do to women."

He considered my stance and said without rancor, "You know, there are travesties on both sides of the sexual divide."

Of course he was right. Meanness. Hurtfulness. Lack of loyalty. None was a sex-linked characteristic.

I'd wanted, in that moment, to tell Tom, to tell everyone hounding me, that while my affection for them was not always obvious to the casual observer, I really did like men. I admired their straight angles and easy heft and the direct, sometimes ruthless, way they let one another know what was on their minds.

I loved tall men, compact men, and medium-sized specimens. I appreciated a well-developed musculature but also felt both charmed by, and protective of the intellectual whose pale fragility had become entrenched after years of library living.

I found appealing men who had thick heads of hair, those who were neatly (honestly) balding, and those who'd gone the decidedly offbeat way of the clean and shiny ponytail.

Unbeknownst to those who pitied me—you know, alone in the world and all—I kept close tabs on the males available out there. I did want to get married and have children and share my pretty terrific life with someone, but I also knew I couldn't force it to happen.

Wouldn't force it to happen.

In fact, I took a completely opposite approach.

If after dating someone a few times, I had the distinct feeling that our seeing one another wasn't ever going to lead to anything permanent, I quickly extricated myself from the relationship. Sometimes I was awkward about it, occasionally I was beastly. Most of the time, I just made it clear by my unavailability that, hey, buddy, you'd probably be better moving on. I wasn't into the drama of prolonged goodbyes.

This meant I spent a lot of time alone, so it wasn't all that unusual, when I found myself jogging through a local park or past a college athletic field, that I stopped to ogle a boisterous crowd of males from the perspective of a comfortable bench or bleacher. As they tossed Frisbees or played vigorous games of flag football, I appreciated the golden hairiness of their legs and forearms in summer sunshine—or their backsides walking past in tight jeans. I took secret delight in seeing their biceps bulk and ripple as they strained against the challenge of a beefy tackle or dived to make a great catch. Bottom line, pun intended, I considered the Maker's handiwork, in having created men, to be unassailably D-I-V-I-N-E.

I was distinctly aware of the negatives men brought to life as well.

I'd been known to detect the smell of an over-heated and under-washed man at fifty paces.

You know it. You've smelled it. The pungent man-odor that trails behind a young male who's just mowed the lawn or played tennis in 95-degree heat. I'd often yelled at an offender, usually one of my brothers, "Hey, take a shower!" but furtively, incon-sistently, I envied the way men rarely apologized for looking, living in, or creating a mess.

It must be liberating not to care.

Which brings me to a tangentially related point: I am impressed by men who exude enthusiasm for their latest professional or personal endeavor and admire, too, those who are quietly pensive before answering a question that draws on their studied expertise. I'm drawn to the modest intellectual and am grateful as well for the talented craftsman. Electrician; car mechanic; a particularly gifted carpenter who can create, from my vague and some-what uninspired description, the bookcase, coun-tertop, or china cabinet of my dreams.

In sum, wherever and whenever there abides in man a passion for quality, I am duly stirred.

On a spiritual level, ultimately the part of me that matters most, I'm drawn to the agnostic who admits to doubts in his disbelief but who tries to live by a strong moral code despite the uncertainty. I find even more appealing and comforting the believer who tempers faith with the awareness that not every person he meets has discovered, or has been discovered BY, the grace of God.

In my time dating, nearly fourteen years, I've cared for a variety of men. Roman Catholic, Baptist, and non-denominational Christian. I'd even found appealing, no matter that they aren't technically monotheistic, a Mormon male or two. It's a searcher's heart that attracts me. Just as surely, it will be a man whose life is committed explicitly or implicitly to God who will find himself paired with me for life.

Sound hokey?

Only to those who've never felt at their core the Spirit's warm, slow burn.

On hearing the aforementioned list of my likes and dislikes, many would probably relegate me to the "Man Mad," pile, but let me state for the record, they would be sorely mistaken. If anything, my strong feelings for men have made me behave with greater restraint and tempering, both traits that I come by naturally.

You see, being neither blonde nor exotic, I am a woman men can and have easily overlooked. I don't believe they consider me grotesque or off-putting; many chat easily with me and flirt. They ask me out. Still, there are times when I've had the sense, as a manly gaze drifted over my shoulder to the va-va-vooms coming through the door, that I knew the passion I fire in men takes more than my modest physique as "kindling."

This handicap, if you will, has served my purposes. I've had the luxury of concentrating on school and advancing in my field while gorgeous girls are picked off by men for whom looks or sexual attraction are a primary motivator. I've also had the time to pursue an intense relationship or two with men for whom intellect and humor have counted for more than a boss set of headlights and a tight caboose. (Sorry. The legacy of my grandfather's WWII lingo dies hard.)

In my solitude, I've often taken the approach, with men, of, "Look but don't touch." I figure there'll be plenty of time for manhandling when I find the one with whom I am destined to be joined.

In the interim, I see myself as not that different from other women. I love children and want a few of my own someday. I'd like a good man to take home to my parents, someone who'll stand by me in good times and bad; who'll protect me from the world's pain and know how to argue with me when the time is right. I want a man who'll see me and all my flaws and all my peculiarities and who'll still want to hold me at night, lying through his teeth, "Hey, Parry, you're not weird."

Until that man falls into my lap, my plan is to live my life straight out. Getting the most from my job; making a difference in the small sphere of my world; spending a little more time on hot North Carolina beaches with girlfriends and, in the grips of a second or third cold beer in as many hours, keeping a keen eye out for potential mates and saying as an especially handsome one strolls by, "Praise the Lord, and pass me the binoculars!"

I am human after all.

FIVE

The day before leaving, I made the dreaded call to family.

I knew that while my mother loved the idea of sacrifice in the abstract, both admiring and supporting the efforts of missionaries through prayer and donation, if following God's will involved the slightest risk to the health or safety of someone close to her, more specifically someone who had made the short but grueling trip from her womb to the dangerous world outside, Mom lobbied hard and vocally against that person putting him- or herself in harm's way.

Her reaction on hearing of my proposed escapade was not, therefore, surprising. "You're going WHERE?"

Shades of Alana.

There followed a stream of questions, highly detailed and interspersed with a rant of colorful expletives that would've made the most seasoned prison inmate blush. She wasn't thrilled, no matter my trip's high purpose, and she didn't hold back citing every last reason why I should not go.

For the record, my mother is a voracious consumer of all things news-related—CNN, MSNBC, the fair and balanced FOX. At my mention of the small and impoverished country that was our mission team's destination, she shifted into full panic mode. "Haven't you read about what's happening in that part of the world," she demanded of her educated daughter. "It's where they killed all those school children . . ."

"That was in Russia, Mom. And it was four years ago."

"No, it was more recent than that. The Russians sent in their tanks only a few months ago."

"Into Georgia, Mom, they went into Georgia and that was over an oil pipeline. Nothing to do with children. Or Americans."

"Georgia?" she challenged incredulously. "What are you talking about?"

"The former Soviet Georgia," I clarified patiently. "Not the one north of Florida."

I had to smile.

While my mother watched three to four hours of news programming every night, she was often simultaneously preoccupied with whatever needle-work lay at hand. Knitting. Crocheting. Tatting. The last was a complicated and delicate threadwork whose practice had nearly died out, but Mom was one of a handful of women helping resurrect it in her corner of the world.

Bottom line: Mom's attention to news content was often diluted by the need for precise counting or needlework, thus her problem synthesizing an accurate overview of international events.

"I'm going to be all right," I assured her. "Really. I'll be gone less than two weeks. If we steer clear of drug traffickers and Al Queda, I'm sure we'll be left alone."

"Parry!" she scolded. "Don't even mention those thugs!"

It was fun yanking her chain.

I reminded her, "*Matante* Lucie spent years in Zaire." Now again, the Congo. "The times were dangerous then, too, but she survived."

A missionary, *Tante* Lucie had witnessed criminal acts that, to this day, she only made oblique reference to. She confirmed information in magazine articles or books, if asked, but clearly she wanted to leave the worst of her memories in the past.

Fifteen years older than my mother, a retired *Tante* Lucie was back in the United States and working in a New York City hospice now, but for more than a generation she'd helped build clinics in the most remote parts of Africa. Ironically, there were times now when she was probably in greater danger in her South Bronx convent than she had been riding a Jeep through the African wilds.

"It almost killed *Me´mere*, her being over there," Mom said softly. I heard the tears in her voice and felt her fear, but I also remembered my grandmother's grace, letting go.

"*Me´mere* didn't stand in *Tante* Lucie's way," I reminded her.

I'd been witness, at age nine, to *Matante*'s first home visit in a decade; to her joy at using indoor plumbing and eating hot dogs and ice cream and cake. I had seen her running barefoot with my cousins in an impromptu game of baseball, long skirts hiked to her knees, euphoric in the Valley's cool summer air.

I'd been there at her leave-taking four weeks later, waving goodbye. *Me´mere* Cyr's bearing had been formal and upright as she bit back her sadness. *Pe´pere* was gone. She lived alone in her little house in town, the farm long since sold.

I remember her dignity hugging *Tante* Lucie goodbye.

Kissing her.

Straightening her veil in a mother's small gesture of love.

The quiet sacrifice had left a vivid and lasting impression on me, and I could tell from her reaction that Mom had been affected as well. "Go then," she said. "I'll keep busy." Which for her meant morning Mass. Votive candles. Hissy fits as she warned God that He'd better keep her only daughter safe.

I gave Mom my itinerary and contact information: an e-mail address and telephone numbers for the State Department in Washington and for American embassies in Vienna, Budapest, and our country of destination as well. "You'll never have to use any of this stuff," I predicted. "But, it's good to have."

She was silent at her end, probably too sad or too worried to speak. "I'll talk to you when I get back," I promised. "Tell Dad I said goodbye."

"He'd have stayed to talk a little longer if he knew why you were calling," she assured me. "You know how he hates the phone."

I did. "Tell him I'm sorry, too."

My grumpy but lovable old man.

"*Au revoir*," I said then, affecting a Parisian accent.

Hearing me use proper French, she often called me a snob.

I grinned when Mom whispered back, "*Au revoir, la p'tite.*" For the first time in her life, she sounded downright Parisian.

SIX

Rand had style, I had to give him that. To save us all time, money, and the aggravation of airport parking, he hired a limousine to collect us, beginning at Beverly Duke's NW Washington manse and working his way around the Beltway to my complex just off the Toll Road.

From here, it would be a straight shot to Dulles.

"We're pushing the two-hour pre-flight arrival time," he called to report. "Can you be ready at the curb?"

"Sure."

"We'll be there in twenty minutes."

"See you then."

I struggled with the two massive paisley carryons I'd originally purchased for their unmistakable appearance on airport turnstiles and realized, pushing them through the building's front door, that no male thief, straight or gay, would ever be caught dead stealing the garish turquoise and peach print.

Two benefits for the price of one, I thought. How did I do it?

I positioned myself under the massive awning outside, and before long I was shivering in a strong west wind, a Maine girl gone wimpy after a dozen years away. I pulled a scarf over the lower half of my face, watched for the promised limo, and reviewed a checklist of my suitcases' contents one last time.

If memory served, I had extra underwear, tampons, and mini-pads — my period due to make its ill-advised appearance on the day we flew home. Packed tightly in whatever spaces I'd found, there were towels, a small pillow, vitamins, and protein snacks.

In a passport holder, I'd arranged the documents needed to get through airport checkpoints as well as a cache of American dollars and euros, the latter accepted throughout the region to which we were traveling. I'd also thought to bring a disposable camera and paperbacks on the off chance I had the opportunity or desire to use either one. The comfort of my tush always a priority, I'd included two rolls of toilet paper, flattened, a resource purported to be in short supply abroad.

"Enough." I'd packed and re-packed three times already. If there was something I'd forgotten to take along, someone in the group would have to provide, or I'd muddle through. No amount of planning or worrying or checking Internet travel sites could anticipate every contingency, but in the short time given to me, I had tried.

I heard before I saw the Caddy. The engine growled. The tires squealed rounding a corner. The right rear fender grazed a hedge of crimson-leaved shrubbery as the ungainly vehicle entered the semi-circular drive and lumbered past.

Rand emerged from the shotgun seat as it came to a stop, hands reaching already for my gear.

"Did someone cancel a wedding?" I quipped.

"I requested black," he growled. "Not that the reservations manager cared."

One of the back doors opened, and Ken Fortin threw out a leg the size of a tree trunk. "Parry? How the hell are you?" The affable giant pulled me into a crushing hug.

I moaned, "Ahhhh!" as he squeezed, pretending that he'd robbed me of my last breath.

Ken and I knew one another from dozens of consultations, and although we never socialized, we had a habit of jawing like old friends when thrown together. "I can't believe you're coming on this trip," he said. "I wouldn't have pegged you for the type."

"Why? What type do you think I am?" I asked, launching the larger of my carry-ons in his direction.

Holding Exhibit One at arms length, he observed, "Kinda girly. I don't see you roughing it."

"Then you don't know me all that well, mister.

"As for the luggage," I explained, "I use it because it's easy to spot."

"Mission accomplished," he teased.

"I am NOT girly," I insisted petulantly. "I'm from good peasant stock. Farming people. Check out these muscles."

I affected a bicep curl. Allowed him a peek at my calves. "I'll have you know, my good man, that I was a champion potato picker in my day!.."

"That all may be true," Ken said, grinning. "But you always have your hair cut nice, and you smell good. All of which says girly to me."

"You don't get out enough," I told him.

"That could very well be . . ."

Rand stalked peevishly back in our direction. "You two want to take old home day into the car. We're still running behind."

Ken winked and bid me enter the car's interior. Once we were in, he introduced me all around.

His partner Paul, still tall and still athletic, flashed me a grin. "Miss Parry," he said, greeting me with an exaggerated twang.

"Paul," I acknowledged. "Good to see you."

Linda Wellington waved hello, and Beverly Duke managed a nod.

"Ladies," I said deferentially. We knew one another from the OR but only rarely spoke.

"This is Rich Marberry," Ken continued. "He's an electrical engineer who consults with UMC occasionally."

"Rich," I said sliding in next to him on the far side of the limo. "Nice to meet you." We shook hands and at his cool, almost limp touch, I sensed he wasn't the former Ranger.

"Ted Ellison. Ted's a heating and air conditioning guy."

Ted wore a spotty beard and glasses cloudy with fingerprints. Hardly the trained killer type. "Ted," I acknowledged, saluting him across the pile of suit-cases between us.

"Last but not least, Jake Spangler," Ken announced.

A solidly built man probably in his mid-thirties, Jake looked to be about five feet nine and really in shape. Seated conveniently closer to me than Ted was, he reached for my hand and gave it a firm, efficient press.

"Rich and Jake are going to be installing a back-up generator and updating as much of the hospital wiring as they have time to," Ken explained.

"Provided we can make sense of these," Jake qualified. He held up a set of blueprints. "Didn't get 'em 'til last night, so we're gonna have to cram.

"Pleasure to meet you, Parry," he added politely.

I gave Jake a discreet once over. He had laughing green eyes speckled with amber flecks. The fan of his dark eyelashes contrasted attractively to sandy, sun-bleached hair he wore clipped short. From his accent, his manners, and a cowboy boot displayed prominently across one knee, I suspected Mr. Spangler was a Southwest boy.

The very kind of man to whom I was most vulnerable.

That said, I turned my attention to the other passengers. Asked about their families; how they had managed to get the time away. I sat back listening to their answers and enjoying the ride, eight of us and our considerable belongings wedged into the rear passenger compartment while Rand hunkered down next to the driver, feeding him a constant stream of superfluous instructions.

Turn here.

Don't let that car go first!

Can't you PASS this truck?

It was a minor miracle the limousine driver didn't drop him by the side of the road. Instead, he disgorged the lot of us at the Lufthansa terminal a few minutes before four.

Rand, ever-imperious, sprang from the car, directing us to help with equipment as we lugged our own bags to the curb. He stood guard, matching container labels against the list on his clipboard. "Sterile sponges, towels, and suture sets.

"Portable autoclave.

"Traction bars and ropes; hack saws.

"X-ray film. Tough to find now that digital's pretty much taken over."

Not a soul was listening to the man.

Instead we were following our instincts and putting personalized airline tags on everything we took along.

Rand had pre-arranged to have things checked curbside, as he reminded us several times, "No need to take anything all the way inside."

Okay. Got the message.

When all our personal bags had been piled on carts, Rand herded us inside as a group. We collected boarding passes from kiosks, joined the disgruntled masses shuffling toward TSA checkpoints, and rode the ugly mobile lounges to midfield, the process taking us a full forty-five minutes.

Had I mentioned I hated traveling?

Somehow we shuffled into the area surrounding our assigned gate with time to spare and accepted Ted's offer to guard carry-ons as we dispersed in search of a last American meal. "Anyone happen to notice Chinese?" I asked without irony.

"Bei Jing Express has a counter up about five gates," Jake volunteered. "Decent for airport food."

"Have you eaten there?" I asked. I didn't want a second-hand recommendation.

"Lots," he assured me. "I travel for my job. I have the menu memorized if you'd like to make your selection now."

"Moo shoo?" I inquired.

"Pork or chicken. With or without pancakes."

"I'm set."

I started to leave then remembered Ted. "Would you like something?"

He smiled gratefully. "Won ton soup and an order of egg rolls?"

"You got it."

"Make that two orders of egg roll." More in keeping with his girth.

Jake looked up from the blueprints he was studying. "Mind if I join you? Chinese sounds good."

"By all means. Anybody else? Going once, going twice . . ."

"Whopper for me," Linda said. "I need beef to tide me over."

Beverly responded to the invitation by holding up a bottle of overpriced designer water and a plate of sashimi, neatly shrink-wrapped.

Elegant food, I thought. Mannequin food.

Sitting hunched over a pile of folders, Rand had a cell phone pressed to his ear and was berating some unlucky slob at the other end of the conversation, someone who'd clearly blown an important assignment. Food was the last thing on his mind.

I caught a glimpse of Rich, Ken, and Paul sauntering in the direction of a steak place we'd passed, so that left only Jake and me.

Fortuitous.

We made the short trip to Bei Jing and ordered our meals. We ate at a small clutch of plastic tables, our eyes tracking the parade of people moving past. Some were bedraggled from flights coming in, others frazzled as they rushed to their gates. Gone were the dignified passengers of travel's golden age, I thought, people who'd dressed to impress as they left home.

"You know," I said to Jake, "when you look at old pictures of people taking plane trips in the '40s and '50s, the men are wearing shirt and tie. The women have on tasteful ensembles with heels and matching purses.

"Flying was glamorous, once upon a time. As was train travel. Decorum played a role."

Now? A much different story.

People herded onto planes and buses and trains dressed in a variety of get ups. Jeans. Shorts. Cheap business suits that wrinkled and crinkled and overall, looked pretty bad. "It's a paradox of the modern age that as fabrics become increasingly easier to launder and care for, we Americans have never been a sloppier looking bunch."

Stretched out t-shirts. Pant hems undone. The occasional midriff overhanging a waistband, especially poignant when worn by chubby teenaged girls trying to fit in.

Jake concurred and pointed out, "It isn't enough we schlep around in worn and rumpled clothes, we have to carry incredible amounts of equipment wherever we go.

"It's like we're afraid, for a weekend—or a minute—to be without every convenience of life."

I agreed with that observation. "The last time I went camping, there were maybe five tent sites for every thirty RV spots. So while my friends and I pitched a tent and tried to blow life into our campfire, we got to do it in the shadow of air conditioners, washing machines, and side-by-side refrigerators."

A slight exaggeration, maybe, but it had seemed that way.

"You're going to the wrong campgrounds," Jake told me. "I know a bunch of primitive spots within an easy drive of D.C." Places he and his friends went to really get away. "I can recommend a few when we get back."

"I'd like that," I said, meaning it.

I would like that very, very much.

"You done?" he asked as I was reading my fortune cookie. "We're gonna be boarding soon."

"Oh. Sure."

I picked up the food for Ted, and we walked back. After delivering the soup and egg rolls, I claimed the last seat saved for the group. In the row directly behind me, Linda engaged Ted in warm conversation. Over her shoulder, I glimpsed photographs he pulled from his wallet. Between bites, he showed himself with a plain and tall woman (named Sarah, perchance?) and their trio of extraordinarily beautiful children. The youngsters' faces, broad and filled with light, beamed intelligence.

Beside me, Paul had pulled a Nationals' ball cap down over his face and was catching a few pre-flight zzz's, his body evidently exhausted already, trying to digest the slab of Angus beef he'd eaten as a hedge against protein deficiency. Beyond him, the vainglorious Beverly sat preternaturally still in her scoop of padded airport chair. Her straight black hair was youthfully styled, I noticed, and her make-up subtle but striking. Her lips were a smear of delicate coral, and her eyelids smoldered blue-gray. She wore bronzer on her cheek-bones, a color that might have seemed brash on someone less sophisticated, but on her? I had to say it looked great. In fact, she looked like she could've been part of a window display—separate, perfect, somehow above it all—and I wondered briefly why she'd volunteered to go on this trip.

Things often got sloppy overseas.

From across the aisle, Rand's voice interrupted my musings. Engaged in another heated conversation, this time with Ken, he huffed, "I can't believe the incompetence. The machine just got to Budapest yesterday.

"We put that thing on a boat three months ago!" he fumed. "Now the transport company is saying they can't guarantee getting it to us in time for our first case.

"Idiots!"

What machine could he be talking about. Suction? Heart monitor?

"We need decent images!"

Ah. X-ray. I gleaned from the men's continuing conversation that UMC had donated an old portable to the cause.

I felt for Rand.

While none of us expected state-of-the-art technology in the developing world, we definitely needed access to basic intra-operative x-rays. Much of what orthopedists did depended on the accurate alignment and positioning of fracture fragments and/or hardware. Even the most experienced and talented surgeons depended on portable fluoroscopy, radiographic video, if you will, or its forerunner, plain x-ray films, in ensuring the accuracy of their work.

"Could we pick the machine up and somehow take it with us?" I interjected. It seemed a reason-able alternative. "Maybe get a trailer or a rental truck?"

Rand executed a half turn, and his eyes shot me a glare of supreme annoyance. "You don't suppose I already thought of those options, do you?"

Put in my place, I apologized. "Sorry . . . of course, of course you would have." For good measure, I devolved into stutter mode—which happened when I was made to look the fool." I—I just th-thought . . ."

Okay, Parise. Stop.

An old, elementary school taunt rushed power-fully back to me in my moment of distress. *"Parise la cerise*! Parry the cherry!" The French and English wordplay had made me feel the dolt more than once.

I flushed scarlet, hence the applicability of my nickname, the chiding of youthful voices harmo-nizing with Rand's accusation now. As a diversion, I reached into my purse for a magazine and caught Jake, just the other side of Rand, studying me.

Great, I thought. A virtual stranger feeling sorry for me.

I saw him wink and roll his eyes. "Consider the source," his expression implied.

He had Rand's number.

I grinned, acknowledging Jake's kindness, but fell back into thinking I might've made a mistake going on the trip; perhaps one of my more spec-tacular ones.

Was Rand going to treat me like this the whole time, I wondered? If so, how was I going to react?

Say nothing?

Call him on his rudeness?

Stage a slowdown that might derail his ambi-tious work plans?

The Lufthansa gate agent saved me from pointless speculation by picking up the phone on the counter before her and in a pleasant voice, welcoming us to Flight 5210 non-stop to Munich with connections to Budapest and points east.

As a unit, we rose and reached for our things. Bulky jackets that we hadn't wanted to pack. Our bags. Last-minute items purchased at airport gift shops. One by one we presented passports and boarding passes to attendants guarding the jet way door, then we made our way slowly onto the plane.

My mind re-visited Rand's rebuke, and I wondered again what working with the man was going to be like if he was already this difficult.

"Don't," I warned myself. "There's no point in anticipating trouble."

I was a competent professional with solid skills. Rand, while brilliant, was a human being who ate, slept, and evacuated in the same way all humans did. I was on this trip at his behest and was doing him a favor. He had better behave or I could, and might, walk off the job.

My nerves settled, I telegraphed a prayer to the heavens, my supplication going something like, "You'd better help me out here. Remind Mr. Genius that his brilliance is an accident of nature. Nothing he did to deserve it. Easy to lose to an accident; to disease; to a greedy patient suing over the most human of mistakes.

"You're in charge," I informed God. "Now act like it."

SEVEN

Having inherited Judd Henderson's e-ticket, I must also have gotten his seat assignment on an aisle, a location meant to accommodate his long and lean frame.

Rand decided that particular arrangement couldn't stand, and as a result there followed a complicated re-shuffling of people and the contents of overhead bins. Somehow I wound up on the other side of the plane sitting next to a window, hardly ideal for a nervous-Nellie flyer like me. Rand, who wanted to be free to roam after we took off, commandeered the seat close to mine on the aisle and pointed Jake to the center seat between us. Right away, he started picking Jake's brain on the subject of electrical circuitry and x-ray equipment.

Single phase.

Multi-phase.

"I think they have a phototimer on their one operational unit, but they've never been able to calibrate it in any reliable way. Can you help with that?" Rand demanded to know.

In the time it took for the plane to push away from the gate, sit out on the tarmac waiting for clearance from air traffic controllers, and to become airborne over traffic-snarled I-66—the Sunday evening rush of weekend travelers in full stagnation—the men had abandoned me, in a flurry of kilovolts and miliamperes, to sleep.

I startled awake over the Atlantic more than an hour later, pulled abruptly from a recurring dream that never failed to leave me feeling depressed and disappointed. In this version, I was living in my two-bedroom condo, and yet not. The layout and atmosphere of the rooms seemed vaguely familiar, but there were extra rooms and closets and a secret circular staircase leading to a library filled with pristine first editions. Standing before the stacks, I picked out several volumes, the bibliophile in me ecstatic. Willa Cather, Edith Wharton, Ernest Hemmingway. Hegel's impenetrable *Phenomenology of the Mind.*

All mine!

Without any effort or desire on my part, I was transported to a sunroom overlooking a spectacular summer garden. Beyond a wall of French doors lay an in-ground pool with a mosaic of aquamarine tiles at its bottom. The water sparkled Caribbean blue and stately cedar columns provided fingers of shade to a bevy of attractive friends, none of whom I recognized. These strangers reclined on chaise lounges, sipping wine coolers and calling for the help to bring more sunscreen. *Plus de crudités.*

A bucket of ice.

In this dream world, I turned my back on these demanding creatures and explored rooms filled with rich textures and colors and sounds, all of them heretofore undiscovered. I was aware, as I had been during other similar dreams, that I wasn't actually living the experience but yearned nonetheless to wake to find that it was real.

I'd talked to a psychologist friend about the meaning of this dream, and she'd spewed vague academic doubletalk that boiled down to my needing or wanting to tap new areas of my life; that maybe I was searching for change.

Blah. Blah. Blah.

Blinking awake in the plane's humming, darkened interior, the explanation struck me as plausible now. My life really was changing. I'd left behind my manic work routine and was flying across the Atlantic into the unknown. In just over twenty-four hours, I'd be working alongside one of the most brilliant surgeons in the world, in a place I'd never seen, with people I barely knew. I'd be eating new foods and meeting patients whose life circumstances couldn't be more different than those of the population I regularly served.

Suddenly the plane quivered and dropped, and I stifled a gasp.

Unfazed by the turbulence, Jake turned in his seat, leaned over, and asked, "Have a nice nap?"

I struggled to disguise my rising terror, answering softly, "Nice enough. Did you and Rand clear up the x-ray problem?"

"As much as we could at 40,000 feet," he confided. "Everything's theoretical 'til I get my hands on the equipment."

He smiled. "Rand's back talking to Rich. Probably asking the same questions he asked me."

Probably.

"We will have access to some kind of imaging device over there, won't we?"

"Oh, sure," Jake said. "The hospital has an old, functional machine. Problem is, it's stationary. No way to take films in the OR.

"If the portable doesn't make it in time, Rand will have to do what he's done before."

"Which is?'

"From what he said, I guess he'll open the patient. Make the surgical changes necessary. Put the patient on a stretcher and wheel him down to the first floor x-ray room on a ramp that's open to public use."

"He can't be serious!"

"I think he is. Says the tech will take a few shots of the leg or arm; then back to the OR the whole procession will go to wrap up." He grinned. "Or sew up."

I didn't laugh.

My mind was considering the exams likely performed in an all-purpose x-ray room every day. Intravenous pyelograms—IVP's—used to check kidney function. Fluoroscopic examinations of the upper and lower GI tracts. Chest x-rays on patients sick with everything from pneumonia to TB.

I envisioned legions of micro-organisms marching unbidden into surgical wounds.

"Rand thinks the portable will cut surgical time by a quarter," Jake said.

The plane lurched a second time and a chorus of involuntary exclamations rang out. The fuselage vibrated squeaky accompaniment in a brisk headwind.

I started to sweat and to breathe in shallow pants. I imagined, illogically, that the least movement on my part would further imperil the plane.

"Bumpy ride," Jake commented.

"Just a bit," I managed, lips stretched into a grimace.

He took note of my dread. "There's no need to be nervous, Parry."

"Easier said," I insisted, positioning my hands like twin vises on the armrests. I recalled a former pastor's admonition. "God doesn't always answer prayer. He answers desperate prayer."

That I could supply.

Jake touched my arm unexpectedly. "Would it help if you had a hand to hold?"

In a different place, at another time, the offer would've seemed forward. With my body in full fight-or-flight mode, a paradox not lost on me, the words were a kindness.

"Couldn't hurt."

We dropped again, WHOA! A terrifying bounce into an invisible trough. The wind buffeted the plane side to side, then up and down, a small toy in the hand of an invisible and cruel airborne giant.

Jake wrapped my icy claw in his warm and solid hand. He didn't speak or pursue any other communication, just pushed back in his seat and closed his eyes.

Next to him, I struggled not to pant, an action I knew from experience would bring on the hand and foot cramping of hyperventilation. I avoided all but the smallest motion, fearing a sudden move could send us in a free-fall to the sea.

Over the next half hour, I slowed my respirations. I tried to relax. I felt Jake's confidence and strength passing to me in a kind of emotional osmosis facilitated by the joining of our hands.

Bit by bit, atmospheric instability lessened, though it didn't entirely go away.

We dipped.

We bobbed.

We veered in sudden, strong gusts of wind, but eventually we equalized.

When things had been steady for a while, Jake opened his eyes and asked, "Feeling better?"

"I think so."

"You up for a quick game of BATTLESHIP?"

I laughed out loud. "You're kidding?"

"Not at all. Nothing like a maritime engagement to put nasty flying conditions in perspective."

"I thought you were Army."

He grinned. "What gave it away?"

"The handshake. The haircut. Okay, rumor."

"I was Army for most of my career," he admitted. "But I taught a while at Annapolis.

81

Learned a little bit about Navy life while I was there."

I extricated my hand and challenged, "All right sailor. Bring it on." My smile, while shaky, intimated that I was hoping for more than plastic subs and destroyers.

EIGHT

After almost an hour of destroying one another's fleets, we put the game away. I retrieved trail mix from my luggage and shared it with Jake, dessert to our long ago Chinese. Picking through cashews, cranberries, and bits of chocolate, we traded stories.

I insisted he go first.

"Not much to tell," he said. "Texas born and bred.

"Undergrad at UT; Masters at A&M."

"Divided loyalties," I observed. The Longhorns and Aggies were longtime rivals.

"Not at all. I grew up just outside of Austin, and my folks couldn't afford me living away. You might say my four years at UT were coerced. I'm Aggie through and through."

Simultaneously we said, "Gig 'em," and laughed.

"You didn't go to A&M, did you?"

"Next best thing. I dated an Aggie in college. A nice Kansas boy I called 'Blue-eyed Joe.'"

"Where was that?"

"Boston. He was in med. school."

"Is that where you trained?"

"No. That was North Carolina."

"Duke?"

"Wake Forest."

"You left North Carolina for D.C.?" he asked in disbelief. "I didn't think anyone did that willingly."

"A body goes where the jobs are," I confessed. "But I'd move back there any time."

I loved the bungalows being restored in Winston-Salem's West End and the well-established homes of Buena Vista. I missed the starkly beautiful Moravian stars that lit doorsteps during the Christmas season and afternoons browsing the shops at Reynolda. Beyond that I was addicted to sugar cake and wafer-thin ginger cookies made and sold in old Salem, and I loved red bud trees in full bloom, painting spring color back into the Piedmont's deciduous forests.

"Be careful," Jake said, noting my wistful, wishful expression. "We all think we're going back someday. Then a year passes. Five.

"I've got friends who are still renting townhouses after ten years in D.C. because anytime now the right opportunity's gonna come along . . ."

I felt my heart tighten at his words. I knew people like that, too. I'd felt sorry for them.

Rand, who'd returned and was pecking away busily on his computer keyboard, interrupted our exchange without apology or excuse. "Parry. Why don't you and I review a few cases."

His tone implied it wasn't a request.

"Sure. Jake, you don't mind do you?"

"Not at all."

We had talked long enough in the tentative, superficial way that people did when both were interested but nervous about revealing too much. It seemed a good time for a break.

"I'll switch places with you," Jake suggested. "I can take a nap while ya'll plan."

The two men backed out of the row, and I high-stepped over backpacks and computer carrying cases bulging from under the seats. We filed back in and re-settled.

While Rand flipped open his laptop, I extricated a pen and a small spiral-bound notebook from my canvas purse. For the next ninety minutes, he and I reviewed about twenty-five cases, not the dozen or so I'd anticipated, and the flow of minutiae that spilled from Rand's brain was staggering. The information complemented the limited histories visible to us both on the computer screen.

Proximity to Rand gave me a new perspective on the man. For one thing, he didn't look nearly as old close up as he did at a distance. His unruly hair was flecked with gray at the temples, true, but his skin had the firm and smooth vitality of youth. His eyes, chocolate brown and unfathomable, danced with excitement for his work. Most important, while he often looked like an unmade bed—shirt chronically escaping his belt and khakis a roadmap of wrinkles—he smelled of old fashioned bar soap, something spicy with underlying nuances of nutmeg or clove. His fingernails were clipped and immaculate, the palms and fingertips of his surgeon's hands worn soft and smooth from repeated and vigorous scrubbing.

For a moment, I imagined his fingertips pressed to my cheek or my forehead and the flash of his boyish smile. His laser-like intensity focused only on me.

Get a grip, St. Amand.

I was on board a plane with people committed to work, and here I was practically auditioning for the next insipid installment of *The Bachelorette*!

Where Randall Szabo was concerned, that could be seen as an exercise in futility. Much better women, certainly more aggressive women, than I had tried and failed to attract his interest. Stories circulated through the OR women's locker room from time to time, a few funnier than the rest, and the upshot was that Rand was too obsessed with his work to notice the machinations women went through trying to impress. A couple of gay staff were equally miffed at Rand's cluelessness, no surprise then that the cruel consensus at UMC was that Rand was asexual.

I wouldn't go that far. He was socially awkward, that much was clear. He knew only one way of communicating. As the expert; the boss; the person in charge. When it came to flirtation or small talk, he was at a complete loss.

I shook my head, clearing it of pointless speculation, and focused hard on Rand's words, his explanations, and his hopes for the days of surgery to come. When my hand started cramping from nonstop note-taking, I got Rand to slow down by indulging my curiosity. "Not to criticize, but how is it you know so much about these patients, Rand? There's very little here about their personal lives."

Test results were visible on the screen, certainly—EKG strips, metabolic panels, x-ray reports that were spottily translated—but Rand was recounting the particulars of complex personal histories. And he wasn't working from notes.

Earlier, he'd described a young patient who played soccer every day despite a serious ankle injury, a boy hoping to keep his skills sharp enough to win a scholarship to college in the U.S. "A couple of Ivy League schools are seriously pursuing him," Rand revealed. "Even hurt, he's better than 95 percent of the competition."

He also mentioned a second teenager, a boy named Janos who lived on a dairy farm and walked five or six kilometers every day to a school for high academic performers. Early mornings and late afternoons, he helped his father milk and care for a herd of seventy-five cows, no matter that he was doing it one-handed after a tumble from the hay loft, months earlier, had left him with a broken hand.

Rand recounted the story of Katalin, as well, a twenty-year old violin prodigy recently recruited by a major Paris symphony. She was ready to accept the offer but had been waiting three months for a surgeon to release the tendon in her faulty index finger, restoring her talented hands to full function. "She's hoping the symphony won't rescind its offer."

He continued, "Katalin lost her father in a mining accident when she was only eight years old, and her mother died last year of breast cancer. She's living with a rather short-sighted aunt who would prefer she set aside her music and begin contributing positively to family finances right away."

He paused in his recitation of tragic life events to say, "I've been told that her playing moves audiences to tears."

If not, I thought, her story surely would.

In explaining his intimate knowledge of our patients' lives, he admitted this much. "Matthias and I talked." Our host.

"Recently?"

According to Linda, Rand had been in the hospital fourteen hours a day for the last several weeks, clearing his backlog of cases. With the time difference, he would've had to carry on conversations with Matthias in the four or five hours between midnight and dawn, a time more wisely allotted to sleep.

"We discussed these cases back in August, but a couple are recent."

"I don't see any notes," I said, once again playing the skeptical detective.

"Notes? Why would I have wasted time taking notes? These details are easily recalled."

By a human encyclopedia, maybe. Or a walking PC.

I challenged his claim. "You remembered all this from conversations you had eight to ten weeks ago?"

"A single conversation," he corrected. "And yes, most of what I know I learned then." He asked impatiently, "Shall I go on?'"

I inferred from his tone that my commitment to the cause would be questioned if I didn't say yes, so I agreed, "Sure. Go ahead."

We went through the rest of the pending cases, as they were known to Rand, and by midnight, Eastern time, a raging headache was threatening to implode my right eye. Beside me, Jake still slumped against the fuselage in full slumber mode.

"I need to use the facilities," I indicated to Rand. "Sure."

I stashed my notes, and he unfolded himself from his seat, allowing me just enough room to emerge. I thanked him, ignoring the unavoidable, full-body rub, and headed toward the rear of the aircraft. The line to the bathroom was down to three, and Rand's right hand, Linda, was just ahead of me patiently waiting her turn. She looked tired but determined not to let it show.

"Are we having fun yet?" she asked. "I saw you talking to Rand."

"No," I corrected. "You saw HIM talking to me."

She laughed.

"The man must have a computer chip for a brain," I surmised.

"There are those who've made similar comments," she assured me. "Only not as charitably."

"I can imagine."

A morbidly obese gentleman bullied his way out of the lavatory just then and interrupted our conversation as he squeezed breathily past. Linda and I retreated into empty seats on opposite sides of the aisle, letting him through before resuming our places in line.

"Wait until you work with him," Linda continued. "If you're not absolutely on top of things every second, it won't be long before you fall behind."

I swallowed hard.

"He's a machine," she added. "I think he has radar in his hands and eyes that let him see 360 degrees around the room even when they're pointed straight ahead. He's cutting and sewing and keeping tabs on the sponge count, all at the same time."

"You aren't making me feel any better," I said, attempting a friendly reproof. "I think my entire blood supply just turned to ice."

She grinned and said, "I'm not trying to scare you, Parry, believe me. Just a word to the wise: be a hundred percent in the game. If you are, Rand'll be a dream to work with."

"He's in. He's out. Case over.

"It's like a being part of a guerilla force or witnessing the detonation of a neutron bomb."

"A what?"

She grinned and apologized. "Sorry. I forget how young you kids are.

"The neutron bomb was a weapon developed during the Carter administration. A nuclear device designed to produce radiation levels lower than those of conventional bombs. The intention, using them, was to annihilate people but leave structures intact.

"A truly MISguided missile."

Suddenly more serious, Linda returned to the original topic of our conversation. "Look," she said. "Rand's patients flourish because his repair work is flawless. He gets right to the injury and doesn't make a mess in the surrounding tissue. And he's radically efficient, so patients are under about a half as long as it'd take for the average surgeon to get the job done.

"His skill and speed make post-op care much easier. Fewer anesthesia-related complications. Infections. You know the drill."

Maybe this would work out after all. I wanted the best patient outcomes as much as Rand did. I might have to work twice as hard making that happen, but I could do it. I could rise to the occasion.

The door to the bathroom opened, and it was Linda's turn to ascend the throne. She waved regally, using the wrist pivot made popular by Elizabeth II imitators, and then disappeared into the bathroom's Lilliputian confines.

Eager for its own go, my bladder cramped jealously, and I was reminded in my urgency of Dad's irreverent take on voiding. "There's nothing in the world so underrated as a good leak."

Well, that was the polite version anyway.

I laughed out loud. Suddenly, powerfully, I missed the insanity of home.

NINE

We dragged ourselves off the plane in Munich around eight o'clock local time. We smelled of fatigue and frustrated sleep.

The group divided along gender lines, Rand positioning himself under a monitor and holding up one hand, our self-appointed safety officer warning, "Not so fast. Our connecting flight boards precisely at eleven." He pointed across the corridor and down two gates from where we stood. "Right there."

The irritable sleepwalker in me wanted to cry out, "We can read, man," but I held back. It wouldn't do to antagonize him. Again.

"Be on time," Rand cautioned.

"Roger that," a voice sounding suspiciously like Paul's responded, and we all laughed. Anticipating that Rand might hand out airport maps or make us walk in a line holding hands, we waited, but nothing else happened. A long night and the prospect of an even longer day had muted even Rand's verbosity.

Beverly, Linda, and I watched the six men merge into a single, disheveled organism, Jake the one neat exception. His jeans still held a crease, his shirt was barely wrinkled, and his hair looked like he'd taken the time to comb it.

More plusses in his column.

Beverly, who'd been reserved and quiet all the way over on the plane, chose that moment to break her silence. "Ladies," she said. "Follow me. I know just what we need."

A complete makeover? A full-body massage? A personal staff ready to primp and pamper me back to recognizable human form? "You don't happen to have a porta-potty in your pocket?" I asked aloud. I had an aversion to public restrooms and often held off (or "in") using them.

"Better than that," she responded. "Come this way." She took off at an energetic trot, fashionable pumps clacking rhythmically on spotless marble.

Slower to rouse, Linda and I barely managed to trail her at a distance.

It took ten minutes of continuous walking through the modern, light-filled terminal, before we discovered our destination.

"Women's showers!" Linda exclaimed. "What a Godsend."

I nearly cried.

"How did you know these were here?" Linda followed up.

"I checked the Internet before leaving."

"Kudos my friend," Linda congratulated before starting to dig through her purse for cash.

I stood between the two women, ambivalent about our good fortune.

On the one hand, this was a public facility, which meant bacteria, athlete's foot, and who knew what else lurking on the shower floors. On the other, I'd slept in my clothes and had roughly another twelve hours of travel ahead. My hair was dirty and had grown to twice its ordinary volume after hours trying to find a sleep position that wouldn't leave me permanently crippled.

No contest.

I paid the requisite fee and followed my new friends inside. In the face of pronounced jet lag, I abandoned all modesty. I found an empty stall and stripped naked. Jumped into the path of water blasting from the shower head and cried in forever gratitude, "God bless the Germans!" The amenity was a stroke of pure genius.

I scrubbed twice, powering off the travel grime accumulated on my skin. A unique blend of body oils and the smarmy dirt of public seating, it coated all exposed body parts—and induced mental vague-ness, I could swear it—no matter the mode of trans-portation involved.

Once disinfected and toweled dry, I yanked on a change of underwear and applied a hit of anti-perspirant under the wings. I tangled with a hair dryer and a fat styling brush, subduing the tangled mass that was my hair.

Boom!

I was reborn.

Linda left her cubicle a few minutes after I did smelling subtly of lavender water, but it was Beverly who emerged completely transformed.

Gone was the severe and polished look she usually wore. Where her hair had been straight angles and traditional bob, she somehow wore it spiked and reeking of attitude now. Her complexion had lost its applied pallor and was a natural shade of rosy pink. It glowed. Fine lines at the corners of her eyes and lips, once pancaked into submission, lent her beauty depth and approachability. In the place of her prim and perfunctory smile, she was grinning ear to ear.

No wonder.

The girl was letting loose!

Gone was the tailored pantsuit she had worn flying; likewise the stylish and uncomfortable pumps. She had pulled on a hoodie emblazoned across the chest with the Iowa State logo, running shoes, and ratty jeans—not the kind purposely torn or stone-washed to give the impression of age but pants with some mileage on them in the form of stains (paint? grass? a smidgen of axle grease?). Corny calico patches at the knees were an unexpected touch, and the loop on the side . . . Oh my goodness.

THEY WERE PAINTERS' PANTS!

Linda was the first to speak. To ask in all seriousness, "Bev, are you all right?"

The new Beverly answered without elaboration, "For the first time in a while, I believe I am." She didn't offer any more than that, and we didn't push. Instead, all three of us collected our gear and went off in search of breakfast.

We opted for a hearty, almost celebratory meal at one of the airport's better café bars. We ordered bread and jam . . . jam and bread—I could almost hear the Von Trapp family harmonizing in the background—and hearty sausage, a food with which Germans have a centuries-long love affair. Our server suggested a selection of delicious cheeses, and we decided on our own to request pots of strong breakfast tea, an antidote to all the sleep-inducing fats we were about to consume.

When the food came, we indulged, and the more we ate, the more Beverly morphed into a talkative and friendly woman that neither Linda nor I had ever met. Linda, who'd worked with the woman for close to a decade, kept shaking her head in pleased incredulity. I was satisfied to watch and fill my mouth with the next delicious bite.

For her part, Beverly grew more animated and girlish, the flow of confidences spilling from her, once begun. She had grown up in Iowa, she said, which explained the shirt. An only child, she had lost her parents in a car accident at the age of four. "I don't have any real memories of them," she told us. "Just a couple of pictures."

She withdrew a single black and white photo, folded to fit a plastic sleeve in her wallet. She stared silently at it for a moment, then gently touched each corner before sliding it across the table for us to see.

Her parents were a stunning couple. The father had sharp, handsome features and a head of wavy hair worn pushed back from his brow—a young Charlton Heston full of daring. Her mother, blonde and stunningly Scandinavian, smiled into the camera, vivacious and self-assured. They looked like a couple for whom nothing but happiness was in store.

"There were no relatives willing to take me in," Bev confided softly. No aunts or uncles. Grandparents who had been too ill or too old to give her a home; she'd never known which. Not surprisingly, Beverly had spent almost ten years in foster care.

"I was fourteen when I was finally adopted," she said in a voice thick with disappointment. Or shame. Youngsters adopted in late childhood often believed there was something fundamentally wrong with THEM.

"The Wilsons weren't bad people, but I always suspected they took me in to help out on the farm."

Not the best plan as it turned out.

First, Bev was a girl and not especially strong. "I was definitely not interested in the smelly world of fertilizers, cows, and feed."

Second, by the 1980s, family farms in the United States were well into their long, slow demise. Many were in crisis, losing ground, literally, to burgeoning agribusiness. "The Wilsons' operation went under the year after they took me in." Hardly a confidence builder for a young girl already feeling disenfranchised. "They lost the farm," she explained. "And any savings went to their creditors."

Family furniture, some original to the homestead, was sold at auction.

"We moved to Des Moines with the little that was left, and Malcolm," Beverly's adoptive father, "got work as a carpenter's assistant. He was good at what he did, but without anyone local to give him a recommendation, he had to prove himself.

"Luckily for the family, it didn't take long for everybody to see that he was a great worker who could be trusted to manage projects and bring them in under budget." After only a few months on the job, Malcolm Wilson was given a raise and more responsibility. "He worked six days a week. Twelve to fifteen hour days.

"I look back now and realize how much determination and humility it must have taken to start over. He was older then, than I am now.

"A lot of men might've run."

She stopped to butter a slice of dense pumpernickel and bit into it. After a few moments, she resumed her impromptu memoir, saying, "Malcolm got a reputation for doing quality work. He bought his own tools, adding to the few he'd taken from the farm, and he started his own business about three years after we got to town."

Which would've been about the time Beverly was finishing high school, I calculated.

"As the oldest of the bunch, I was expected to help bring in money. I got jobs babysitting and cleaning houses with Myrna," her adoptive mother, "on weekends. In my senior year, I tutored math and biology.

"I really wanted to join the drama club and play field hockey, you know, the regular high school stuff, but there was never time."

The summer before her senior year, Bev started bringing home college catalogs and scholarship applications, hiding them under her bed and pulling them out after her younger sisters fell asleep. It was in those nights of surreptitious daydreaming that she came up with her plan.

She would get into a good college and win a scholarship. She'd work like a beast if she had to and someday have all the things she'd missed early in life. A real family. A home. Pretty clothes.

Her wish list was a long one.

"I'm not sure how I got interested in nursing; maybe I figured I'd always have a job or that I could live anywhere I wanted to, going into that profession.

"It wasn't like studying English lit. or psychology, where maybe you got a job in your field or maybe you wound up pushing burgers and fries at McDonald's.

"I'd never known a nurse or even talked to one about the work involved; I just knew there would always be hospitals and sick people who needed human beings, not machines, to care for them.

"The only other profession I saw as viable was teaching, and frankly, I'd had enough of trying to pound math and spelling into my spoiled sisters. I couldn't imagine facing a classroom full of goof-offs like them for a lifetime.

"I studied hard to keep all A's, and I aced the ACTs.

"I planned on moving to Chicago because my parents had met there.

"On the very fringes of my earliest memory, I remembered hearing my mother's voice and seeing her smile at Daddy when she talked about their first date. Walking Michigan Avenue in a snowstorm.

"I don't know why that stuck with me . . ." she said thoughtfully. "Maybe I was just a romantic little girl . . .

"When the time came, I applied to Northwestern. The nursing school there offered one full academic scholarship every year, and I set my sights on it.

"A friend of mine who's the admissions director there now told me not long ago that the office had received more letters of recommendation for me than for anyone in the history of the program. They only required three, but I saw to it there'd be more. I wrote to old teachers and asked all the people I'd ever worked for, for help.

"Even Estelle, my favorite lunch lady volunteered to write one. My biology teacher contributed a five page, single-spaced letter. I'd helped her with a couple of research projects for her Masters degree. I guess she was impressed.

"The staff in the admissions office was overwhelmed. Didn't have much choice but to pick me."

It was lucky she wasn't living today, I thought. Without pages of extracurriculars, I doubt she'd have made the first cut to an exclusive school like Northwestern, never mind the scholarship. Friends at work bemoaned the high-pressure state of affairs their children endured applying to colleges, and the crushing disappointment they felt when acceptance letters from their preferred schools failed to materialize.

Bev drew a deep breath, looking relieved.

As Mason Duke's wife, she had an image to maintain, but here, away from everything and everyone with high expectations, she apparently felt free to be Beverly Griggs Wilson.

Striver.

Achiever.

An orphan on her way to helping other children alone in the world.

I was no psychiatrist, but I saw something in Bev's shining eyes and relaxed demeanor that hadn't been there a few hours ago. Where she'd been tightly wound and had flinched at the slightest sound or touch, she seemed happy now.

What had motivated the change? Maybe she'd worried, on the flight over, that she wouldn't be able to sustain the Beverly Duke persona among children of loss; children who would likely have seen through the façade of her sophistication to the kindred spirit who shared their pain. Maybe Bev had chosen this as the time and the place of her "outing," before the truth of her early life came out later in an unbridled, emotional rush.

We finished eating and decided we had time to explore. When we congregated with the males after a leisurely hour, they were impressed by how rested and refreshed we all looked. Beverly's appearance, in particular, drew comment.

Even Rand weighed in asking cluelessly, "Hey Bev. Something happen to your hair?"

Her hair? Wake up man! The woman was changed from head to her Timberland-encased toe!

We boarded our connecting flight moments after our reunion and spent just over an hour airborne. On the ground in Budapest, it took a while collecting all the luggage and equipment we'd checked through. All of it was miraculously there but negotiating the airport in a group of nine, again at Rand's insistence, took much longer than it might have.

When we finally made it outside, we found the day overcast and the weather crueler than it had been in Virginia—impressive, given how unseasonably cold and raw it'd been there. Waiting for our bus to appear, we donned winter apparel: some pulled on fleece and others down vests; Bev wore a stylishly cut coat that looked to be a soft cashmere blend, her transformation clearly having its limits.

Dressed in a sweater and scarf, I was the last passenger to board the dilapidated vehicle that emerged from heavy traffic to stop for us. I plodded listlessly up the steps, the invigorating effects of my earlier shower completely dissipated. Every inch of me ached. I felt nauseated and disoriented from lack of sleep, and I knew from Rand's frequent reminders that we had a long way yet to our destination.

"Let's get the show on the road," I mumbled, hoping for nothing more than an empty seat to myself and the chance to get horizontal.

Jake waved to me from the back of the bus.

We hadn't spoken since deplaning in Munich, but we had smiled at one another a time or two over the heads of our companions and ignored Rand's constant guidance.

"You've lost the pep in your step," he said as I approached.

I growled and tossed my suitcases overhead, the paisley print inducing a headache as I heaved them. I collapsed into the one remaining seat, next to Jake's. "I'm not a good traveler," I needlessly warned.

"Promise not to make any demands," he vowed. "I won't even talk."

"Good."

I stood and pulled a fleece vest from where I'd wound it into the straps of my suitcase. I bunched it up and propped it against the bus window to use as a pillow.

I kicked off my shoes.

"Care to stretch out?" Jake asked softly, pointing to his lap.

"Inappropriate," I answered grumpily.

"In any other circumstance, you'd be right. But you're dead. Let me help."

Just like that, he broke me. "Okay," I relented. "But no funny business."

"Scout's honor."

He collected the leaden weight of my legs and draped it across his thighs in a gesture that seemed both natural and harmless.

"Thanks," I whispered in acquiescence. "I'll owe ya."

First gear engaged, and the bus jerked forward. We eased into a bolus of late afternoon traffic.

Second gear.

Third.

My head whipped back slightly with each increase in speed.

We edged past taxis clogging the lane directly ahead, and my eyes closed involuntarily.

"Parry?"

"I thought you weren't going to talk."

"We'll have to show our passports at the border . . ."

Of course.

I flipped my holder from its hiding place inside my sweater and let it fall across my chest. I slipped its cord from around my neck as an afterthought, explaining, "In case you have to hand it over."

"Good enough."

It would have to be. In moments, I was gone.

TEN

Much as I yearned for endless sleep, it didn't happen.

I drifted in and out of light dozing, studying a different sector of Budapest every time my eyelids drifted open. I saw church steeples and red tiled roofs. From a distance, I glimpsed a stretch of river-front, the Danube presumably, and later saw signs of industrialization that were an ugly but neces-sary part of urban life everywhere. Together with the gray and gloomy day, the passing cityscape disappointed.

Our driver maneuvered the roads and streets dexterously, and soon we were on a highway headed out of the city. The road was busy in some spots, slowdowns almost indistinguishable from the congestion that plagued American highways. In other places, it moved smoothly. It wasn't all that long before we cleared the outskirts of Budapest and were driving into barren countryside.

Still no shut eye.

"Having trouble?" Jake asked.

"I think I've reached a tipping point," I confessed. "Parise Marie St. Amand may never sleep again."

He laughed. "You will. Traveling doesn't lend itself to rest.

"Want me to read to you?" he asked. "I've been told my voice has a narcotizing effect."

My turn to laugh. "Sure. Got anything interesting?"

"How about that handout of Rand's. I haven't had much time to look it over."

"Me either."

"It's settled then." He swung my legs back to the floor, stood, and reached for his briefcase. He fiddled with the zippered pockets until he found what he was searching for, then resumed his seat.

I rearranged myself, legs forward, fleece vest transformed into a blanket. The bus heater wasn't very powerful, or maybe we were too far back to feel its effects. Whatever the problem, I was freezing.

Jake noted my shiver and stood a second time. He retrieved a jacket and tucked it gallantly around my legs. He sat close, sharing body heat as he read.

The country to which we were traveling had a population of just over six million, Jake informed me, and it covered an area of about 75,000 square kilometers. The Danube formed a portion of its western border. Austria lay to the west; the farming plains of Hungary were east and south.

"A protectorate created from the ruins of the first world war, the nation has been, at various times in its history, a refuge for Austrians fleeing Hitler and Italians fleeing Mussolini. It has provided safe haven for people escaping more restrictive Communist regimes, among them a substantial group of Ukrainians."

In the face of Communism's collapse, the nation's monarch had been restored to the throne, though his power was mostly ceremonial. Today, the country was ruled by a democracy similar to England's, having both a bi-cameral parliament and a prime minister in charge of the nation's day-to-day political and foreign affairs. As with many of its European trading partners, the recent global credit crisis had been hitting the small country hard.

Lithium mining, one of the nation's primary industries, had been dealt an especially serious blow. While overall car sales in the U.S. were seeing steep declines, the more expensive "green" hybrids, whose batteries depended on lithium, were faring worse; hence the blow to mining. "Tourism to the country's new, state-of-the-art ski resorts, only beginning to gain in popularity, is projected to decrease by as much as FIFTY PERCENT in the coming winter, as both Europeans and Americans economize."

And we thought we had it bad.

I stopped him. "You know, this is too much a rehash of the news I've started avoiding at home."

A constant diet of network heavy hitters was a recipe for depression, I'd come to believe. Their reporting marched in lockstep with that of newspapers and wire services. In the most prosperous nation on earth, Couric, Williams, and Gibson, their producers and correspondents often ignored healthy sectors of the economy and the things happening there, even as they showcased the worst of the whiners.

That's not to say there wasn't financial suffering abroad in the land; only a fool would have made such a claim. But there needed to be perspective and balance; a sense that not all was lost when over 90 percent of the public still had jobs. A Polish friend of mine teaching in the Johns Hopkins International Studies Program not far from UMC couldn't believe the country's collective bellyaching. "Polish leaders would kill for similar numbers. Most of Europe would."

Melodrama had become a way of life for news organizations.

An acquaintance of mine, a native of New Orleans who was a dyed-in-the-wool Democrat, had had her consciousness raised by the bias in Hurricane Katrina reporting. "All of them, standing there in their khakis and waders and sweat stains," she snarled. "They were completely oblivious to the best that came out of that storm.

"My parents were shocked at the heroism and sacrifice that never rated so much as a footnote in the early coverage."

Multiply that phenomenon across the news landscape, and you had news organizations adept at promoting the worst in human nature and, almost as annoying, pursuing relentlessly anyone with the misfortune of committing a valiant act—digging up the smallest, insignificant detail of a hero's life and serving it up to us *ad nauseum*, his or her virtue robbed of pretty much all meaning by the time the press finally let go.

"Anything in there about the arts or literature?" I asked. "I'm in the mood for something uplifting."

He flipped through the stapled pages and started reading again. He described murals in the country's churches; the excellent state of the country's classical education; the political and economic neutrality officials were trying to cultivate in the face of a volatile and violent world.

I listened closely as Jake provided details of fine textile manufacturing and the writings of Nobel-laureate novelists—two in the last fifty years—but started to drift a little at talk of the country's efforts luring high tech development with the promise of low taxes.

Somewhere between talk of the legal system and emerging foreign policy, I slept, jerking awake later with a startled, "Wha-what?" as the bus came to a hard, sudden stop.

"We're at the border," Jake explained.

"Oh."

I studied my surroundings in sleepy confusion and pulled my hair into the coated elastic I often wore as a bracelet. Straightening my sweater, I gave Jake back his jacket, with thanks, then stood to stretch and satisfy my curiosity. I peered through the bus' dirty windshield and struggled to make out what was happening just ahead of us on the road.

There were at least a half-dozen vehicles in line, none of them moving. "We may be here a while," I said, dropping back to my seat. Sheepishly I added, "Sorry I zonked out on you."

"That was the point."

"Still, a little rude. You did a good job catching me up, though."

"My pleasure."

The bus inched forward. One vehicle down. Five to go.

Linda peeked over her seatback. "I enjoyed the tutorial, too."

"You probably knew most of it," Jake responded.

"Some. But things here are changing."

"They're changing everywhere," I contributed.

"Does it usually take long to cross the border?" Jake asked Linda.

"Five or ten minutes at most. They usually just wave their own citizens through. But not tonight, it would seem."

Night? It was almost dark, wasn't it?

I glanced at my watch. "How far to the orphanage?"

"A couple of hours. Depending on the roads."

"Are they well maintained?"

"If the area's had a lot of rain, we could come across a few washouts or get stuck in the mud. I've seen a little bit of everything since I started coming on these trips."

Another ten minutes passed before we felt ourselves moving closer to the guard station. Linda was the one to get up this time. "They're inspecting each car individually," she reported. "That's not the usual protocol."

I tensed, remembering Rand's reference to official State Department warnings. Maybe he should have taken them, and I my mother, more seriously.

Shouting erupted outside. Uniformed guards pulled a man from a rusty Fiat and threw him spread-eagled to the ground. Firearms were trained on his passenger.

Next to me, Jake shifted into high alert, while at the front of the bus, Ken and Paul craned their necks for a better look.

No one spoke.

A soldier burst out of the border station, jumped behind the wheel of the Fiat. He disappeared, wheels screeching, around the back of the building. The line of cars remained stationary, as though their drivers were reconsidering. The ancient Mercedes directly in front of us U-turned and sped away in the direction from which it'd come.

Should we do the same, I wondered. There was still time.

Our bus drifted into the abandoned space ahead, then Rand stood and turned to face us. "I don't think I have to say this, but I'm going to anyway.

"I have all the appropriate papers for the medical supplies we're bringing into the country, but if ANY of you have ANYthing considered illegal IN THIS COUNTRY, now's the time to tell me. Narcotics. Anything recreational.

"I can't imagine your having been that stupid," he said bluntly, "but let's just say you had a supreme lapse in judgment and took along something questionable. In your suitcase. On your person.

"Speak now."

Utter silence.

"Good."

He sat back down.

Another twenty minutes, and it was our turn to be searched.

A guard with impeccable bearing entered the bus, and Rand handed him a sheaf of documents. "Thank you," the unsmiling young man uttered in English.

Not surprising. School children in this part of the world studied it from the very earliest grades. Unlike the U.S., where parents tended to be paranoid about their children losing proficiency in their mother tongue if immersed in a foreign language, Europeans had a long history of appreciating the advantages that multilingualism, practiced well, brought to the culture.

I agreed. Learning a new language made you appreciate the value and peculiarities of your own; the cultural basis that led to interesting idioms. I'd spoken French with my parents all my life, and I was grateful for their unapologetic use of it in our home.

Ditto instruction that our school district provided from third grade through twelfth.

Unfortunately my language ability didn't matter much now.

The youthful guard couldn't disguise his disdain as he asked, "All Americans?"

Rand answered respectfully, "Yes."

Scanning the papers, the guard directed, "I will need to see medical supplies, first. Then, passports and suitcases."

He and Rand left the bus together with the driver, and a few moments later, the compartment beneath us slowly creaked open. The inspection that followed was long and laborious.

Untie this. Unwrap that. "Where is this item?" the guard demanded as he compared Rand's list to the cargo. There were no niceties involved in the inspection, just the continual barking of requests and clarifications and Rand complying with every last request.

Thick plastic wrapping was ripped open; likewise trays swathed in sterile cloth covers and boxes filled with surgical screws. Specialized equipment. Virtually all of it would have to be sterilized again when we got to the hospital, I thought, a not-so-productive use of our time.

Rand returned dripping wet from the rain recently begun and flustered. In his wake two guards now followed, the original and another who glared threateningly at us. Each man took one side of the aisle and brusquely requested papers. They pulled bags from the racks overhead and searched through them; grabbed others from under our seats and fumbled carelessly through the contents. They scrutinized passport photographs and steadied flash-light beams on our tense and pale faces.

They moved on.

By the time they reached Jake and me, a pile of contraband had formed behind them in the aisle. I saw a handheld videogame player of Ted Ellison's and several apples—the food, not the computer—that Beverly had bought at the airport in Budapest.

"No foreign produce!" the guard declared as he appropriated the fruit. An embargo had been imposed on the Hungarian apple crop, we would learn later, a move considered to be more politically motivated than scientific.

Several over-the-counter medications appeared on the discard pile, items not on the list of banned products Rand had provided. I decided I would relinquish Dramamine to the cause, if it came to it, but I had to hope that we had something similar in our cache of legitimate drugs if a bout of vertigo befell me.

Watching them, I suspected the guards wanted these things for themselves or for their families; appropriating them was just a benefit of the job.

We wasted almost an hour and our emotional well-being at the crossing, heaving a collective sigh as the guards waved us off into the night.

The rain intensified, and road conditions grew worse. The driver, uncharacteristically timid for a European, was doing about thirty five—make that sixty KILOMETERS an hour. (I was making an effort to adapt.) We were stopped twice at small-town checkpoints, and both times I heard Linda mumble, "This is new."

It was late evening by the time the building that was our destination appeared in the deep, wet darkness. The imposing three-story stone structure was set on a hillside with a broad southern view. While rooftop crenellations and a massive portico were impressive, what we could make out of the surrounding grounds seemed modest. Well tended.

To a man (and woman), we were numb with fatigue, the kind of tired that only sitting in place for hours could bestow.

Disembarking, Rand quickly revived. He pointed to a cluster of roofs barely discernable through the murk and told us, "Over there's where we'll be working."

Easy walking distance, I estimated, presuming we had the energy.

"Let's get this thing unloaded."

The men emptied the belly of the bus, and the driver was generously remunerated. We all pitched in, as we had twice earlier, and it wasn't long before both we and our gear were inside.

"*Bienvenue. Bienvenue,*" the voice of a sparrow-like little nun welcomed us. Barely my height, she was a hundred pounds (no more) of pure energy. Her eyes danced as she glimpsed Rand and drew him into a hug. "*Le beau Docteur Szabo. Vous avez bien voyager?*" She pronounced Rand's surname as one would the French word for wooden shoe, *sabot,* and asked if we'd traveled well.

"*Bien, ma soeur. Et vous? Ça va?*" Yes. And how are you?

"*Ah! Toujours merveilleuse.*" Always wonderful.

Had we taken a wrong turn into France during the short time I'd managed sleep or were we in Quebec? I would've recognized our hostess' *grossaillage*—a distinctive and guttural rolling of the r's—anywhere.

And Rand? That he would be fluent in Hungarian was understandable, given his background. But one didn't make the jump easily from Hungarian to the romance languages. His mother tongue, linguistically speaking, was in a league of its own.

"*Soeur St. Helena*," Rand began, "may I introduce my colleagues." He went through the whole crew, keeping me for last. "*Ici nous avons Parise St. Amand.*"

"*Ma soeur,*" I said, coming forward with my hand extended and, out of parochial school habit, my head slightly inclined. Sister.

"*Voyons! Ou as-tu peche´ c'ta petite canadienne-lâ?*" she teased. Where did you find this little French Canadian?

"*Je suis ame´ricaine,*" I corrected as she hugged and quickly released me. "*Acadienne.*"

"*Ah, pas d'diffe´rence.*" No difference, she grinned mischievously. Acadian. French Canadian. All from the same genetic pool. The effervescent little nun added with a smile, "You and I must speak later," and she sounded for all the world like a friend.

Soeur St. Helena turned and shook hands all around, beckoning us in out of the night. She directed a younger nun, suddenly materialized, to show us to our quarters and pulled Rand aside for a brief, intense exchange.

As instructed, the newly arrived *Soeur Madelaine* took us in hand. "We apologize that we must relegate you to our basement," she explained as we followed in her wake, "but you will find, with our capacity crowd, that these are the quietest and warmest rooms in the building."

I lingered at the back of the pack to more closely study my new digs.

There was often a temptation, when traveling to an area of great need, to think that one would find universally primitive or slovenly conditions there, but poverty didn't always manifest itself in that way.

It certainly didn't at St. Maria's.

"The ladies' bedroom," as the young nun called it, was tidy and smelled of a fresh cleaning. Small but fastidious. Table lamps lent a warm and intimate glow.

"The gentlemen will be housed in the larger room around the corner.

"As you may know, it is our habit not to acti-vate the furnace until later in the season," she said, corroborating what we'd been told. "While in the upper floors you may feel the chill, these rooms tend to be insulated and comfortable."

It wouldn't matter. Our sleeping bags would provide more than enough warmth. Given their ratings, we'd probably roast.

"Please remember that electricity is turned off from midnight until five a.m.," she informed us.

Not a problem. I hoped to be sleeping soundly through those hours.

"The girls," about thirty-five of them, "will do all they can to afford you privacy in the baths."

We'd visited the one assigned to us, two floors up, on the way. It comprised three showers and a single tub. Five sinks. Three cramped toilet stalls.

We'd have to be quick about our business.

Jake and Paul came in carrying our camp beds and started setting up. *Soeur Madelaine* expressed her regret again. "We are sorry to have appropriated your beds, but we received several new charges in September. Their needs had to be our priority.

"It is good of you to have replaced them."

Her comment prompted me to ask. "How many children do you care for altogether?"

"One hundred and forty-two." She paused a moment. "No. One hundred forty-three. A tiny one came to us just last week."

"And how many bedrooms?"

"There are ten dormitory rooms. Apart from the nursery."

"So, roughly a dozen children per room?"

"Yes," she confirmed. "We arrange six sets of 'bunk' beds in each room. You will be able to see for yourselves when we introduce you to a few of the older girls tomorrow." She checked her watch. "They have retired for the night to study."

"And the nursery?" I asked. "How is that organized?"

"Infants and toddlers, of whom we currently have about seven, sleep in one large space. They have cribs prior to the age of two and later small beds low to the floor.

"One worker oversees them at night, two during the day. The remainder of our children are of pre-school age, two to five, and there are about sixteen of them with us presently."

"How many sisters in the facility overall?"

She didn't seem to mind my curiosity, but Rand, hovering nearby, had some advice for me. "Parry, how about we save the Q&A for after we've had something to eat? Dinner's being kept warm."

"I'm sorry," I said sincerely. "I'm impressed by how neat everything is. It must take a small army to keep things this way." Immaculate but lived in. Welcoming.

"The staff is not as large as one might think," *Soeur Madelaine* said with a smile. "We all do double duty. The children clean up after themselves, as well. Before and after classes; prior to play. On Saturday mornings there are general chores.

"There are only five religious," she said, "but we are helped by several employees and volunteers from the community who work for food and a room to call their own." Turning, she suggested, "Shall we go?"

"By all means," Rand responded, his eyes shooting me a silent reprimand.

I smiled. Once again on his bad side.

As the men disappeared, Linda, Bev, and I changed out of our traveling clothes and primped a bit. We followed the small map *Soeur Madelaine* had drawn directing us to the dining room and met the men for a small but delicious meal of stew and hearty peasant bread.

Much later, after tepid showers taken quietly so as not to wake the children in adjacent rooms, and well after Linda and Bev had fallen quickly to sleep, I found it impossible to settle. Though Rand had issued explicit instructions that we were not to float around the orphanage unnecessarily, I decided it might be a good time to tour the building on the pretext of a late-night bathroom run.

I felt the floor next to my cot for my flashlight, found it, and got up out of bed. I put on slippers. Tripping clumsily over Bev's open suitcase, I caught myself on the foot of her cot, recovered, and stealthily opened the door. Safe outside the room, I flicked on my light and padded down the hall and up the wide staircase where, over time, many feet had worn a noticeable concavity in the stone. A cone of yellow light swept away shadows and illuminated a path for me through the orphanage's deep darkness.

I located the deserted bathroom and remembered, when I was done, to dispose of toilet paper in a can, not THE can. I washed my hands and, finding no towel, wiped them dry on my pajama bottoms.

Exiting the room, I ran full face into *Soeur St. Helena* and gasped an expletive.

Nice job, I silently congratulated myself; way to make an impression.

Our hostess ignored my *faux pas*, asking graciously, "You have found everything you needed, *m'amselle?*"

"*Oui, merci.*" Yes, thanks. Then a correction. "*J'n'ai pas trouve´ d'serviette.*" No towels.

"We have a circular cotton roll on the back of the door, if you'll recall. It's difficult to find when one is not familiar," she assured me.

"Of course."

"You don't seem very sleepy after your long trip," she commented. "Would you like a cup of herbal tea to help calm you?"

"I couldn't bother you."

"Nonsense. I'm on my way to the kitchen to make one for myself this very moment. I'd love the company."

Before I could politely decline, she had me bustling down the passageway, our lights bouncing up walls and through the frosted windows of class-room doors; converging as we rounded a corner.

"Here we are."

The kitchen was spacious and clean. Pots and pans hung from overhead racks and two industrial-sized stoves were flanked by rows of open-shelves. Across the room stood oversized refrigerators and a walk-in freezer. "How do you keep the food cold?" I asked. The electricity had been off for over an hour with three and a half to go.

"Propane."

Of course.

"We use it for cooking as well. These appliances are recent acquisitions," she shared. "Generous donations." Quickly she turned on the burner under a kettle, lit a match, and watched a ring of blue flame leap to life. "They have vastly improved life for our kitchen workers."

I could see where they would. On a different matter, I confessed to her, "I was quite surprised to hear French spoken when we arrived. Rand, Dr. Szabo, hadn't breathed a word."

"A man of secrets, that one."

"Agreed."

"But he is devoted to us and we to him," she said admiringly.

"That's obvious. How did you two come to collaborate?"

"The story is a rather long one, and so I will give you the abridged version."

She climbed a small footstool and reached for a ceramic pot. Setting it on a counter, she scooped loose tea into an infuser. "Chamomile?"

"*C'est bon.*" Fine.

"The order to which I belong is first and foremost a missionary order, as you may know, and one of our primary occupations is to provide needy children an education. To do that, in this setting, we must care for the physical needs of the population as well.

"In the years after the Wall came down, and the political climate in this part of the world began to change, we in Canada had been praying that our work might take a new direction as well. We felt called to this part of Europe, reading of the crowded orphanages and growing destitution as the economies made the adjustment from Communist centralization to free market.

"After a few months of concerted prayer and fasting, we were approached by a gentleman, a former world class runner from this very town, as it happened, who'd defected from the Mexico City Olympics. Somehow he had made his way to Canada, and over the years he had worked very hard and become a wildly successful merchant in Montreal.

"Before we knew any of this about him, we had noticed him occasionally attending Sunday Mass in our chapel or stopping by to pray mid-week. While he was unfailingly polite, he was also reticent. Coming alone and staying after the recessional hymn to pray at the very back of the chapel. Walking forward to light a candle at the altar of Our Blessed Mother a time or two.

"On the Sunday in question, *Monsieur* Miroslav, as we call him, broke his silence. He approached our Superior, and the two of them spoke for some time. He explained how he had come to leave his country during a time when other Soviet bloc nations were pressuring leaders here to become, how do you say it, more hard line, and those leaders were showing strong resistance.

"Talks were held.

"Tensions ran high.

"Ultimately an invasion occurred, weeks before the games. Hundreds of thousands of Warsaw Pact troops had steamrolled into Miroslav's homeland.

"He told how, in the shadow of all that was happening at the games, he was able to slip away from his coaches and to request political asylum, quite fearful of what would happen to him as an outspoken critic of both the Kremlin and of Communism.

"He spoke also of the guilt he'd long felt abandoning his family to the invasion's totalitarian madness."

The Superior, *Soeur Jeanne D'Arc*, had put *Monsieur* Miroslav in contact with the General, the head of their religious congregation. "Slowly we learned more about him and about his plans for his native land."

She paused to pour the fragrant brew into small tea cups. When that was done, she led me to a small office at the very back of the kitchen, lit a candle, and directed me to draw a chair close to the desk.

We turned off our flashlights.

Soeur St. Helena blew gently to cool her tea and continued recounting the history of St. Maria's. "Rather than buying himself a larger home or more expensive cars, *Monsieur* Miroslav felt it incumbent on himself to help those here who had not been given the same blessings and opportunities he had.

"While he held planning sessions with us and got the permissions necessary to move his project forward, he traveled here every chance he got, studying both his homeland and this community specifically, coming up with ideas on how best to help.

"He learned there was a continuing spike in out-of-wedlock births, due in part to the changing behavior of young people, who were beginning to fashion their social interactions more and more on what they saw in western publications and film, and in part to the relatively high cost and low availability of birth control.

"Under the Communist regime, abortion had been relatively common, but with the fall of Communism, the people's political will was reasserted. A number of countries, this one foremost among them, passed strict laws prohibiting the slaughter of the unborn.

"The United Nations actively chastised those laws, claiming they unfairly limited women's basic human reproductive rights, but a few nations held strong to what they considered a greater moral imperative.

"The country has paid a steep price for adhering to its principles."

"In what ways?" I asked.

"Loss of foreign aid; nutrition and education programs. There also seems to be increasingly limited availability of micro-loans for women wanting to start their own enterprises at home." She paused and smiled. "For all the humanitarian gibberish it espouses, the United Nations can be imperialistic and dogmatic if it chooses to be."

No kidding.

She went on. "I should explain, perhaps, that feminism evolved differently here than it did in the west. For one thing, women here were forced into jobs outside the home as early as 1948. They saw the uglier side of 'equality.' Trying to do right by their children even as their lives were dominated by demanding employers, crushing quotas, and exhausting factory work.

"With Communism gone and a market-based economy gaining momentum, young women began to see freedom as the right NOT to have to work; NOT to have to limit the size of their families.

"While both *Monsieur* Miroslav and the Church were convinced that the government's action in limiting abortion was objectively good, they also realized, in practical terms, that the country needed help dealing with a growing population of children whose mothers, many of them unemployed and unmarried, could not adequately provide."

There was a nearly identical trend in the west, I thought, though affluence there minimized the worst of its effects. Young single mothers in the U.S. received food stamps and housing vouchers. Medical care for their children. Those of high school age often had the benefit of in-house day care or subsidized care elsewhere. Again, though those policies and services were objectively good, they often promoted behaviors that harmed the very people they were designed to help.

The Law of Unintended Consequences was the biggest problem with the liberal agenda. A much maligned Dan Quayle—admittedly not an intellectual heavyweight, but a decent man at heart—and others like him had had reason to take the Murphy Browns of the world to task. There was little to be gained by teenagers or young single women becoming parents. Most of them struggled for years at low income jobs and many dragged children through a succession of bad living situations. The resulting instability increased children's vulnerability to a variety of social ills, not the least of which were sexual abuse and a much greater risk, among male children raised without fathers, of later criminal behavior and prison time. Things had reached the point in the U.S. where, in at least one recent *Washington Post* editorial, even people who considered themselves progressive were starting to say, "There's got to be a better way."

Of course there was, but most people were too proud of their open-mindedness to consider it. Abstinence education wasn't a popular notion in our times, but there were programs that had enviable successes. Furthermore, statistics showed that parents who simply taught their children the value of self-control and marital commitment often saw those children grow into more responsible, less sexually active teens and young adults.

They got the message.

Sexuality was an appetite like any other. Enlightened, educated, and properly motivated human beings could rein it in.

Should rein it in.

It made for a balanced life and a lot less drama.

Unaware of my internal digression, *Soeur St. Helena* continued, "*Monsieur* Miroslav decided that abandoned children would be among the first beneficiaries of his charity. He spent almost a year looking for property, and in consultation with us, settled on the purchase of St. Maria's.

"It was an easy decision for him. A nostalgic one, you might say. This property had been the place where his father had been a groundskeeper for almost twenty years, a place where *Monsieur* Miroslav himself, as a boy, had worked alongside other young men planting and harvesting crops, pruning the orchards, and raising a variety of farm animals."

She paused, then added, "It was the place where his father had spoken to him secretly of their faith and helped him grow in service to God."

She sipped her cooled tea and continued, "When we arrived, it was obvious that the property had been horribly neglected for some time.

"Fortunately, Miroslav could envision it as it had been in its best days, and he decided, with our help, to devote himself to its restoration, elevating both the building and the grounds to a higher purpose."

She snapped her fingers. "Before we knew it, the building was ready for occupation. Within two years, it was filled nearly to capacity."

"I'm sure it wasn't that simple," I said.

"*Oui pi non.*" Yes and no. "God did the heavy lifting," she revealed with a smile. "He gave those of us drifting lazily into middle age renewed energy, and provided us with people from the area eager to devote themselves to God's work, something long forbidden here.

"Your Dr. Szabo and his friends came to us through his cousin Matthias, whom I'm sure you'll meet directly. It has been a wonderful fit."

I felt the camaraderie already.

"*Soeur Madelaine* tells us you care for nearly one hundred and fifty children here. That takes tremendous dedication."

"That is true. You should also know that annually we produce several of the country's top scholars from their midst."

"Impressive."

"It is meant to be. You see, we may not be able to provide the children with the parents they miss and long for desperately, but in every other way that is important, we tend to their fundamental needs.

"Within the limits of our time and energy, we teach them to work. To achieve. And to make beautiful lives for themselves out of the suffering they've known."

Patting my hand, she added, "All of this is done with divine help, Parise, it goes without saying. God is the engine to our imperfect machine."

Her words and her display of faith humbled me. I finished the last of my tea and handed her my empty cup. As I rose to go, I could only add to her apt metaphor a whispered, "Amen."

ELEVEN

We rolled out of bed the next morning, Tuesday, some of us less enthusiastically than others.

We had our first introduction to the orphanage's children at the appointed breakfast hour of 6:15 a.m. They filed into the dining hall, freshly scrubbed and uniformed, the boys in white shirts with dark blue sweaters and trousers; the girls wearing skirts, crisp blouses, and cardigans in the same color scheme. A current of curiosity ran through their ranks as they studied us, their new guests, at a distance. A few smiled shyly; others wore sadness in dark under-eye circles and tentativeness. A few extroverts waved, and one boy, likely a self-appointed greeter, made a grand bow and called to us in crisp English, "Good morning!" while friends giggled at his audacity.

The nun closest to Mr. Personality clapped him and his column back to order, and the room quieted as *Soeur St. Helena* entered the room and took her place. At her signal a tall, male student rose to say grace, and all heads bowed.

The prayer finished, cheerful morning sounds quickly erupted and filled the cavernous space. The children's morning chatter played counterpoint to the bang-and-clang of kitchen activity that drifted out to us through a wide set of swinging doors.

Rand directed us to sit together eating our breakfast of muesli, black bread, and strong coffee—the last an extravagance provided only to guests—and we complied. But, after Linda, Bev, and I finished eating, we cleared our dishes from the table and wandered the room, introducing ourselves to the children and entertaining the questions they asked in adequate enough English.

"Do you know Mr.GeorgeBush?" one boy asked, pronouncing the name as a single word. "Or BarackObama?"

"Have you visited the World of Disney?" this from a lively little boy.

"Not yet," I responded to his question. And God willing, I never would. Amusement parks gave me headaches; as did zoos.

"High School Musical, yay!" a teenaged girl exclaimed.

I smiled. Even as the children lived in relative isolation, it was obvious they kept tabs on popular American culture, if belatedly, through the blessing and curse of the Internet. According to *Soeur St. Helena*, there were no television sets on prem- ises other than the two connected to DVD players and used to screen movies once a month. Several computers, complete with software filters, had been donated recently for the children's use, however, and aged ten and older, students were granted individual access thirty minutes every other week. Clearly they shared what they learned.

At seven o'clock, a bell rang, and our time with the students promptly ended. They stood as one, pushed in their chairs, and quickly cleared both the tables and the room. Classes began at 7:30, we'd been told, and the children were allowed—or more accurately, required—to run and play games of kickball for the half hour before second bell. While the physical activity was commendable, I sympathized with teachers forced to begin the day in classrooms filled with the steamy, aromatic scent of sweaty children. Had I been on staff, I might've joined in the games, if only out of self-defense.

In pairs or singly, we drifted back to our rooms. We threw on jackets, hats, and gloves, then left to congregate in the main hall. At Rand's direction, we readied supplies for transport, carrying bundles or pulling loads behind us on hand carts. As a group, we followed his lead down the orphanage's long, unpaved driveway toward the main road.

The day was beautifully bright and crisp, a north wind having cleared the last remnant of rain cloud hovering at the horizon and propelling fallen leaves before us now in delicate arabesques. In daylight, the vastness of St. Maria's was more evident. To the west, an apple orchard stretched to a high hillside and beyond. To the east lay a patchwork of fields where much of the produce consumed by the children was grown. Together with vegetable crops of all varieties, there were fields of herbs and medicinal plants.

"They go through amazing amounts of Echinacea during cold season," Rand told us as we and our supplies bumped along.

"We think they're doing their part to curb the abuse of antibiotics," Linda suggested with a grin.

"Or maybe compensating for our stubborn love affair with them?" I suggested.

"In either case, the nuns should be awarded a collective Nobel," Linda said, and we all concurred.

Rand continued the guided tour, echoing much of what *Soeur St. Helena* had shared the night before. "In late summer the kitchen staff spends weeks canning and building up the root cellar," he indicated. "And the children help with that."

He pointed to a cluster of outbuildings in the distance. "They raise poultry, pigs, and cattle. There's also a herd of dairy cows which," he said as he sniffed the air, "I believe you may have noticed."

And how.

"Are the children used in caring for the animals," Bev asked, putting a distinct emphasis on the word USED.

She was probably having flashbacks to her young life with the Wilsons and the frustration of working hard, then having to hand over pay. The weight of too much responsibility at a young age and the resentment it incurred could die hard.

I sympathized with Bev and the feelings of deprivation that she still felt, years removed from the experience. But I had a slightly different take on child labor. In fact, I had begged my father to let me start working with him at potato harvest the year I turned ten. Raised in town, I was desperate and nosy to find out what the farming life was like.

I'd heard both my parents speaking fondly of their rural childhood from the time I could remember, and going to harvest with Dad—his vacation as he called it—was about as close as I would ever get to sharing in the experiences of his young life. In the face of my pesky promises to work hard and to stay out of the way of dangerous farm equipment, he'd relented the fall of my fifth grade year, my mother muttering audibly in the background, "She probably won't earn enough to cover the cost of her lunch."

As it turned out, I picked my section clean like a pro, earning enough money for lunch, though some days that first year, barely. The work was hard and the northern Maine weather unpredictable. There were times I grew weary and miserably cold, forced to hide behind barrels as flash blizzards blew through, hiding from the storm's icy sting. Other days were glorious, brilliant with fall sunshine, the trees' irrepressible oranges, yellows and reds, and the air fragrant with the leaves' heady decay. As a teenaged harvest worker, I remember loosing my hair to the wind and not being able to get a comb through the mess later that night at home, a high price for my stab at freedom.

During the regular school year, I'd worked for a while as a mother's helper. Every other Saturday and an evening or two a week, I earned extra cash and used it to buy clothes, tapes, and the books to which I was becoming increasingly addicted.

Based on my admittedly limited experience, I'd concluded that child labor, when wisely and judiciously combined with education and opportunity, had its place. It could be a springboard for achievement and success when little else was available. Granted, I'd had the benefit of a mother and father who put strict limits on when, where, and for whom I could work; and any child should have a similar advocate. An aunt, an older friend. Someone who could check for signs of burnout or abuse.

In the case of orphans, the opportunity to work and to earn seemed even more critical. It could give them a sense of independence and power they otherwise wouldn't know, and more crucially, it gave them the skills on which to build a solid future.

Mine wasn't a popular opinion, and I knew it. I'd had words with contemporaries the few times I'd dared gently but firmly to voice it. A few disagreed so vehemently, they felt free to hurl at me remarks they considered to be terrible insults.

"Ann Coulter wanna-be," a bewhiskered law student had once called me.

Another friend of a friend had asked, "Are you some kind of Laura Ingraham clone?"

Most recently, a Congressional aide inebriated on cheap Scotch and his own ego had accused me, spewing spinach dip onto his donkey-emblazoned tie, of being a female Rush Limbaugh. That last comment had hurt, I admit it. I didn't much care for the radio talk show host, though my dislike had more to do with the style and delivery of his bombast than its content or ideology.

In responding to these enlightened critics, I described to those who would listen what often happened in parts of Asia where well-intentioned westerners had campaigned to have children banned from all factory work. Instead of sending their children to school after they were freed from the demands of employment, impoverished parents had sold them into sexual slavery, often to pedophiles from the U.S., there to evade prohibitive western laws.

Those were the kinds of desperate choices available to families in the third world.

How much better would it be, I suggested, to allow children to work a few hours a day, their safety ensured, and to require factory owners to provide classes the other half of the day, creating and educating a middle class while improving conditions for everyone?

More thoughtful individuals conceded that my idea had merit, though they wondered how, practically, it could be implemented. I agreed it might be difficult, but we owed children everywhere, not just ours in the affluent West, to make the effort.

Unfortunately my detractors and many like them had been raised in affluence and private schools, so they wrote me off as a conservative ideologue with no heart.

I knew that opinion had no basis in fact. I supported two children in Africa, one in Zambia, the other in Kenya. My parents had been raised in very poor households and had achieved what they had without trust funds or inheritances. Let my critics stew in their ignorance. I knew a lot more about hardship and deprivation than they did.

So, it seemed, did the community at St. Maria's.

Rand assured Bev, "Only the older children work with the animals during the school year, and the time they spend on chores is limited. A local man is in charge of the operation, and he has a staff whose numbers rise and fall with the demands of the season.

"During the summer, though, it's all hands on deck. The children feed the animals and muck out the stalls. From the age of eleven, they spend two to four hours a day helping out. Less for the younger kids; the full four hours when they hit fifteen.

"A lot depends on the weather and what other responsibilities they have."

The daily schedule always left time for fun which, according to *Soeur St. Helena*, the children had in spades.

"I see," Bev said, seemingly placated by Rand's explanation.

Linda added, "When the children leave here, Bev, they're prepared to face a world that's rarely kind."

"Aside from my personal ties to the area," Rand interjected, "this combination of education and work and lots of hearty play is one of the reasons I wanted to partner with St. Maria's. It produces young people who can hold their own pretty much anywhere."

"And it's not all about manual labor," Linda explained. "Students who demonstrate an aptitude for music, for example, are given the chance to excel."

I thought of the advantages St. Maria's children had over their American counterparts, children who often floundered in foster care. It occurred to me that the kids here not only had a leg up on them but on the average American high school graduate as well.

I'd seen and lived with enough roommates to know that there were a lot of people who weren't adequately trained to fend for themselves. Sure, they could order take-out or lay down plastic for the next electronic must-have by the age of eighteen, but there was more to self-reliance than that.

Half of the people I knew couldn't cook and seemed proud of the fact. A number of my friends couldn't or wouldn't do laundry, dropping off shirts or fine wool garments at the dry cleaners as though there were some magic to getting clothes clean.

"Buy a bottle of Woolite," I'd wanted to scream at more than one inept cohort, "and for God's sake learn to hand wash!"

Was I sounding like an irascible old biddy? If so, it was only because I'd seen too many friends indulge their helplessness while at the same time griping about how outrageous their credit card bills were.

Asking me, in desperation, how I managed.

Hello! It didn't take a degree in economics.

I pointed out the wisdom of frugality, and for the most part they made fun. Sometimes they hooted at my parsimonious hints. There had to be something else, something trendier than buying second hand or using coupons to account for my bank balance.

"Not really. Anyone can do what I do."

To which they laughed and countered, "Parry. You're so anal!"

Well who needed the Preparation H now?

It took about twenty minutes, but we finally reached the hospital, a low-slung concrete building whose architecture harkened back to 1960s' form and function. Sporting lots of utilitarian concrete and ugly steel trim, the edifice didn't strike me as a place where much healing went on. The façade could've used a good pressure washing, new windows, and a crew to plant vegetation on the denuded parcel of land where it sat—trees, flowers, anything!

What a frightening place for a sick person to enter, I thought, hesitating at the threshold. Everything about the building reinforced the mistaken notion, expressed occasionally by elderly patients. "Hospital is the place where you go to die."

The interior was no more welcoming than the forlorn exterior.

The odor hit us first, the combined smell of urinary ammonia, unwashed bodies, and vegetables boiled to a pulp—the latter unexpected since Rand had just finished telling us just there was no kitchen or cafeteria on site.

We entered the cave-like gloom from intense and sparkling sunshine, suffering a temporary loss of vision. We stood a moment, waiting for our eyes to adjust.

The foyer, as it came into focus, was packed with people. Some in wheelchairs, others leaning on canes. Still others lying on litters that family members probably had used getting them here. For every person who looked to be a patient, there were two to three companions, and beside them, bags filled with the necessities of life.

The room was a maelstrom of human suffering.

Rand drew us aside. "Things are different here. People take unexcused leave from their jobs to care for sick family members. They stay for days or weeks until the person they came with either gets well or . . . doesn't."

Nodding our understanding, we gingerly made our way through a crowd that sensed we were there to help. Strangers smiled at us and politely created a path that would get us more quickly to our destination.

Rand diverted us down a hallway to the left.

We discovered a second open space that served as a waiting area for the clinic. Like the lobby, it was filled with people quietly and patiently waiting their turns. "They come from as far as seventy-five kilometers," Rand told us, already speaking in European terms.

Fifty-five miles.

"While that might not seem a great distance to you, remember that most folks in the region don't own cars. Some are able to talk a brother or richer cousin into lending them a rattletrap. Others come by wagon from isolated mountain areas.

"Most take trains. The nearest depot is about twenty kilometers; so they walk from there, or hire a taxi if they've saved enough money."

As he spoke, I imagined how treacherous the trip would be in winter or during spring rains, when snow, mud, or rock slides were a hazard. The mountains whose slopes we had seen in the distance seemed bare. Not much vegetation to stabilize the soil when the spring runoff started up.

"Family stays with patients," Rand told us a second time. "They sleep beside them on the floor, or if they can afford it, find a room nearby. They wash and feed their loved ones as they're recovering."

Hospital staff were too few, he admitted, and older caregivers, steeped in the Communist way, didn't always feel compelled to work hard. He pointed to a window that overlooked a windswept concrete courtyard pockmarked with carbon stains. "In good weather they cook their meals out there."

Our initiation complete, Rand turned to the women of the group. "Linda, Bev, Parry. We're going to join Matthias making rounds in a few minutes. When we're done, we'll come back to the clinic and start pre-op checks."

At last.

"Ken and Paul, when Matthias gets here, he'll set you up with patients he thinks might benefit from therapy. You'll see a lot of chronic back and neck pain. Shoulders and knees. There might even be a couple of stroke patients who would be better served by occupational or speech therapists, but you're the best we have to offer."

We chuckled at the men's expense.

"Ken. Before I forget. *Soeur Charles Regis* wants you to come by and spend some time with that little boy you've been helping," Rand suddenly remembered. "She assures me you have to see his progress first hand."

"Sure. Sure. Soon as I can."

Ken had described his recent plunge into long-distance consultation to me on the short flight from Munich to Budapest. Thanks to computers and digital cameras, he and Paul had started reviewing cases from the comfort of home—looking at x-rays and medical reports and the patients themselves using Skype. Based on what they saw, they recommended exercise regimes for people who might otherwise never fully recover from their injuries or overcome chronic conditions. It wasn't a perfect system, Ken was the first to admit, but he and Paul kept at it, fine-tuning things as they went.

A little boy named Balint had recently become Ken's special project, and the trip was his first chance to see the boy close up. "I'll check in with the good sister as soon as I can," he promised Rand again.

Rand shifted his attention to the non-medical types. "Jake and Rich, why don't I introduce you to the physical plant folks, and you all can get started."

They nodded; neither man the type to need hand holding.

Ted was the only person missing from the group. As planned, he'd stayed behind at the orphanage to study its antiquated heating system. Furnace to steam radiators, he saw it as his responsibility to make sure the system functioned as it was intended to. "If I got the time," he'd told us that morning between impressive mouthfuls of food, "I've already seen a bunch of other problems that could use my attention."

A man in a lab coat blew into the room suddenly and was introduced, in some cases re-introduced, all around. Matthias Szabo was tall, robust, and bearded. He vaguely resembled Rand, but the moment he opened his mouth, it was obvious he was a completely different person. Warm, effusive, and comical, he shook our hands and welcomed us as though he'd known us a lifetime. "It is so kind of you to come all this way.

"Please. Follow me."

We dropped Ken and Paul first, assigning them to a rotund little nurse named Anna. "Come, come," she encouraged them pleasantly. "We have much work."

Back in the hospital lobby, Matthias drew Jake and Rich a map. "You're expected," he explained as he labeled the repair shop with a big red X. "Please ask for Zoltan."

That done, the rest of us trailed Matthias onto the wards, which were more crowded and confused, if possible, than the hospital's public areas. Patients lay in old, metal beds whose paint was chipped and scarred. While separated from one another by walls of stained curtains, a modicum of privacy maintained, the sounds and smells of misery easily filtered through.

We were in a time warp. Discarded glass syringes and IV bottles, not seen in the States for at least fifteen years, were everywhere. On table tops; on the floor; swinging from poles. Soiled blankets and clothing had been shoved under beds, the disposal of contaminated linens obviously not of overwhelming concern. Bedside suction devices, a rare find in modern hospitals, cluttered the space between beds. Likewise IV tubing and metal (not plastic) bedpans and basins. "Clean" bed linens, stored on open shelving, were a dull and dingy grey.

Hello bleach!

The contrast to the fastidiousness of St. Maria's was startling and worrisome, but we somehow ignored the lapses in sanitation and did what we'd come here to do. We started examining the patients on our surgical list.

The first, an elderly woman named Viktoria, had been admitted to the hospital for a hip fracture. In a perfect world, she would have been operated on a.s.a.p. to decrease the risk of blood clots or permanent joint damage, but immediate intervention here wasn't an option. As a result of having been confined to bed for more than two weeks, she was considered high risk, but the fact she'd survived this far spoke to her overall health and resilience. Rand, Matthias, and I concurred: the septuagenarian had a good shot at recovery.

In another part of the ward, we examined two bad shoulder breaks then moved on to a pediatric case. In a far corner, we discovered a young boy named Lorant who'd walked in alone from the countryside a few days earlier. Three fingers on the teenager's right hand had been badly crushed in an accident, the skin bruised and scabbed in several places. His misshapen hand was infected after almost a week without attention.

Rand leaned over to study Lorant's hand, then looked at the grossly overexposed x-rays provided. Through Matthias, he told the youngster he absolutely needed surgery. While two fingers might be saved and their function partially restored, the third would have to be amputated. There was no other alternative.

Hearing the one terrible word, the boy withdrew his hand. He vigorously cried out what sounded like a loud and non-negotiable, "No!"

"Tell him he'll lose his hand if he doesn't let me operate," Rand insisted. "Or worse. The infection's far gone. I'm surprised he's not septic."

"He was when he first came to us," Matthias said. "We have given him the strongest intravenous antibiotic we have, but unless you operate, I fear the infection will gain ground."

He lowered himself to the bed and laid a hand on the frightened boy's shoulder. With infinite gentleness, he pled Rand's case.

The boy's own case.

I imagined him explaining that the loss of a single finger could mean a near-normal life while struggling to find work with only one hand, the outcome he was courting by refusing our help, would be infinitely more difficult.

It might've seemed cruel, telling this already terrified boy what could happen in a worst case scenario, but he needed to know the full truth of his situation. He needed to know that if he refused surgical treatment, he'd probably never have to concern himself with a job.

The boy wavered. Tears streamed down a face still caked with farm mud, and his eyes darted around the room desperately, an animal inexplicably caged. It was obvious he wished there were someone else to take on the burden of deciding, someone to comfort and protect him from us; from our news.

Unfortunately, there was no one.

With less certainty, Lorant shook his head again, "No," declining our help a second time.

Rand stood and moved away, files in hand. "Next case," he ordered, and reluctantly Matthias and I followed his lead.

We spent another hour interviewing patients and taking notes, Matthias supplementing the information Rand and I had reviewed on the plane. After we finished on the ward, all four of us reported to the clinic and spent what remained of the morning meeting with patients and conducting pre-op physicals, helped in our endeavor by two nurses fluent in medical, not just conversational English.

This was the part of the work I loved. Getting my hands on patients myself.

Touching.

Listening.

Looking into eyes of a mother whose young child had been inexplicably favoring one arm or leg over the other, determining what the problem might be.

Physical contact and incisive questioning, even through a translator, were the tools with which the nuances of precise clinical information could be mined. And that, in turn, was the key to effective treatment.

By coincidence, I met Janos, Katalin, and a boy named Erik in the clinic that morning, each of them corroborating the stories Rand had told me about them on the plane. The hours passed quickly, and soon the group—minus Rich and Jake, busy somewhere in the bowels of the hospital—strolled back to the orphanage for a lunch of cheese, chunky applesauce, and spicy hard sausage.

We returned, bag lunches in hand for our engineer comrades, to the news that the long-lost x-ray machine had finally made its appearance! Tied into the bed of a truck equipped with a heavy-duty lift, it had arrived a half hour earlier, both the vehicle and the cost of the transportation a last-minute gift from a well-endowed trauma hospital in Budapest.

There was universal rejoicing as an administrator named Jan gave us directions to the loading dock where the machine awaited our inspection.

"You ladies head over to central supply," Rand said, waving Linda and Bev to an afternoon of re-sterilizing our supplies. "Parry and I are off to look over the wayward portable."

It was sitting lone and unattended in the open air when we found it. "What luck," Rand observed. "They left the technique chart taped to the control panel."

In his place, my first words might have been, "Thank God it's not raining," or, ""Phew! No one stole it," but I guess in terms of what was most important to our patients, yes, the chart was definitely a good thing.

Technique charts were specific to each x-ray machine, though there tended to be a great deal of consistency among them. The charts were used by radiographers in determining the amount and the quality of x-radiation needed to adequately expose a body part. In making best use of a chart, the shooter considered both the thickness of a part and the kind of tissue being penetrated—fat, muscle, or bone—before setting the factors needed to get a good x-ray picture. Kilovoltage (kv), milliamperage (ma), and length of exposure, usually set in milliseconds, were the primary factors involved.

The X-ray techs with whom I'd been friendly, both at Wake and UMC, had taken the time to explain the process to me, because I bothered to ask, and in general terms, I understood it this way.

The thicker—or more dense—the body part, the more powerful the radiation needed to adequately penetrate it. The higher the kilovoltage, the more the penetrating power it had. Extrapolating, I knew lower settings were used x-raying fingers and hands, higher settings for bellies and skulls. Chests, while thick and relatively large, were air-filled; they required less radiation than one might initially assume.

There were other image characteristics one had to keep in mind when shooting, things like the desired contrast, image density, and detail, but in bone work, I'd surmised, close enough was usually good enough.

Relatively recent developments in the use of digital radiography had broadened the spectrum of acceptable exposure, rendering much of the foregoing explanation obsolete. Digital equipment replaced technologist experience and expertise with computer algorithms, so that now image manipulation could be accomplished after the fact.

While the change was good in the sense that it meant an overall decrease in patient exposure and fewer repeated films, older technologists thought the new technology allowed younger techs to get lazy. The more professional among them considered it vital that the basic principles of radiation exposure not only be taught but be adhered to; they themselves relied on the tried and true.

As expected, this unit wasn't digital.

"You're going to shoot our OR films," Rand told me unnecessarily.

"I can do that."

He would never have expected Judd Henderson to snap pictures, but hey, I was here, and I was cheap. I could be conscripted.

I walked around the machine. It was an old General Electric model, the kind I'd seen a hundred times in the halls of every hospital I'd ever worked in. The thing carried its own massive battery under the hood supplying juice to the tube head, a cathode/anode arrangement used to actually produce the rays.

The oversized battery made the portable versatile; techs could snap pictures in the wards, in halls; in the event of a medical disaster, they could even shoot outdoors. One important complication, however, was that it had to be plugged into an outlet periodically to recharge.

"Where's the adaptor?" I asked.

"Adaptor?"

"This machine uses alternating current to recharge the battery. Europe has direct current. Ergo . . ."

Some kind of converter was required. Any American who came to Europe with a hair dryer understood the concept.

Rand's reaction was a succinct and monosyllabic, "Damn!" Apparently this was one detail that had escaped his attention.

He pulled open the drawer where film cassettes were usually stored but found nothing there. He cussed furiously.

Helpful.

I flipped the machine's ON-OFF switch, hoping that it had retained enough charge for us to be able to at least move the beast inside.

No luck. The battery was completely unresponsive.

I didn't want to add to Rand's wrath, but I had to speak up. "Rand, we can't even move the machine with the battery the way it is. No charge; no motion."

He glared at me, eyes spitting fiery accusation.

"It's a bit of a Catch-22," I explained just for the joy of seeing him get more flustered. "The battery is what makes the machine portable, but it's also the weight of the battery that keeps the machine from being completely 'mobile.'"

Put another way, "We need to get this thing plugged in, or it won't budge."

Rock, meet hard place.

Rand shot a second round of hairy-eyeball mortar my way then disappeared into the building without another word.

I spent a guilty moment relishing his discombobulation.

It was perverted, this pleasure I took in his frustration, and yet the thought that I, Parise St. Amand, had caught the illustrious Randall Szabo unprepared was just a little too wonderful not to indulge.

I noted the exact time, date, and location of my minor triumph and promised myself never to forget.

I planned a dozen ways in which to use the newfound leverage.

With nothing more for me to do getting the machine up and running, I headed back to the clinic. The overworked staff there could use my help.

As I smugly sauntered away, it occurred to me that the conventional wisdom was true: It was the little things in life that made it worth living. Despite my best intentions not to be cruel, I whistled as I walked.

TWELVE

The next four days were a blur of muscle, blood, and bone.

While the rest of the world was in the throes of the worst economic downturn in a generation, our small band was completely oblivious to any financial angst. We got up in the dark, showered in the building's stony chill, and hiked to the hospital, jacket collars turned to a brisk November wind. Except in generalities, we had no idea what was happening beyond the small and isolated community that was our temporary home. All our energy, focus, and intent was directed toward one thing: our work.

The hospital's resourceful handyman, Zoltan Chovanec, had saved the surgical side of the mission from disaster on Tuesday by plundering his trove of surplus parts on our behalf. Swearing us to secrecy, he'd provided an adaptor able to handle the x-ray machine's high voltage load, quickly charging the machine where it sat vegetating on the loading dock's concrete apron. At my request, he'd moved the lumbering machine to an empty clinic office where I took pictures of patients recently admitted and used the process as a test both for the machine and for my limited radiographic skills.

I shot chest films, skulls, and abdomen x-rays, the latter a tool used in looking for free air in elderly patients complaining of belly pain, and finding, invariably, that they were FOS—crude hospital shorthand for "desperately constipated."

Determined to get the best pictures I could, I used other equipment also donated to the cause by UMC. I taped leaded devices called grids to x-ray cassettes. I knew they enhanced picture quality by absorbing excess, i.e., 'scatter" radiation, and were used primarily on thick or dense body parts. I'd watched technologists handling them a hundred times, but doing so myself was infinitely more challenging than I could've imagined.

If the x-ray tube's central beam wasn't precisely perpendicular to the plate, technologists had told me repeatedly, the lead strips in the grid could and would absorb most of the x-ray beam before it reached its ultimate target, the coating on x-ray plates that converted x-radiation to light. I blew at least three films to the dreaded "cut-off" before I got the knack of things.

In short order, I also learned a few key translations for, "Lie down," "Take in a breath and hold it . . . hold it!" and the ever-important, "Breathe now!" supplementing phrases with hand or body motions whenever additional communication was needed.

Pull up your shirt. Pull down your pants. Roll up on your side.

I was a champion at charades.

The most challenging part of the job, working alone, was running back and forth to the hospital's one-room radiology department and getting the slightly resentful male technologist there to develop my films.

There was an automated processor in the department which, despite its antiquity, worked well. The gears squeaked and the films came through in the ninety seconds typical for units of that vintage, or so I'd been told.

The technologist's didn't seem pressed for time either. Whenever I showed up winded from the 100-foot sprint and carrying an armload of exposed cassettes, I found him sitting at his desk reading or enjoying a glass of tea—not much of a surprise since I was doing most of the work that usually went to him.

Still, he didn't rush to help when he saw me, in fact he continued reading for a minute or two, then ever-so-slowly closed his book or took a long, slow sip of beverage. Standing, he put his chair back in its proper place, straightened his tie, and offered me a seat while I waited. Disappearing into the darkroom, he took ten minutes or more developing the few films I had. Even accounting for his bumbling around in the dark as he reloaded cassettes, the man was infuriatingly slow. When I had the audacity to offer to run the films myself, he pretended not to understand and then, contradicting his confusion, insisted, "I go. I go."

I decided my problem came down to gender or nationality—maybe both—and that maybe he saw it as an affront that he had to share his esteemed role in the hospital with an American female.

The reason didn't really matter to me. I just wanted to get through my workload as efficiently as possible, which was why, on my third trip over with a load of 14 x 17-inch cassettes, I was inspired to bring along a couple of chocolate chip granola bars to share.

"Snack?" I offered Mr. Slowpoke.

He studied me wordlessly but watched as I bit into the bar I'd brought for myself. I chewed and subtly yummed it up; slid the second one across his desk. He left it behind as he vanished into the darkroom, but when he came out, in record time, he succumbed to the lure of Quaker Oats.

From the moment he tasted Peanut Butter Chocolate Chunk, my new friend seemed cured of ill will. Call it old fashioned and unenlightened, call it contrary to feminist rhetoric, I don't care. The way to a man's cooperation, if not his heart, really was through his stomach, and I had no problem bribing this one if it meant getting the job done.

When he finished eating, he introduced himself as Laszlo.

"Parry," I reciprocated. We shook hands.

When I offered to teach him how to use the portable in words he seemed to understand, he appeared to be torn. As I turned to go, though, he followed. For the rest of the afternoon he helped me shoot films and insisted on running them back and forth himself to develop.

Before he left for the day, we scrubbed down the portable with disinfectant and steered it into the two-room OR that would be its new home. We high-fived one another on a job well done.

I gave Laszlo the granola bars I had left in my pocket to take home to his kids, and he thoughtfully gave me a tour.

We were golden.

Compared to the rest of the hospital, where peeling paint, dust, and a panoply of micro-organisms abounded, the OR was amazingly modern and clean. It was tiled, floor to ceiling, and lit with adjustable operating room lights similar to, if older than, those at UMC. Supplies were labeled and stored in glass-front cabinets or on metal shelving, medications and assorted intravenous set-ups in the former; sterile instrument trays, metal basins, and linens on the shelves. The air, unlike the moist and presumably infectious atmosphere of the wards, was chilled and filtered.

When I commented on the OR's comparative modernity that night at dinner, Rand responded, "The Quebec group provided much of what you saw."

"Who?"

The Quebec team included a pediatrician, a heart specialist, and an orthopedist from *Soeur St. Helena*'s hometown of Montréal, Linda explained. The group generally visited in the spring, alternating with the D.C. group that came in late summer or early fall. Like us, they took over supplies and equipment as space and money allowed. They, too, scavenged engineering and construction talent from under the noses of semi-complicitous hospital administrators, and just that spring had contributed a new anesthesia machine, training a bright, Vienna-educated nurse anesthetist in its use.

Adrienn Kunu.

"The young woman we met today before leaving?"

"The same."

"Well, here's hoping she's ready to have her training put to the test," I toasted, raising a glass of cider from our hostesses' cellar.

"Here. Here," the group echoed.

In the days that followed, Adrienn proved herself a tireless ally. She never stopped. Never complained. She never let any detail of her patients' care go unnoticed.

More important than any of that, she was a huge fan of Third Eye Blind and Sugar Ray, bands I'd loved in college. Between patients, the two of us sang; we danced; we bonded in the way girl-friends did, laughter as the international language of friendship.

Rand was too busy for that kind of frivolity.

Our very first case turned out to be Viktoria's hip. Probably not the patient I'd have chosen to put at the head of the line, but I think Rand was so taken with the old woman's spunk and determination, he had to give her a shot.

While he scrubbed, and the nursing team set up trays, I scrambled to get the x-ray machine in place before sterile draping was arranged. The lateral, or side view, was the trickier of the two shots we would need to ensure that the hardware pounded into the hip's bony mass was well positioned, so I maneuvered the tube head into place for that picture first.

Less than an hour into the operation, I snapped a picture at Rand's request and prayed that the grid I'd positioned with exquisite care was still where it needed to be. I extricated the cassette from its holder without contaminating the field and ran it to the x-ray department like a woman with her clothes afire. There and back in under five minutes, thanks to my new best friend Laszlo, I held the film up to an overhead light for Rand to check. Conventional view boxes were a luxury here; doctors made do with whatever bright light happened near.

I got a quick thumbs up, then set up for the second shot.

Carefully, nervously, I guided the machine from beneath the extensive draping and got it into position for a frontal view of the joint, the picture that would seal the deal. It turned out even better than the first, and like a finely tuned machine, we began the job of closing.

We finished the hip nailing in record time for the facility, though nowhere near Rand's personal best, then moved on to the rest of our demanding day. During our second case, we reduced a femur fracture and hung it in traction. We manipulated and casted a forearm fracture and followed that with a broken ankle.

We took a half hour break around two, annihilating a lunch of cheese sandwiches, raisins, and cider delivered to us in Matthias' office by smiling Jake. I watched as he distributed the food. Napkins. Pieces of chocolate I knew didn't come from the nuns.

He sat with us in the crowded room as we ate.

"You doing all right," he asked after Rand and the ladies excused themselves.

"A little tired," I responded. "But it's good tired."

"Portable working okay?"

"Amazingly, yes. I still can't believe how Zoltan saved the day."

"He's incredible," Jake acknowledged. "For a guy completely self-taught, he has the most solid grasp of electrical engineering principles I've ever run across." Popping in a Dove lozenge, he continued, "Zoltan trouble shoots like a master. I could use a dozen more like him at work.

"You can always teach someone book smarts," I contributed. "It's a lot tougher to make them more hardworking."

Agreed.

"Even his English is nuanced," Jake revealed.

"How so?"

"He gets the jokes Rich and I make . . ."

I grinned.

"What's with the smile?"

"You don't want me to tell you."

"I do."

"No. You don't."

"Parry," he said menacingly.

"All right. All right. You and Rich? Making jokes?"

"What about it?"

"You're engineers."

"Point being?"

"Yours is not a profession known for its comedic bent."

"Ouch."

I followed up by asking, "So, do the two of you make jokes in Geek speak?"

"You raggin' on me?"

"No." I met his direct gaze. "Maybe . . ."

More seriously, I admitted, "Maybe I'm just the leetlest bit envious."

"Of?"

"Your competence. Your brilliance. All of the above."

He didn't speak, but his eyes softened. "You hardly know me," he observed.

"I know enough."

The room was suddenly still and silent.

He looked shyly down at his feet.

It occurred to me that I might've just shown my hand, something Parise St. Amand never did. But then, by his silence, so had he.

Jake rose to go, and I tracked his deliberate movements as he cleared away leftovers and a few pieces of trash. He turned and our eyes briefly locked.

"See you tonight, then," I said.

He gave me a little half smile. "It's a date."

Somewhere inside, I felt the tingle of romantic confirmation. He liked me, too.

"Bye."

"Bye yourself."

I had to hurry, joining my colleagues for our first afternoon case. Rand was amputating the finger of our young country boy, Lorant, a late addition to the schedule.

Matthias had joined us for dinner the night before at *Soeur St. Helena*'s invitation, and he'd agreed with me that we couldn't leave the situation as it stood. A boy as young as Lorant didn't have the maturity to see beyond his own terror.

It was that thought, expressed between bites of dumpling and stewed prunes, and emboldened by sips of the fire water Matthias had brought to share, that helped the two of us decide we'd take on the role of parents on Lorant's behalf.

We'd snuck away from St. Maria's sometime after Rand left the table—and after the effects and scent of alcohol on our breath had completely dissipated. Arriving at Lorant's bedside, we'd patiently explained to the boy that surgery was the best chance he had for a normal life—for a family and a future that could be bright, if only he let it happen in the way that it should.

Lorant's fever had climbed to over 101 degrees by the time we saw him, and his hand was swollen to the point where the slightest movement was excruciating. We saw in his eyes the dimming light of hope.

It wasn't a hard sell.

Seventeen hours later, I stood next to Rand and watched as he cut into the boy's hand, both of us instantly aware that things were worse than we'd expected. Though the amputation was quickly achieved, Rand devoted over an hour painstakingly examining and debriding Lorant's wound. Bent over the field, he aligned small splinters of bone and inserted pins where they would do the most good, deftly clearing away infected flesh. The procedure stretched into a ninety-minute ordeal, Rand doing everything humanly possible to save the boy's injured fingers. He knew what was at stake, what kind of life a one-handed farmer or tradesman had to look forward to in an agrarian economy, so he pressed on, sweating and persevering, giving Lorant the best chance at rehabilitation that he could.

Making good on Matthias' and my promises of the night before.

Every few minutes, I irrigated the surgical site and sponged away the perspiration that gleamed on Rand's forehead, drops of it threatening to drip into, and contaminate the wound. Watching him, I saw the tender, considerate side he kept well hidden.

The days that followed were every bit as demanding and intense as our first.

As wearying.

Because so many of our patients had been injured weeks or even months earlier, we expended as much time and energy undoing the effects of improper healing as we did setting things right. The surgeries were difficult and intricate and they ate up commensurately more of our resources.

As tired as we were, we attacked each new case as though it were our most important. I found myself playing the role of human ping-pong ball, bouncing from the OR to recovery to the wards, and back again, helping Rand and the nurses when they needed me in surgery, checking on patients groggily stirring awake in the recovery room. Through the same interpreters who'd helped me in the clinic, I gave strict instructions to the floor nurses, returning later to be sure that Rand's directives had been followed to a T.

Over those first few days we handled fractures of all kinds: greenstick and spiral; simple and compound; displaced and non-displaced. We repaired a torn rotator cuff, excised a synovial cyst, and set a fresh and excruciating fracture/dislocation.

I rushed here and ran there. I removed bandages from wounds we suspected weren't healing as they should've been and pushed the antibiotics hard. I lectured nurses on the absolute necessity that they WASH THEIR HANDS—the whole time flashing back to M*A*S*H re-runs my parents had watched off and on during my childhood and to the staff of the crazed 4077th. I couldn't help but think how much like those conditions ours here seemed to be—minus the gunfire, the casualties, and the home-made hootch, of course.

Like the M*A*S*H crew, we were in a battle against time, and we worked in relatively primitive conditions. We laughed hard and often, teasing Rand, our very own Charles Emerson Winchester, out of his gruff intensity, and flirting with Matthias, the affable B.J. come to life.

One glaring difference between Team Szabo and the fictional Army unit, though, was that we had the blessing of simple and delicious meals.

"Man this is good," Rich raved as he devoured the food set before him at night. "They don't give us much, but what there is sure hits the spot."

Stews.

Potato dumplings with a caramelized onion kick.

Pot pies filled to the flaky crust with vegetables and gravy.

None of us left the table hungry.

"It's like the miracle of the fish and the loaves," Jake said as we cleared away dishes our third night there. "In the midst of poverty, we're more than adequately fed."

I stared at him, a man of science and mathematics who was both poetic and scripturally knowledgeable and thought, someone pinch me.

As miraculous as our diet was the fact that the entire crew—working, eating, and sleeping together—got along. Sure, we debated the merits of our respective professions, the medical staff claiming they worked harder than the engineering types, naturally, but at the end of the day, the old 'familiarity breeds contempt' adage was trumped by a palpable sense of respect and cooperation. Falling into bed at night, I was thankful for new friends and new stamina; for living life on a whole new plane and with a whole new purpose.

Every day I was strangely grateful for the privilege of working myself to exhaustion.

THIRTEEN

Saturday was a half-day at the hospital, so we all got back to the orphanage by 2:30.

Instead of collapsing in heaps, which would've been both understandable and forgivable given the work we'd dispatched in three days, we put on our play clothes and joined the children on their afternoon off.

Preparing for the cold, I dressed in flannel-lined jeans and a thick sweater, then headed toward the fields, hoping to join the teenagers in a raucous soccer match.

European football.

I passed Linda on her way to the nursery.

"I'm gonna put in a couple of hours rocking and diapering babies," she confessed. "My children are going to be single forever, looks like. I may as well get this grand-mothering out of my system while I have the chance."

"I thought you were getting a cold?"

"I might be." She held up latex gloves, a surgical mask, and a bottle of hand sanitizer. "I'll make sure I don't share."

Bev was staying inside, too. She'd made plans to meet with a group of tweens, girls who seemed drawn to her despite her new, pared down look. I couldn't blame them; Bev had *VOGUE* imprinted on her like some kind of subtle watermark. Linda, while attractive, was ***Better Homes and Gardens*** and I, on my best days might've been a recruit for an ***L.L. Bean*** cover shot.

Wholesome, fresh-faced, freckled. You know the type.

Out in the cold afternoon air, I saw that Paul was playing the perpetual sports dad. He was hauling Frisbees and American-style footballs out of the duffel he'd lugged three thousand miles, and fully energized, was directing a gang of boys and girls in a free-for-all out by the barns. Jake and Rich were in the thick of the action, too.

No sign of Rand, though. He was probably in the library writing synopses of articles in *The American Journal of Orthopedics*, preparing for a conference and completely unaware of the concept of play.

For more than two hours, I ran and elbowed past youngsters. I jumped up and down on the sidelines for warmth when I had to and watched the children try to impress me with their natural athleticism.

As darkness descended, and the dinner hour approached, activity slowed. The kids got silly, and the adults, now ravenous, migrated toward the dining hall for the evening meal. Someone in the large group of us walking past an outdoor thermometer noted that the temperature had dropped to minus eight degrees Celsius already—twenty-five degrees Fahrenheit. That was cold.

I glanced at a rising half-moon and felt the air's distinct wintry quality as it struck my face. "Feels like snow," I said to myself.

Ken, a Southern boy red-faced from the afternoon's exertion, heard me and was unbelieving. "Don't be crazy," he told me. "It's barely November."

Paul backed him up, agreeing, "It's much too early to snow."

The Mainer in me didn't bother to contradict. I knew the signs; I'd spent more than two-thirds of my life in New England. There was nothing more certain than the moon's hazy glow through a veil of atmospheric ice crystals to predict a storm. Slung low on the horizon, it was as good as a promise that we'd wake up the next morning to snow.

I headed inside and thought, let 'em learn.

When we met up again at the dinner table, news of my prediction had spread, and Paul was taking bets. "C'mon. Our little alarmist here says we'll see flakes by sunrise. Who wants easy money?"

"You really don't have enough to keep you busy," I joked.

Next to me, Jake said, "Count me out. The girl's got Yankee blood."

Well not exactly, but I suppose to him it would've seemed that way.

"Thanks for the vote of confidence, Jake."

In a soft aside, he assured me, "I always back a winner."

Somewhat more dubious about my meteorological expertise, Ted and Rich opened their wallets, and Linda unzipped her fanny pack. Bev, the only other native northerner, couldn't seem to decide.

Getting into the spirit of things, Rand surprised us by holding up his satellite phone and saying to Paul, "Give me a minute. I may want some of that action . . ."

"No fair!" Paul challenged. "You can hook up to the Internet with that thing."

"Well, I'd have to plug it in to the broadband unit first, which I believe is downstairs, but the answer would be yes. Yes I can."

People laughed and started putting away their money.

"Cowards," Paul said. Then to Rand, "Show off."

There would be no gambling action for anyone that night.

The next morning we slept in.

I didn't get up until well after seven, even then hoping to beat the rush getting ready for nine o'clock Mass. It wasn't until I glanced out a bathroom window on the second floor that I was vindicated.

At least six inches of the white stuff covered the ground, and from the storm's intensity, it was a good bet there was a lot more on the way. It took everything in me not to race back downstairs and pull Paul out of bed. Push him out the door. Wash his face in the snow the way my brothers had brutishly washed mine too many times to remember.

By afternoon, the wind picked up.

As we filed into the chapel for a musical performance that the children had prepared for us, the world beyond the windows was featureless, fathomless white.

Eight of us from the team made up the core of the children's audience. In the throes of a premigraine aura, in his case a colorful kaleidoscope, Rich had begged off. Hoping to thwart a full-blown headache, he'd stolen down to the men's bedroom where he could count on darkness and rest.

"Do what you have to do," Rand had advised before he left the dining hall. "You need any meds?"

"Not yet. I think I'll be all right as long as I hide from the light."

A fellow sufferer, Linda sympathized, "By all means."

We seated ourselves and, politely silent, waited for the program to begin. Minutes before three, a group of the older youngsters entered, stage left, and walked across the altar. They sat down in chairs arranged in a broad semi-circle. The remainder of the children, upwards of seventy, filled the chapel rotunda and the marble steps leading to the sanctuary.

The boys and neatly combed girls were dressed in Sunday finery, wearing black trousers or pleated wool skirts where yesterday they'd sported overalls, old sweaters, and hair blown silly by the wind.

Muddy and pink-cheeked from play then, they were almost unrecognizable in both appearance and demeanor as they stood before us, reserved and ready to sing.

The chapel was at once a vast and an intimate space. Old stone walls, polished marble floors, exquisite stained glass windows high overhead that bespoke medieval notions of worship and devotion. The oak pews smelled mildly of tung oil and glowed golden in candlelight beaming from the altar and holders stationed along the aisles.

Matthias, having braved the weather in his rust-riddled truck, snuck in just as the children were drawing a collective breath to begin. The first strains of violin floated plaintively through the chapel as the hallway clock struck three o'clock. Vivaldi, I thought as I heard it, or maybe Mozart. The notes were lively and immensely appealing, a complete contrast to the somber and serious business of blizzarding that whined and whirled outside.

As the piece's final passage faded, the choir, directed by lively *Soeur Marie-Celeste,* immediately launched into song. Youthful and thin, the nun's hands moved with deft and delightful enthusiasm. The children, inclined toward her in full concert mode, were animated and smiling.

Though none besides Rand and Matthias understood the words that the children sang, it didn't seem to matter. Their voices sounded angelic, until the moment they segued into a more spirited selection and suddenly turned playful. Soon enough, all of us adults were clapping to the beat and humming along. We cheered the tiniest girl in the choir as she successfully finished a solo and then took a deep and deserved bow.

The program proceeded to Hayden and Brahms solos, and then to an awe-inspiring rendition of Ave Maria, a duet sung by a pair of spectacularly talented adolescents. My eyes filled at the familiar Latin words, the song favorite of my father's. A few minutes later my friends and I were invited to join in an English version of the Lord's prayer that the children had learned especially for us. At the end of the concert, at the very last echo of Handel's Hallelujah Chorus, we rose to our feet and called, "Bravo!"

The children acknowledged our applause with their smiles, and later, when we stood mingling with them in the hall outside, it occurred to me how much a departure this performance had been from the few events I'd attended at my niece's and nephews' schools. There had been no boom box here or electric amplification of any kind. No canned accompaniment to overwhelm pure young voices. All we'd heard was the delicate dance of fingers on piano keys or the lively whistle of a flute; at times the lament of a sweet violin underscoring the singers' talent.

The children, while precocious at moments, didn't emote the subtle sexuality that American stage children often did. No hip was suggestively angled or tummy exposed. I hadn't seen the first hint of lip gloss or mascara or blush, despite Bev's tutorial, the way I would have in a production at home.

These children had been all the more beautiful for the lack of artifice.

I had a sudden memory of myself at my niece Annabelle's dance recital. Girls as young as kindergarten costumed like tiny street walkers, their sad, often inadvertent objectification bringing back images of JonBenet, whose haunting, video-taped performances would live into infinity. I'd worried, looking around at the audience that night, if there was a sexual predator in its midst, a man for whom dress-up, and the fantasies it stirred, was exactly the sick reason he was there.

I'd said a quick prayer on the innocent young girls' behalf that he was not.

We left the chapel as a group, adults and children strolling the corridor toward the dining hall for a late afternoon meal served by the nuns. Kitchen employees were given Sundays off to be with family.

The meal was delicious—thick chicken soup, sandwich quarters, and curls of homemade fruit leather, a childhood staple I still loved. We laughed as much as we ate, teaching the children words and expressions they were unlikely to learn from textbooks, and while I will not, under penalty of death, enumerate the exact content of said tutorial, I will confess that there was a mildly improper theme to the new vocabulary, as per the children's request.

When the dinner hour was officially over, Jake and I pled the children's case to *Soeur St. Helena.*

Because of our collective eloquence, they were allowed to stay on an extra hour. Together with Paul and Linda, we supervised impromptu games of password and charades—an opportunity for the students to showcase both their knowledge of English and their considerable imaginations—keeping the din to a dull roar.

Just after six-thirty, *Soeur St. Helena* and her helpers returned, herding the children up to their rooms. It was time to prepare for the week ahead, they explained, to lay out clothing and organize assignments that should have been completed the day before but may have not.

The children shuffled off, turning several times to bemoan their plight. Our friends left, too, Linda insisting, "It's going to take a week for me to recover from all this."

Jake and I stayed behind, alone in the empty dining hall whose lights *Soeur St. Helena* dimmed on her way out. We spoke softly. Warmly. He asked me questions about Maine, my family, what I had been like as a child.

I was curious about his life, too.

"I have four younger siblings," he told me. "A brother, Pete, and twin sisters, Natalie and Jane. A baby sister who's just now graduating from college. Temperance."

"Interesting name," I commented.

"I think my Mama was giving Pop a hint," he grinned. "She's a tiny bit of a thing, and my guess is she was tired."

"I hear you."

"I can see that you do," he told me.

I blushed. "So, aside from the fact you're a first born, what else can you tell me?"

He grinned. "That doesn't say it all?"

"Not quite."

"Okay then. Well, I'm a good Baptist boy. I teach Sunday school and volunteer on service projects. Flip a few pancakes for the church's annual Mother's Day brunch."

I liked that.

"I played football and baseball in high school. Went to college on a ROTC scholarship, so I guess you could say the Army owns my degrees."

"Uncle Sam owned much of mine," I commiserated. "Where'd you serve?"

"I spent a lot of time in Germany with an engineering unit," he revealed. "Got transferred to NATO headquarters in Brussels about halfway through. Before I resigned my commission I had two posts stateside. I taught at West Point for two years then got sent down to Fort Meade."

A facility known for its intelligence work and impenetrable security.

"While I was there I taught at the Naval Academy."

"A checkered work history," I observed.

"I prefer to think of it as a slightly unconventional career path."

"Should I be afraid?"

"Of?" he asked.

"Of the things you know. Or may have done."

I'd read my share of spy novels and, having lived in Washington, knew that folks in the intelligence community could very tight-lipped. Add to that the Ranger angle, the mental toughness and endurance that typified the breed, traits great in a soldier but sometimes hard in a marriage. I didn't know how the secrecy and need to be in complete control would play out when combined with the peculiarities of my life, already circumscribed by HIPAA regulations, confidentiality, and the habit of making split-second decisions saving people.

He stopped and turned to face me. "Do you feel afraid?" he asked.

I looked up into his friendly eyes. "Not yet," I answered softly.

He pushed a strand of hair back from my face and gently pressed an index finger to the ball of my cheek. "Trust that instinct, Parise."

At his touch, I suddenly found it hard to breathe. To see anything beyond the shine in his eyes.

We got up finally and started again toward our basement rooms. When we reached the door to my room, it was closed. Bev and Linda were in and probably asleep, anticipating two more long days of surgery and a third wrapping up before the long trip home.

"Did you know Rand's arranged for us to stay in one of Budapest's best hotels on the trip back?" I asked Jake sneakily.

Linda had been searching through Rand's briefcase the day before and happened to see the reservation. She'd let Bev and me in on the secret, the three of us already imagining our tired bodies in fragrant baths and 600-count sheets.

"Really?" Jake said, feigning surprise.

"You knew," I accused. "How long have you known?"

"Rand might've mentioned it . . ."

"And you didn't think to share?"

"He asked us not to say anything."

"Us?"

"The boys and me."

"You're all in on it?"

"It would seem that way."

I attacked with both fists, playfully pounding his chest.

He caught my wrists. "Hey. He wanted to do something nice for ya'll." He drew me close. Spoke softly. "Who knew you'd feel left out?"

"It is nice," I agreed.

"Nicer than you think," he enthused.

"How so?"

"You'll see."

"Come on. Spill!" I demanded.

"You'll see," he echoed, pretending to zip his lips. Before I could torture him for additional information, he leaned down and gave me the lightest of kisses, shy and almost adolescent in its tentativeness.

I felt its imprint linger.

He turned, ambled away, and as he turned the corner toward his room, pantomimed the lip zipping a second time.

"Go away!" I called in a stage whisper. "Return to your lair of co-conspirators!"

He smirked and disappeared.

Inside our room, I quietly laid out clean scrubs and found a book. I slid into my sleeping bag and read for more than an hour by the tiny beacon of my Itty Bitty Book Light. Before settling, I silently left the room for a last potty visit.

Alone in the echoing bathroom, I brushed, flossed, and slathered Oil of Old Lady, an apt moniker for the moisturizer suggested by my brilliant nephew Hal. Traipsing back to my room, I rounded a corner and very nearly tripped over Ken and Jake camped out at the top of the basement stairs. "What're you two doing here?" I demanded. "Cooking up more surprises?"

"Can't sleep," Ken confessed, while simultaneously Jake declared, "Kinda hungry."

"You two need to get your stories straight," I advised.

"Have a seat," Jake invited. "Night's still young."

"I guess I can stay a few minutes." The stone surface was glacial, so I perched my cheeks at the very edge of the step.

"Chocolate for you?" Jake asked.

"Get behind me Satan," I invoked, though I enthusiastically studied the selection. One hand plunged into the box of Godivas, I asked, "You guys aren't depressed are you?" Dark chocolate was my medication of choice on low days.

"Not really," Ken declared. "In my case, just stunned."

"By?"

"Tell her," Jake encouraged. "She'll fall in love with you . . ."

Impossible, I thought; my heart was busy elsewhere.

Ken popped a chocolate with a pretzel chaser. He smacked his lips as he apologized, "You probably noticed I didn't stick around playing games with you and the kids after dinner . . ."

"I figured you got enough of that at home."

Ken had five children ranging in age from twelve to nineteen. He'd more than paid his parental dues.

"That I do," he allowed. "But it's not why I left. I finally got up to the nursery like I'd promised I would."

"You went to see your little guy?"

"Balint."

"How'd it go?"

"Great," Ken responded. "I know I told you a little bit about the boy already, but I didn't tell you the most impressive part of the story. I guess I didn't really know it 'til tonight.

"First you have to know that *Charles Regis*," the foreshortened version of her name that she was often called, "is known in these parts as a miracle worker.

"Last fall, authorities brought her this boy. He didn't weigh more than about eighteen pounds. He couldn't sit or stand. Couldn't roll over.

"In the States, a kid like Balint would probably have had the benefit of early intervention but
here, where resources are hard to come by and atti-
tudes still not all that open to providing help to the
disabled, the child had been completely neglected.

"When they first saw Balint, the nuns thought
he was somewhere between six and ten months old,
at most a toddler, and they were convinced he had
some kind of neurological defect.

"When Matthias examined him and went over
what few medical records that came with the boy,
everyone discovered how wrong they were.

"Balint was four years old!

"*Charles Regis* described him to me via e-mail,
and I saw pictures. The boy's head was large and
mushroom-shaped after years lying in a crib. The
consensus was that he was hydrocephalic." A condition caused by an excess build-up of spinal fluid in
the brain and spinal canal, it's most often treated
with shunts that drain off excess fluid into the
abdominal cavity. "What they found was that the
boy was physically normal."

"All his problems stemmed from neglect."

I was speechless in the face of Ken's sad
revelation.

"The kid didn't have the strength to do the most
basic things because no one had ever taken the time
to hold and play with him. And he was malnour-
ished. We learned later that his mother was a drug-
addicted prostitute who'd ignored the boy from the
day he was born."

My heart broke again for a child I'd never met. I'd read about his kind of abuse in textbooks, certainly, and while I believed it existed, I'd never known of anyone whose case was so severe.

While I also understood that poverty made people desperate, to not even hold or comfort your own child; how did a person harden his or her heart so completely?

Ken went on. "When *Charles Regis* e-mailed me about Balint, I wasn't sure I'd be able to help. She and I had collaborated before, helping kids with CP, " cerebral palsy, "or a few with minor developmental delays.

"But this was beyond anything I'd ever seen or done.

"It took a while to devise a protocol for the boy. I hit all the pediatric databases I thought might help and researched therapies used in similar cases. I called everybody whose expertise I thought would be useful.

"Paul and I came up with exercises we thought might work, and I e-mailed a few the nuns could start with. Keep in mind, this little fella couldn't hold his head up or grab things with his hands. Nothing."

"The sisters started in right away working with him," Ken resumed. "Three or four times a day; whichever one of the nuns had a few minutes, she went in and exercised his arms and his legs. Picked him up. Played with him. Read him books.

"It wasn't long before I started getting positive reports. 'Balint reached for my hand.' Or, 'Balint rolled over today.'

"I raised a toast the day they told me he sat up on his own for the first time, propped against pillows." Ken disguised his tender feelings with a snort adding, "I'm embarrassed it took so long for me to get upstairs to check on him after we got here, but we've been so tied up at the hospital . . ."

An understatement. He and Paul barely breathed.

He picked up the thread of his story. "When I reached the nursery last night, there were kids playing with toy trains and trucks and dolls. A couple of teenaged girls were reading to pre-schoolers or braiding the littler girls' hair.

"You can bet *Charles Regis* jumped up from her desk the second she saw me come in. Ran over all excited. 'You've come to see Balint,' she said, wearing a big, old grin.

"She could've been announcing, 'You've come to meet the Queen!' She was so hyped up.

"I apologized, but she wouldn't hear a word . . ."

"'Don't be silly. Balint hasn't gone anywhere, though he could. He's only made more progress. Come, he's waking from a nap. He tuckers himself out so, you know.'

"It worried me when she said that. I thought for a second maybe the boy had some kind of heart defect that Matthias had overlooked, or some other condition that wouldn't allow sufficient blood flow to support all his new activities.

"The possibilities raced through my head as I followed *Charles Regis* into the boy's room. When we got there, she told me to have a seat in the corner and to wait a few minutes before approaching him. Balint doesn't always warm to strangers.

"None of the chairs would hold me," he grinned. The man weighed a solid 260, and nothing pint-sized would do. "So, I sat down cross-legged on the floor."

Probably not easy for a guy his size.

"There was only this one tiny nightlight on in the room, so it took a minute before I could see.

"When I did, I saw that *Charles Regis* had plunked herself down on the bed next to the boy and was talking softly to him. Gave him a little peck on the cheek.

"I swear I heard him giggle.

"Can you imagine that? After all he's been through and how much he's suffered, this little guy still has joy in his heart."

I could imagine it. I'd seen the very sickest patients be thankful and kind, and I'd felt through the squeeze of a hand or a slow and patient sigh, their gratitude. Young Balint's ebullience, now that people were plying him with care and attention and love, was easily believable.

"*Charles Regis* talked to him for a couple of minutes and stroked his cheek and hands. All of a sudden he popped up like he had somewhere impor-tant to go, and he sat there looking around the room like he was seeing it for the first time.

"He spotted me and stopped. Probably wasn't sure he liked the idea of an intruder. An older girl wandered in and cried out his name. She ran over to him and squeezed him so tight he squealed.

"They tangled a second, I guess he didn't like being trapped even in the name of love. He pushed the girl away, and she left.

"'Dara,' he called after her. He babbled a bunch, peeved as all get out that she'd run off, then he shot me another uncomfortable look. I couldn't tell if he was warning me to keep my distance, or if he wanted me to carry him over to where the action was.

"*Charles Regis* got up and walked away, too, and little Balint stuck his thumb in his mouth. Poor kid. He looked from her, to the door, and back again.

"I started to get up, thinking if she was just going to stand by and watch him get frustrated, I sure wasn't. But she shook her head, 'No.'

"Then I saw why. Balint had scooted his bottom to the edge of the bed, and he was dangling his legs over the side. He sat looking down at the floor another coupla seconds, then over at the door.

"I made another move to help, but she waved me away again. 'He'll do what he has to do,' she said in a firm whisper.

"First thing I knew, the little guy had slipped down the side of the bed in that snaking, slithering way toddlers have, and he was running toward the door. Past me. Past *Charles Regis*."

He couldn't go on.

Neither Jake nor I could speak.

We knew now how this wonderful story would end.

A tiny boy in impoverished Central Europe, a boy without money or family or influence had been forever changed. By the nuns. By the children around him. By this big bruiser of a man who'd reached out to him from thousands of miles away.

Balint was upright and running into his new life, a child who would grow into a strong and capable man, in large part because of the transformation Ken had helped make happen.

The chocolate and goodies before me lost their appeal, the satisfaction I might've felt filling up on them dwarfed by the significance of the sweet story.

I stood and hugged Ken, aware of Jake's fleeting fingertip touch on my naked ankle as I leaned forward.

"See you both in the morning," I whispered. The moment begged for reverence.

A few minutes later, I was back on my subterranean cot, enveloped in a down sleeping bag and the warmth of my flannel pajamas. I settled into a comfortable spot, my back pressed to the wall, and fell instantly into a fugue of sleep so deep and so complete that when the pounding began, a few hours later, I was only distantly aware of its regular thump, thump, thump.

At first, I reacted to the disturbance by pulling my sleeping bag to my chin and flipping my pillow over my face to cover it. Someone, somewhere in the building was making an emergency repair or being purposely annoying. Either way, I was going to light into the person responsible if it didn't stop soon.

I burrowed into my cozy nest and tried to go back to sleep, but the clamor intensified.

Bang.

Bang.

Bang-bang-bang.

Across the room, Linda protested, "I'm too old for this."

Six nights on an unforgiving canvas sling provoked impatience in the most tolerant of people, which, bless her heart, Linda wasn't quite. Every night she vowed death to anyone who dared disturb her before five forty-five.

Given the depth of my exhaustion, it couldn't be anywhere near that late.

From Bev's corner, I heard the nylon rustle of a sleeping bag, then something hitting the floor hard. A series of furtive movements followed, then an expletive. Moments later she informed us, "Good heavens. It's not even four o'clock!"

Who could be up at this hour and the better question was, why?

A male voice called through the door. "Ladies." Our new collective identity. "Ladies. Get up!"

The voice sounded like Rand's, but we all knew he was too smart to be rousing us at this hour.

"Go away," Bev bellowed, sounding uncharacteristically like a longshoreman.

The door to our room opened, and in the wash of a powerful flashlight beam, Rand stood fully dressed.

"Ladies," he repeated. "Get up."

Had the man even gone to bed?

"You need to get dressed."

In my semi-comatose state, I thought maybe a patient had gone bad and instantly my mind went to Lorant. He hadn't looked all that good when we left him on Saturday afternoon; maybe the infection had returned or a new and opportunistic organism had gotten a foothold in his weakened system. If that were the case, I'd be hard-pressed to help in his treatment on less than four hours sleep.

"I need you all to meet me in *Helena*'s office in ten minutes," Rand directed.

I sat upright in bed. "If you want me to get out of bed, you'd better give me a good reason, Mister. We have a pretty complicated shoulder repair first thing in the morning," I reminded him through my blindness. "And I'm so tired I can't even think."

He hit me full face with the harsh light. "You want to know why we're meeting," he asked. "Here's the Reader's Digest version.

"There's been a *coup d'etat*. We have to figure out a way to get ourselves out of this country and fast. Good enough reason?"

I came completely awake, frozen in mid-bitching mode. "*A coup d'etat*?" I echoed. "Here or in the U.S.?" Either way we were in a pickle, but it made a difference.

"Here. Now get your ass up to the office. I don't want to have to rehash the details of this thing." With that he slammed the door, and the room was thrown into total darkness.

All three of us sat, momentarily stunned.

Scared.

Silent.

My do-something nature kicked in. I threw off my sleeping bag and vaulted from bed. I felt the floor for the clean civvies kept alongside my scrubs. Quickly I climbed into clean underwear and tights. Then, heavy cords and a turtleneck. It wasn't my best (thinnest) look, but it was warm. I found a wool cardigan and added that, teeth chattering more from fear, I suspected, than cold.

Linda and Bev turned on their flashlights. "I can't believe this is happening," Bev said tensely. "We're caught behind enemy lines."

A bit of an overreaction, since we didn't know any details, but there was a chance she could be right.

"Let's not panic," Linda warned before I had the chance. "Things like this happen all the time in these little countries."

In some countries, yes, but not here. According to the overview Jake had read to us, there had been little political change in the region for forty years, until the fall of Communism. Before that, the last rumblings of discontent had occurred in 1918.

While BBC reporters had started filing stories of growing foment between the head of the country's military and the pro-American prime minister last summer, not even the most pessimistic of corre-spondents would have predicted the government's overthrow.

I was almost ready to leave when I saw that neither of my roommates had moved. "Rand's serious," I told them as I leaned to tie my boots. "We have to hurry."

Linda stirred, but across the room Bev was pretty much catatonic. "I can't believe this is happening," she managed through lips that barely parted. Her face had turned ashen and lifeless.

"We need to go upstairs and get the full story," I said reasonably. "All this could be hyperbole."

Not that Rand was prone to it. His problem was thinking he always knew best.

"Do you think that could be it?" Bev asked hopefully. "That Rand might just be misinterpreting a news report on that thing he uses . . ."

The sat phone.

I didn't think that was the case, but I allowed for the possibility. "Why don't we stop speculating? Here, I'll help you find something to wear."

I searched through her bags and found cotton velour sweats and clean underwear for her to put on. I turned and checked on Linda, who was margin-ally more engaged. "I'm going to run up ahead. You guys good?"

"Sure. We'll be up in a minute. Right, Bev?"

Bev turned a steady stare on us. "Right," she managed.

"See you in a few," I said before slipping out the door.

Out of my roommates' sight, I climbed the stairs two at a time and sped through the labyrinth of hallways. I ran past the chapel and primary grade classrooms that were absolutely still. The only sign of life, other than my panting, was my pitiful light bobbing up and down the old walls, leading the way.

When I got there, *Soeur St. Helena*'s office and the small conference room next to it were ablaze with the glow of kerosene lamps. The men of the group stood in a cluster whose center was the slight superior. Anxiety pulled at all their features.

"Where are the others?" Rand demanded.

"They'll be along."

I didn't think he wanted to hear that Bev was scared out of her gourd and rooted to the spot, or that Linda would have to cajole and lead her every step of the way here. "The cold slows them down," I obfuscated. "Maybe we should talk a bit before they get here."

I had a sense that neither woman would take the news well. Better to distill the details and feed them the info in more manageable doses.

Jake read my expression and instantly understood. "Parry's right; maybe Linda and Bev don't need to be filled in on the worst of it right away."

Rand conceded, "All right. Matthias, why don't you brief us."

Matthias? I hadn't seen him. What was he doing here?

He pointed us to chairs, walked to the head of the table, and pinned a map of his country to a corkboard. He turned to face us. "As some of you know," he began, "I like to relax in the evening by speaking with ham radio colleagues around the world.

"It is an out-of-date pastime, given the universality of cellular telephones, but I enjoy it."

Nice to know, but . . .?

"A few minutes after midnight," he explained, "I was chatting with my good friend Akos, whom I have known since university. He lives on the outskirts of the capital." As though giving us a geography tutorial, he pointed it out on the map, a place not far from the country's border with Austria.

"Akos knows hundreds of people in the city, many of whom work in the government. He also has a network of friends who live scattered throughout the region."

Interesting but surely not the reason why we'd been shaken from sleep.

"As he and I were speaking, his home telephone began to ring. Then his cellular."

People here were mad for them. Young adults carried them everywhere. Few people had landlines because they were too expensive, and the government, wanting the advantages of a wired generation, encouraged the use of cells. Less infrastructure to build and maintain.

"Akos is not inclined to answer either telephone when he and I are engaged in a heated discussion, but tonight the callers were quite persistent.

"Not wanting to be disturbed, he pulled out the wall connection to his landline and set his cellular telephone to the shaking mode."

Vibrate.

"Still, it kept going off and interfering with our debate. Akos is by nature a worrier, so when the interruptions continued, something, perhaps his paranoia, told him to respond.

'Just a second,' he said, interrupting our discourse. 'I will dispatch this person inconsiderately ringing me so late at night.'

"As soon as he answered his cell, I heard someone yelling at him on the loud setting."

Speaker.

"'There's been a takeover, Akos,' this person declared. 'The king is dead. The Prime Minister as well.'

"Akos made this friend, this Tomas, slow down, but his words were rushed and difficult to understand. He was blubbering and crying.

"Perhaps I should mention, Tomas is an employee of the Interior Ministry.

"Was. Very high up. He talked daily with the Prime Minister and admired him greatly. There was tremendous emotion in his voice as he described all he had witnessed.

"Because of his flat's proximity to Parliament, Tomas had heard and seen much of the initial attack on the royal residence and the Prime Minister's, both located just up the hill from where he lives.

"The violence began around eleven o'clock, Tomas reported, starting with the sound of gunshots and explosives. He got up from his bed and looked out his bedroom window in time to see fire erupting from several buildings, filling the night sky. Military vehicles raced into the royal courtyard moments after the explosions.

"There were tanks and trucks bursting with soldiers dressed in riot gear and carrying automatic weapons. Everywhere there was running. Shouting. Shooting into residences and nearby government buildings. Executive offices were ransacked.

"Presumably the guards were killed first.

"Tomas was certain there had to have been a staging area not far because almost no time elapsed between the initial gunfire and the streets being awash in troops.

"Given the storm and the ice," Matthias continued, "there was chaos everywhere. The king's personal staff ran out into the storm with overcoats thrown over their night clothes. Some had bloodied faces and serious injuries. Arms dangled at their sides. Some people limped noticeably.

"Tomas saw one man vomiting blood."

Matthias described how the violence and fear had spread outward in waves through the streets around Tomas' building, then beyond it to nearby neighborhoods. "Soldiers jumped from the backs of transports, more and more of them appearing out of the frozen night, securing buildings both public and private."

He paused and gathered himself before divulging the rest. "While Akos was on the telephone with Tomas, I could hear gunfire growing louder and more frequent in the background.

"Then suddenly Tomas cried that he had to hang up.

"Akos terminated the conversation and told me he was leaving immediately to evaluate the situation for himself.

"I tried to talk him out of it, but he was determined. I have not heard from him since," he declared. "I have called him, but there is never an answer. I've also called friends who live close to the border to ask if they know anything; if they have seen anything."

His voice grew grave. "The borders have been closed to all Americans, quite specifically," he announced. "Whoever is responsible for this takeover has the country locked up, how do you Americans say it, 'As tight as a drum?'"

That would be the expression.

Looking grim, Jake asked Matthias, "Is there anything else we need to know?"

"Quite unfortunately. Two things.

"First, I have verified that the king and his family, in addition to both the prime minister and foreign minister and their families, are gone."

This was bad. The government had been friendly to the current U.S. administration, one of several in Central and Eastern Europe that had stood solidly with us over the war in Iraq, while allies whose economies and infrastructures we'd rebuilt in the wake of Hitler's deranged lunacy couldn't distance themselves fast enough.

While I hadn't given the Iraqi invasion my unqualified support, Saddam's murder of 300,000 countrymen and the torture of countless others would certainly have justified such an action, even without the suspicion of WMD's. More than that, I resented the fact that our allies, whose backsides we'd saved not once but twice in the last century, and whose economies had long been bolstered by our foreign aid, that they dismissed our concerns and interests out of hand.

I snapped back to the moment. Matthias had said there were two things we needed to hear.

Jake moved his chair closer to mine and asked Matthias, "What else is there?"

Matthias hesitated but knew there was no point in delaying.

"Go ahead," Jake encouraged. "We need to know."

Matthias looked each of us in the eye. "They've put a bounty on the heads of any and all Americans found in-country," he revealed. "Fifty thousand euros.

"Apiece."

There was more coming; we all sensed it. "The bounty is to be paid whether the Americans are captured living or dead," he softly confided.

Bev and Linda picked that most inauspicious of moments to appear.

FOURTEEN

No one moved; we barely breathed.
We'd all been so obsessed with the mission, the work, and the fulfilling of our promises to people once strangers—now friends—that we'd let down our guard. A guard that we, like my mother, fed with the constant monitoring of world news. CNN; MSNBC; the networks or BBC. In deference to our commitment, we'd completely dropped the information ball.

Bev sank into a chair, and Linda put a hand out to shore her.

"Do we have an exit strategy?" Ken asked, sounding more like a Congressman at a military briefing than a man terrified for his life and his friends'.

"Matthias has been making calls. *Soeur St. Helena* has as well," Rand emphasized. "There are ways of leaving the country, but they're dangerous.

"Dangerous," he repeated so we understood clearly. "And in one case, physically grueling as well."

"In one case?" Jake echoed.

Ted and Rich, sitting to Jake's right, wore their best poker faces, but I thought I heard the distinct knocking of their knees.

"We have drivers willing to hide and cross three of you into Hungary and another three into Austria," Matthias explained. "A friend of mine owns a small factory, not far, that manufactures cast iron bathtubs for 'high end' western markets."

Matthias had spent a year in Boston completing a Harvard post-doc; it sounded to me like he must've spent time watching HGTV as well.

He explained, "Josef sends a shipment out every Monday to Budapest, and he has agreed, if we get three of you to his warehouse by 6 a.m., to conceal you on the next load going out.

"It may be a treacherous ride, given the road conditions, but it is unlikely that the shipment will be closely scrutinized. Border guards are not equipped to lift the tubs to check beneath them, and given the short time between the *coup* and this crossing, they are unlikely to suspect Josef, whom they know, of having had the time or the imagination to organize such an escape.

"Josef has promised to drive the load himself, and I'm told, he plays the fool with the guards quite convincingly."

The risk seemed reasonable given what we now knew was the alternative.

"That takes care of three of us? What about the rest?" Paul asked.

"This part of the plan is a little less certain, but we're fairly confident it can work," *Soeur St. Helena* said, entering the conversation for the first time. "We have a shipment of oats, ordered in October by one of our Austrian customers. It's due to be delivered on November 11th."

The very next day.

"We are going to deliver the goods ahead of schedule, as we sometimes do. The paperwork was signed and dated the fifteenth of last month." She slid a copy of the contract to the center of the table. "We can remove the equivalent of three people's weight from what is contractually required and then hide three of you within the shipment. The truck will be weighed, but again, given our pre-existing arrangement, it is unlikely to be searched."

This second plan sounded more uncomfortable than the first and, to my view, more risky. What if the load shifted and someone had a difficult time breathing?

As though reading my mind, Rand elaborated, "I've had the farm manager and his assistant construct boxes to hide people."

What? Their caskets?

"This tubing will assure they get plenty of air."

He held up several lengths of urinary catheter tubing that, I assumed, had never seen the inside of a patient.

I wanted to laugh—or gag—at the thought of sucking air from the thing, but given the gravity of our plight, I resisted my own sick sense of humor. Use of the tubing was inventive.

"The requisite stamps have been affixed to our contract by local authorities, and they are clearly genuine," *Soeur St. Helena* assured us. "There should be only minimal inspection of the truck's contents as it crosses the border."

"The operative term being, 'should,'" Rich commented.

"It's true," Rand allowed. "There IS risk, but given what's at stake, I think these are two viable routes of escape."

How many options did we realistically have?

"Okay, six of us have a way out," Rich re-capped. "What about the last three?"

Rand pulled a cylinder from his briefcase. He laid out several topographical and road maps of the region. "We'll have to walk out."

The last piece of the puzzle.

This would be tough. We were Americans accustomed to warm homes, three squares a day, and relatively little in the way of vigorous physical exertion. Now, three of us were going to have to hike to freedom in the dead of an early winter? Over completely foreign terrain?

Added to that potential misery was the fact that only one of the three was even vaguely familiar with the local language and customs. I assumed from Rand's use of the word, "we," that he would be one of the walkers.

Did he understand an entire nation's military would be hot on the tails of these hikers?

Rand confirmed my assumption. "I'll be one of the three heading out on foot."

Next to me Jake insisted, "I will, too. I came prepared."

So, the rumors were true. As though to verify them, Jake pulled out a sophisticated handheld. "I downloaded the latest topographical and military maps before leaving. We have GPS capability."

Of course.

"A former colleague helped me plot out several routes of egress," he told us, his voice firm and calm.

Rand ignored him and addressed a different topic. "The women of the group will leave via motorized vehicle; that's non-negotiable." Turning in the direction of his trusted colleague, Ken, who'd started to object, he explained, "You have cardiac issues, Ken. That's a pass on hiking out in this cold."

I was surprised to hear him divulging personal health information, but I understood the need for speed. Given Ken's age and his weight, the news wasn't a total surprise. "Sorry," Rand apologized. "But we don't have time to invoke confidentiality."

Besides, we weren't in the U.S. Did HIPAA even apply here?

With everything that was in him, I could see Ken wanted to stand up and appeal the decision. Instead, he revealed, "Paul's a diabetic. He should ride out, too."

Now that was a shock!

Paul was the picture of health, but looking normal was one of the more frustrating aspects of diabetes. It did its ugly work out of sight, destroying blood vessels and kidneys and retinas, until one or another system eroded to the point of life-threatening illness, and there you were.

Even when it was under control, diabetes could be insidious. In this circumstance—hiking in winter weather; eating unpredictably; stressed by the possibility of capture and worse—walking out of the country was no activity for a diabetic.

That left Ted and Rich.

I studied both men. Middle-aged. Out of shape. Ted was at least fifty pounds overweight, and his was soft fat, not the compact, bulky kind with muscle as a base. Rich, while slender, was a smoker; I smelled it on him every morning.

I doubted either man had much in the way of stamina.

"I'm going to walk out," I announced without fanfare.

Jake's reaction was an immediate and intense, "Out of the question."

Rand joined him. "Parry. This isn't open for discussion. The women need to be protected, first and foremost."

"I disagree. I think this is not only open to discussion but to reason. I'm the youngest person here by at least five years. I have no chronic illnesses. I've never been a smoker or a drinker.

"I work out."

Well, most weeks.

I proffered my ace in the hole: "I've hiked farther than what you're proposing, just for fun."

The summer after my college graduation, Blue-eyed Joe and I had started in southern Maine and tromped all the way to Katahdin. Friends and relatives had replenished supplies at critical junctures along the way. We'd gone what, a hundred twenty miles?

"Where was that?" Rand asked.

"The northernmost segment of the Appalachian Trail."

"Did you hike it in winter?" Linda asked, her face etched with motherly concern.

"The fall," I exaggerated. We had reached Katahdin on Labor Day, effectively the first day of autumn.

"No," Jake said again, though with more gentleness than insistence.

"I'm up to this," I said.

I turned to Rich and Ted and smiled. "With all due respect, gentlemen, you're born and bred to warm weather. And, you've been sitting behind desks for the last twenty years.

"It would be dangerous for either one of you to try this." I circled my gaze back to Rand and Matthias. "Do we have forecasts for the next few days?"

Matthias nodded gravely. "More of the same. The region has not seen cold or snowstorms this severe or this early in fifty years. Some are speculating that the military took advantage of the unusual weather pattern in the timing of its *coup*."

"That's it," I insisted. "I'll make the trip. I'm a northern girl." I was up to the challenge.

Ken and Paul looked miserable in their impotence. If it hadn't been for their health issues and the disadvantages that those might inflict on Jake and Rand, they would've told me to butt out. Instead, they sat mutely by as I lobbied to be one of the walkers. "It's not so bad, a hundred kilometers? Sixty, sixty-five miles. Seventy, if we had to detour . . ."

I turned suddenly to *Soeur St. Helena.* "*Vous avez des skis nordiques?*" I asked. Did they own cross country skis?

"*Oui, certainement, mais ils sont vieux . . .*" They were old.

"*Des bottes?*" And boots?

"*Peut-etre.*" Maybe.

"We can be out of the country much faster if we ski out," I enthused. "Three days. Two if we push it."

I knew even as the words came out of my mouth that the estimate was overly optimistic. Cross country skiing was fine and fast on groomed trails, but we wouldn't have that advantage.

Matthias chimed in, concurring with my unexpressed second thoughts. "It won't be that simple, Parry. There will be armed patrols along all the major routes out of the country and guards at strategic crossings. You will have to break your own trail."

"Not a problem, unless the new regime's already managed to string a fence around the border," I joked. "They haven't, have they?"

"Not to my knowledge," Matthias smiled. "Though there may be those in Washington able to advise them on how it should be done . . ." A reference to the immigration fracas at home for which no resolution appeared imminent.

I smiled then returned to the idea of the skis. "Why don't I check out the equipment? All this is conjecture until we know what the possibilities are."

"Granted," Rand agreed. "You're the only one of us with any experience. Why don't you and *Helena* look them over?"

"Done."

We excused ourselves and proceeded quickly to the back of the silent building. "We have snowshoes as well as skis," *Soeur St. Helena* confided as we hastened through the dark hallways.

Now those I knew we could use.

Everything in the storage shed was neatly labeled. I pulled out a pair of waxless skis, perfect for people like me who didn't have the time, dedication, or experience to be a waxing purist. There were poles and boots in several sizes as well.

Soeur St. Helena handed me a second set of skis. "These were *Soeur Veronique*'s when she was here. They might do for Jake." Indeed, they looked like they'd fit a large woman or compactly built man. "Veronique was a robust farm girl from northern Quebec," she confided with a smile.

'Nuff said.

I went through the rest of the selection, twice, and while I found several sets Jake and I might use, there was nothing in the collection to accommodate

Rand's considerable height and mass. Over six feet, he had thick arms and legs. He was broad through the chest. I gave him at least two thirty, and nothing I'd found would likely accommodate that heft.

"We'd better go with snowshoes," I said, spying the collection to which *Soeur St. Helena* had earlier referred. They'd allow us to wear our own warmer, sturdier boots and would be more practical scaling hillsides.

"Perhaps you should take the skis along just in case. They're light. You could load them on this toboggan," she suggested. "Along with the rest of your supplies."

Food, water, sleeping bags. It would be impossible to carry on our backs all that we'd need for four to five days of winter hiking.

"We commonly see people here pulling them along," she said of the sled.

"Really?"

"It's an efficient and inexpensive mode of transporting goods."

A toboggan would also be ideal getting Rand down a slope quickly, say, if we had to outrun authorities. Jake and I could ski, and Rand could center his rump on the sled's broad, flat surface. Meet us at the bottom of a hill.

"Sold."

We stacked and hauled everything to the orphanage's back doors and together made our way back to her office. People were talking quietly when we came back in. Only Jake sat alone, studying the screen of his GPS.

"We have what we need," I said without embellishment. There'd be time to review the particulars with Jake and Rand after the others were set to go.

"Good," Rand said, obviously trusting my judgment. "So Linda, Beverly, and Ken, you'll be in one group. Paul, Ted, and Rich in the other.

Immediately Ken objected. "I think each of the teams ought to have a 2-to-1, male-to-female ratio. Rich, Beverly, and I in one group, say. Paul, Ted, and Linda in the other."

Right away I saw the wisdom of Ken's plan. One take-charge guy per group. Linda, the stronger of the women, paired with the less imposing of the men in Paul's group. An increasingly timid Bev could be cared for by the competent males in her group, Rich and Ken.

Rand was pensive for a moment, obviously resisting the urge to override Ken's idea. "You're right," he allowed, words I would never have expected to pass his lips.

Paul asked a follow-up question that had occurred to me. "Will we have weapons?"

It was Matthias who answered. "We have knives for everyone that we will distribute." He reached into his jacket pocket. "And I have this for the group walking out." He deposited a handgun in the center of the table; from his other pocket, a box of ammunition.

"We can't leave you here unarmed," I said to him. "Things could get bad if word of our escape and your role in it gets out."

Matthias smiled. "For the time being, Parry, it may be more hazardous than not for me to keep this in my home. It is common practice, in a military takeover of this kind, to quickly disarm the most vocal or popular critics."

Matthias likely had a reputation as both.

Rand didn't respond to the offer of firepower. Instead he surveyed the faces around the table. "It looks like we've made the most crucial of our decisions. Now we have to move. There are a lot of preparations to be made and not much time in which to make them.

"Linda, Ted, Paul. You'll ride with the bathtubs. I don't think Ken would fit at all comfortably."

Ted might be a snug fit, too, I thought, but his soft body was probably more malleable than Ken's.

"Locate your documents and take whatever necessities you can fit into your pockets. Food. Water. Whatever else you deem vital. Remember you'll be in very cramped quarters.

"Matthias will arrange to have Josef deliver your group to the American Embassy in Budapest once you've made the crossing," Rand told Paul. "Someone there will facilitate the arrangements to get you home."

He threw Matthias his satellite phone. "I recommend you use this to make any calls. It's possible this new government has disrupted cell tower operations."

"They could also be listening in on local frequencies," Matthias said knowingly.

Rand turned again to the first group. "I'm sure the embassy staff will be able to help you negotiate with the airlines or book you into hotels until our scheduled departure date."

Friday coming.

"Whatever costs you incur; it's on me."

Paul started to object. "That's not necessary . . ."

Rand was immovable on that point. "No discussion. I expect receipts when I get back."

The words were spoken softly but firmly, Rand's generous heart on display.

Paul nodded assent.

Rand spent a few more minutes giving practical advice. "I recommend wearing as many of your clothes as you can. I don't think the cast iron will provide much warmth and sleeping bags are too bulky to fit."

On to the next matter. "Ken and company. You'll be traveling by truck into Austria. Again, take as much food and water as you think you might need to hold you for the day. I'm not sure when or how the men will be able to dig you out of the oats, or how long you might be kept waiting at the border. I'd go light on the liquids, if you know what I mean."

They did.

"Be quick getting ready. When you have everything you need, head out to the barns. You'll see the lights.

"The men have been instructed to get you situated in the grain with your 'scuba gear," Rand said, again holding up the clear tubing. "In case you're concerned, just know this will be threaded through casings the men are installing at the corners of the truck bed as we speak. Your air supply will be safe."

Listening to all the details, it occurred to me that someone in our midst must have experience with clandestine escapes. I turned and studied Jake, but his face was impassive.

"The oats will act as insulation and keep you warm while you travel," Rand was telling the members of the second group. "But there is a danger the load could shift.

"You may have to be patient while you're buried under there," he told the three.

Ken and Rich understood. Between them, saying not a word, Bev seemed resigned.

The six riders rose to go, and in the room's flickering lamplight, our gazes met and held. The looks we exchanged were filled with fondness and mutual high regard.

Matthias and *Soeur St. Helena* shepherded everyone through the door, two by two. Linda and Bev; Ken and Paul; Ted and Rich, bringing up the rear. As they disappeared, the lights over the conference table flickered to life.

Five thirty a.m.

In this moment of welcomed illumination, I had never felt more alone.

FIFTEEN

W hen the others had gone, Jake leaned in close and whispered out of Rand's earshot, "I guess we shouldn't have stuffed ourselves silly last night."

Equally lighthearted, I volleyed back, "I don't believe I did."

To the twelve-ounce bag of jerky and half a pound of pretzels he and Ken had annihilated, I'd had maybe two ounces of chocolate. I'd seen their empty wrappers, the official rationale for their gluttony, that we'd eaten only two meals earlier in the day.

"I can barely button my jeans," Jake confessed.

"Your problem," I said without pity.

Rand cleared his throat and fixed a look of irritation on us both. "If you two are finished with the Weight Watchers meeting, we have slightly more important matters to take up."

The man had bionic hearing.

"Sorry. I thought a little levity might be useful," Jake offered.

"I'm sure the guys with the guns will appreciate that."

I sighed. This wasn't going to degenerate into a 'you're-not-the-boss-of-me' exchange, was it? Things were bad enough without male posturing.

Jake started to apologize again, but I stepped in. "You're right, Rand. Let's get down to business."

"Fine."

"Fine."

We moved to Rand's end of the table, and Jake reached for his handheld, a piece of equipment I had no doubt was unavailable to the average American.

True I was somewhat ignorant of electronic gadgetry, a fact that stemmed not so much from my being a technophobe as it did from my quibble with cost. New toys meant money. New toys strategically released to markets hungry for them meant even more money. Companies had products in the pipeline years before introducing them, the plan being to maximize profits under the guise of meeting customer need.

Quite literally, I didn't play the game.

I owned an Apple laptop and a cell phone—the latter used for my personal safety on the road and in consulting with patients or emergency room docs when on call. At home I subscribed to a satellite service and owned a DVR, but I only did that much so I could keep up with the few programs I enjoyed and couldn't watch on the nights they aired because I was almost always at work!

Another reason I eschewed electronic toys was that I had trouble enough keeping pace with the technological demands of my job, I didn't go looking for the latest and greatest when it came to personal entertainment.

Enough was enough.

All that said, I completely contradicted myself as I watched Jake manipulating his hand-held. Cognizant of the danger in which we found ourselves, I silently acknowledged that, whatever hardware Jake had thought to take along, I was thankful for. This wasn't a game; it was life and death. If an advantage could be had electronically in outrunning our pursuers, so be it.

Rand laid out his maps and his papers. He handed each of us a list of essential supplies for the hike. Then, in a move that made me wonder just who was in charge, he yielded the floor to Jake, saying, "So, Major Spangler. What do you think?"

Jake started in. "Okay. Before any of us packs anything, we need to be sure it can't be identified as American. Cut the labels out of your clothes and repackage food products in locally available storage bags or foil. The kitchen staff will give us what we need, won't they, Rand?"

"They will."

Jake continued. "Don't forget to scratch out product names on things like your toothbrush, your sunglasses, anything that has the smallest logo on it.

"We'll need to take our passports, but they'll have to be well concealed."

"How about in our underwear?" Rand suggested.

"The obvious choice, but too easy to find."

"How about a hat or a jacket," I suggested. "Or our boots." I untied one of the ankle-highs I was wearing and turned the cuff inside out. "See. Here. We can open the lining, slip in the passport, then re-sew the fabric.

"They'd have to take apart our boots to find them."

"Good thinking," Rand complimented.

Jake shot me a grin. "That is a solid idea," he said. "Can you get that done?"

"I'll need to borrow needle and thread."

Though organized, I rarely traveled with a sewing kit. The grudging feminist in me wouldn't yield that much territory to my practical side.

I offered more advice. "We should dress in layers. Hiking over snow can work up a sweat."

"Noted," Jake said. "But back to the issue of labels. Don't forget to check your sleeping bags."

"Even with the tags gone, don't you think the design and fabric might give them away?" Rand asked thoughtfully.

"They might," Jake answered. "But we'll never make it without them. It could get damned cold out there and blankets won't cut it.

"We aren't in the movies."

Strange Jake would put it that way. The last few days, the last few hours in particular, I'd felt like an actor in a film. Like I was watching myself. There was something about deprivation and danger and distance from the known that colored and intensi-fied every moment.

"What about our emergency medical supplies?" I asked, getting back to the conversation. "Everything in the kit's labeled in English. If we get stopped, it'll give us away."

"We can legitimately make the claim it was donated by a Canadian group," Rand responded. "Given the nuns' Quebec connection, that's not so far-fetched.

"Kind of a plausible deniability," he added.

I hated the catchphrase popular in and around Washington. It suggested cynicism and that it was a good thing for those in positions of power to be kept in the dark on the particulars of illicit activity. No matter that they might've set the illegalities in motion, fat cats could make it their business to know as little as they could about questionable situations as they evolved.

The Big Lie, as it were, so much more believable than a smaller one.

As much as the concept disgusted me, both in theory and in practice, now that we were caught in a life-threatening dilemma, I had greater appreciation for its usefulness.

"Make the claim?" Jake said, echoing Rand's earlier words. We'd evidently left him back a way. "How do you think we're going to tell anyone anything without their immediately making us as American?"

"I speak Hungarian," Rand instantly reminded him. "The expat community in the region is large. It won't raise eyebrows."

"Really?" Jake confronted. "I'm no expert, but the Hungarian you speak and the version I've heard coming from Matthias don't sound much like the same language.

"People will peg you as a foreigner the second you open your mouth. And from there, it won't take long to figure out the rest of the story . . ."

Jake's was a salient point.

I smiled.

Just outside of Wilmington, North Carolina, there was a street by that name. Well, not a street really; more like a winding set of car tracks in tall, summer grasses leading to a clutch of secluded beachfront homes. I'd followed them one day and discovered the enclave on a sandy spit of peninsula. I'd intended to compliment whoever I could find on the wittiness of the name, but before I could follow through, the skies had opened up, and I'd been caught in a deluge. Hightailed it back to my car.

The cleverness had stuck with me.

Refocusing, I saw my companions facing one another, nose to nose. Jake was emphatically staking out the position that, while Rand considered himself fluent in his parents' native tongue, he had an accent that was easily discerned. He often hesitated, moreover, trying to remember a word or an expression. Rand addressing authorities, if it came to that, would raise a giant red flag.

"And here's another glitch," Jake continued. "There's some kind of national identification card in this country. If we get stopped, what are we going to show?"

"Matthias has thought of that," Rand said, regaining composure. "He has a guy making them for us."

"A guy?" Jake asked doubtfully. "And just what is this 'guy' using for photos?"

"He's cropping us out of that group shot we took last Tuesday." Set against a stretch of dreary hallway, we'd been smiling broadly at the news that the portable x-ray machine had arrived.

"He's supposed to be some kind of expert forger," Rand added. "Matthias promised to bring back the cards after dropping Paul and his group." News that still didn't solve the problem currently under debate.

Jake asked, "Did he happen to mention if he'd seen any road blocks on the way in here this morning?"

"A couple," Rand answered, seemingly relieved at the change of topic. "He was stopped just outside the hospital by a patrol, and he told the soldiers there was a really sick kid out here who couldn't be moved. A bad case of influenza.

"It was the only thing he needed to say. Folks here are scared to death of flu and the pneumonia that can come as a complication. They do everything possible to prevent the spread of it through their families.

"The patrol couldn't wave him through fast enough, but he made sure he left them with the impression that he was going to be back and forth at least a couple more times today. Checking on the boy."

Matthias was great on his feet.

"One of the guys who stopped him was a kid whose mother Matthias saved last year. He won't be giving him—or us—any trouble," Rand added.

"As long as he's the one on duty," I contributed. "I'm sure they rotate shifts."

Another of the many problems facing us.

"What time is Matthias due back?" Jake asked.

"In an hour. Maybe two. He'll be bringing other things we're going to need." Glaring at Jake, Rand added, "Maybe he can help us figure out what to do about my language 'deficiency'."

There was a prolonged and uncomfortable silence, a stalemate broken only by a knock at the open door. We turned to find *Soeur St. Helena* politely waiting, her face a mosaic of concern and age that it hadn't been a week ago.

A day ago.

"They're ready," was all she said. "They'd like to say goodbye."

We followed her toward the staging area at the very back of the building, but I detoured to my room at the last minute to get something I thought my women friends might need. As I swiftly made my way through the halls, I could hear the children beginning to rouse on the floors overhead. For now they were safe and unaware of how significantly their world had changed. I begged God, on their behalf, to keep them as sheltered from this new reality as He could. To keep them safe.

When I arrived at my ultimate destination, minutes later, I found my colleagues standing in a small and forlorn cluster. Ken, despite his size, seemed diminished by the way in which he and the others were being forced to leave. "I'd hoped to say goodbye to my boy," he told me despondently.

Balint.

"He'll be fine," I assured, hugging him hard. "He's got a great new start in life, thanks to you."

Ken's eyes filled, and he managed to nod in agreement. He held up a fist in the universal sign of triumph.

Next to Ken, Bev was reserved, her eyes liquid with fear. She asked in a voice I could barely make out, "Could you see that the girls get the rest of my things?"

Soaps. Her manicure and make-up kits. A few nice undergarments, bras and camisoles, for girls who wouldn't be grossed out at the thought of second hand in the way American teens surely would.

Childless and without biological siblings, Bev had imbued her new friends here with the status of family. Stunning Vivien and stately Annett. Thirteen year-old Kata who'd hung on Bev's every word and unconsciously adopted her measured movements.

Bev pulled something from her jacket pocket. A tortoiseshell comb. "Please give this to Lilla," the tiny girl whose beautiful voice had charmed us at the concert yesterday.

"I'll take care of everything," I promised.

"And I will help," *Soeur St. Helena* vowed.

Bev smiled her thanks.

I suddenly remembered my parting gift. "Here," I said quietly to Linda. "Divide these as needed."

She looked down into the paper bag I offered and grinned. A half dozen maxi pads. "In case the urge is impossible to resist," I explained.

"Thanks. They could save us a lot of embarrassment." Which was the idea.

One of the dairy workers blew in from out-of-doors, icy air trailing him like an invisible tail. "We must go," he insisted. "Daylight is near."

He was right.

Everyone hugged. The men. The women. *Soeur St. Helena*, acting as the group mother. All of us were trying with the intensity of an embrace, a pat, or a final wave to express the sentiments and fears we couldn't speak aloud.

After the door closed on our friends, and we watched them walk away through the frosted window, Jake stated the obvious. "It's time to get our sorry butts in gear."

We swallowed hard and turned to go.

SIXTEEN

B ack in my deserted room, I inventoried my belongings.

"Yes" to thermal underwear and "no" to the too-cute top worn yesterday. I threw dental floss on the "keep" pile, vowing to take an eternity's worth of the stuff to my grave. For the next few minutes, I sorted the essential from the superfluous, hearing my mother's voice echo across two decades, "How in the world did you get yourself into such a scrape?"

Scrape. It was the word my parents used scolding us kids whenever we got in over our heads. The very sound of the single syllable turned my innards to a quaking, quivering mess, and transformed me from a competent adult into a child who still feared her parents' anger or disappointment.

I had been tenderhearted and not a little gullible as a youngster, a curious and overly helpful gradeschooler who somehow found herself embroiled in trouble of other people's making from time to time.

One such incident stood out starkly in my mind, and for years made me flush crimson resurrecting it.

The imbroglio involved Scarlett Dumond, a girl who'd lived in the house on the corner of my dead-end street. My history with Scarlett had been a troubled one. She was my age, but we'd never been in the same classroom at school, nor were we friends. She was the kind of girl light years ahead of me in her knowledge of, and involvement with things my parents (and I) considered forbidden, among them the particulars of reproduction.

My first real run in with Scarlett had come on a cool and beautiful autumn day. I was sitting astride an oversized concrete planter, singing outdated songs from Miss Stuart's music class, and waiting for my best friends Sam and Alan to join me. I was ten, a fifth grader, and compared to Scarlett, I was still very childlike and innocent.

As I should've been.

Scarlett had wandered by, ignoring me as usual, but a few minutes later she had circled back and approached me. Unsure of myself in her presence, I'd started to babble and trip over my own tongue, telling her about my latest Girl Scout badge, or a wonderful book I was reading, or some other geeky thing in which she had no interest.

"So," she said, barely letting me finish a thought. "Guess what I know?"

"About what?"

"About where babies come from," she boasted. "About sex."

My mind froze on the last word. I knew what it meant, or suspected I did, but the details of it were mysterious. "They come from mothers," I ventured. Everyone knew that.

"But where from their mothers?" Scarlett demanded to know.

That question had long puzzled me. Was that what a belly button was for, I wondered. Did it somehow pop open and close again after birth? Mother's didn't regurgitate their offspring, did they? Was there some other avenue of "delivery" of which I was unaware?

In the face of my obvious ignorance, Scarlett blurted out her outrageous confidence in language that would've drawn a stern lecture or worse at my house. She laid out the facts of life for me in vivid and mildly graphic detail, and in a moment long mourned, I felt my innocence take a serious hit.

I fought the overwhelming urge to vomit, my heart beating out of my chest. Life was stranger, even in its common, everyday occurrences, than I could ever have imagined.

Sam and Alan had arrived on the heels of Scarlett's revelation, and one of them tossed me a baseball mitt. Unaware of what had just transpired, they ran off in the direction of the vacant lot where we always played, leaving me to stare at Scarlett's retreating back and wishing that she'd never been born—especially if she was right about procreation!

From that moment, I'd vowed to avoid the girl. If she had more to share, I didn't want to know it. Hear it. Feel it reverberate through my tainted soul.

By the time we hit seventh grade, Scarlett was in a wholly different league. She'd started hanging out with much older kids at the poolroom, a local dive that proper children didn't frequent. I saw her in the company of thuggish-looking boys who smoked and spit and used the F-word to punctuate their loud and obnoxious conversations and caught glimpses of her at high school soccer and basketball games, flirting with older boys and flipping back the straight, golden hair I secretly and desperately envied.

Occasionally I saw Scarlett on Friday or Saturday nights when I was walking back from the movies with a crowd of my equally uncomplicated friends. Dressed in tight pants and low-cut shirts, she paraded up and down Main Street until a car filled with high school ruffians screeched to a stop next to her. The boys inside whistled at Scarlett, threw open a back door, and one of the bolder ones pulled her into his lap before the car raced off into the night.

In contrast, I was straight arrow and straight As; a kid who spent most of her free time memorizing lines for school plays, reading books, or playing records on her parents' decrepit stereo.

On the day of my last and grossly ill-advised involvement with Scarlett, I was weeks from my thirteenth birthday. Hurrying home from a play rehearsal, my mind was busily anticipating applause, a final bow, and my brothers' grinning faces shouting encouragement from the audience, when Scarlett appeared before me on the sidewalk just in front of her house.

Without warning, she grabbed me by the arm and shook me. "An old man just tried to break in my house!" she screamed. "I'm all alone! You have to help me!"

"Where's your mother?" I asked, immediately dubious of her claim. Mrs. Dumond didn't have a job. She should have been there to protect Scarlett.

"She's doing groceries. Please! You have to help me!" she cried, nervously pushing her messy hair from her face.

The explanation seemed believable, but I asked anyway, "Where's Glenn?" Her older brother.

"I don't KNOW!" she screamed. "I don't KNOW where ANYONE is!"

Scarlett's clothes were in disarray. She was red in the face and obviously terrified. "I'm afraid the old man's gonna come back!" she cried, eyes scouring the street for any sign of him.

Despite my history with her and my mother's advice to keep my distance, I couldn't resist the instinct to help. Every bit as terrified as Scarlett, I told her, "Stay here. I'll get help," and I ran to find the nearest adult. In this case the owner of our tiny neighborhood grocery store less than a block away.

Louie would know what to do! He wouldn't let anything bad happen to Scarlett or to me!

The store was crowded with high school kids as I burst through the door. They were lined up three deep at the cash register, waiting to pay for Twinkies, Doritos, and assorted other junk food. A couple of skinny girls were drowning their appetites in diet soda.

I pushed past all of them, breathless and afraid that all our lives were in jeopardy. Who knew where that dangerous old man had gone? What he could do?

Louie was cleaning up colorful spill of grape juice, when I found him, and I dramatically divulged every detail Scarlett had entrusted to me. The old man. The beard—a detail that frightened me almost as much as the rest of the story—the rattling of the door knob as the man had tried forcing his way in.

Louie called the police without hesitation, and on his say-so I stayed put, conveniently frightened into paralysis.

It had all been a hoax. A way for Scarlett and her friends, hiding in nearby bushes, to get a laugh at my expense. Who better to set up than Parry, the good girl? The who-does-she-think-she-is smart girl?

The S-word had flown back and forth over the supper table THAT night. My father at one end of the table, shaking his head in disbelief at my naiveté; my mother implying, again and again, that people who allowed themselves to be swept along in others' malfeasance were either too gullible or too mentally inept to sustain life.

Twenty years later, I reflected on my new circumstance and admitted, "Well, I'm in the mother of all scrapes now!"

No parental back up.

No Scarlett Dumond—a wild woman-child, fond of the drink, last I knew—to blame.

It didn't seem possible that good intentions could have gone so very badly awry.

"Suck it up!" I advised. "You'll get through this." In the way I always had. One foot in front of the other, eyes focused on what lay directly ahead. I had used the technique to good advantage in getting this far in life; it would have to work again.

Prayer, my conscience prodded. A little of that couldn't hurt.

I'd get to that later, I thought dismissively. First there were a dozen more practical matters to address.

I picked out cotton and wool socks; a couple of turtlenecks and sweaters that could be layered. I added the pair of bibbed snow pants that *Soeur Madeleine* had offered as I rushed past the open door of her room earlier, a gift from her sister two Christmases ago.

"I'll mail them back," I promised. "You need them here more than I do in Washington."

"When you're able," she'd said. "There's no rush."

I moved down my list to the next item.
Food.

I pawed through my things and found cashews and salmon. "Yes" to the first, but salmon? The package graphics were a dead giveaway, the company fine print, as I squinted to check it, listing a U.S. address and an 800 number.

A donation to the orphanage then.

I packed toothpaste picked up at the Munich airport and soap. Deodorant whose label I busily attacked with a razor blade. Toilet paper. A single flattened roll easily fit in my backpack.

What about the sanitary products I had left? My period wasn't due until the very end of the week, but stress affected my cycle. I didn't want to be caught in the wilderness without "coverage," as it were, so I whipped handfuls of tampons into my pack and pulled one out to be sure it was in a plain wrapper. I threw in mini-pads in for good measure.

Jake was suddenly there and knocking on the door. "Need any help?" he asked.

"I'm good."

"You almost done here?"

"I am. Let me just zip up my backpack."

"I'll do that," he offered as I looked around the room one last time. "You know, we should probably get some breakfast."

Our last meal.

"Lead the way."

St. Maria's breakfast hour was just about over by the time we reached the dining hall. A few student stragglers were headed outside to play even though a cold and harsh wind was blowing.

Jake and I waved to a few boys whose team had beaten ours badly at charades, but we didn't let on we were leaving. "Peter," Jake called. "Imre."

"Hello Miss Parry!" the boys called. Then a proper, more reserved, "Mr. Jake."

"Guess we know who they have eyes for," Jake observed.

Whom, I silently corrected. Aloud I confessed, "The young ones always like me. I suppose compared to the nuns and two women old enough to be their grandmothers," Bev and Linda, "I must seem incredibly hot."

Jake stopped and looked at me. "You are hot."

"If you say so." Blind man.

"I mean it," he said, his tone final. "You're very pretty."

Objectively I knew he was right. I was neither ugly nor strikingly beautiful. There were occasional moments—fresh from a workout or after a really great date—times like this one when I was blushing furiously, when, yes, pretty was the word that came to mind. But I'd never let myself say that out loud; I rarely even thought it. My parents had done a great job of keeping us humble.

With as much grace as I could manage, I relented, saying, "I'll try to remember that."

"It's all I ask," he said with a smile. "Now let's eat. It could be a while before we get another hot meal."

Over the next several minutes, we shoveled in as much food as was reasonable. From the deserted dining hall, we made our way back to *Soeur St. Helena*'s office. She was deep in conversation with Rand when we walked in, our boots still sitting before her on the desk.

"Matthias just called," Rand told us. "Given what you said about the state of my language proficiency, he's devised a new plan."

"We won't be hiking out?"

"No, that part hasn't changed," he clarified. "But he's thought of a cover that he thinks may make things safer for us."

"Anything you can share?" Jake asked.

"I don't have all the specifics, but in a nutshell he thinks the three of us should pretend to be deaf. That way we wouldn't actually have to talk to anyone if we were stopped."

"Deaf?" I had to be sure I'd heard correctly.

"That's right. He's had cards printed up—introducing us. We won't be using our real names obviously, but something that sounds native. There'll be a second set of cards that asks where we can buy food. Find a place to stay. Get directions to transportation."

I got it.

And then I had to speak up. "You're telling me, after all that's happened around here, the takeover, the ban on Americans, the bounty on our heads. You don't think this plan is the slightest bit, I don't know, obvious?"

Juvenile.

Insane.

A hundred other descriptors came to mind, but I settled for the one. Looking at Jake, then at Rand, I saw I'd made my point.

Behind her desk *Soeur St. Helena* smiled. "I was explaining the very same objection to Rand as you entered."

"Do we have any other ideas?" Jake asked.

"As a matter of fact," she volunteered, "I do."

Before she could elaborate, Rand turned to her and insisted, "It's too dangerous."

"Why, it's not at all so," she asserted. She pulled open a desk drawer and retrieved a manila envelope. She laid it on the desktop and slid it toward Jake. "Here's my plan."

He opened the envelope and drew out three black leather pamphlet-sized books emblazoned in gold.

I recognized Canada's Royal Coat of Arms.

They were passports.

"Rand's right," Jake said, instantly comprehending. "We can't let you relinquish these."

"And why not? Matthias' friend was going to forge copies of the national ID for you to take; he could just as easily modify these."

Could he?

The determined nun turned an insistent stare on Rand. "Matthias did say the man was the best at what he did."

"Expert. Yes. He's 'retired' from an intelligence agency that shall remain nameless."

KGB, I thought instantly. Or another of the dozen other possible intelligence agencies on the continent.

But the men were right. We couldn't leave the nuns here without papers. What if authorities appeared and demanded proof of citizenship? Hauled them in and made them talk? Everyone from the children to *Soeur St. Helena* would be in danger; the farm's workers and all their families as well.

"You need not worry," she assured us. "*Monsieur* Miroslav will not let anything untoward happen to us here. He is generous, shall we say, to local authorities and to a few faithful friends who are paid handsomely to oversee our safety.

"It's very unlikely the new government will want to take over the care of a hundred and fifty children, one of whom is sick at the moment with a very bad case of 'influenza'." There was an impish tone to her delivery as she smiled again and stood.

Fixing her attention on Rand, she summoned her reserves. "Make the call to Matthias," she ordered. "Explain to him what we've just decided. Convince him we're right.

"Oh. And speak to him in French on the off chance authorities are intercepting the exchange. It's doubtful anyone hereabouts speaks it."

English maybe. Hungarian, undoubtedly. But French? The chances were infinitesimally small.

Rand saw he was outgunned and appreciated, too, the simplicity of the new plan. Grudgingly, he told her, "I'll make the call." Then he left to do so.

Soeur St. Helena picked up the passports and put them back inside the envelope. "I will have a workman run these to Matthias immediately."

Locals came and went at all hours. Milking the cows. Driving oats to Austria. Headed to the capital for supplies. "Give me a moment to summon Erik from the dairy," she asked of us. "He's my most reliable employee."

With both Rand and *Soeur St. Helena* engaged, Jake and I quietly debated the virtues of the escape plans recently revealed. He thought the deaf ruse might work; I argued against it. "Do you remember what *Soeur Madelaine* told us? People with handicaps tend to be hidden away here. Cared for out of sight of neighbors who might ridicule or taunt them. If that's true, how likely do you think it would be for three deaf-mutes to be traveling together?

"*Helena* is right. We could pull off the Canadian thing without any trouble. Rand and I both speak French. We'd be believable.

"On the other hand, none of us knows sign language. How would we communicate? With a few cards? Please. It's lunacy to think we could pull that off."

Rand came back into the room. "It's all set. It seems Matthias sees things the way *Helena* does."

Amazing. It was the second time in a short time span that Rand had admitted someone else was right. And by extension, that he was wrong. Who could've imagined we'd live to see that?

"Don't we have something we need to be doing?" he asked impatiently. Clearly he was eager to have the moment pass.

"Absolutely," Jake said. "We should be looking through all our supplies again and making sure we've wiped away any trace of home."

Rand picked up our hiking boots and said in a low voice, "You may want to check out these first."

"Why's that?" I asked. "They haven't been touched yet."

He grinned. "They have."

I examined my pair for evidence of tampering. I felt for lumps or bumps, and there were none. "Are you saying my passport's in one of these boots?"

"*Oui, ma chere*," *Soeur St. Helena* answered as she came back in. "It is."

She pointed to the heel of my right boot and explained, "We removed the stitching from the lining along the sides and the back. We folded the pages of your passport crosswise and moistened them. Then we applied petroleum jelly to the cover to make it more pliable." The same way my brothers had softened and molded their baseball gloves to a ball.

"We added a thickness of the cotton sheeting roughly equivalent to that of your passport, along the backs and sides of both boots, so they would be identical in appearance. Then we re-stitched each lining."

"Are you sure you didn't hire a plastic surgeon?" I challenged. "The stitches are nearly invisible."

She snickered. "We used suturing material that Rand thoughtfully provided. As for the intricacy of our needlework, my colleagues and I are expert from years of making quilts for the children."

I'd seen them. On beds. On walls. One with spectacularly intricate patterns adorned the orphanage's wide entry, the beautiful splashes of color diminishing the institutional feel.

"I thought the stitching would be stronger if we used catgut," Rand explained. "Happened to have some."

"We may have a couple of CIA recruits on our hands," I joked as I stepped out of my shoes and into my newly transformed hiking boots. The extra padding made them snug but not uncomfortable. "Good fit."

Jake slipped his on and found them acceptable as well. "Let's get to work then."

Soeur St. Helena excused herself again, and the men and I migrated into the next room. We dumped the contents of our backpacks across the broad conference table and started going through things, one item at a time.

As it turned out, we'd done a pretty thorough job, but pretty good wasn't enough. We spotted a couple of tags that could easily have given us away, t-shirts whose logos and size information were imprinted with some kind of rubberized ink that had to be scraped away with a knife. We discovered Nike swooshes on several pairs of socks which, while common, weren't worth the risk. Labels on two vials of water purification tablets were printed in English, so we soaked the bottles while we re-packed, then peeled the paper away.

"This really necessary?" Rand asked Jake. "English is spoken in Canada."

"It is. But most products sold there are labeled in both French and English; it's something small but to the right eyes, a giveaway. Why risk it?"

Again, Jake was right, and Rand was out of his element.

Soeur St. Helena returned. "What's next?" she asked.

"Why don't you two get down to the kitchen," he suggested to Jake and me. "You can pack the food. Mrs. Holic has prepared a few things for us to take."

"The question is: will we be able to carry them?" Jake asked with a grin. The food here, while tasty, leaned toward the leaden side of the scale.

"I just spoke with her and asked her to use a light touch," *Soeur St. Helena* assured us. "Why don't you go see how well she listened."

Evelin Holic, God bless her, was almost as wide as she was tall. Weight aside, however, I'd never seen anyone move more efficiently or happily around a kitchen. She was the first one to arrive in the morning, constantly chopping and mixing and monitoring the facility's food preparation, and she'd been the last of the kitchen workers to leave, at least during our stay. She had welcomed us home every evening as we shuffled in exhausted.

Evelin had never let on that staying beyond her usual work hours was an inconvenience, moreover. In fact she implied by her smiles, by her bustling back and forth, and by her encouraging, "More! Eat!" what an honor it was to feed us. Invariably, her cheerfulness and humility made me feel the too-fortunate American chump.

"Go," Rand said encouraged. "*Helena* and I will be down in a few minutes."

"Done."

As Jake and I made our way past the first floor classrooms, the reality of our predicament suddenly overwhelmed me. I felt my intestines moan at the thought of the danger ahead.

I was a woman. A young woman. No matter that I was to be accompanied by two able-bodied men probably willing to die rather than let anything bad happen to me, they weren't the ones in control.

I'd read stories and seen enough movies to know the horrific things that could happen to someone like me in war. And make no mistake, this felt every bit like the real thing.

I grew cold and clammy thinking of what could happen. Felt the urgent need to go. "Jake," I said. "Why don't you go ahead. I need to visit the 'loo'."

"Going British on me?" he laughed.

"Just a little affectation I like to indulge from time to time."

"Cute," he teased. "Don't be long."

Safe in the second-floor bathroom, I communed with the porcelain god, another St. Amand family trait rarely discussed outside of reunions or raucous family dinners. It was common knowledge in our family that the least little thing smacking of excitement, good or bad, transmitted itself instantly to the gut.

Or as we so fondly called it, our second brains.

Researchers studying the intestinal tract, in the last decade or so, had documented its many similarities to grey matter; the ways in which neurotransmitters and neurons there were identical to those that made up the brains in our heads. Both "organs," it seemed, regulated heart rate and respiration; they initiated the body's responses to stress.

As I wrapped up the paperwork, it occurred to me that the St. Amands had probably received more than their fair share of intestinal enervation alleles when the Maker was divvying them up. Hence our collective "movement," so to speak, when faced with the perilous unknown.

I hurried downstairs to find that Jake and Evelin were almost done. They'd packed food in water-proof containers and stacked them for the trip. Our kitchen friend had added bags of muesli and dried fruit to the stash and small wheels of cheese she was sure would stay fresh in the cold. Among the supplies, I discovered tea bags, a small aluminum pot, and three cans of sterno gel.

"You no snow, eat!" Evelin warned, her chubby finger pointing to bottled water.

I promised solemnly, "No snow eat."

It wasn't long before Rand appeared with *Soeur St. Helena,* and the four of us carried supplies to the storage shed. "Should we be taking this much?" I asked. "Even with the toboggan, it's a lot to haul. It could make us look more suspicious."

"If anything, a large load will make you seem more like you belong," *Soeur St. Helena* insisted as she opened wide the shed doors. "As I told you before. People often walk the roads here pulling their possessions behind them. Going to visit family. Uprooting for better jobs in the city.

"Visiting a friend in hospital."

"The weight could slow us down," I cautioned.

"We can try it," Jake said. "If we have to, we can lighten the load later."

Rand agreed. "Better too much than too little starting out."

The orphanage's second morning bell rang, and we watched through the shed's open doors as students streamed past, lining up. I fought the impulse to run out and hug them goodbye, settling for a silent and heartfelt farewell.

Beside me, Jake advised, "We'll want to carry a few essential supplies on us in case we have to make a run for it."

An astute recommendation.

We rummaged through the supplies. I retrieved the Imodium that Rand had saved from the border guards' ransacking, jerky for protein, and dried fruit for a glucose charge, squeezing them into my backpack.

Rand pocketed the satellite phone, a couple of water bottles, and matches.

I noticed Jake palming the GPS and two bags of trail mix. A single water bottle. "The rest can stay on the sled for now."

Rand looked at me and asked, "You sure you have everything you need, Parry?"

I grinned. Foraged for a few seconds. I extricated a roll of toilet paper and a giant handful of feminine products, unabashedly showing them off. I warned both men, "Woe to the man who tries to help himself, friend or foe."

As the last of the student stragglers ran past us to the back door of the building, Rand told us, "Matthias won't be back for a while. The change in our plan means more work. Things are going to take a little longer than we counted on.

"I propose the three of us get some shut eye."

The suggestion made sense. I was already feeling lightheaded from lack of sleep. Giddy almost.

"Go on," *Soeur St. Helena* prodded. "I will wake you on Matthias' return." She laid a hand on my shoulder and encouraged the men. "You will need to be fresh when he comes."

SEVENTEEN

Matthias had been back for close to an hour, and we were running terribly behind.

It had taken a while to pin down the details of a new back story he insisted we concoct. Ultimately, we'd decided—*Soeur St. Helena*, Matthias, my fellow travelers, and I—it would be best to stick as close to the truth as possible.

So, we became medical relief workers. Rand was a physician and I a nurse; Jake the construction expert accompanying us to our next assignment where he would help build a new clinic associated with an obscure Canadian organization Matthias had researched on the Web and knew to be active in the country. *Les Me´decins Internationals.*

Our story evolved in this way. Two nights earlier, the truck we'd been driving had taken a washout too quickly in the darkness, and we'd broken an axle. Jake, reborn as James Carter, had walked to the nearest farmhouse for help. A generous soul there had given him a toboggan on which to load our gear; he had no tools and no skills with which to help repair the truck.

"James" had been directed to a place where we might find assistance, and after loading the sled the three of us had gone off in search of it. We'd gotten lost. We had no idea where the truck was anymore. Where our benefactor was. We had been wandering for some time and only knew we should be headed toward a small town north of capital.

On an official looking document that Matthias' forger had produced—printing it; re-folding it; spilling water on it to make it seem weathered— were the particulars of our assignment.

No. We had no idea what had happened here in the last few days.

What? No. We were Canadian, not American . . . And so the script went.

Compared to our first ruse, this one seemed infinitely more plausible. And we had passports now to back up our claims.

"These are impressive," Jake complimented Matthias. He opened each one and compared the new data pages with those that had been removed. Where once there had been photos of *Soeur St. Helena*, *Soeur Madelaine*, and *Soeur Charles Regis*, there were now pictures of Rand, Jake, and me carefully enlarged and cut to fit. The paper, complete with a maple leaf design subtly visible in the background; the appropriate thickness of the sheet; and the bold black print precisely reproduced, were indistinguishable from the original. The pages had been inserted into the document with exquisite care.

"It would take an expert to detect that these have been tampered with."

"Let's pray we don't run into one," I implored.

Matthias reminded us, "You realize you should show these passports as a last resort. You should avoid all check points and official border crossings at all costs. It would also be best for you to appear native."

He handed me a package and said, "To that end, I have traded Evelin's daughter Agnes some of the clothing that Linda and Beverly left behind. For these."

I opened the bag he handed me and discovered pants, a long-sleeved shirt, and a thick woolen overcoat that could have been a man's.

"These should help you to look like you belong."

I held the garments before me, gauging fit.

Matthias observed, "I believe you and Agnes are about the same size."

Leave it to a man.

I'd seen Agnes. She was of slender to average proportions, as I was, but was at least three inches taller and, given her more athletic build, probably fifteen to twenty pounds heavier. Where I had curves and strategically placed soft spots, Agnes was solid muscle. I'd watched her helping her mother in the kitchen, lifting crates and scrubbing floors. She looked like she could run a three-hour marathon and still have the energy to pick up after her gaggle of four equally robust children.

In spite of my reservations, I rolled the unwashed clothes into a bundle, the unfamiliar smell of them hitting me hard. Not quite clean and certainly worn, they bore another woman's imprint. Her essence. They left me mourning the clothes I was going to jettison, wondering for the briefest moment if I'd ever get home again to tackle chores as mundane as laundry.

To reclaim my life.

"Time is short," Matthias reminded me gently. "You all need to change."

"Gentlemen," *Soeur St. Helena* beckoned. "I have things for you as well.

In an empty bathroom stall, I stripped off jeans and the blue Fair Isle sweater I'd thrown on in the middle of the night. I folded each piece of my clothing and laid it aside. For just a moment, I wrapped my arms around myself and rubbed the fabric of my thermal underwear against my skin, inhaling the familiar scent of aloe and white lilac fabric softener that had become for me the smell of home.

I briefly considered staying behind and riding out the revolution at St. Maria's disguised as a nun, but I knew doing so would only be putting all these wonderful people at greater risk. Endangering lives of those already sacrificing a great deal to help save me.

It wouldn't be right.

I donned the camouflage Matthias had provided, each garment bearing the bouquet of Agnes' hard country life. It was a privilege, I knew, not a hardship to wear them. Agnes had little in the way of worldly possessions, and she looked forward, at most, to modest future wealth. That she would give the clothes off her back, helping me return to the kind of life she could only dream of, was an unbelievably generous act, one that would be diminished if I turned up my nose at it. If I thought somehow that my life was better or worth more than hers.

Back in the shed, I found Jake and Rand divested of their American clothes, wearing jackets, tattered trousers, and worn winter hats donated by the men working St. Maria's barns.

Soeur St. Helena insisted on completing the look. She called each of us forward and smeared well-seasoned compost on our clothing and through our hair. She patted it on our faces and necks for effect.

"Dig through this bucket with your fingers," she instructed all of us.

"Through dirt?" Rand asked. "What in the world for?"

"Your clean fingernails will betray you. You've been on the road. Sleeping outside. You haven't washed in days.

"Now dig."

He complied, then Jake and I did as well.

"Try not to brush your teeth too often until you cross the border," she added. "Dental hygiene isn't big in this part of the world." An observation, not a judgment. "As Westerners purporting to have been here a while, you would have learned to fit in."

I wasn't sure what would kill me first: the soldiers waiting to capture us or my bad breath after days on the run. My mother was neurotic about dental care, and she'd passed on the trait. We'd always visited the dentist twice a year growing up, and she'd gone without new clothes, new furniture, or a better grade of groceries just so she could finance our braces. Following *Soeur St. Helena's* advice would go against everything my mother had "drilled" into us.

Matthias came back in from a trip to his rusty truck. "You may need these," he said handing out knives, a large coil of nylon rope, and sunglasses. "Rand, did you take the gun?"

"I have it," Jake responded. "And I know how to use it."

"Good." Matthias glanced at his watch. "We should leave soon."

His words were met with silence.

"I was hoping for a few minutes in the chapel," Jake said quietly. "Would you mind?"

Matthias checked the time again. "Ten minutes," he allowed. "No more. I will meet you outside."

Given the lateness and the likelihood of capture so close to town, he'd offered to give us a ride past the closest government checkpoint and around the far side of the mountain that dominated the local landscape. Making up for the time his forger friend had needed.

"We'll be brief," I promised.

Jake and I turned to go, and without waiting for an invitation, Rand quietly followed behind. We traveled the first floor corridors to the front of the building, muted classroom sounds drifting out to us as we walked past. Teachers' firm voices giving instruction. The lightheartedness of a collective class giggle. From one room, a student's voice showcased understanding.

We reached the empty chapel and went our separate ways.

I walked to a side altar, knelt, and lit a candle. Silently, I asked God for His mercy and strength. This ordeal was real, I reflected, and our coming flight fraught with dangers we could only imagine. Though we pretended to know what we were doing, the truth was these circumstances had little precedent in our lives, certainly none in mine. Compared to the silly situations I'd inadvertently fallen into as a child, this was dramatically and dangerously different.

I rose from the kneeler and slid into a nearby pew. I caught a glimpse of Rand, sitting alone in the last row, eyes staring straight ahead, as mysterious as ever on matters of faith.

Close to the altar, Jake had settled before the grand piano, a lovely instrument that only a day earlier had featured prominently in the children's impressive performance. He began to play a melody that sounded vaguely familiar, the notes flowing delicately at his touch.

As he moved through the piece, the memory of it came back to me.

A warm summer evening in rural Virginia. Children running beneath stars and turning clumsy cartwheels on the grass. Toddlers collapsed tiredly in their mothers' laps, heavy heads pressing into softness.

There had been a man, then, too, bent to a keyboard in much the same way Jake was now. An acoustic guitar had leaned on a stand, not far, and a violinist somewhere on the darkened stage had provided accompaniment.

The singer's name came to me: Fernando Ortega.

A friend had dragged me to the concert as a belated birthday gift and I, who had an aversion to over-produced Praise music, had been taken with this gentle more thoughtful version of the style.

Though Jake wasn't singing, I heard Ortega's voice and simple lyrics drifting on a fragrant night breeze. The melody was clear and clean, and through it I heard children exclaiming at fireflies, taunting one another in the way they often did, offering real-life counterpoint to the plaintive violin solo that was a bridge to the song's final lyric.

Jake's playing faded to deep quiet, and the three of us got up to leave.

There was no more delaying the inevitable.

EIGHTEEN

Per Matthias' instructions, I crawled into the space behind his truck's bench seat, the only one of us who could wedge herself into such a compressed space without risking asphyxiation. The men were secreted under a tarp in the truck bed, where customarily Matthias kept his supplies. "The local constabulary is aware that I bring food and clothes and medicine to the homebound," he explained. "I doubt anyone will insist on seeing for himself."

The local constabulary was one thing, I thought as I settled in; guards sent by the self-appointed dictator and ordered to shoot Americans on sight, quite another.

Every minute spent bumping hard along the impossibly rough roads, I prayed that we didn't run into soldiers, or if we did, that my churning gut wouldn't betray me. There was no question we were risking capture, perhaps worse, in accepting Matthias' offer, but we had faith that he, if anyone, could pull off an encounter with the enemy. We were banking on his local reputation and his popularity to keep us safe, shaving ten kilometers, six or seven miles, from the arduous walk ahead.

I felt the truck slow.

"A new checkpoint," Matthias updated tersely. "I had hoped they had not had the time."

How charming Matthias' English was, I thought, How precise. He never used a contraction or slang; he enunciated every word. In that one way he was like Rand, though overall he was openly generous and optimistic where Rand tended to growl when times grew tense.

The truck stopped abruptly and with it, my frivolous thoughts. My heartbeat intensified to the point I felt it reverberating the length and breadth of my body. My mouth grew parched and sweat trickled in the valley between my breasts. I panted in the dry, hot air blowing manically from the truck's heater, set for some reason to high.

Matthias rolled down his window, presumably at a guard's signal, and cold air rushed in. Footsteps crunched on roadside gravel as someone approached. I heard Matthias utter the name, "Gabor?" in the form of a question.

The person Matthias was addressing called that same name back over his shoulder, then his footsteps retreated.

With the truck engine idling, neither one of us spoke. No one moved.

There came the sound of running footfalls, intensifying, and a second male voice shouting out in greeting to Matthias. There followed a rushed exchange between the two men and subdued masculine laughter. A brief conversation that didn't involve Matthias being pulled from the truck.

Miraculously, the truck gears shifted, and we were driving forward again. Matthias rolled up his window and affected a final goodbye with several staccato beeps of the horn.

"Gabor has been transferred to this new location," Matthias murmured as he accelerated. Clearly a boon for us. "But I am afraid that he has bad news."

"What?" I queried. How much more could there be?

"The new government has begun billeting soldiers in communities throughout the country. And the orders vis-à-vis Americans have been modified." There was an ominous hesitation to his delivery. "Americans are to be taken captive and promptly removed to the capital."

"For what purpose?"

"Gabor would not elaborate, but my guess is that the new president may soon attempt to negotiate a deal with the United States government." The more living Americans he could assemble, the thinking likely went, the more power he could wield. "The rumor is that the national coffers here contain funds insufficient to cover bounties."

Little surprise there. Every country in the world was hurting in the wake of the United States' credit crisis. The banking industry's greed and the acquisitiveness of borrowers together had laid the groundwork for the financial pandemic rapidly worsening everywhere. As credit dried up, Americans had stopped buying. Countries around the world had been forced to stop selling, manufacturing, and reaping profits critical to their overall solvency. It didn't take Milton Friedman to predict where the lack of money and confidence would end.

"Officially, the U.S. doesn't negotiate with kidnappers," I reminded Matthias.

"Perhaps," he responded. "But if the numbers grow substantial enough, there will be pressure brought to bear on your President. There are exchange students here. And teams of scientists from your CDC and NIH conducting studies," he continued. "A small army of NGO volunteers."

He'd probably worked with any number of them.

"This administration won't respond well to pressure," I told him. "The President and Congress have just written a $700 billion check to rescue their banking friends; I doubt there are funds left in the Treasury earmarked for the rescue of hostages."

Of course, lack of money didn't seem to be an impediment to federal spending these days; the long, slow slide into trillion dollar debt had started with the New Deal and had only become more entrenched as citizen expectations expanded. For their part, many thought that if individuals could borrow against the accumulated value of their real estate holdings, as determined by appraisers, why shouldn't Treasury borrow against the future industriousness of the nation's citizens?

It had worked for Social Security, until now. Why not other entitlement programs?

Accountants and Harvard MBAs and upper level management-types across the American business landscape shared in the blame for our collective financial delusions. Together they'd learned to hide corporate liabilities with aggressive creativity and to overestimate assets. The more devious among them had contrived Ponzi schemes of unprecedented vastness that had robbed individuals and companies and non-profits alike of a generation's accumulated wealth.

Why not use imaginary revenues to pay a ransom?

It wouldn't be fair to taxpayers, that was why. Seven hundred billion wrongs did not make a right. We and people like us who'd traveled to the region of our own accord and despite official warnings, had taken a risk. We'd entered a part of the world where American popularity historically waxed and waned; we couldn't rightfully expect rescue now that fate and the balance of power here had turned against us.

The prospect of capture and subsequent torture left me terror-stricken, the child in me wanting nothing more than to have someone ride up and whisk me away. The adult realized that Jake, Rand, and I should fend for ourselves. We'd gone into the situation fully aware of the dangers; it was vital we do all we could now to extricate ourselves. Evading patrols and soldiers and whatever other pursuers thrown at us, we would have to use every resource that we had.

The American in me knew we could do it; the realist wasn't sure.

The truck slowed again and stopped.

"We have arrived," Matthias stated calmly. He threw open the driver's side door and hopped out of the truck. He released the bench seat and pulled it roughly from the wall.

I unfolded my legs and sat up straight. Through the window, I saw Matthias at the tailgate already, drawing back the tarp; Jake and Rand were instantly upright and lowering our fully-loaded toboggan into the snow.

I quickly left the truck, pulling on mittens and hat.

Rand lifted our snowshoes out of the truck bed and handed me a pair to put on. Jake busied himself securing the load, testing both the ropes and the bungee cords that crisscrossed the sled's brown canvas cover.

I moved more slowly than I would've liked to, tired in spite of my determination not to be. Except for the fitful few minutes of sleep I'd managed during my nap, I had been up five hours already and moving most of that time. I'd run from one end of the orphanage to the other; one floor to another; one room to another, making the hundred small preparations to go.

I'd packed; I'd peed; I'd prayed. It was time to get about the business of escape.

Once we were appropriately shod, Jake urged softly, "We should go."

He was right; we needed to be off. In the shelter of an evergreen wall, though, I selfishly prolonged the time left to us under Matthias' care. I hiked thick woolen knee highs over my pants and put on sunglasses against the day's snowy glare. I shrugged into Agnes' heavy wool coat and wound a scarf around my face to protect it from the harsh wind blowing steadily from the west.

In a final reconnaissance, Rand studied a landscape daunting in its starkness. Vast fields fell away from the foothills where we stood in a slow and steady decline; evergreen forests; a distant river that winked in pale sunlight as it snaked in and out of view.

"We need to go," Jake repeated after running out of straps and buttons and ropes to triple check.

The men shook hands with Matthias and stood back as he picked me up off the ground in a gentle, ursine embrace. They watched as I kissed his hairy cheek. "Get some sleep," I ordered. "Your patients depend on you."

"I will."

He wouldn't. His country was in trouble, and he wasn't one to sit or lie idly by.

He shook hands with Rand again and drew him into a cousin's brutish hug. Who knew when they would see one another again?

IF they would.

Matthias said something to Rand in their mother tongue, then he turned and saluted Jake.

I couldn't stand to watch as he turned to go, so I leveled my gaze to the northern horizon. I heard him move quickly to the open truck door and jump in. He gunned the engine, and it growled as he floored the accelerator.

I fought every instinct not to turn and call out, "Wait, I changed my mind!"

I ignored the voice virtually yelling now, in my mind. "Who the hell do you think you are, Parise St. Amand? Setting out on this fool's exercise?"

I wasn't devious. I wasn't brave. One cross-eyed look from a soldier holding a gun on me, and for sure I'd give myself up. Give up anyone who'd helped me.

Wouldn't I?

The transmission heaved as Matthias shifted into reverse, and the engine emitted a high-pitched whine backing out of the windbreak and out of our lives. I heard the alternating sounds of revving, clutching, and shifting as Matthias drove away, leaving us to our fate.

Seconds passed, and no one moved. Instead we listened to the wind's lonely, winter lament.

I thought of a novel I'd recently read in which a character cited Mark Twain's take on courage. Bravery wasn't the absence of fear, Twain reflected, it was more resistance to it and the eventual mastery over it. None of us came by courage naturally; it was something we chose to live.

The observation had struck a note. Stayed with me. I had looked at my own life, at the choices I'd made, and I knew that courage had evolved as I plowed through whatever it was I had to do. Behaving as though I didn't have a choice.

Pretending, if I had to, that there was no going back, so I could get through whatever lay ahead.

Action as conviction.

Standing bereft of family, friends, and nation, in that moment, it took every molecule of confidence I had in my experience, having overcome, not to run desperately in the direction Matthias had gone.

It was time to face a new reality. We were three civilians trying to outrun an entire nation's military, three indulged Americans pitting their stamina against soldiers hardened by years of deprivation and shifting loyalties. Tough men, and women presumably, used to making tough decisions.

Jake's voice startled me back to the moment. "I'll take the lead," he offered. "And pull the sled."

"Okay."

"Parry, you walk behind me.

"Rand, bring up the rear."

Conventional wisdom dictated that the slowest member of a hiking party should assume the lead position and set the pace, but it was doubtful Rand was up to the strenuousness of the work.

While relatively fit, I was too small to effectively break trail.

That left Jake.

"We'll try that for now," Rand answered, allowing himself the option of taking over.

I glanced at Jake. He was the only one of us familiar with outdoor survival and orienteering; the one who'd led men on grueling operations and consistently returned with his unit intact.

Rich had spilled a few details about Jake's military record to me after a little too much plum liquor a few nights earlier. "He doesn't talk about how good he was," Rich confided. "But I hired him. I've seen his file. Guy has steel for guts."

Jake was the natural choice to lead us into the unknown.

He knew it.

I knew it.

Most important, Rand knew it. He just hadn't reached the point where he could speak the certainty aloud.

We set off.

In the first few hours of high-stepping through newly fallen snow, we worked like dogs. We headed downhill across slightly sloping terrain and remembered Matthias' earlier warning, "You may want to maintain silence among yourselves. The less sound you produce in this wilderness, the less likely you are to be detected." So, we spoke only when we were close enough to make sense of one another's muted words and signaled to one another at a distance otherwise.

Jake grew confident and assertive in the freedom of fresh air, clearly a man accustomed to taking action on his own and others' behalf.

He issued orders wisely.

"Let's go this way."

"Stop a second to rest."

"Here. Have a snack."

He was a man for whom intellectualizing, beyond the basics of smart planning, served little purpose.

As we made progress on the open terrain, we rarely heard from Rand, who was having trouble keeping up. Beyond the occasional word of encouragement, we said little to him as well. It took all our energy making headway through the snow.

Before very long, my thighs were burning; likewise my throat and lungs. I longed to sit and take a load off, but it wasn't until we reached the safety of a tree line that we stopped to rest, and to let a distant Rand catch up.

"This is pretty intense," Rand panted as neared us. Hat off; gloves shed; worn dairyman's coat thrown onto the heap of our supplies. His face was splotched red and white from exertion, a sign that he was working inordinately hard given the easy terrain and warming conditions. We hadn't covered more than three miles in our time out, but neither Jake nor I had the heart to tell him that.

"You exercise much?" Jake asked as Rand drained a twelve-ounce bottle of water.

"I play a little handball and go fishing once in a while with my uncle," he responded.

Obviously not an Olympian.

"It's hard to get to the gym with the schedule I keep."

That was the same excuse I'd used a hundred times.

Without a hint of recrimination, Jake said, "We need to keep a steady pace." Eyes fixed on Rand, he added, "We have to cover between twelve and fifteen miles a day." Of the sixty total Matthias estimated the trip might be.

Not should or could. MUST.

"How far've we gone so far?" Rand asked. "Five, six miles?"

"Just over three," Jake replied.

"You're kidding?" Rand rebutted. "I feel like I've gone ten."

"Maybe three and a half," Jake generously allowed.

"Why don't we get moving," I suggested. "If we stop too long our muscles will get cold and stiff. It'll be that much harder getting back up to speed."

I'd seen inexperienced hikers indulge themselves and live to regret it.

We rose from the warmth of the massive rock whose surface we shared and grabbed our gear. We skirted the edge of the nearby woods and kept both the trees and the river, now close, between ourselves and stretches of country road visible in the distance.

For the next couple of hours, we stepped gingerly over roots and down small dips in the land. We climbed up gradual hillsides and down, the land undulating mildly toward the western horizon. Sometimes I kept pace with Jake, other times I purposely started falling back a little as an encouragement to Rand, who was growing visibly tired as the last of the morning s-l-o-w-l-y passed.

Just after one, he and I rounded a peninsula of fir trees grown impenetrably close to find that Jake had laid out lunch for us across a table of the toboggan's flat cover. He'd even taken the time to boil water for tea.

"You run here?" Rand panted.

"No. Just one shoe in front of the other."

Instead of the smart retort I expected, Rand offered only a non-committal, "Thanks for setting up."

"My pleasure," Jake replied.

We made benches of our backpacks and felt the sun burn warm on our already flushed faces. We were ravenous after a few hours on the trail, my own body behaving like it had been at it for a day.

Strange, I hadn't felt all that tired as long as I was moving; pushing; finding the next interesting thing to whisper to Jake or to Rand as we hiked. But sitting and hungrily stuffing bread, cheese, and dried apples into my mouth, I suddenly wanted nothing more than to curl up in my sleeping bag, hidden from the wind, and to spend the next hour or two snoozing.

I couldn't give in. A nap would be the end of any forward progress for the day. Best to finish eating and get right back on the trail.

"I think I might have a couple blisters," Rand diagnosed. The mildly euphoric effects of exercise had waned, and now he was grimacing in pain. "I should probably check my foot."

He took off his right boot, peeled back two pairs of damp socks, and revealed his assessment to be correct. There was a blister on the inside of his heel and the watery fluid draining from it was tinged with blood. The surrounding area looked tender to the touch but was otherwise unremarkable.

Falling into p.a. mode, I got out our medical kit and dug through it for the antibacterial cream I knew was there. Found it. Slathered a generous amount on Rand's wound and covered the affected area with a wide bandage. There was a smaller blister on the ridge of his big toe, and I pointed it out. "Let me take care of this one, too."

Rand raised no objection, though he winced a time or two. As I stowed away the kit, he put on clean socks and somehow squeezed his enormous foot back into his boot.

Looking on, Jake asked Rand, "You good to go?"

"I guess."

We cleaned up our trash and suited up.

It was hard to get started again, almost like pushing through a wall of molasses. We moved slowly, each step forward exaggerated and painful as we struggled to get back in the swing.

We had no choice, though; the journey was do . . . or die.

Two o'clock. Three. Clouds scudded in from the north like a miniature armada, and any sunshine disappeared. The temperature fell. The land and our movement across it grew more challenging. There were increasingly more small ravines; long, wide folds in the land that were undetectable at a distance and time-consuming as we approached and passed through, not around them.

We sidestepped steeply down the side of each dip, then grabbed at plants and rock outcroppings trying to get ourselves up and over the opposite walls. Matthias had told us we might encounter this kind of exhausting topography and that negotiating it would be the high price of avoiding roads and the military likely patrolling them. We'd been prepared, but still, it was draining work.

About 4:30, daylight was in rapid decline, and Jake started talking about finding a place to spend the night. He and I stood on the floor of a gully, fighting to get ourselves and the toboggan up the eight foot embankment in front of us. We pushed; we strained; we gave it every ounce of reserve that we had, and still the thing scraped noisily against exposed rock.

"Take a break," Jake ordered setting down his end of the toboggan.

"Happy to." I dropped mine.

Looking down, I saw that my ski pants—correction, *Soeur Monique*'s ski pants—were splattered with mud and fraying already at the hem.

Dusk was no more than a half hour away, complete darkness maybe an hour.

Five hundred feet behind us, Rand was breathing hard and moaning involuntarily at the trip's rigors.

"This is rougher than I thought it was going to be," Jake confided. "On the bright side, we haven't met a single patrol."

True, though we had come across a number of farmhouses, two that had shown signs of occupation.

"What about the detour we took?" I reminded him.

"Hey. No one told us we might run into aggressive sheep," he laughed.

"Maybe our aroma had something to do with them pursuing us."

"Could be. We better hope no one sends out any smell patrols." He took a drink of water, recapped the bottle, and said, "How about I hike ahead and find shelter while you wait here for Rand?"

"Sounds good."

I lowered myself to a seat made of the toboggan's curly end, happy to wallow in my fatigue. My clothes were sweat-soaked. My calves were on fire, and each of my thighs felt like it weighed a ton.

In no time, I started to really feel the cold; to be the cold. My eyelids drooped sleepily.

Rand appeared at the edge of the ravine, whining like a grade schooler, "Are we there yet?" and I snapped to.

"Shh," I warned, finger to my lips.

"Sorry."

"And, yes, we're almost there," I whispered. "Jake's scouting for shelter."

"My legs won't hold me going down this slope," Rand confessed softly. "They sure as hell won't get me UP that one."

"I hear you."

Above me, his breathing was ragged and deep.

"Stay where you are," I encouraged. "If we have to, Jake and I can pull you up."

I seriously doubted my words, even as they left my mouth, but I wanted to give the man hope.

Jake appeared. "Nothing in that direction that can shield us from the wind or the soldiers probably out on patrol. But I think we passed a pretty good spot not too far back."

I stood and declared, "Backward, ho!"

"Let me have the sled," Jake directed.

I relinquished the rope, and he grabbed it. Somehow he pulled the toboggan up and out of the ravine, then bounded back down the trail like a gazelle.

I crawled up to where Rand still hadn't moved. Stood there next to him. Neither of us took a step. There was no point in backtracking only to find we'd have to move again.

A minute later, we heard Jake's muted beckoning. "Guys. Over here!"

All righty then.

I steered Rand down the path we'd already beaten, soldiering through my own exhaustion. Jake was undoing the sled's canvas cover when we found him. He'd unfolded it to its full dimensions, about ten by twelve feet, and had left one edge tethered to the side of the toboggan. While we watched, he attached the opposite side to a strong, horizontal stretch of tree limb, Rand and I, for the moment, superfluous.

"Ta-dah," Jake presented. "Not the Ritz-Carlton, but it should protect us."

He was right. The dirt-colored canvas would shield us from the view of traffic skirting the perimeter of the valley floor a dozen miles or so due east. To the west, boulders and a morass of interwoven tree limbs and vines broke the wind.

"Great job," I said.

"We can't make a full blown fire," Jake warned. "On this moonscape, we'd be made in a minute. But we can set up the burner behind this rock to boil water for tea."

"Works for me."

I caught my fifth or sixth wind and helped set up camp. With a broken pine branch, I swept the ground directly under the canvas roof of small rocks and assorted debris. I laid our sleeping bags side by side, positioning Jake's closest to the shelter opening, a given that he'd assume the role of guard. I put Rand's hard against the shelter's far side, where he'd already dropped and propped himself against a tree, as still as a statue. I situated mine, of necessity, between the men's and hoped I wasn't steamrolled by a restless sleeper in the night.

Hearing no complaint, I organized dinner. I sliced bread and combined nuts, raisins, and cheese for a main course. I opened a jar of Evelin's preserves to smear on the bread and discovered, next to it, the packet of dried venison she'd thoughtfully provided. A gastronomic reward for our tough day.

Rand announced candidly, "I need to take a leak," and lumbered from away from his spot.

Interesting, wasn't it, how quickly fatigue eroded one's veneer of good breeding? In no other circumstance could I imagine him so crudely broadcasting his urinary need, but here, with us? It seemed normal.

I turned my attention back to the meal, and Jake busied himself taking readings with his GPS. He walked the perimeter of our campsite and climbed a near-by bluff. Carefully positioning a flashlight, he consulted both the electronic maps and the conventional ones Rand had packed. When he was done, he confirmed what I'd suspected. "We only covered about eleven miles today." Sixteen kilometers.

Even with Matthias' help, we hadn't gone even a third of the way! For sure we'd have to work harder if we expected to make a timely exit into Austria.

Chastened by the truth of our situation, I stopped feeling sorry for myself. I felt more keenly the punishment we'd incurred pushing and punishing every joint, muscle, and sinew. I knew if I didn't get a long stretch of uninterrupted sleep, and soon, there was no way I'd up the ante the next day.

Rand returned, looking relieved, and the three of us gathered under the improvised awning, to dine. "Rand, why don't you offer grace?" Jake proposed.

"I . . . I . . ."

We listened without comment to his stammer.

"In my family . . . we . . ."

What? Didn't say grace? Had never said grace? Agnosticism, I'd heard, was often the religion of convenience in the intellectual home.

I wouldn't know; my parents considered themselves blue collar.

I was on the verge of offering to say a prayer myself when Rand said, "Sure. I can do that," and by so stating, defused my unwarranted assumptions.

Maybe it was the reality of our powerlessness or the trouble he'd had keeping up, but beaten, hungry, and wet, Rand bowed his head and prayed humbly. He borrowed from the Lord's prayer, at first, adding something generic and new-agey like, "Oh great Spirit who looks over us." He continued by asking for strength and perseverance, ending with a pretty convincing, "Thank you for bringing us safely here."

To which, Jake and I added the contribution of two very sincere amens.

Legs swathed in sleeping bags, hats pulled low over our ears, all three of us dug in.

I chewed slowly and thankfully, determined to make the meal last as long as it could. It was only six o'clock, give or take a quarter hour, and though my body begged for the relief of sleep, bedding down this early would mean I'd be awake by three. Given the countryside's utter darkness, the treacherously uneven land, and the fact that somewhere in the impenetrable night, soldiers with day-vision goggles could be sweeping the windblown plain looking for us, a pre-dawn departure seemed inadvisable.

Next to me, the men's talk degenerated into a detailed critique of the Washington Redskins' performance so far this season, not exactly the scintillating conversation for which I'd hoped. They speculated on whether the team owner would or wouldn't fire his newest coach. There was precedent (even) I knew.

In a succession of lackluster seasons, Daniel Snyder had given the boot to several talented coaches, most of whom had gone on to brilliant work elsewhere. Norv Turner. Marty Schottenheimer. Spurrier and Gibbs—the last a Hall of Famer in his first go-round with the Skins. The very competitive Snyder had barely given any of these men time to unpack before showing them the door, and the Redskins record was worse for his impatience.

He was older now, and his wife had faced a serious health crisis not long ago. It was possible that time and a brush with mortality had tempered Snyder to the point where he might actually give the new guy the chance to build a better team.

Personally, I liked the spikey-haired Zorn. He was attractive, for an older man, and affable in the interviews I'd seen. I agreed with Jake and Rand, while being careful not to divulge my superficial rationale, that the fellow from Seattle deserved a second season at the helm.

As I prepared a modest dessert of almonds and tea cake, Jake and Rand started in with players' statistics and talk of the draft, and that was the point at which I allowed my mind to wander.

My thoughts strayed to the other members of our mission team.

Our friends.

They would've reached their destinations by now and were probably warm in hotel rooms, getting ready for bed.

Smelling good.

Feeling good.

Finely (and finally) fed.

Imagining them, I floundered in self-pity and envied them their good fortune. I resented the feeling of wind and wet and residual hunger not nearly assuaged by our cold meal.

"Tea's ready," Jake announced, handing me a metal cup filled to the rim with a strong black brew. I warmed my hands on the container, taking slow, cautious sips.

How civilizing, I thought. How welcomed in the bleak night.

Using a single hand, I pulled Agnes' heavy coat close, and the oniony aroma of goulash wafted from the wool. My benefactress was somewhere safe, too, hugging her children or correcting their table manners. Her husband would've come home drained from his factory job, and they would've settled, by now, to a meal.

I imagined the family in the cottage Evelin had described, crowded around the hand-hewn table Agnes' husband had crafted himself, the lot of them sitting knee to knee. The couple devoted cold evenings to helping their children complete school assignments or spinning magical bedtime stories to hasten sleep. A small bedroom was reserved for Agnes and her husband on the home's drafty north side while a second, slightly larger, was tucked into the eaves along the cottage's southern exposure, Agnes' four growing children sharing the two beds wedged cozily inside.

I would've given anything, in that moment, to be safe with them.

Poor with them.

Warm with them.

The wind picked up and whistled through tree tops whose desolate branches were raised, in supplication, to the sky. Clouds obscured any moon or starlight. "Better lock up," Jake suggested, the men's football conversation come blessedly to an end. "I don't know how much longer we're going to be able to stand to be out in this wind."

Following *Soeur Helena*'s instruction, I purposely did not brush my teeth, so it took only minutes for me to dispatch bedtime preparations. When I came back to camp, the men had cleared away any sign of the meal.

I helped Jake ready supplies for the next day, and we re-situated the toboggan where it could best block the wind. We cosseted ourselves against the increasingly frigid night, insulated by the relative warmth of down. Before zipping my bag closed, I thought to pull clean underwear, socks, and shirt from the backpack I used as a pillow, and I folded them into the sleeping bag with me. That way, when I dressed in the morning, it would be with warm, not ice cold, clothing.

Our last small flashlight extinguished, Rand turned his face to the shelter wall. To my left, Jake lay flat on his back, eyes closed. It wasn't long before Rand's even breathing converted seamlessly to soft snores, while beside me Jake opened his eyes.

He turned his face toward mine, asking softly, "You all right?"

"Sure."

He perched on an elbow. "You were impressive today."

"Really? How so?"

"I pushed you hard, and you showed stamina. More than I'd expected."

I didn't know whether to be flattered or offended. At my best, I abducted and adducted about 120 pounds on the leg machines at the gym. I pulled down between 90 and 110 on the lats, and made the rounds of the Stairmaster, the elliptical, and the bike. On easy days, I set the treadmill to about 4.5 m.p.h. with an incline of 5.

I had a lot more fight in me than I'd shown today.

"Mind over matter," I whispered, never having been more aware of that truth.

"Back at the hospital," Jake continued, "I could tell you were a hard worker. But you're small . . ."

"Compact," I corrected.

"Duly noted." He paused and then added, "I thought you might, I don't know, you might hold us . . ."

"You may want to stop before you put your foot in it," I warned.

"No. No. I want to say this."

"Your funeral."

He started again. "I thought you might hold us back. But you proved me wrong. I'm glad you pushed to be the one to walk out with us."

In the darkness, I studied his warm eyes and the corners of his mouth lifted into a grin. I saw he was a hopeless optimist.

"Thanks for the change of heart," I told him.

He leaned in close, touched my cheek with the back of his fingers, and confided, "I'd take you over a dozen wanna-be Rangers any day."

The spot where his hand made contact radiated warmth for several seconds after he pulled it away. Reluctantly, I whispered, "Goodnight."

"Goodnight," he echoed.

I turned my back and closed my eyes; in moments I'd dropped into the abyss of sleep.

NINETEEN

I had never been a huge fan of sleeping on solid ground, and our first night in the wilds did nothing to change my mind on that score.

I stirred awake every two to three hours, feeling every bump and hard spot and lump coming through the compacted snow. Like a new age Princess and the Pea, I turned and stiffly searched out a stretch of sleeping surface that didn't poke or cramp or otherwise irritate me to soreness. In my half sleep, I wandered close to one or another of the men between whom I lay sandwiched, having absolutely no motive in sheltering myself behind a manly back other than to hide from the ferocious winds straining the capacity of our ropes to batten down.

Sometime toward morning, the wildness calmed, and I fell into dreamless slumber. When I opened an eye to the day, dawn was a smudge along the crown of mountaintops to the east, and Jake was up getting things ready for our imminent leave-taking.

Food was out.

Water on.

Everything but our sleeping bags and canvas roof had been loaded on the sled.

"Give sleeping beauty there a poke, would you?" Jake enjoined.

I looked over to where Rand lay curled into himself like an oversized caterpillar, oblivious both to our movements and to the rising light. Before waking him, I struggled inside my sleeping bag, getting off dirty clothes and jamming my body into clean ones. I forced myself to get out into the cold and poked Rand. He only groaned at my touch.

I gently shook his shoulder a second time, and he shrugged away from any contact, huffing impatiently, "Parry. Lay off."

Hardly in the mood for his petulance, I whispered harshly, "You want to give us away?"

He quieted but didn't stir.

I granted Rand a few minutes' reprieve, though he didn't deserve it, and rolled my sleeping bag tight. When he refused to budge after another poke, I dribbled drinking water on the exposed skin of his neck.

He caterwauled like a wounded buffalo, "What's WITH you people? Can't a man get any sleep?"

"You've had your quota," Jake responded unsympathetically. "Now we've got to get outta here. Like it or not, we're taking your sorry behind."

I left the two of them to hash things out, and in the privacy afforded by a stand of short-needled pines, did my morning business. Hovering over the frozen soil, I felt incredible soreness in my legs, my thighs, and my freezing backside. Indelicately exposed, I imagined the luxury of a hot shower and the familiar scent of Dove. Regretfully, I realized I would've had both in Vienna or Budapest, if I hadn't insisted on getting my own way.

Back at the campsite, tensions were palpable. Jake had finished a quick morning meal and was drinking the last of his breakfast tea. Rand was rolled into his sleeping bag, though sitting now, stuffing his face with jerky. There was more of it on his plate.

"We don't have too much meat left . . ." I hinted. "Maybe we should conserve."

"He knows that," Jake apprised. "But evidently it's HIS, and HE can eat it when and where he wants to."

So, that was the way things had gone.

"Schnot what I shaid," Rand garbled. He swallowed and clarified, "I said I was dying for lack of protein. You can't expect someone my size to subsist on nuts and oatmeal."

"It's only for a few days," Jake told him. "If you eat more than your share, what do you think will happen to Parry and me? We're already carrying your sorry ass."

"What the hell does that mean?" Rand demanded, straightening and clenching his fists. He was clearly primed for more than a little verbal back-and-forth.

"If you haven't notice, we've been pulling the sled. Setting up camp. Taking it down. Parry and I have done about 99 percent of the work while you barely manage moving your fat feet.

"Face it Szabo, you can't keep up with a girl half your size!"

That said (shouted!), Jake took three long strides over to where Rand was sitting and appropriated what was left of the meat. He broke off a hunk of cheese and sliced more bread. "Eat this. Then get out of that sleeping bag, and do what you have to do. We're pulling out in five minutes."

The two men glared at each other for several long, brooding seconds, then turned away.

I ate quickly and drank my tea.

Jake and I got the last of the supplies re-loaded, and precisely five minutes after Jake's warning, we started into the day. A resentful Rand, still not ready, was forced to carry his sleeping bag draped across his shoulders. It was to late to try and position it properly on the sled.

A subdued lot, we shoed non-stop across the fields of crusted snow. The temperature rose slightly as the morning passed and with it, the snow pack began a slow and steady melt. Though what remained was deep enough to require snow shoes and dense enough to allow the toboggan's glide, we anticipated that the afternoon would bring a more dramatic thaw.

At our morning break, we made quick work of drinking, going "potty," and grabbing a snack. I could see in Rand's face and in his hair, dripping sweat, that he was really tired. I heard it, too, as he heaved himself up the moment Jake said, "Let's go."

I wanted to be sympathetic but knew we couldn't afford that luxury. Rand had to break through the wall of his self-indulgence to realize that, fit or not, the next three days were going to be a test of his toughness. He had muscle mass enough to handle the demands of our trek; he just needed to believe that he could.

We ate lunch in the early afternoon but rather than stop and set up, we decided it was better to chew as we walked. "From now on, we only stop when we absolutely have to," Jake told us. For bathroom breaks. To sleep at night. When we couldn't soldier through our exhaustion another second. "Every minute we lose is an advantage to the enemy."

Around two, we crested a small hill, and below us, maybe a mile or so away, we saw all the proof we needed that Jake was right. Three trucks painted in flat, olive drab encircled a campsite, and a half dozen uniformed men were setting up temporary shelters.

"Matthias' information was accurate," Jake observed softly. "Let's divert."

We backed away from the hilltop before our presence there could draw attention and made a wide circle to the southwest. When it seemed safe, we crossed a narrow side road and remained absolutely silent prowling catlike through a mile or more of naked hardwood trees, afraid that the land's contours wouldn't completely absorb the sound of our voices or occasional stumble.

An hour after we'd dodged that bullet, perhaps literally, I noticed Rand cutting into my lead. Eyes trained on the ground for obstacles, he'd greatly decreased the number and awkwardness of his falls. When we paused to refuel, he unpacked supplies and restored them to the sled before setting out again. He snuck an occasionally resentful look in Jake's direction but uttered not a single word resisting his lead.

For my part, I treated Rand as I might a recalcitrant child and through my silence, backed Jake. He'd been right teaching Rand a lesson in camaraderie. We needed one another, and more important, we needed one another to be selfless. Any less jeopardized us all.

I imagined that Jake's words had been tough for Rand to hear. He was a man who'd probably never had to rely on anyone EVER for help. If the things I'd heard about him were true, he was someone who'd raced through life unhampered by the little inconveniences the rest of us assumed were part and parcel of being human.

Trouble in school. Competing for jobs. Trying to balance a budget.

Though his parents might have had a difficult start, Rand was an All-American success story, a guy who'd rarely, if ever, heard the word, "No."

Well, he'd finally hit a wall. His wall. Only time would determine if he could successfully break through.

We forged ahead.

Temperatures continued to hover around freezing, cloud cover coming and going on the whim of a strong and icy west wind. The hike grew hypnotizing. The snow's fierce brightness; the endlessness of the terrain; the need to be as quiet on the landscape as we could.

We were three souls trapped in a world of whispering white.

Just after four, we approached a ridge bordered on its northern edge by stand of windblown spruce trees; to the south and east, shoulder-high shrubbery. In the granite hollow beneath the ridge, there looked to be adequate room both for us and for our gear, a spot where we might dare build a real fire. It wasn't something crucial at this point—we were hot and sweaty from hours of exertion—but later, when the sun went down and the night cold descended, the heat from a decent blaze would be welcomed.

"How about we stop here for the night," I urged. It was early, but I doubted we'd find a more perfect spot.

Jake consulted the GPS and made a few calculations. "Okay. We've gone far enough," he noted with pride. "Close to fifteen miles."

Amazing what a little kick ass could do!

Five minutes later, Rand appeared and saw that we had stopped. His face broke into a euphoric grin as he asked, "We spending the night here?"

"That we are."

"Great."

He shoed over to where Jake and I had started setting up the canvas lean-to and demanded, "Let me help." I handed him my corner of the canvas, and he took hold. His cooperation continued through dinner and early evening. It made itself evident as we laid out our sleeping bags, and he suggested that he position himself in a way that would protect Jake and me from the wind.

"Thanks," Jake accepted. "Appreciate it."

The soft smell of atmospheric moisture woke me the following morning, the kind of humidity that intensified the decaying smells of dead leaves and grasses nearby. A vague, blue-grey dawn confirmed that to which the loamy smells alluded, thick cottony clouds having filled the sky overnight.

It wouldn't be long before precipitation of some kind would be falling.

I pulled my arm from my sleeping bag and checked my watch's illuminated face. Six forty-five. "Boys," I said without mercy. "Rise and shine!"

A momentary rebellion erupted from Rand, but I quickly realized that the sounds emanating from the mass of his abused body were unintentional. I cut him a break, as they say in the south, and he slowly rose to the occasion.

Jake didn't speak much beyond a perfunctory, "Morning all," then he stooped to zip and roll his sleeping bag into a snug cylinder. He thought-fully collected dinner's debris and disposed of it discreetly in the brush; no point in leaving a trail.

I relinquished my sleeping bag to Rand when he reached for it and accepted the men's gallant suggestion, "You go first," slowing only to grab my flattened roll of t.p.

Without the cover of darkness to shield my fluorescent behind—melanin long ago having mutated out of my family's genetic make-up—it took a while for me to find an suitable spot between a wall of low-lying shrubs and a rock pile. Modestly situated, I gathered underwear, tights, and bibbed ski pants into a single fold and propped myself against a immense boulder for support. Did my thing.

I was pleased to find that the men had laid out a breakfast of muesli, canned milk, and applesauce when I rejoined them. I plunked tagless tea bags into a pot to steep. Constant Comment, I judged, from the distinctive scent of citrus and cinnamon rising fragrantly into the air. It was a combination I'd loved since grade school, slyly stealing sips of it from my mother's morning cup.

Fed and fortified, we were on the trail by 7:20, all business.

As we walked, our eyes scanned the fields, the farms, and the forests spreading out from us in all directions to the horizon. Vigilantly, we watched for any vehicles even remotely close to where we were, and sought out signs of anyone traveling on foot.

Sustaining the scrutiny gave me sympathy for troops on patrol, for the sense of foreboding that surrounded them when they weren't precisely sure where danger lay, and for the effects of unrelieved stress that they suffered, night and day. Every snap of a branch or distant animal call made us jump;

caused us to wonder who, if not us, had made the sound.

The first part of the day passed uneventfully, and the temperature soon spiked to a balmy forty-two. We made the decision to shed our snowshoes. While enough of a snow pack remained to allow the toboggan's slide, it didn't call for anything more than a hiking boot, slugging through.

The rutted unevenness of harvested fields; the muddy spots where we plunged in mud to our ankles; the wet soles of our boots sliding across the occasional rock pile—all made the going tougher. Our trail, such as it was, evolved into one long obstacle course where the slightest misstep threatened injury. Conversation became an unwarranted indulgence; we devoted our full attention to staying upright.

Having stuffed granola and dried fruit into our pockets, we snacked as we walked and cut out every inessential break. We made incredible time as we grew in our collective determination to cover ground.

"Seven and a half miles," Jake announced as he inhaled cold beans and black bread for lunch.

"I think I can push a little harder this afternoon," I said, considering myself fully capable. "At the very least, we can pound out another fifteen-mile day."

"We'll see," Jake answered, pointing to clouds amassing to the west. "We may be meeting with a little resistance from Mother Nature."

"Rain?"

"The forecast was going either way this morning when I checked."

Rand insisted on pulling the sled that afternoon, saying with determination, "I can do it." He'd been working hard, and the last few hours he'd moved ahead of me a couple of times. Which wasn't right. The man had been a desk jockey for most of his life, and now, with a couple days of concerted effort and a little back-to-nature nourishment, he was outperforming me?

Okay, he was almost a foot taller than I was and had the advantage of testosterone. I was supremely resentful of the fact that no matter how hard I worked and with what intensity, my 28 percent body fat and a small woman's frame would be a forever plague.

Get over it, I lectured; it was what it was.

I threw Rand sidelong glances for the next hour and took silent solace from the fact that he couldn't get pregnant or have a baby—the refuge of the truly desperate female—then I re-stated his achievement in more comforting terms. Rand's success was OUR success.

Now move.

Some time later, with Rand still in the lead, all three of us heard and then saw activity around a clutch of farm buildings roughly a half mile to our south. Instinctively, our footsteps veered north, distancing us from the group of four rough-looking men.

"Let's hope they don't notice us," Jake whispered.

"Or worse, that they don't jump into that truck parked over there and head our way." This from Rand.

Jake waved us toward a clutch of trees and prodded us to speed. He signaled Rand to stoop a little, making his profile less conspicuous. Together the men grabbed the toboggan rope and made the thing fly.

I hustled keeping up.

We portaged the sled across a muddy stretch of road and maintained the press of our rapid, determined pace. We heard a truck door slam. Then a second. We turned to discover that the entire crew of four had squeezed into the cab of the vehicle whose engine was coughing to life.

Damn. We were out in the open, less than fifty feet from the road over which the truck was going to pass in the next minute.

What to do?

Jake whispered furtively, "Head north and MOVE! And for the love of God, if they yell to us, pretend not to hear."

What? We were going with the deaf routine again?

I forced my feet forward despite my reservations; Rand and Jake did the same. We kept our backs to the road and leaned into the hillside ahead.

The gravelly roar of the truck engine drew closer.

"If they honk or stop or yell, not a sign we've heard."

No problem. My heart was a tom-tom, beating out an alarm; I couldn't hear anything anyway.

""You got our paperwork?" Jake asked, referring to the phony certificate from *Les Me´decins Internationals* festooned with the government's imprimatur.

"In my pocket."

"You be our spokesman. French at first. Stumbling English if you have to."

We heard the slip and slide of tires on the road's rough surface, then the distinctive sound of a skid as the truck braked. We didn't acknowledge the trumpet of its horn blasting to get our attention.

A man's voice bellowed, and still we didn't turn. Maybe he'd take the hint.

A truck door slammed, and there followed the tromp of a heavy tread traveling fast in our direction. I steeled myself as though for a collision. Muscles tensed. Breath held. Field of vision narrowed to take in only the trail immediately ahead.

I whispered an entreaty, "Let's not deviate from the plan.'"

The man pursued us, who knew why, and as he came even with me, he reached out and grabbed my arm. Swung me around to face him.

I gasped when what I really wanted to do was to scream, "NO! Let me go!" Face to face with a kid no more than nineteen or twenty, I cried out the Acadian equivalent, "*Lache-mwai donc*," and lurched away out of my assailant's grasp.

Rand turned and timed his reaction perfectly, launching into a well executed tirade. He dropped the toboggan's rope and shoved the young man, who immediately let go of my arm. Our pursuer held up his hands in apology and spoke several sentences that sounded more or less friendly.

I could see in Rand's expression that he understood him but wouldn't make the mistake of trying to converse. Instead, he withdrew our forged papers and his passport from his coat pocket. Made it obvious we weren't local. By God, we were Canadian citizens!

Let this guy be able to read!

That was a major blind spot in our plan, I thought suddenly. While the country had near universal literacy, what if this young man had never seen a passport. Had no idea what it meant. Our preparations had been predicated on the assumption that any confrontation might be with people of average intelligence, education, and experience. This grimy, homespun boy seemed questionable on all counts and could, in his ignorance, still get us into a mountain of trouble by just mentioning us to friends.

He said something to Rand, who gestured and pointed away somewhat from the true direction in which we were headed. Rand added a single word of explanation in Hungarian (and spoke it clumsily), and that our new acquaintance appeared to understand.

The young man pointed to his truck, gestured toward Jake, Rand, and me, and then pointed to the truck a second time.

He was offering us a ride.

No, Rand. Say no, my mind cried!

Rand seemed to briefly consider the boy's offer, to weigh the advantages of a respite. In the final analysis, though, he grinned his appreciation and shrugged a pretty obvious message: thanks but no thanks. "*Je regrette,*" he added. Sorry.

He was letting the boy down easy, I guessed, not wanting him to think we were ungrateful or defensive in any way.

Rand pointed due west, intentionally deceiving the boy again, and he thanked him, "*Merci.*"

Jake reached over and clasped the young man's hands between his in an exaggerated handshake. "*Au revoir,*" he said slowly.

The boy patted my arm, where before he'd grabbed it hard. He inclined his head in a show of apology and stepped back as though trying to excuse his earlier misbehavior.

I returned his gracious bow and bestowed my forgiveness with a softly spoken, "*C'est rien.*" I stared steadily at him as he left.

He ran downhill, leaped back into the truck where his friends waited, and crowded in behind the wheel. At his explanation, the others leaned forward, studying the sight of us waving goodbye. They were probably trying to understand why three people who looked as tired and bedraggled as we did had said no to a lift.

Shortly, though, and without further acknowledgment, the four men rattled off.

Watching the truck disappear, Jake assessed the situation grimly. "We're in it deep now."

TWENTY

Rand concurred with Jake's no-nonsense appraisal.

"We have to throw those geezers off our trail," Jake declared. "They stop and think a minute about what's happened in the last few days, and then remember us. They could get suspicious.

"Or make others suspicious," Rand added.

We began a steady sprint toward the river and shadowed its course as it flowed in the general direction of the border. Over tangled tree roots and riverside debris, I lengthened my stride. The men pulled me up over fallen tree trunks and offered to carry my pack.

"I'm good," I said in response.

From time to time, we turned to make sure that no one followed, or studied the landscape just ahead to be sure no one had appeared to intercept us.

"Even if that guy believed us," Jake grunted as we pounded ahead later, "anyone hears his story, it's gonna set off alarms.

"Three Canadians, pulling a sled and refusing help. Probably not something they see hereabouts every day."

Propelled by worry, Jake set a tough tempo, but he remained even-tempered and controlled. He mentioned our young pursuer again, saying, "If he or his friends talk, and it gets back to local authorities, someone will be asking questions."

He didn't finish the thought.

Didn't have to.

We all knew that the upshot of our little encounter could be weapon-wielding soldiers combing the countryside before the day was out.

We shifted into overdrive. No obstacle in the form of rock slide or swampy riverbank delayed us for long. We kept vegetation and rocky prominences between ourselves and open spaces as much as we could and didn't let up until big fat flakes started to fall from the sky.

"We needed this," Rand declared. "The more it snows, the harder it'll be to track us."

"And a good strong wind would help, too."

"I think we're going to get lucky," Jake observed. "It looks like this weather's gonna get bad, and fast."

Pointing to a hamlet barely visible through the worsening snow, he revealed, "I think we better plan to spend the night; a solid hour's effort, and we're there."

The clutch of homes and shops looked closer than the mile and a half, maybe two that Jake estimated, but in the vastness of countryside, distances deceived. I looked beyond the town to where a few farm houses were scattered across a windblown hillside to the north. A desolate place to live, I thought. An even more desolate place to make enemies.

We pushed hard into the onslaught of wind and icy snow grown suddenly fierce. Even though we'd been chugging along like locomotives for almost three days and were on the brink of collapse, somehow Jake's drive and confidence convinced Rand and me that we had those couple of hard miles left in us.

We moved ahead, engines stoked from the protein snack of nuts and cheese we consumed as we walked. For the next half hour we stopped only briefly to climb back into our snowshoes. Struggling through the deepening snow, I breathed harshly in and out through my mouth, gulping air and feeling its cold irritation in my throat.

I took a spill, and Jake stopped to help me. Brushed me off.

"Why don't I take out my flashlight?" Rand suggested. "It's getting hard to see."

"Bad idea," Jake said breathily. "Light moving across a field will zero people in on us p.d.q."

Rand's oxygen-deprived brain was betraying him.

The air turned chowdery, and the diminishing light made the going increasingly tough. We couldn't make out the buildings that Jake had pointed out some time earlier. We should've been approaching them by now.

It didn't matter. Jake had a sense of where we were. He kept us moving and motivated. Every time I thought I couldn't manage another step, he urged me on and propelled Rand forward, too. "Almost there guys. We're gonna make it."

My nose was running, my hair was wet and plastered to my scalp under a smelly wool cap. Every few minutes, I was tempted to stop, burrow into a snow drift, and yell at Jake, "For the love of God, just come back for me in the morning."

Instead, I held on.

Suddenly he was declaring, "We're here," and in the obscurity, I saw a lone farmhouse, pale light outlining windows that appeared to be heavily draped.

There were no other visible signs of life. No tiny faces of children peeking out into the storm. No vehicles. No car tracks, to and from.

We'd gone beyond the town, I realized, probably Jake's plan from the start. His real trajectory had limited the risk of contact.

"Rand. Polish off your acting skills," Jake directed. "We'll knock. If anybody comes to the door, ask if we can spend the night. Out there." He indicated a structure about thirty or forty feet beyond the house, some kind of old shed or garage that appeared solid enough.

"You sure that's smart?" Rand challenged. "What if word of our run-in has reached local officials? Small town. News like that might travel fast."

"Maybe. But it's unlikely anyone's going to send out a search party in a storm just to find three Canadian doctors.

"They'll figure we had to stop."

With a note of finality, Jake added, "We have to take the chance."

He had grown tired enough to run the small risk of discovery, especially if it meant a chance to sleep indoors, out of the cold.

"We could camp in those woods," Rand said, offering an alternative. He gestured uphill toward a copse of towering evergreens whose outstretched limbs, interlocking, created a black hole in the landscape.

"This is going to be a massive storm," Jake reminded him. "Even if we could set up our shelter," the toboggan cover, "it'd be impossible to keep it from collapsing under the weight of the snow." He re-issued the direct order. "Ask if we can bunk in that old building, bub."

Rand didn't seem convinced such a move was smart, and truthfully, neither was I. But I'd glanced at the weather maps Jake consulted, and it was that, more than anything, that helped me plant a foot in his corner. "Go ahead," I urged. "We need a night under cover."

Rand accepted the decision, and we killed all conversation approaching the farm house door. On the porch, he pulled me forward to stand before him. If a woman answered, it was certain she would feel threatened by the sight of two men. Unshaved. Unwashed. Slightly malodorous. Better that I, less physically imposing and marginally better smelling, be her introduction to the group.

My knock went unanswered, so I tried a second time. We were trying, without benefit of open discussion, to decide if one of us should turn the knob or put a shoulder to the door to force it open, when we heard the slide of a bolt and saw the door's hesitant opening.

Beyond weather-beaten oak, a young woman stood before us, visibly pregnant. Her eyes were red-rimmed and her long hair braided and pulled back into a stringy, asymmetrical mess.

She greeted me, and I nodded hopefully.

"*Bonjour*," I said, speaking softly. I reached for Rand's sleeve and pulled him forward to act as our spokesman. He stood quietly, not making the least move to force his way in. In the light from a kerosene lantern, he handed her our documents, provided in French, English, and her native language.

She flipped to the latter, read, and seemed to understand.

He handed her a card that Matthias had insisted we take along just in case—a castoff from our original plan. It would tell her we were looking for a place to sleep. Another bore a picture of plated food, and Rand gave her that one, too.

Her reaction glancing at the second card told us we'd overstepped. She shook her head and shook her head, "No."

No to all of it.

She started to close the door, but Rand broke into a French rant and thrust a handful of euros through the opening rapidly closing to us. He yelped dramatically when his wrist was momentarily trapped. At the sight of money, the woman drew open the door and stared hungrily at the bills.

Cash as a universally successful negotiating tool.

Cradling his forearm, Rand clumsily motioned toward the rear of the house and the oversized shed. That's where we want to spend the night, the action told her. *"Pas de trouble."* No trouble.

She studied the three of us, giving the request prolonged consideration.

I pressed my hands into a prayerful pose and beseeched her mutely with my unwavering stare. We only wanted a place out of the cold, I tried to communicate with my eyes. I hugged myself and made my teeth chatter for effect.

Rand added two fifty euro notes to the lure.

The woman withdrew the card with a drawing of a bed on it from the pile she'd thrust back at Rand. She held it and pointed, as Rand had, in the direction of the outbuilding. Yes, she nodded, she would give us place to stay. Then she fished out the card with the drawing of the food and shook her head solemnly, no.

My dreams of a hot meal were dashed, but I didn't care. The possibility of sleeping away from the biting cold and wet snow seemed heavenly. We thanked her with a chorus of "*Merci*s," and she shyly acknowledged our gratitude.

Turning, we filed from the porch and stepped unprotected back into the storm.

Rand flicked on his flashlight and lit a path for us through the feathery murk. There was little danger, at this point, in doing so. Now we belonged.

Approaching the shed, we heard the house's back door slam open and saw our hostess appear, a kerosene lamp lifted high in one hand, a too-small coat clutched across her swollen middle with the other. She called out, and we stopped, waiting as she plowed her way out to us barelegged through snow drifting to mid-calf.

Reaching us, she held out the key to the padlocked shed doors. Rand slid off a mitten pearled with ice to accept it. His fingers wrinkled and stiff, he fit the key into the lock, pulled open the doors against the weight of the accumulated snow, and stood back as Jake and I rushed inside.

In the dimness, Jake's light raked the walls, the floor, and a small overhead loft. Rand pointed and used his fingers to pantomime us climbing to the building's upper level. Our hostess approved with a nod and mimicked the motion Rand had performed.

She left, and we studied our surroundings. Bales of hay were stacked neatly against the back wall to the height of a man, and there was more of it stored overhead in the loft. Tools hung from spikes in an orderly wall display, with more arranged on a workbench nearby. In the corner closest to us stood a small tractor, a vintage machine nearly identical to the Massey Fergusson my grandfather had kept garaged nostalgically after his retirement, unused through much of my childhood. The tractor had a bouncy seat on springs and tires nearly my height, just like *Pe´pere*'s. An exhaust pipe mounted just above the workings of the engine had a flip top lid that would likely fly open on acceleration.

I remembered the dozens of stories my grandfather had told me about raising crops and harvesting them; of the hard life he and *Me´mere* had known imposing order on their loud and lively batch of kids. Of how much he missed turning up the soil, growing his crops, and living his life in fresh air now that he was too old to do so.

My eyes teared.

Would I get to make memories like that with my children and grandchildren one day; would I play the role of respected elder? More fundamentally, would I ever know the feeling of falling into forever-love, or would the one truly selfless act of my life and the events it had set into motion, preclude those precious possibilities?

This was no time to indulge my fears. It was time to act and to strengthen my resolve.

I joined the men hauling our sleeping bags and food and backpacks to the loft, each of us avoiding all but the most perfunctory exchanges. When we finished, we illuminated the space with our flashlights and started hushed and tentative conversations.

"She can't be living alone out here," Jake noted. "Not as pregnant as she is."

"Someone will be coming home tonight," Rand predicted. "We'll need to be vigilant."

Agreed.

Jake pulled Rand's phone from our supplies, connected it to the broadband unit half the size of a laptop, and fired it up.

"Will you be able to get anything in this weather?" Rand asked.

"I'm gonna try."

He paced the loft trying for a signal.

Miraculously, he accessed an international news site, something we hadn't had the time to do since leaving St. Maria's. Stiff and sore, I waited for an update, and Rand occupied himself slowly rearranging hay in a protective, insulating wall.

Jake suddenly spoke. "We have to make this a short night."

"How short?"

"We have to be out of here by five. Four if we can manage it."

"Why the rush?" Rand wanted to know.

Jake seemed to weigh the wisdom of full disclosure.

"Don't b.s. us," Rand directed. "I think we've all proven we can handle whatever you've got."

I seconded Rand's request in a word. "Now."

"All right.

"The government announced today that it wasn't going to negotiate with Washington."

"What? Why not?"

He handed me the device, and together Rand and I scanned the Reuters headline. The piece described, though it did not provide photos, a public execution. A half dozen American graduate students had been accused of spying, a charge which on the face of it seemed bizarre. They had been convicted and summarily executed.

What possible information or technological secrets would have justified American spying, I wondered. What hardware or scientific advancement? The flow was more often from West to East, not the other way around.

We scrutinized quotations from recently-appointed officials, men who predicted more killings if the U. S. failed to release their fellow countrymen being held captive by our forces in Afghanistan.

"Neo-Taliban sympathizers," Rand explained, where the article had not.

"They're there," Jake corroborated. "I've seen incontrovertible proof that the military here has been sending 'advisors' to help arm and train the Taliban." He didn't mention the source of his intel, but I suspected he'd had his own private briefing before leaving the States.

Whatever relief I'd felt at the thought of a warm and restful night was shot. The three of us sat in drained, despondent quiet.

"How far do we have left to go?" I asked Jake.

"I've made a few calculations," he said. "And I've looked at our options again. We could take a relatively undemanding route from here, which would put us at about nine or ten miles. But frankly, that's the way lazy Americans would be expected to go. The Army will have it covered.

"There are a couple of other routes; one I've discounted as too dangerous. The last is a ball buster." He colored. "Sorry Parry . . ."

I waved off his apology. While I was someone who valued faith and strong morals, raw language had never really bothered me. Three older brothers. A career in health care. I would've been sunk if every time I heard an expletive, I fell to my knees begging for deliverance.

Jake explained the complicated course. We would have to travel first through pretty rugged forest. Then would come a narrow white water crossing, "Over a bridge I hope to God is still there." Finally, we'd have to climb about halfway up a thousand foot elevation before coming down the other side to the border. "The good thing is, if we decide to go this way, we cut the distance to just over six miles."

I could do that.

"We'll have to be out of here by four, four-thirty. The snow should be tapering by then. Stopped if we're lucky. There's a stretch of open field between us and the beginning of the woods; we'll need to cross it as early as we can. Before light if we can manage it."

"We'll need to hit the hay early," I said, pounding one fist on a bale.

The men groaned.

"All right. I'll stop." I rose from our impromptu conclave, stretched, and told them, "I think I'm gonna use the facilities." I'd seen an outhouse just a few feet from the shed door.

"I'll go with you," Jake offered.

"I'll be fine. Really."

"To hold the door shut," he explained. "Before taking my turn."

"In that case, you're allowed."

"I'll rustle up some grub," Rand volunteered.

The cowboy lingo was cute, I thought, but Rand's pallor and sluggish movements suggested he was running on fumes.

"Thanks," I said. "No matter what anybody says, Rand, you're a good egg."

He managed an obscene gesture, and I laughed. Another inhibition down the drain.

When Jake and I reached the shed doors, we pushed them open and together shuffled to the outhouse about twenty feet away.

Lucky Jake had offered to play doorman, I discovered. The outhouse door had no hook-and-eye fixture or bolt to hold it closed. Without him, every gust of wind would've threatened to reveal me, in squatting splendor, to the world.

My flashlight teetering on a shelf above the wide one-holer, I used a stash of baby wipes to affect a thorough cleansing. Three full days of all-out exercise and not a shower or bidet in sight; this particular contraband, and my duplicity hiding it, was worth any consequence.

My defense if discovered? "Hey, I'm a chick! I can't just shake and run."

Newly cleansed, I traded places with Jake. Back plastered to the outhouse door protecting his modesty, I suddenly spotted twin headlight beams about a half mile down the road. I turned and directed a warning into the door, "I think someone's coming."

No hint of reply. Maybe Jake hadn't heard me.

I cracked the door open and repeated my advisory.

He reached out from the throne to grab and shut the thing, uttering a loud, "Do you mind?"

"Someone's coming, Jake," I cried into the narrow opening. "A car."

"Shit!"

Precisely.

I turned to check on the vehicle's progress, but it was almost impossible to gauge in the stormy darkness. I guessed it wasn't more than a third of mile away. Fifteen hundred feet maybe.

The car struggled uphill, engine straining against the incline and a wall of wind-driven snow. I made out a driver hunched over the wheel, peering into the darkness and trying to decide where the pavement ended and the softer, deeper snowbanks began.

"Hurry," I urged. We were outside without a spokesman or our papers or an effective way to explain ourselves to the home's presumed owner.

"Go ahead in," Jake ordered. "I'll bring up the rear." So to speak.

I rushed toward the shed and heard the car getting close. Inside, I pulled the doors shut and called recklessly, "Rand. We have company."

"The husband?"

"Someone in a car. I can't tell."

Jake was pulling on the shed door now, breathless from his foreshortened toilet time. "S'gotta be the husband. Who else?"

"You two get up here," Rand suggested. "I'll handle this."

I climbed the stairs like a goat and removed myself to the loft's farthest reach. Rand pulled on his heavy coat and armed himself with my t.p., an item that would make clear to the interloper his destination.

Rand took the staircase slowly, no doubt hampered by his aching muscles. He crossed the shed floor and went out, timing his exit to coincide perfectly with the wash of headlights profiling him starkly in the open doorway. He waved as though welcoming a long lost friend.

He had guts, I had to admit.

As Rand closed the door to the wind's battering, I saw that Jake had wedged himself behind the tractor primed, if he were needed, to leap to Rand's defense. From where I stood, I heard only a little of Rand's exchange with the person newly arrived. Over the car engine's low rumble, there floated snatches of men's raised voices, the homeowner's coming in the form of angry exclamations and easily drowning out Rand's almost incoherent French.

Suddenly there was a crash against the shed door and then a second.

"We need to do something," I whispered fiercely to Jake. I pounded down the stairs and commanded, "You stay here."

Jake disagreed vehemently, "No!"

I held my ground. "He won't keep this up if he sees a woman."

He hesitated.

Something really big collided again with the door, and this time the wood splintered along one edge. I pushed open the broken panel and saw Rand. Mouth bloodied, he was clutching the right side of his face and was bent over one knee as though trying to catch his breath.

A few feet away, a uniformed six footer was ready to have at him again.

I launched into a tirade, screeching and crying and making to protect my husband. Assured that Rand wasn't badly injured, I got up and ran at his attacker, fists raised to take him on. My adrenaline-driven hysteria was mostly for show, but I prayed that, at the sight and feel of me defending Rand, the man would realize his overreaction and back off.

Before I could pummel him in earnest, the man restrained me with a vice-like grip. I emitted loud and anguished noises, buying Rand time to recover. Above the chaos, a scream emanated unexpectedly from the back stoop, and I looked over to see the pregnant woman calling her husband off.

I stopped flailing, and my captor loosened his hold. He turned to his wife and allowed the content of her calm and considered reproach to sink in. There erupted a series of exchanges between them and, caught in the crossfire, I pretended to grow agitated once again. I moved closer to Rand, pulled our papers from his bleeding hand, and waved them insistently in my attacker's face, no matter that the ink on them had smeared in the falling snow.

He snatched them from me, still shouting questions at his shivering wife; still studying us with hostility and suspicion. He straightened his coat and rearranged the tie to his uniform. He inhabited, with requisite dignity, the attire that was a symbol of his role and importance in the world.

Leaning into the headlight's glare, he read over our permits. He scrutinized the information found there in triplicate: home, city, country; our surnames; dates, signatures, and the required stamps of approval provided by authorities in his own Ministry of Health.

He looked to Rand and me, at the surrounding yard, and into the little of the shed's interior visible through the broken door. He was trying to ensure, I imagined, that neither his home nor his wife had been violated.

Abruptly, the officer demanded to know, "*Vous avez des passeports?*" You have passports.

Quickly recovering from the shock that he spoke French, Rand responded, "*Oui. Certainement.*"

Our names had given us away. I was Parise Pelletier now and Rand was my husband, Jean-Robert. We had been unofficially married by Matthias, who'd decreed that no respectable, unmarried women traveled here with unrelated men.

Hands shoved deep into my pockets for warmth, I felt for the passport that was my lone shield against capture. I found it slipped under my balled-up mittens; quickly retrieved it; and offered it up for consideration.

Our interrogator grabbed and studied the damp document with a practiced eye, turning from one page to the next, seeing there the regulation blues, greens, and yellows, and requisite maple leaves. He signaled Rand to hand over his as well, which he did without hesitation.

I edged protectively toward my new spouse in the way a wife might have. Crouched to kneeling, I wrapped an arm around his shoulders and kissed the side of his face. I comforted him—a performance embellished for the benefit of my skeptical audience of one.

Our host looked through the passports a second time. He noted the stamps there, and I was glad I'd taken the time to memorize both the places and the dates of my earlier travel.

While he was busy, I examined the markings on his uniform sleeve; the bars on his shoulders; the patchwork of colored ribbons on his chest. I didn't know a lot about military rank or meritorious decoration, but I was sure that only an officer of some stature sported that kind of hardware.

My heart sank.

Jake's earlier prediction was spot on; the three of us were in this mess to our beleaguered backsides. While it appeared we'd evaded trouble from our earlier encounter, the laws of chance had gone against us in another way. We were embroiled one-on-one now with a man who was probably a player in the new regime. A man who could, in the next few moments, pull out a gun, throw us all in his car, and drive us to our deaths.

The officer's wife called out to him again in a loud and long declaration, and whatever words she spoke seemed to have the desired, settling effect. He put out a hand to help Rand get up and made a show of brushing the snow from his clothes. He excused himself to me as well, saying a polite, "*Pardonez-moi, Madame.*" Excuse me.

"*Certainement.*"

"*Docteur* Pelletier."

Rand nodded.

Our host pointed toward the door of the shed, encouraging us to go on, go ahead inside.

I thanked him, helped Rand, and hobbled away, the considerable weight of my husband's arm draped across my right shoulder, slowing me somewhat. Silently I hoped Rand was acting, and that he was not as badly hurt as his limp implied.

Reaching the doors, I opened them wide so our host could drive past us and shelter his car inside. I caught a fleeting glance of Jake's face behind a tower of hay bales and gave the very slightest indication that I'd seen him. Stay where you are, the motion declared, everything's fine.

It was the final act in what had been the performance of a lifetime.

TWENTY-ONE

There was something about sustained physical challenge coupled with terror that reduced life to its essentials. *"Mange, shi, pi dors,"* as my brothers might put it. Eat. Poop. And sleep. The triumvirate of need, regularly fulfilled, made for a happy, healthy life. In this situation, somewhat irregular on all fronts, my friends and I were the worse for our recent deprivation.

"We'd better eat," Jake said, unenthusiastically pointing to the paucity of food before us. The rations had grown exceedingly familiar—crusty bread, dried fruit, the salty bite of jerky—and given the day's effort they were disappointing.

I said nothing about the meal that could be construed as negative, but inside I missed the modern extras. Fresh, crisp greens and sliced cucumbers. A baked potato dripping butter served alongside a sizzling rib eye steak. The tang of a juicy navel orange.

Rand, whose eye had swollen to the size and color of a ripe Concord grape, sat folded into his sleeping bag, waiting for Jake and me to make our selections.

"Aren't you hungry?" Jake asked me.

"A little," I lied. I was famished. But nothing I saw seemed worth the effort or the calories to ingest.

Jake helped himself to a modest share of the food and set down his plate as he asked, "Think he made us?"

Rand answered, eyes closed, "Maybe." His face was flushed and his breathing rapid even though he'd been resting for the better part of an hour. I worried there was something more than fatigue wrong with him.

I challenged his opinion nonetheless. "There's no maybe about it," I rebutted. "I saw how the guy looked at you.

"At us."

"What way was that?"

"Suspiciously. Cynically. He may not know exactly who or what we are, even though we gave him all the proof he asked for. But I guarantee, he suspects the worst."

"Why would you think that? He seemed to settle down after seeing the passports," Rand insisted.

"For the moment."

"What does that mean?"

"It means he could decide to check them out. I imagine he has access to computers. Ways of crosschecking passport numbers. If the real names matching those numbers come up, we're sunk."

Jake directed his curiosity at me again. "What makes you think he doesn't believe our story, Parry?"

"He's military," I explained. "The sight of us here in the middle of nowhere had to give the guy pause. He let up at his wife's pleading, but everything in me says he didn't quite buy our cover.

"Given enough time, he'll come at us again."

And then what? We weren't trained operatives—or at least, Rand and I weren't.

Jake looked back and forth between us. Whose judgment to trust?

"I guess we can't be sure what he believes," Jake announced after a brief hesitation. "But the fact that he's military and that he might have heightened suspicions AND access to information networks. It all makes my plan to leave early all the more imperative.

"We get out of here no later than four."

The issue settled, it was time to eat. I chose from what was available and sat back. I was biting into a dried apricot when I noticed how quiet it had gotten. Rand was waiting; Jake was, too. "Would you like to say blessing?" he asked.

"Sorry." Lapsing again. "Sure."

Too tired to think of something original, I fell back on the words that hung framed on ivory vellum in the space above my dining room table at home. The Moravian blessing I'd first learned visiting friends in Winston seemed especially appropriate now.

"Come Lord Jesus, our guest to be. And bless these gifts, bestowed by Thee. And bless our friends from everywhere . . ." I paused, suddenly overcome by emotion and a strange sense of loss. "And keep them in Thy loving care."

I set down my plate and watched as the men dug in. Jake was urging me to eat when the downstairs door creaked open. Instantly, we silenced ourselves, communicating dread in a wary, visual exchange.

"Here we go!" I mouthed.

As he crested the top of the stairs, we saw that our host had changed into civilian clothes. A heavy jacket, dark trousers, a colorful scarf at his neck. He held before him a wooden tray that held a large stoneware serving bowl, plates, and a *boule* of freshly baked bread. In the small space, the food's aromas easily overshadowed the building's diesel smells.

He startled a bit to see there were three of us and retreated a step. For a moment he seemed to reconsider Jake's presence, then I saw something click. He was remembering our permit and the names listed there.

He relaxed visibly and shifted into hospitality mode. "*Un peu de nourriture,*" he explained. Some food. "*Et quelque chose bon a boire,*" Something good to drink, he said, holding up glasses and a small flask.

He flashed a conspiratorial grin.

Rand motioned feebly for him to join us, but in response, he only deposited the tray at the center of our weary circle. The draw of steaming food overcame my caution, and I bent to the tray, to the bowl mounded with vegetables and beef and gravy so thick I was tempted to dip my fingers in it and lick them clean. Better yet, I wanted to slather it over a body grown permanently chilled after three days in the relentless cold.

Our benefactor leaned forward as though to shake hands with Rand but instead handed back the money we'd paid earlier to his wife. He folded the bills into Rand's hand and spoke a few words of explanation. "*Ma femme n'est pas elle-meme*," he said apologetically. "*L'enfant.*" His wife wasn't herself. The baby.

"*Pas de soin,*" Rand told him. Not a problem.

Before Rand could remember his manners, asking our host his name, or introduce Jake, our host had gone as quietly and unobtrusively as he'd come. Whatever the real reason for his kindness, we quickly decided we weren't going to say no to the food. We split it three ways, falling to it like wolves, the remains of our own paltry dinner instantly and completely ignored.

The meal had interesting and strong flavors compared to the milder institutional fare we'd eaten at the orphanage. I tasted garlic and peppery root vegetables, chunks of beef warm with smoky paprika. The tang of dill permeated the bread. We ate every last morsel and drop of gravy, topping it off with shots of the same fiery potable to which Matthias had earlier introduced us. It was just the ticket to warm and settle us for the night.

Rand drained his glass a third time to Jake's and my two modest drinks apiece, then he kicked back in a satiated daze. I piled both the glasses and crockery on the tray, and Jake shuttled everything except the dregs of brandy to the house's back stoop.

"I just knocked and left everything out there," he told us on his return. "It looked like they might've already gone to bed."

That seemed like a good idea to us, too.

While Jake and I made our last run to the outhouse, Rand told us he could wait until morning. Either the pace of the last couple of days had gotten the best of him, or the alcohol had packed a greater wallop for him than it had for Jake or me. Whatever the cause, he was hot and sweaty and ready to call it a night. If he wet in his sleeping bag because he was too lazy to walk outside to the facilities, it was—or would be—on him.

Jake set his watch alarm and without delay, the two of us tunneled into the mounds of hay Rand had earlier swept foot-deep in the space set apart for sleeping. We turned out our flashlights and, side by side, were left to our thoughts.

I replayed the events of the last several days and realized, on the edge of sleep, that I'd compressed a lifetime's worth of exploits in just over a week. The rough airplane trip over and the problematic border crossing that we should have seen as portents of the dangers ahead. Thirteen-hour days of surgery in conditions appreciably less than ideal, counterbalanced by the sweet and uncomplicated interactions

with the orphanage's children and the Quebecois
nuns devoted to their care.

I thought of Ken, the gentle giant who'd left a
busy family to witness firsthand the rebirth of a boy
who, without his help, might've been trapped in
his body forever. I saw chubby, slightly frightened
Ted, who'd politely settled next to me at dinner,
each time speaking warmly and proudly of his children. Derek, his oldest, had just applied early action
to MIT. Fifteen year-old Lydia was interested in
design. "Maybe they won't be like their old man
and finish college instead of deciding that a job and
money RIGHT NOW are more important than some
old degree."

I was familiar with the sentiment; I'd heard my
own father and extended family members express it
many times.

Turning over, I pictured the newly-transformed
Beverly and how petrified she must've been,
secreted under cast iron on a truck bed, cold and
darkness surrounding her. I couldn't imagine the
terror she had felt—all our friends would have
experienced—approaching the border and waiting
in breathless silence for guards to wave them
through.

My new friends were likely on their way back to
their lives now, remembering Jake, Rand, and me;
praying for us; waiting for word that we would join
them as soon as circumstances allowed.

I envisioned us sitting around those crappy old
tables in the OR lounge a week or two from now,

laughing and comparing notes, saying "Was that a close call or what?"

It occurred to me that, of all those in the group, I was the only person who'd simply happened on her role as Good Samaritan. Where the others had planned and sacrificed to be able to go on this trip, I'd given up virtually nothing.

Plane ticket, paid for.

Bedding, paid for.

Time off, donated by Geoff and company.

All I had done, and that grudgingly, was listen to my better instincts.

Was that enough, I wondered. If God loved a cheerful giver, what were His thoughts on those of us who tiptoed into the pool, never really jumping into charity's deep end. Was gradual and wary conversion as acceptable to Him as one filled with drama and immediate commitment?

I had always felt a pronounced allegiance to God, but to this point in my life I'd demonstrated little outward proof of my devotion. Worse, I tended to focus more on the things I shouldn't be doing, avoiding sin, rather than following the Christian imperative of doing for those who could not. Widows. Orphans. People serving time in jail.

In the last dozen years, my life had been all about getting an education, paying off debt, and saving the money I needed claiming my share of the American dream. Admirable goals, as far as they went, but reeking of complete self-involvement.

The trip had changed that. It had changed me. It had helped me lay aside my plans, my responsibilities, and my comfort as no church sermon ever had. It'd helped me push my body and my mind to their limits, beyond their limits, and to put my very life on the line, even when the reward for my selflessness could be death.

Lying in the stillness, I had a sudden inkling of what the universe's Mastermind went through as he watched us. Of what it must have felt like, giving the human race the gift of this world and then standing to the side as generation after generation of us turned our backs on goodness and virtue and selfless love, pursuing instead the things that so corrupted us.

Power.

Money.

The kind of pleasures that eroded decency.

How frustrating it had to be seeing us reject what little collective wisdom we had, again and again repeating the mistakes that too often caused innocents (and innocence) to suffer.

And how did our abuse of free will play out?

We started wars. We tortured enemies and indulged greed. We inflicted a thousand small hurts on one another even when, in virtually every situation, there was a choice for good.

I called up scenes from my monochromatic northern Virginia life and compared them to the lustrous, high definition reality I'd been living the last two weeks. I saw Lorant's face in the recovery room as he woke from anesthesia, a mix of relief and little-boy terror at the coming unknown. I smiled at the recollection of old Viktoria as we got her moving the morning after surgery, the stiffness and discomfort she felt no match for the absolute joy of being upright and mobile again.

I juxtaposed the fulfillment I'd felt here, changing lives, with the annoyance sparked in me meeting the demands of UMC's affluent clientele. The intellectual overachievers for whom the world was an endless econometric model to be tweaked; the perpetual politicians who never met a hand they wouldn't shake or an ego they wouldn't stroke; partners in law firms or think tanks or any one of a hundred prestigious corporations, one of whom had visited our offices days before I left, demanding a third arthroscopic procedure on his right knee. The stubborn fifty-eight year-old was unwilling to give up a lifelong addiction to sports and was determined to pay whatever money it took to keep his ranking on the competitive senior circuit, no matter that his joints were screaming for relief.

It occurred to me what a difference my presence had made to Lorant, to the great-grandmother, Viktoria, and to a dozen others who, without our help, would've hobbled through the winter. How superfluous my advice and skill often were to strong-willed American patients who, for the most part, already had it all.

I fell into fitful sleep, and it seemed only moments before Jake's whispers were penetrating the darkness, "Parry. It's time to leave."

I didn't move. Didn't answer.

"Come on," he urged again.

"It can't be time," I insisted, sounding a little like a kid desperate for a snow day. "It's too early."

He pressed a hand gently to my mouth, subduing my complaints. "Parry. You need to hold it down."

I murmured, "Sorry," and pushed his fingers away. Still half asleep, I asked, "Is something wrong?"

"It's time to get up," he repeated. "We have to leave."

My body pressed into the side of a hay bale, I was gloriously warm. I didn't want to relinquish my snug and secure comfort.

Jake showed me his watch. Almost 3:30.

Unbidden, tears of fatigue and discouragement burned my eyelids. ""I don't know if I can do this," I confessed. "I barely slept."

Jake's face loomed close. "You can't give in," he stated kindly. "We're close."

We were running, in Rand's case limping, for our lives.

My body balked. In a few minutes, it would be cold again. Cramping. Its muscles having barely rebounded from the abuse of the last several days, it would have to make the final sprint to freedom.

I thought of Balint and Lorant and the scars they'd forever carry; of Matthias serving the country he loved when he could easily have walked away.

What was I complaining about?

Beside me, Jake provided a new impetus for action. "You know how our host made a show of giving that money back last night and bringing us food?"

"Yes."

"It occurred to me he could just be trying to lull us into a false sense of security."

"You think?"

"I do. I think there's a strong chance he's arranged for a few of his friends to be here at daybreak. Maybe give us a little welcome of their own . . ."

That was all it took. I threw off my sleeping bag with resolve, my life not worth a few minutes' self-indulgence.

Jake put a hand to Rand's shoulder and shook it. Roused him.

I found a corner of the loft that afforded me privacy and there I got dressed. Fresh underwear, shirt and thick tights. The same ratty snow pants of *Soeur Madelaine*'s that I'd worn three days running and knew now I'd have to replace.

"Need some help with the sleeping bags," I asked Jake as Rand stumbled out of his.

"Sure."

Rand stumbled down the stairs and outside for his morning *toilette*. Jake and I realized that if we were going to leave soon, there wasn't time to brew tea or search through supplies for something delicious to eat. We pulled out the remains of the dinner we'd shoved into paper bags the night before. If possible, the food was more tasteless than it'd been then.

Too bad.

We shoveled it in. Brushed off crumbs that cascaded down the front of our sweaters. Spoke not a word of complaint. There'd be time for better food after we crossed the border into Austria, meals that I hoped would be heavy with fats, protein, and flavor. I could tell from the fit of the clothes I had on that I'd lost at least five pounds on this marathon; a little indulgence would be good for the soul.

"You look like crap," Jake said as Rand came back in from the cold.

He was right. Rand was sweaty and even more lethargic than before. When Jake offered him food, he pushed it away saying, "I'll be all right. I just need a little medicine for my foot."

Was that blister still bothering him? He hadn't mentioned it since our first night on the trail.

Rand fell into a malodorous heap, pulled off his boots, and grabbed the toe of his right sock. Tugged hard.

I gasped at the sight of his foot and above it, his lower leg. The back of his ankle was a bloody, festering mess, a vivid red streak rising halfway up his calf. There was also a very worrisome rash.

"Why didn't you say something?" I hissed. Of all people, he should've known the symptoms of blood poisoning.

Leaning against a hay bale, he closed his eyes. "I was too tired to check it at night. Too cold." The rest of his explanation came in gasps. "In the morning, it would've slowed us down."

"And you think this won't," Jake criticized tightly.

I could tell by his clenched jaw he wanted to say (scream!) something more.

Recriminations were useless at this point. Only action would help.

I shot down the narrow staircase to the shed floor and fumbled through my backpack. I got out the medical kit, then rummaged for soap and a facecloth. I grabbed our sterno burner and the pot that was already put away. Rand's wound needed a vigorous scrubbing with sterile water; we'd have to boil some.

I rushed outside to fill the pot at the pump but was stopped dead in my tracks by the sight of the farm house ablaze with light. Upstairs and down, the haze of kerosene illumination was a beacon against profound rural black.

The snow had stopped, and there were no signs of vehicular traffic or footprints along the back of the house to indicate the presence of the "company" Jake had feared. Whatever the reason for our hosts' early rising, I doubted it had to do with our capture. If that were the plan, they'd likely have taken a more subtle approach.

I quickly remembered Rand and his infected leg, and started pumping well water. Turning to go back inside, I heard a muffled scream come from the house. Was our friendly host beating his wife? Hurting her? Worse yet, was he trying to elicit from her our real purpose here?

If so, he'd wind up killing her; she knew even less than he did.

Wait. If information was what the man wanted, why wouldn't he just use a weapon to threaten or beat it out of us? There was no need for a middleman.

I heard another long and loud lament, and then I knew. The wife was in labor. I'd heard that unique and haunting sound before.

I dashed back inside to the men and told Jake, "Get this boiling. You're going to have to help Rand clean up."

"Me? Why me? Why not you?" he challenged.

I wondered briefly if festering flesh was Jake Spangler's Achilles' heel?

No time to give head to my curiosity. "I've got to go," I stated, throwing on my hat and coat.

"Go where?"

"To the house. I think our new friends are having their baby."

"Are you sure?"

"Not a hundred percent, but what else could it be? The wife's in there moaning. Lights are on in every room. The guy's probably in a panic at the thought of seeing blood."

"I'll come with you," Jake declared. "Just in case."

"What about Rand?"

"Still here," Rand managed. "Go. I'll be fine."

I laid a hand on his forehead. "Any nausea?" I asked.

"No."

"Do we have any antibiotics?" I asked, indicating the bag. I didn't remember seeing any. "Something strong?"

"In my backpack. Small zipper pocket."

"Take them."

"Why?"

"Your leg's infected."

"Can't be. I've been putting the cream on it."

"Not enough."

"I figured it was just irritated."

"Well, you figured wrong, Doc. It's bad."

"Can't be . . ." he insisted.

Frustrated by his obstinacy, I started pulling foil packets from his backpack and found the medication I thought would work fastest. "Get me his water bottle," I ordered Jake. There was enough left to wash down a couple of pills. "You should be on an IV, but this is the best we can do."

I popped a pill from a blister pack and pried open Rand's mouth. Plopped the thing in. "Here's some water. Now swallow." I forced a second tablet on him.

He gulped it down.

Why hadn't he taken this stuff sooner? What was he saving it for?

"You think you can wash this foot off by yourself while Jake and I see what's up?"

"Course . . ." The single syllable was a strain.

Jake grabbed something from the floor next to his sleeping bag.

"What's that?"

He held the object to the light.

"Matthias' gun?"

"We'd be fools not to take it," Jake explained as he pocketed the deadly looking thing. "We'll need it if our friend out there decides to shoot first and asks questions later."

HOW DID I GET HERE, I shouted inwardly. This wasn't me. I was a boring and ordinary; I didn't DO JACK BAUER!

I turned to Rand with a last piece of advice. "Here's a bottle of antibacterial scrub," I said. "Use it."

This was what I knew. Healing. Fighting disease. Taking charge in an emergency. Like my long ago Acadian ancestors, I was especially adept at avoiding the manmade evil in the world.

In the room.

I unrolled Rand's sleeping bag. "When you're done," I directed, "get back in here and rest until it's time for us to go." As though there were a chance in Hades we were going to be able to move with him in this condition.

Ego could be a bitch, I thought as I settled him, and here was proof. Rand hadn't wanted to show weakness in the face of Jake's competence, so he'd played macho man. Now the three of us were in greater danger than ever.

"Let's go," I growled in Jake's direction. I grabbed the pot of water, warmed nearly to a boil, then I put out the burner's blue flame. "This will have to do."

If we left the burner on, he'd knock it over and torch the place. Himself with it. Given what had happened the last several days, it was the way our luck seemed to be running.

TWENTY-TWO

J ake and I crept down the shed stairs and in less than a minute, were knocking on the farmhouse's back door. We feigned tentativeness on entering and cautiously looked around.

The kitchen was a disaster. Pots, pans, and covers lay strewn across worn countertops. Likewise towels, and on the floor, a listing mound of sheets. The woodstove had been filled to capacity and stoked. A stewpot bubbled water. The heat that filled the room was a veritable sauna as we came in out of the cold.

A plaintive moan rose from somewhere beyond the ceiling and filled the house. There was little doubt now that I was right. "Mom" was in labor.

"Go back and get me Rand's bag," I told him. "I've got to help."

"Have you lost your mind?"

"They know Rand and I are medical people," I reviewed. "I'm surprised Dad didn't already come out to get us."

Mom. Dad. What else to call them?

With reluctance, Jake headed off.

The house, as I walked through it, was well kept and solid. The first floor was one continuous room—kitchen, small dining area, a parlor with sofa and two solid armchairs—whose walls were painted in bright colors. Yellow. Blue. Green. Touches of red. Stenciled at the ceiling and around doorways were dainty flowers, the attempt at cheerfulness a young woman's likely response to isolation.

I slowly climbed the staircase tucked into the home's southwest corner and discovered a second floor divided into two bedrooms with a sitting area between. The space was furnished with his-and-her rockers, a small table, and a wall of bookshelves filled to bursting.

I ignored the urge to settle myself in that cozy reading room and kept moving, instead, toward the room from which bright lights and activity emanated.

Our host was stunned to see me, though visibly relieved. I pointed to his wife and asked, "*Je peux vous aider?*" May I help?

"*Oui.*" It was his expression, more powerfully than the single word that cried out, "For the love of God, do SOMETHING!!!"

Hoping to be helpful, he added, "*Elle ne parle ni français, ni anglais.*" His wife spoke neither speak French nor English.

Okay then. Sign language.

I gently took hold of her hand and motioned for him to leave us. I picked up a clean towel and sponged her forehead. I dampened a second cloth with water from a bedside pitcher and pressed it to her lips.

She gave me a weary, appreciative smile, and I saw she wasn't as young as I'd earlier presumed. Though the long blonde hair and beautiful eyes gave her a timeless, almost ethereal look, there were laugh lines at the corners of her eyes and creases, nose to chin, that formed a parenthetical embrace of her full, parched lips.

She was easily in her thirties, I approximated, and she must not have spent much time in the sun. Her skin was translucent alabaster, devoid of even the faintest "sunspot," a word I'd used since childhood to describe the freckles that plagued my own cheeks and upturned nose.

A contraction took hold of my new patient, and I saw her ride it out.

I was going to have to examine her to verify progress, but I had to gain her confidence first. More important, I needed gloves. In an age of HIV, hepatitis C, and a host of STDs increasingly resistant to treatment, no thinking medical professional introduced a bare hand into a human orifice if it could at all be avoided.

The peak of her latest contraction past, Mom fell into a trough of rest and recuperation. She opened her eyes and focused, trying to remember where she'd seen me before.

And when.

The light of recognition dawned, and she emitted a few soft words I assumed to be a greeting.

I smiled as though confirming her memory, then straightened the bed linens.

I took her pulse.

Strong.

Steady.

Good.

Picking up the bedside clock, I pointed to its face, and she pointed to the nine. She had been at the work of birthing her child for almost seven hours.

Without evidence to the contrary, I figured this was a first baby. The average first labor was about twelve hours, so even if nature cooperated, we could have a lot of work ahead of us.

Where was Jake???

I wouldn't know anything for sure until he got back.

The woman groaned in resignation, and I saw in her posture and expression that the next contraction was on its way. I saw her brace herself against the rising pain and close her eyes in concentration.

Not quite four minutes had passed between pains.

Jake was suddenly there, thrusting the medical bag toward me like a hot potato. He turned to go, and I pulled him back. Drawing him close, I pressed my mouth to his ear. "You stay. I may need help."

All color left his face. I indicated he should take the chair by the head of the bed and mouthed the single command, "Sit."

He squared his shoulders and complied.

In the hard throes of a contraction, Mom was oblivious to our exchange and to Jake's movement in her direction.

Not surprising. Women often told me that labor made you turn in on yourself, that the people and activity around you dissolved into a blur of inconsequential nonsense as every cell of your body was consumed by the active pushing of a massive human bolus from your loins.

That seemed the case here.

The contraction retreated, and I touched my patient's knee. I made a show of putting on latex gloves. They were Rand's size and huge on me, but they'd have to do. I improvised, inquiring could I have a look-see, and she accepted the indignity.

Pushing the sheet only to mid-thigh, I retained a modicum of her modesty. I made her bend her knees and positioned myself on a chair at the foot of the bed to perform an internal exam.

No matter that I was a woman myself and that the procedure had immense diagnostic value, this was one examination I'd never liked performing. Early in my training, I'd probably done a hundred and fifty to two hundred pelvic exams, each one more unpleasant, in my view, than the last. My feelings had nothing to do with a particular patient or type of patient, nor was it a matter of their hygiene; the whole process simply lacked appeal.

There are those who might think my aversion strange, but believe me when I say, it is not. Ask any medical professional. There's almost always something about her job that she hates to do.

An x-ray tech. friend of mine can't stand doing mammograms. She'd long ago been trained to perform the study and, when scheduled to do so, did it without complaint. But, at the end of a busy day mashing mammary tissue between Plexiglas plates, she freely admitted that she wanted nothing more than to run screaming from the room.

Similarly, my friend Alana couldn't stand giving enemas.

Another nurse I knew hated suctioning her patients in Intensive Care, the very sound of it making her want to vomit.

We all set aside squeamishness or distaste, however, and did what was required of us and eventually even the distasteful became routine.

I'd been fortunate. The patient surrogate hired by Wake Forest Medical School to train us in performing pelvics had been extraordinarily gifted. In plain and unemotional language, she'd passed on the nuances of a thorough but pain-free exam. "Warm the speculum.

"Proceed more slowly.

"Angle your instrument just the slightest bit posteriorly."

I'd practiced on her at least a dozen times, felt her hand, her hips, her precise words guiding my novice's movements, until one day, she'd given me the go-ahead to examine clinic patients.

Thanks to Regina's brilliant tutelage (I swear on my life that was her name. She even pronounced it like the city in Saskatchewan, a rhyme to the relevant body part), I became both adept and fast at the work. Patients commented on the delicacy and gentleness of my touch; how they hadn't felt a thing. They recommended me to friends, to mothers, even to their young daughters when it was time for a first exam, and I became a victim of my own perseverance.

Examining this Mom, I found she was eight centimeters dilated and almost completely effaced. Great. I advanced my fingertips to find that her water had broken, my palpation a corroboration of what I'd suspected seeing the wet linens in the kitchen. Instead of a relatively hard little head at the opening to the cervix, though, I detected only soft, pliable flesh.

Buns or lower back, if I had to guess. The baby was breech.

My mind raced through the list of possible causes. Placenta previa—a definite disaster if it happened here—was unlikely; poor uterine tone; a fetal anomaly that precluded the head-down position. Without modern medical tools, there was no way to tell what, if anything, had caused the baby to present its backside to the world.

Where was Celeste when I needed her?

Celeste was a friend and a nurse midwife whom I'd met along with her husband Desmond on a three-day Bike Virginia excursion my first year at UMC. Given her almost thirty years of birthing experience everywhere from the wilds of Swaziland to the refined row houses of Capitol Hill, it had been natural and inevitable that we become friends.

On that first trip, we had gravitated toward one other, sharing breaks, eating meals, and cycling side by side on long stretches of flat countryside. We'd chatted with other group members, certainly, and didn't purposely segregate ourselves, but we wound up trading funny and occasionally gross medical anecdotes when it was just the two of us alone. Predictably, Celeste's repertoire had vastly over-shadowed mine.

In the first year or two of our acquaintance, we'd spoken often on the phone, catching up, planning dinners, trying to schedule outings that invariably got cancelled or postponed because one or the other of us got called into work. Recently, we relied on Christmas cards and the occasional call to keep in touch.

I remembered vividly that her take on breech births was more matter-of-fact than that of the average ob-gyn. Where the latter often tried an external cephalic version, turning the baby from buns to head-down presentation, or performed a C-section when labor's push did not come to shove, Celeste was comfortable delivering a baby whose little bottom or feet presented first. "You just have to be patient," she'd told me more than once. "And therein lies the problem.

"The passage of time is not always good for the doctor's bottom line, while surgical intervention almost always is."

I had seen a few versions performed during my OB rotation at Wake, and I'd been tested academically on the particulars of the procedure. I knew that three to four percent of babies came into the world breech, determined (I imagined) not to leave the warmth and comfort of their first homes.

It was useful to know how to maneuver the most reticent of those children into a more conventional position, if only to spare the mother hours of effort, but in Celeste's experience, it was no more dangerous to deliver a baby bottom first than it was a normal presentation. "I delivered a half dozen breech babies in my first year of practice alone," she'd once confided. "No big deal."

The statistics on breech deliveries were good, but few obstetricians believed the odds were worth the legal risk. One disastrous delivery in the hands of an effective litigator—someone like North Carolina's pretty boy politician recently fallen from grace—could forever ruin a career.

A life.

I didn't seriously consider the risk of version here, attempted without benefit of sonography or an experienced attending physician in the wings. I couldn't run blood work, a non-stress test, or even establish an IV access—all considered essential to the successful external version. Most important, Mom's membranes had ruptured and that meant a version was impossible, no water left to help float the child to head down position, no cushion of water to protect its head as it entered the birth canal.

The only choice now was a breech delivery.

I scoured my brain trying to remember every hint or observation Celeste had ever made in my presence regarding this kind of delivery. One foot presentations were the worst, I recalled her saying, and it was imperative, if one were imminent, to reach inside and secure the second little leg. Bring it down.

That wasn't the situation here, thank goodness. I detected no feet at all.

"I let my Moms labor," I recalled Celeste saying. "The weight of the child usually delivers the head, unless . . ."

Unless what?

I racked my brain for the remainder of that critically important memory, but nerves or inexperience or panic wouldn't let it come.

What HAD she said?

No use. I couldn't force it.

I walked to the head of the bed and sat down next to my patient. I held her hand and encouraged her with my smile. At the same time, I conjured images of Celeste and me, going over again and again all the snippets of conversation I could remember. Thought of that one particular exchange most relevant to me here.

How could I have known there'd be a field test?

Calm down, I advised myself. Retrace your steps. Remember the context.

I saw the two of us sitting on a rural Virginia roadside, waiting for Bike Virginia's end-of-the-day pick-up. Desmond had hurt his knee, and out of sympathy, maybe sloth, Celeste and I had fallen behind and lingered with him, waiting for the van to appear.

It had been about five o'clock, the sun lazy and low over the Blue Ridge. A dinner prepared by volunteers was waiting to be served to us precisely at six.

We'd been hungry and tired, Des lying sweaty and inert, his bicycle shorts saturated from the day's sixty-mile effort. The course had been flat, mostly, but we'd hit at least three killer hills. Had walked part-way up those.

I'd consumed a gallon of water, re-hydrating, and had coasted downhill whenever I could, reveling in the views and the feel of the wind as it blew my hair back in a giant, puff ball.

While Des dozed, Celeste and I had compared notes on our most challenging or memorable cases.

I re-wound the tape. Played Celeste's words again. "The weight of the baby will help deliver the head unless . . . Unless the head . . . Unless the head gets hung up on the symphysis!"

I envisioned her face as she described the procedure, the way she'd moved her hands.

Come on! What exactly had she said to do??? Still nothing.

A new contraction hit, and Mom's body was utterly absorbed in its singular demand. I joined my hands with hers transmitting strength and encouragement. I recalled the utter confidence of Celeste's advice, but still the words wouldn't come. I shook my head, purposely wiping the slate clean.

My thoughts strayed to Rand, fighting his own battle back in the shed. Were we going to have to pull him behind us on the toboggan later, getting him the rest of the way? Would he have the strength to walk if we needed him to? Would our proposed route through forest and partway up a mountain even allow transport? Presuming we got him to it, could Rand cross the footbridge Jake hoped was still there without someone nearby to help support him?

Suddenly Celeste's words flashed through my mind. It was almost like she was there, talking to me, backlit by a summer sunset, demonstrating what to do.

If a Mom was having trouble expelling the baby's head, it was best to build up her hips, she'd advised. You supported the baby's body as it came out, and then, ever so gently, rotated the baby's head until it could get free of the pelvis' bony prominence.

I relaxed for exactly half a second. Now that I remembered the tutorial, I immediately questioned, could I actually follow Celeste's advice? Did I have the skill and judgment required?

I fell into a sweat of unprecedented intensity. Maybe it was the stove going full bore downstairs. Maybe it was the life (the lives!) entrusted to my care. I was soaked through, and if I could've peeled down to my underwear, in that moment, I would have.

I walked back down to the foot of the bed, waved Jake over, and waited for the next contraction to hit, realizing they were coming about every three minutes now. Mom clamped her eyes shut and centered her body's every muscle on the work of bringing a new life into the world.

I smashed my mouth into Jake's ear for the second time that morning. "Get Rand in here. The baby's breech. Tell him I need his help."

Not that he would know all that much, really. Orthopedists worked in an entirely different domain. But I knew I would feel calmer having him close. The depth and breadth of his medical knowledge was infinitely greater than mine, and while I possessed a useful skill set, I knew my limitations.

Rand had seen more. Done more. And, he was brilliant. If at some point I needed to improvise, he was the person I wanted at my right hand.

I watched as another wave wracked Mom's body. Legs pulled instinctively toward her chest, she clutched her knees. I stepped to the head of the bed and helped her curve forward, helping in the struggle to GET THAT BABY OUT!

She had endured two more contractions and increasingly shorter rest periods by the time Rand shuffled into the room. Following on his heels was the nervous and now-confused father. I suspected from the desperate look of him that Rand had given him some kind of update, and now real fear was kicking in.

Can I trust the two of you, his eyes asked? Do you know what to do?

I grabbed his hand and squeezed it hard in reassurance. "*Mon mari peut m'aider.*" My husband could help me, but his leg was hurt. "*Il a mal a la jambe.*"

I saw him think back to the papers we'd shown him earlier. "*Il est me´decin,*" he recalled. "*C'est bien.*" A doctor. All right.

I directed Dad once again toward the door. I didn't work well with an audience, and if I had to ask Rand a question in English, my medical French too limited to be trusted, I wanted to be free to do it with impunity.

Dad seemed to understand the importance of cooperation, though he went briefly to comfort his wife. He kissed and reassured her, and only then left the room. I motioned Rand forward to examine her.

He seemed marginally improved in the time since ingesting the antibiotics, but the changes I saw might have stemmed more from my desperate hope than reality. The medication wouldn't have had time to work.

Rand gloved and masked; he examined our patient in full contraction, palpating the mass of her hard and substantial abdomen. At the head of the bed, I checked her vital signs again.

Holding steady. Similarly the fetal heart beat, which I could make out now with the help of a stethoscope.

Rand nodded to me over the protuberance of her belly and signaled me to join him. He stayed seated, clearly weak, and the two of us turned our backs to Mom. I leaned my head into his. "Things seem all right," he said, lips millimeters from my ear. "But I'm going to try and get some history from the husband. Adam.

"She's Judit, by the way."

Adam and Judit.

I helped him stand, then watched as he lurched painfully away. I hoped both men knew enough French to get me the information I needed.

Judit's labor pains seemed to be lasting longer now, her body intent on unloading its cargo! I had no idea if she had complicating conditions like Rh factor or diabetes. There was no way of determining oxygen levels—hers or the baby's—and no real options available to us if either became dangerously low.

I watched her and listened to her breathing. I checked her heart rate and the baby's again. Her blood pressure. Though tired, she seemed up to the task of finishing this. I encouraged her to squeeze my hand as she met and survived another wave, then soothed her in the moments of the contraction's waning.

Where was Rand???

I smoothed Judit's hair and wiped the perspiration from her face as I had before. I gave her the tiniest sip of tepid water because aspiration was not a concern. There was no way Rand or I could attempt a C-section here without anesthesia or the necessary surgical instruments. If we were forced to deliver the baby using only a scalpel and our hands, it would mean Judit had died, and the danger of her vomiting and then inhaling the contents of her stomach, aspiration, was moot.

I pawed through our medical bag and through the pile of supplies that the couple had probably been advised to have on hand. I lined up the things we would need if delivery were successful. A clamp for the umbilical cord and a tiny rubber bulb syringe to use suctioning out the baby's nose and mouth. A sterile scalpel and suturing materials in the event of extensive tearing, or Lord help me, an episiotomy.

Extra gloves.

Disinfectant.

Gauze.

How had women managed to birth their offspring the last few thousand years without all these aids? In filth? In squalor?

The answer to those questions was as simple as it was cruel: they hadn't. Many had died, if not in the actual process of giving birth, shortly thereafter of sepsis, embolus, or puerperal fever.

None of those would happen here, I vowed. I hoped not to let it.

On the heels of my resolve, Rand finally returned. He waited until Judit was in the clutches of a contraction before briefing me. She was in good health, he'd learned from Adam, but her due date wasn't for another two weeks. She had seen a doctor for pre-natal care, but Adam had hesitated, with the bad weather, driving the forty-five kilometers to the hospital.

Running out of gas.

There was little money, Adam had explained, and the tank was well below a quarter. He hadn't been paid in weeks.

That last comment confirmed our suspicions that the *coup* was not well financed.

Unable to get his wife to a doctor, Adam had tried reaching a local midwife. With the storm, cell service was spotty. He had resigned himself to doing the best he could alone.

Rand had explained to Adam that I had midwifery training, but that he was a doctor who usually repaired bones. We were overdue to our next assignment, first because our truck had broken down and second due to the storm. Still the two of us would do all we could to help his baby and wife.

Adam hadn't questioned the story, told in Rand's rusty French; he just wanted someone to help. "They've lost three babies already," Rand revealed. "Two to miscarriage and a still birth just last year."

This wasn't good.

Adam and Judit were a couple desperate for a child, and I was the person they were counting on for a successful birth. Everything had to go right!

There was very little pause now between contractions. I examined Judit and located the baby's buttocks at the mouth of the birth canal. She was completely effaced and fully open at ten centimeters. This was going to happen all on its own.

I pulled Rand close and made him sit. I whispered in his ear, "We're going to deliver the breech."

He was sweating and clearly in pain, but he nodded, in that one motion indicating he would help me if he could.

I motioned Jake from the doorway where he was trying to be invisible, back to the head of the bed.

I indicated that he should support Judit's back. Not now, I indicated holding one hand up. "When I say so," I mouthed pointing first to myself then to my watch.

I really wished Jake knew French!

Positioning myself at Judit's feet, I pushed up my sleeves. I put on a clean pair of gloves and felt myself bathed in sweat. Forehead. The cradle of my inner elbow. The ring of my waistband.

I prayed as never before, "God help us."

Our mother grew more weepy and exhausted. Her hair was plastered darkly to her head, and the sheets that covered her were soaked from hours of sustained work. She begged for her mother, a long, subdued sob that made her sound like a toddler crying herself to sleep.

I stood and tapped Judit's hand to get her attention. I made a face. Eyes closed; lips compressed; nose crinkled with utter concentration. I put a finger over my mouth indicating she should make no sound but force all her concentration toward her pelvis. Hands in a v-shape, I motioned downward as though diving.

Judit suffered through another half hour or so of contractions.

Jake remained at his station, wrapping Judit's left hand in his and holding tight.

Progress was excellent. I stood again and got Judit's attention. I held up one finger, then two, then three. No more than that and the baby would be here.

The next contraction was on us. Judit took in a deep breath and screwed up her face in just the way I'd earlier demonstrated. Jake pressed her forward in support.

The baby was coming. Cute hiney. Then a back. A little red bag between his legs announcing his gender to the world. He was small, probably a function of his early arrival, but of greatest concern was his skin, a dusky blue, and the fact he was smeared in meconium.

Both bad signs.

We had to get him out.

The contraction loosened its hold, and Mom relaxed. I faced Rand and whispered behind the cover of sheet and legs, "Be ready. We have more work to do."

He knew; he'd seen the baby's worrisome color and the meconium as well.

The next contraction hit, and we reprised our roles except this time Rand and I appreciated more clearly the gravity of the situation.

Judit did her work! He was almost all the way out! Buns, back. Little legs wriggling.

I still didn't like his color.

More important, his head wasn't coming.

Damn.

Another contraction hit and despite its intensity, the little boy I was holding made no more forward progress.

It was time to put Celeste's advice into action.

I pointed to a pile of sheets and towels. Rand shot me a questioning look. I directed his attention to the sheets again and showed him using my elbow where he should position them. He stood uncertainly and picked them up.

I moved smoothly and seamlessly to the opposite side of the bed, hands still supporting our little boy's body. I pointed again toward Judit's rear and hips, but Rand had no idea what I was asking of him.

"Shove them under her butt," I hissed. "The baby's head is stuck."

He glared at me as though shot.

This was no time to worry about our situation or how I might've just blown it. IT WAS TIME TO SAVE A LIFE.

One-handed, I grabbed the pile Rand was impotently clutching and somehow held on to the baby's slimy backside with the other. Jake, who seemed to have a better grasp of what I wanted, lifted the mother's hips for me about four or five inches.

"Higher," I whispered, bending closer.

There.

I carefully swung back into position at the foot of the bed and felt for the baby's head. Just a little turn to the right, I guessed, and tried that.

No go.

Rand was trying to get my attention, and no wonder. The umbilical cord was taut, encircling the baby's neck twice. If not oxygen deprived, the child was dangerously close.

"Scalpel," I said softly.

Rand had it unsheathed and ready.

I rotated the baby's head left, and felt it give. The whole of his head and neck slid down to me past the obstacle of the mother's pubic bone, and in seconds, his body was completely delivered. Rand quickly clamped the cord and sliced through it, and together we shook and pinched the boy's tiny feet to get him to breathe.

The room was deathly quiet, Judit fallen back on the bed.

Rand reached for the nasal aspirator and cleared the baby's mouth and nostrils of blood and mucous. The baby had been stressed on his journey out to us, and he'd done what such babies naturally did. He'd evacuated the material accumulated in his bowels during pregnancy. To anyone knowledgeable, that meant the additional danger of pneumonia.

He still hadn't breathed.

The crisis wasn't over.

I inverted the tiny body and patted him forcefully between his fragile shoulder blades—a vestige of angel wings, I'd often thought. We were desperate to clear his airway and lungs. I laid him back on the bed, pinched shut his nostrils and exhaled a newborn-sized breath into his lungs.

Then, a second rescue breath.

Suddenly the glorious sound of a human cry filled the room. It was a gargle-like exhalation, followed almost immediately by angry little outbursts that demanded to know: How dare you manhandle me?

How indeed.

We quickly examined the baby's mouth and nose a second time and were relieved to see no sign of meconium in either opening. I wiped his body with a damp cloth, and wrapped it, a healthy pink now, in a towel that smelled of soap.

I listened to his lungs and detected, for now, "All clear."

Alleluia.

One hand on the infant for security, I leaned over and grabbed a flannel blanket from the crib that would be his new home. "Get me some warm water," I whispered to Jake. In a bit we would take the time to thoroughly wash him.

Adam ventured into the room just then wearing a hopeful look. He smiled at his wife, beaming beatifically from the bed. I laid the baby on Mom's chest to keep him warm, so close that the two were eye to eye, and Dad leaned in close. The three introduced themselves to one another with soft coos and tentative touches, caught up in the invisible bond that would forever make them a family.

I turned my attention to the afterbirth that would soon make its gelatinous appearance, laying my hand on Judit's lower abdomen. I felt for the uterus beginning its clean up work. Contracting; expelling materials no longer needed by the miniature human within. I massaged the area, helping move nature along.

Busy falling in love, Judit paid my ministrations no mind.

A short while later, Jake came back carrying a pot for a wash basin and a bar of soap that he'd found. I waved him aside. The bath would wait.

He pointed to his watch.

It was after eight o'clock, the group's pragmatist was telling me. Time for us to go!

Long past time, the desperation in his eyes told me.

"Thank you," a voice said in perfect English.

It was the father's voice. Adam's.

Neither Rand, Jake nor I acknowledged understanding; we had given no indication so far, that we were anything but French-speaking Quebecois.

"You speak English, no?" he confronted. "You are American." There was no doubt in his voice.

For the second time, none of us answered the man.

TWENTY-THREE

We'd been discovered. The single thought paralyzed my brain.

I watched as Rand slowly sank into a chair, and Jake took a step forward as though to protect us. His hand was in his jacket pocket—the one with the gun.

I could neither speak nor move. Given half a chance, I'd have soiled myself.

Our host spoke again, asking a second time in English, "You are American?"

Jake answered, "Yes."

I saw that he was ready to act, depending on Adam's next move.

"You should not be here," Adam declared in a hard voice. Then, more softly, "But I am very thankful that you were."

What did his gratitude mean?

Was he going to turn back to his new family, euphoric at the sight of its most recent small addition, and let us leave? Even if he did, would he do his best to set his cohorts on our trail the moment we disappeared?

Adam looked down at his wife and at the infant son nuzzling already at her breast. There were tears in his eyes. "I am Colonel in my country's Army," he spoke without turning to face us. "It is my sworn duty to enforce the laws of my land."

Here it comes, I thought wretchedly. Country first.

"But I am required to be faithful first to the laws of my God."

Release weakened my knees and spread through me like a river of warmth.

Soeur St. Helena had spoken to me of the people's residual Christian nature in the face of a forty-year religious drought. Proving her observation correct, Adam warned, "There is not much time. The search is, how you say, becoming more intense?"

"The search?" Jake tested him. "A search for us?"

"For you and for your fellow countrymen."

As we already knew.

"General Bacenko is a madman," Adam explained. "He will not rest believing there is even one detested American within the borders of his country.

"Three of you escaping his capture would send him into fits."

Adam was on our side. I could breathe again.

Jake demanded to know, "What do you mean, the search is 'becoming more intense?'"

"The new leaders are taking example from our more wealthy neighbors," Adam explained. "Very soon, they will begin flying the borders with aircraft, and they will conduct surveillance using, how do you say, sound devices . . ."

"SIDS," Jake guessed knowledgeably.

"Just so."

"What's SIDS?" I asked. In medical circles, the acronym stood for Sudden Infant Death Syndrome, a topic I would certainly never raise in this situation.

"Seismic intrusion detectors," Jake supplied. "They use sensors in the soil to detect the presence of people or machines in an area. There are other kinds of surveillance devices that can be used as well. Some use thermal mechanisms, others electro-magnetic. Newer ones can detect changes in environmental smells using chemical recognition.

"An operator who's really good at using SIDS, the first device I mentioned, can identify various kinds of intruders just from the fluctuation in the transmissions.

"A person. An animal. A car versus a tank."

"Yes," Adam agreed. "Technology that was once used to interdict drug traffickers or deserters will be co-opted for the hunting of Americans."

After checking briefly again on his wife and child, he told us, "General Bacenko will use any machine or monies or personnel at his disposal in pursuing his obsession, while the poor of our nation have less and less of what they need to survive."

Matthias had implied as much briefing us.

"You must leave quickly," Adam urged. "The technologies of which we speak will be implemented quickly. Any delay and you may be shot a few kilometers from safety." He paused and then added grimly, "If you are discovered here, we all will be killed."

In the midst of his happiness, I saw that Adam was frightened, both on our behalf and on his family's. He finally had happiness in his grasp; a child who'd survived a rough delivery and a wife who grew increasingly beautiful as vitality returned to her face. If not for our presence, and General Bacenko's in the prime minister's residence, he had a chance at a good and wonderful life.

"Your friend is sick," Adam commented unexpectedly to Jake and me.

"Your son could be, too." This from Rand, speaking slowly and with difficulty. "You should take him to your doctor."

"He appears healthy."

"For now. But he could develop trouble with his lungs." Rand stood, placed a hand on the baby's chest, and explained, "He could have breathed in a dangerous substance as he was being born."

Adam seemed suspicious. Had we sabotaged the birth? "What is this 'dangerous substance?'" he challenged.

Evidently there had been no birth preparation classes for these two.

As your baby was being born," I began. How to say this so he understood? I went with a juvenile version of the truth. "He went caca."

That was a universally recognized term, wasn't it?

I pointed to the baby's bottom, then to the black waste material smeared on bloodied gauze. "This, " I said. "He might've breathed this in."

I saw comprehension. "Your wife should also be examined," I told him. "I don't think she will have any trouble in her recovery, but I can't be sure.

"I am not a midwife," I confessed. "I work as an assistant to a bone doctor. Like Rand. I mean Jean Robert." There was no time to parse the peculiarities of the American medical system, or to elaborate on our duplicity. It was enough for him to know that neither Rand nor I was expert in the field of maternal and child health.

Adam's eyes widened; were there any more half truths, they asked. He turned to Jake, clearly the logistics coordinator of our merry band, and enquired, "Have you determined a path . . . a route of escape?"

"I have. We were preparing to leave when Parry saw your lights."

"Parry?"

"Parise."

"Of course. It was your idea to help?" he verified. "You must have known it was dangerous."

"You and your wife were kind to us. It was right to help."

"And so you have," he said with grace. "Thank you."

He directed his next comment to Jake, ordering, "Let me see this plan, if you would."

Jake didn't bite. Maybe Adam would help, I saw him thinking, but maybe he would use the information to cut off our best avenue of escape.

Adam sensed Jake's unexpressed wariness. "Fine then. I will propose one of my own." He kissed his wife and son. To the three of us, he signaled, "Come."

We followed him to the area immediately outside the bedroom. Energetic despite the long night, Adam unlocked the cabinet portion of the desk and withdrew several maps. He flipped through them and selected two.

While larger than ours and more detailed, the maps were similar enough that even I recognized the region they covered. Adam unfolded the desk's writing surface and encouraged Jake to join him. "I am charged with border security," he revealed. "I am aware of the dangers you will encounter."

I crowded behind Jake, looking over his shoulder as Adam worked. Without hesitation, he drew a red line that traversed a forested area, crossed a river, and skirted an elevation of moderate size. From there he drew a relatively short, straight line to the border.

The route paralleled almost exactly the one Jake had proposed hours earlier. With one exception. "I transport you to this point," Adam said, eliminating the forest crossing with a stroke of his pen. "I do so as I drive Judit and our son into the city."

Jake was quiet, mulling over the offer; Rand sat, his head supported by the wall.

Adam returned to the map, drawing several symbols, also in red. "I know that there is plan to install sensors, SIDS as you called them, in a pattern such as this close to the bridge crossing. To my knowledge, that has not yet been accomplished."

Jake studied Adam's additions and intently questioned him. If there were SIDS, where would the Army have stationed its listening posts? Were there troops amassed anywhere close to that stretch of border? If so, how many? How long would it take them to get to us? To Adam's knowledge, could we expect to see others positioned along this particular route?

Adam smiled. "Except for one unit stationed here," he said, indicating a point on the southwest edge of the forest Jake had proposed we cross, "this is safe exit. I give you my word.

"Your friend is too ill to walk more than a few kilometers," he predicted. "Accept my offer of transport and go from here," past the challenge of soldiers, solid forest, and the arduous path through them both. "In that way, you may be able to reach your destination unharmed."

He leaned toward us and reiterated the offer. "I get you past this checkpoint."

I studied him closely. Did this offer stem from Adam's innate goodness, I had to ask, or from a lifetime spent perfecting the bluff?

Whichever it was, we had to make a choice and do so quickly.

Jake stood and declared, "We go."

"With?" Rand asked.

"We go with Adam."

Those were my instincts exactly.

"Parry. You get Judit and the baby ready," Jake instructed. "I'll pack."

I took his words to mean he was going to ditch everything not absolutely essential to our last mad dash, making space for Rand on the sled.

"Before we go, Adam, I have to ask. What gave us away?"

He smiled at me. "Two things. One, your friend's passport." He looked at Rand.

"What was the problem?"

"It was supposed to have been issued in 2006, but it had a change on the final page not instituted until 2007. A modification in the name of the ministry charged with issuing passports."

Our forger had been so busy getting our personal data right, he hadn't noticed something as simple as that. Something that Adam, in his job, had been trained to spot.

"And the second thing?" Jake questioned.

"The gun you carry in the pocket of your coat. I have rarely encountered anyone in my country to help provide humanitarian aid who was carrying one."

Adam did have a good eye. He spoke again, "We must go now. Clear snow. The main road is open but not so the drive."

"I'll meet you in a few minutes," Jake offered.

Adam went back into the bedroom where baby and mother were soundly sleeping, and it fell to him to gently jostle his wife awake. To explain what we were doing and where we were going.

She balked, and I would have, too. Judit had been stretched, stem to stern, and wrung out like a rag. (The mixing of metaphors seemed appropriate.) Now we were expecting her to get up out of her comfortable bed; put on clothes; AND TO WALK DOWN A SET OF STAIRS before climbing into a car for what would probably be an hour's ride, given the terrible road conditions.

Her new, precious child would have to venture into the miserable cold as well!

No. No. No.

Her refusal was not so much vehement as heart-wrenching.

I joined Adam in stressing the importance of getting the baby medical attention. While she couldn't make sense of my words, I saw her intuit their meaning and respond to my air of authority.

I had helped her in a time when her husband hadn't been able to, and so now, she acquiesced, echoing my words, "We go."

It took the better part of a half hour dressing Judit in clean underwear and a maternity pad; slipping her into her husband's long underwear, more practical than the snug women's equivalent; bathing then enveloping the baby to Judit's strict specifications. Before leaving to meet the men, I sat her in one of the comfortable chairs in the reading room outside and then changed the bedding. That way the room would be clean and comfortable for her eventual return.

When I had finished, I woke Rand, still resting with his head against the wall. Together the four of us moved at a slow and careful pace down to the parlor, where I encouraged both Judit and Rand to sit again. Through the window, I saw Jake and Adam wielding wide-handled snow scoops, relying on brute strength and stamina to accomplish the work of clearing a path to the main road. The toboggan had been tied to the roof rack, and our supplies filled the open trunk. Gone were the cross-country skis we'd earlier carried, "just in case."

No. There they were, leaning against the shed door. A gift for Adam and Judit, or when he grew into them, their precious son. Most of our clothes were probably staying behind as well; we would only take what we wore.

"It's all just ballast," Jake emphasized when he came in and told us it was time to leave.

Somehow we got five adults and the new baby into Adam's small car. Judit and her son, without benefit of an infant seat, rode shotgun. I got the hump in the back between Jake and Rand.

None of us wore seat belts; the car had none; but after all that'd happened, I didn't sweat this one small detail. Between snow banks over three feet high and the male mass surrounding me, I figured I'd survive a low-speed impact.

Adam let the old diesel engine warm.

To my left, Jake was like a thoroughbred at the starting gate. Spirited. Impatient. Exuding his eagerness to be off. To my right, Rand was more like

Big Brown, a once fantastically capable ride and winner; now pretty much out of the running.

Rand looked much worse than he had an hour ago. While he hadn't vomited, he'd started complaining of stomach upset, and he faded in and out of sleep—a likely side effect of the fever. I guessed he'd rallied for the birth, but he was slipping fast now. There was little question that Jake and I would have to drag or prod him the rest of the way.

Adam put the car in gear, and we spun out of the farm yard toward the road. Riding along, even at low speed, the car's back end skidded unpredictably on the snow.

Adam tapped the breaks.

"I speak for us all at checkpoint," Adam declared a few minutes into the trip. "We will continue the ruse of your vehicle having broken down."

He had dressed in his uniform and resumed his military bearing. At his words, we were immediately transformed into Canadians, no matter that Rand's passport was less than perfect.

"I very much doubt a young soldier will note the error in Dr. Szabo's passport," he assured us. He'd insisted on knowing our real names, and given his sacrifice, we'd complied. Hearing him use Rand's aloud, however, stirred new uncertainty in me.

Less confidence that we could sustain this subterfuge one last time.

"If anyone does note the error," Adam explained, "I shall say that I have already addressed the matter with my superiors, and that all is well."

Okay then.

I breathed again.

In the distance, we saw the roadblock Adam had known would be there and beyond it a fork in the road. To the left, one could return to the small community we had seen at a distance late the day before. To the right was the road into the capital.

At the sight of uniforms, guns, and the soldiers' stern expressions, I wavered. I felt like I was either going to faint—or lose the breakfast I'd eaten hours ago. My heart raced with dread.

A paranoid thought occurred to me: Adam could, in this moment, reward us for having made possible the successful birth of his son; or he could climb the next rung on the ladder of the country's ruling military elite by announcing our single-handed capture.

He applied the brakes, and the car swerved the last few feet to the improvised guard station. A young soldier, barely shaving, appeared. Adam rolled down his window and addressed his subordinate with authority. He stated his name and rank, then introduced his wife. He motioned toward the three of us in the rear of the car and, I assumed, explained who we were.

Pulling out his ID and Judit's, he turned and he signaled to us. He told us in French that we should provide our passports and the government permit allowing us safe passage through the country.

I dug in my pocket and easily located my passport. Jake produced his as well. Beside me, though, Rand was fumbling. I tried my best to help, and Adam, aware of what was happening, shared something quite funny with the young soldier. Probably jokes at our expense.

I stuck my hand in Rand's left coat pocket while he searched the right. Both came up empty. I wanted to cry out, "Where in the world did you put our papers???" But indulging my irritation would have been a decidedly foolhardy move.

I felt myself growing hot, no matter that Adam's window was open wide, and the car heater was the most anemic known to man.

Rand was barely holding it together, getting flustered and red-faced and desperate to find the documents. Could they have gotten packed on the toboggan or stowed in one of our backpacks? For some reason, left behind? I added to his misery by throwing open his coat and searching its inner pockets myself.

Still nothing.

The soldier approached the car's back door, and Jake rolled down his window to slowly hand over his passport and mine. The boy leaned in, looking for the rest.

What to do now?

Rand was wearing a vest, something he must have put on just that morning. It had two reasonably deep pockets. The first, on the right, was empty. I forced my hand into the pocket on the left and felt the familiar leather shape.

Let it be!

I pulled at the thing, and the passport appeared. In it, the three copies of our permit.

With infinitely more calm than I felt, I smoothed Rand's vest and closed his coat. I worked the pretense of my unflappability, while inside I was near emotional collapse.

I handed everything to Jake, and he passed them to the soldier who took a mere half-second scrutinizing them.

We were in the presence of a high-ranking military officer, I could see him thinking. If he couldn't trust him, what was the point? There was a second, prolonged exchange, the young soldier nervously flipping through the pages of each passport without even looking down.

Adam depressed the accelerator as a sign we needed to go, and the soldier saluted. He returned the documents to us. The gate in the makeshift blockade lifted, and we were allowed to pass.

Adam smiled, as we drove off, and rolled up his window. "My new friend believes you must have come here by way of the Czech Republic," he said with a smile.

"Why's that?"

"He detected an odor he didn't quite like," Adam said. "And recommended a hostel in the city where there are free showers."

In the back seat, Jake and I smelled success.

TWENTY-FOUR

A few kilometers beyond our careful passage through the checkpoint, Adam left the deserted road at breakneck speed and plowed his car some distance through drifted snow. He pulled behind an abandoned stone structure, a place where there was little chance of his car being seen.

Jake forced the door open against snow pack, and the two of us jumped out. We took down the toboggan and extricated supplies from the trunk.

Adam joined us and pointed due south. "See there. That is edge of forest I indicated on the map. Beyond it, no more than two kilometers north, is the river crossing. A footbridge, dismantled many times, has been recently rebuilt by parties who use it from time to time.

"My unit and I have been assigned to remove it again. It is fortunate that we have not had the time."

On that we agreed.

"For now the bridge can bear weight," he told us, "but safely, no more than one person at a time."

Rand would have to walk.

"Once you have crossed, climb slowly along the southern face of the mountain." He pointed in the distance. "Descend moving north and west."

Jake was clear on the route. They'd reviewed it twice.

"The faster you are able to move beyond the bridge, the less danger you will be in," he reiterated. "After border, it is five kilometers to train."

Three miles.

Piece of cake.

"For safety," he said, providing a last piece of advice. "It is best to approach the bridge from the north and move both carefully and quickly."

"We will," Jake assured Adam. "Many thanks."

Together the men helped Rand out of the car and left him leaning against the back fender while I pumped Ibuprofen into him. That done, I laid a sleeping bag on the toboggan.

Jake grabbed the last of our belongings from the trunk. Sitting Rand at the head-end of the sled, facing backwards, we tucked him inside a second sleeping bag and covered his shoulders with a third. I secured our one remaining backpack on his lap using bungee cords hooked into the rope that ran along the sled sides. His feet hung off the end, but there was nothing we could do about that. For purposes of this move, he was a giant.

Jake and I put on our snowshoes and laid a third pair on Rand's lap.

It was time to say goodbye.

I went to Judit's side of the car and carefully opened the door. I kissed her forehead and wished her luck, laying my hand on the bundle of blankets that protected her beautiful new son. "God bless you," I said.

"Gotte bless," she responded in halting English.

I shook Adam's hand and said, "Thank you," imbuing the words with as much sincerity as I could.

The man was risking his career, his family, and his life to help us. It was vital he know how much we appreciated all that. No earlier action on our part justified the peril in which he was placing himself and those he loved.

"It is I who thank you," he said modestly. "Go with God."

He walked to the car and only momentarily turned for a last look. He quickly jumped in.

Jake and I backed away as he affected an amazingly tight three-point turn and retraced the car's narrow tracks through the snow. We watched as he built up a nice head of steam and blasted through the snowbank a second time, "Foof!" The car rose several inches as it hit, the wheels spun, and the tires hit a base of gravel that propelled the car into the road like a shot.

No sooner had the vehicle disappeared around a curve, we heard the fearsome growl of a diesel engine coming to us from the same direction. We grabbed the toboggan with Rand on it and concealed ourselves behind the skeletal stone structure. We ducked low and held our breaths as a large truck appeared and rumbled past.

Jake snuck a cautious peek. "Supplies," he reported. "No sign of reinforcements."

Good.

I started to get up.

"Wait." His hand grabbed my arm. "Let's make sure it isn't traveling in convoy."

"Let's not wait too long," I insisted. "If I don't get moving, I'm going to freeze in place."

The fifteen-minute ride, as tense as it'd been, had spoiled me. Jake pressed against me on one side, a feverish Rand on the other. My body had grown accustomed to comfort. Crouched in the cold, my muscles were turning to stone.

"Give me a minute to check our precise location," Jake requested.

He worked from the same paper map he and Adam had used plotting our escape, the batteries of his GPS in need of recharging. Ditto Rand's satellite phone. "We'll only use them after we cross the border," he'd told me during the ride. "We'll want to be absolutely sure of our coordinates at that point."

Absolutely!

Quiet settled over the countryside as we stood and set off, our pace more deliberate than it had been on previous days.

Rand was the reason. He was a big. Heavy. His heels dragging, he was a much greater burden than we'd thought he might be.

We stopped. Jake re-positioned the backpack and rolled up the bottom sleeping bag to create a wedge under Rand's knees. "There," he said. "That should help."

We started up again.

While things were better, we still moved slowly. It had been one thing encouraging Rand to move along earlier on the trip, quite a different matter hauling his bulk over snow that wasn't hard packed. This stuff was icy in some spots, soft and slushy elsewhere. Beneath the snow, a world of obstacles hindered our progress. Jagged rocks; foot-sized craters; the barren, muddy remnants of vegetation frozen into shapes that were an impediment to smooth travel.

The ride, both for Rand and for us, did not go well.

Fortunately, Jake was as strong as a pack mule, a hundred and sixty-five pounds of raw determination to which I added only a modicum of auxiliary power. Nothing turbo, mind you; more like the mild kick of a moped engine boosting human pedal power. Occasionally he went it alone, sending me ahead to push aside tree branches that impinged on our narrow path.

It took almost two grueling hours to reach the river whose sounds echoed off rugged cliffs. We approached it cautiously in the manner Adam had recommended.

"How wide is the thing," I asked before I could actually see the river.

"We're crossing it at a ravine, so, relatively narrow."

"How deep a ravine?"

"About sixty feet," he estimated.

"Are you sure?" I asked nervously.

Jake sometimes had a way of interpreting bad news to make it less frightening. He pulled out one of the maps and checked it. "Seventy-five feet," he said. "No more than a hundred, tops."

The continued rise in Jake's estimation wasn't reassuring. "We're going to cross a footbridge suspended ONE HUNDRED feet in the air???" I questioned. Anxiety earlier sublimated took center stage. "Is that right?"

"This reaction's exactly why I wasn't more forthcoming," he said coolly.

He refolded the map. "It's also why I'll go first."

"You bet your Ranger ass you will."

Watch the language, I heard my mother say.

More politely, I added, "You don't think this could be a trap, do you?"

All of Adam's talk about the pressure sensors not having been laid yet, how did we know that was true? He could have called ahead to warn his unit, not wanting to do the dirty work of arresting us himself, yet eager to be given credit.

Jake stopped. "You looked in his eyes, Parry. Did you get the sense he was going to betray us?"

Had I? "No."

"I didn't either. And it's not as though we have any other real options. Not with Rand in this shape."

He was right.

On we went.

It wasn't long before we arrived, and I discovered that our only way home was also my worst nightmare. "It's a swinging bridge," I observed, a detail neither Adam nor Jake had thought to mention. The body of it moved ever-so-slightly in a strong, morning breeze, and at the sight, I felt like I was going to get sick.

Peering over the side of the embankment that formed the river's eastern shore, I glimpsed a gash of turbulent river water foaming at the very bottom of the gorge; water that plunged over boulders and collided loudly with rock walls.

The good news, according to Jake, was that the bridge appeared to have been recently rein-forced. "See this wire," he said. "There's very little oxidation."

Miniscule consolation.

"We need to cross quickly," Jake stated. "If the sensors were set without Adam's knowledge, there could be soldiers already on their way to intercept us.

I suddenly felt like Moses poised before the Red Sea.

"I'm going to make two trips," Jake explained into my bloodless face. "The first just to test it. To see if it can really hold an adult safely and to get myself over there to clear the landing."

The ledge across from us looked overgrown, but there was a chance that the plants and debris were clever camouflage. "I'll come back for the sled on the second trip," he added.

"What about Rand?" I asked softly.

"You'll cross next."

I asked again. "What about Rand?"

"I'll come back for him."

I saw through Jake's plan.

He was going to get me and the supplies over first, so if something happened to Rand, to him—or to BOTH of them—I'd have what I needed to go on.

Jake had taken a few minutes to demonstrate the electronic equipment to me before we left St. Maria's, making sure I could operate both the phone and the GPS handheld. That I could read topographical maps if I had to. If the worst happened, I might not travel fast or efficiently, but I would be able to make it to safety without anyone there to help.

"I don't think that's how we're going to do it," I contradicted Jake now. "You've got at least forty pounds on me. It makes more sense for me to help Rand across."

Jake stared me down. "You'll be lucky if you can get yourself on that bridge," he observed not unkindly. "I saw you blanch just looking down at the water."

"Hey. White's my natural color." Shark bait, a Hawaiian friend had dubbed me once. "You get yourself over. And the stuff. I'll follow with Rand."

Who, at the sound of our exchange, livened up. He rose to standing, the sleeping bag he'd worn as a shawl, puddling at his feet. "I agree with Parry, Spangler. Get this crap across the bridge and await our instructions."

Jake grinned at our collective insubordination. "At ease," he advised.

He got to work rolling the sleeping bags and repositioning them on the sled. He hefted the backpack to his shoulder. "I think we should wear snow-shoes going over," he opined. "They'll distribute weight more evenly on the bridge surface."

"If they don't make us take a header over the railing," I countered.

"The bridge floor is textured metal, but after the overnight temperatures, it's pretty icy," Jake responded. "The weave of the shoes should give us traction."

He stuck to his guns and kept the snowshoes on. As soon as he set foot on the bridge, the weave caught on the raised tread, and the structure swayed slightly, ice and snow falling from it into the void.

He never hesitated. He just lifted his feet straight up, marching ahead and acting as though the strange pace had been part of his plan all along.

I sighed when he took his last step onto *terra firma*.

He waved and then cleaned away fallen tree branches, clearing a space large enough to accom-modate the three of us and the sled. He wore only his boots on the return trip, obviously having learned a lesson.

I watched and considered his m.o. Hands outstretched for balance, feet moving gingerly down the center of the bridge, he didn't stop or slow when the thing swayed, just kept on coming back toward us.

Seeing the dexterity required, I doubted that Rand would be able to make the trip across. He would need someone to help keep him upright. What if he had a dizzy spell and started to fall?

Could the structure bear the shift in his considerable mass?

Would things be worse, though, if there were two of us dangling in mid-air?

I cringed.

Jake reached us and picked up the sled. "The bridge is stable," he assured me. "But I'm sure it can't take more than about three hundred pounds."

"How can you tell?" Not that I didn't believe him; I just wondered.

"I've been on enough of these things with the Corps to know. Trust me. It's probably designed to discourage law enforcement from chasing anyone across.

"A hundred fifty-pounds of man plus a load of "H' . . . Any more than that, and the whole thing takes a tumble."

I turned to Rand. "What do you weigh?"

Already flushed with fever, he reddened. "Two twenty."

Add about twenty to that, I thought. Twenty-five.

"I can go it alone," he assured us, but neither Jake nor I was buying the claim.

"We don't have another choice," Rand said, leaning against a tree. "I'm not going to let you risk your lives."

"Wait," Jake said. "I have an idea. Don't move yet."

I would've stood there forever if I could.

Jake backtracked across the bridge carrying the toboggan and our snowshoes. He secured everything on the opposite shore and spent time digging through the backpack. In minutes, he came back with rope. "I'm going to let you try and get yourself across," he said to Rand. "But you're going to have to wear this." There wasn't much extra, but the length of rope seemed adequate to the task of reaching shore to shore.

"I'll go back over. Then you Parry. Then Rand."

"Take your time," he said to both of us. Then he singled Rand out. "You get lightheaded, you stop and hold on to the railing with everything you've got. We'll wait as long as we have to."

Rand promised, "I can do this," and at the sound of his determination, I was shamed into finding mine.

Once Jake was back over, it was my turn to approach the bridge. My first step onto the unsteady surface was the worst. The world spun with panic-induced vertigo. I took a second step feeling every minor movement of the wind and every little give in the bridge floor.

I looked neither ahead nor behind. I kept my eyes on the few square inches of black metal grate directly before me. One brown boot stepped into the frame, advancing with great and faltering care; then the other. After each step, I released my death grip on the bundle of wires that formed the railing, but only to allow myself the chance to move forward. Step. Release. Grab.

I made progress a few precious inches at a time.

Staving off terror, I pretended I was a rehab patient stumbling toward her future.

I repeated the sequence once. Twice. A half dozen times.

How far had I come? Was I almost there? I didn't dare lift my eyes to see.

Jake's encouragement guided me—willed me—forward, and he wisely ignored his instinct to rush out and pull me to safety. While our combined weights were probably under the bridge's safety limit, he couldn't be sure; and he wasn't going to risk my life trying to save it.

A gust of wind broad-sided the bridge, and it swayed treacherously. I clutched at the handrails and crouched, lowering my center of gravity.

That would stabilize the sway, wouldn't it?

I could barely remember my own name, in that moment, let alone the principles of physics governing the mass of my considerable . . . behind.

"I'm okay. I'm okay," I whispered. "Breathe."

I ventured ahead. One foot, then the other; my hands following my feet in appropriate succession. Approaching the bridge's far side, I felt less sway; more stability. I heard the call of winter birds and the rustle of dead leaves scratching against the icy cover of snow.

I finally dared to look up and ahead.

No more than fifteen feet away was land. Massive. Substantial. Be it ever so muddy and messy, the unfamiliar real estate beckoned me in the direction of home. I took several oversized strides and fell into Jake's open arms.

I cried. For at least three or four minutes, great heaving sobs.

I don't know how, and I don't know why, but in those last few seconds of suspension, I'd decided I wasn't going to die falling from a footbridge in a place whose name I didn't know. I might collapse or be shot dead a mile from this spot, maybe inches from freedom, but by all that was right, I was going to have both feet on the ground when it happened.

Jake sat me on the toboggan. "Don't move."

I nodded my total compliance.

It was Rand's turn to follow us over.

From the first, it was obvious that he was going to have trouble. Every few steps, he paused and then forced himself to get started again.

He was long-legged, and that trait helped. While he moved more slowly than I had, he covered more distance with each stride. A bit beyond halfway, his knees buckled and without intending it, he let his full weight list to one side.

Jake tightened his hold on the rope tethered to Rand's waist, and he tugged. Yanked a second time. I joined him steps from the cliff to urge Rand on.

Jake's measured movements seemed to be the stimulation Rand needed. He straightened and started coming toward us again. Eyes barely open. Mouth agape. Feet shuffling more than propelling him forward.

One.

Two.

Three.

Pause.

He opened his eyes, and I saw in them a flicker of determination.

He summoned his reserves and within moments, he'd reached us. Still upright. Still conscious. Still the overachiever the world knew him to be.

We grabbed and pulled him to safety, and the three of us hugged.

The worst of our adventure was behind us.

"A short break," Jake suggested when we finally let each other go. We resettled Rand in the toboggan and took a few minutes' respite to eat and drink. Finishing, we studied the slightly foreboding climb ahead.

The mountain was squat and russet brown in the patches where snow had melted or been blown away. Its contours were unremarkable except that it was the last barrier to our freedom, the final challenge before our descent back to sanity.

I fed Rand another double dose of antibiotics and prayed he didn't suffer an allergic reaction here, miles from help. The dosage was high, but at this point, it was the only thing in our arsenal that could fight off full blown septicemia. If he started to show signs of a reaction, we had Benadryl on hand; two Epipens in the event of full blown anaphylaxis.

If the second situation evolved, Rand would be in trouble. While the epinephrine would buy him time, he'd need immediate follow-up care, and therein lay the irony. There was a chance, small but real, that he could suffer deadly complications out here in the middle of nowhere, possibly minutes after the danger of being shot by General Bacenko's lackeys diminished to nothing.

Medical care was like that, a delicate balancing act; the overriding and likely good juxtaposed with the potential and much less likely bad. I made similar judgments in treating my patients all the time. Every good professional did.

The best among us shared information and concerns with our patients. We probed. We asked them how much inconvenience or discomfort they could reasonably live with, as opposed to how much risk they were willing to accept. The sooner patients understood that this was a perpetual dynamic in medicine, the sooner they got the quality of care they deserved.

"Ready to go?" Jake asked me.

"Ready," I answered, feeling more hope than I had in a while.

We set off slowly, making decent time.

The grade in the land grew more steep, and soon we were breathing hard. The veins on Jake's forehead were visible below the brim of his knit cap, and the scarf protecting the bottom half of my face grew damp with the moisture of my panting.

The wind died, and temperatures warmed. Ice and snow began a rapid melt, and we started to hear the unmistakable sound of rocks and dirt scraping the bottom of the toboggan.

"Jake. Stop," Rand called over the grating sounds. "I should walk."

He should. But could he?

"How much farther do we have to go?" I asked.

Jake extricated himself from the harness of the toboggan's rope handle and ferreted a map from his pocket. He consulted GPS for only the second time that day.

His face broke into a smile. "A mile, two at most, to the border."

Thank you!

"But we have to get down that thing." He pointed to a depression in the terrain not far ahead. "That could give us a rough time."

Instructing Rand to stay put, Jake and I walked forward about a couple of hundred feet to consider our options.

The rugged mountainside stood hard to our right, and to our left a treacherous rock promontory was clearly something only an expert would dare scale. We saw that the concavity in the soil, as we approached it, was actually a rock slide slick with melted snow. It dropped about the height of a four to five story building before the land leveled off. The slide had steep sides and down the center, there were rocks of every conceivable size and shape.

"Rand will never be able to negotiate this," I predicted softly.

"He made it across the bridge," Jake argued. "And we didn't think he could do that either. Let's go a little farther. Maybe we can find a way down that's easier. If we find the right spot, we can be down this thing in a half hour."

I was doubtful. "The only thing on the bridge in Rand's way was the swaying and a little lightheadedness. On these rocks, the least little misstep, and he's down."

I didn't have to spell out for Jake what that could mean.

"No point in speculating what might happen," Jake reminded me. It was a sin of which I was frequently guilty. "He has to walk, and he's already volunteered to get started."

Jake was right. We had to deal with what was, not the overwhelming multitude of things that might be.

We shuffled back over to where Rand sat with his eyes closed. His breathing was shallow and audible. Jake leaned over and patted him on the shoulder. "One more hurdle."

"I'm up."

Jake reached out to help him.

Watching them, I imagined us safe in Austria. We could take pretty much anything for an hour or two, right? Do anything.

I'd seen what Rand and Jake were made of; I knew myself. The three of us could fight our way through this final level of hell!

"I'll wear the backpack," I proposed.

Rand would go first.

Jake would bring up the rear, lugging the rumpled and filthy sleeping bags and the toboggan that we'd need, once down, getting Rand the rest of the way to civilization.

To help.

I'd take the middle position.

Gloves on. Sunglasses in place against the sun's growing brightness. We walked until we found a way down the rock slide that looked manageable. Without hesitation the three of us started downhill.

We kept to one side of the slide, gaining purchase in the rough surfaces of a side wall. For safety, we grabbed the occasional stray branch or tall and tenacious winter grasses.

Rand rested every few steps, body pressed into rocky, muddy soil.

I started a silent conversation, advising myself against the dangers of letting my mind wander. "Too dangerous," I said. "Keep your attention right here."

Underfoot, the rocks were slick. The tread of my boots played off the surfaces, and I took a knee more than once.

Tore my pants.

Tore them a second time.

"How about I sit down and take my bumps that way?" I joked after a third spill.

The men didn't seem to find humor in my suggestion; they were too busy holding on.

We kept at it for another fifteen or twenty minutes until, about halfway down, the slide made a gentle turn. Ahead of me, Rand seemed frustrated with his slow progress. He started launching himself from one tenuous position to the next, knees bent; head thrown back; long arms grasping for whatever help they could find.

A branch.

A rocky handhold.

The slap of a sapling as he reached for it and missed.

His face, when he turned toward me, was streaked with mud and dotted with tiny, embedded pebbles. If UMC's administrators had seen him in this moment, they would quickly have recognized what a waste of talent and grit it would be turning Randall Atticus Szabo into a paper pusher. This was a man who had been born to fight for his patients the same way he was fighting now for his life. A guy who never gave up.

Behind me, Jake called out, "Doin' okay, Rand?"

"Yeah. O . . . K."

"Parry?"

Past the point of *politesse*, I hollered back, "I'm bedraggled and soaking wet, but other than that, I'm fine."

I leaned my torso downhill and a little to the left. My left foot and lower body followed, then, tentatively, the right side came along.

The rocks were harder edged here, sharp angles that could leave nasty cuts. A base of loose and muddy soil underneath shifted slightly at my weight.

"Careful. Take it slow," I warned under my breath. There was absolutely no margin for error.

I adopted Rand's style of descent: a full body press against the nearly vertical wall of rock and dirt. Side step. Hand slide. Body to follow.

I snuck the occasional look ahead, getting the lay of the land, and heard the men, one above and one below me, breathing hard.

We weren't far, now, I could tell. There was a slightly more horizontal feel to the trail.

Behind me, for a mere millisecond, Jake lost his footing, and a shower of rocks and small stones cascaded past.

"Sorry," he called. "My bad."

"Give it up, hotshot," I shouted. "Your slang's so *passé*."

He didn't respond.

All right, be that way.

I reached for my next handhold, a rock about five inches above my head and maybe two feet beyond. I executed a good, healthy stretch.

Thank you Joseph Pilates.

I felt my way with my left foot and found a level spot. I got the aching bod down the next couple of feet as carefully as I could and dragged my right foot into alignment, settling for a moment to catch my breath.

Preparing for my next measured movement, I felt the ground under my left foot start to shift. There was no reason it should, no obvious cause. Rand had passed this very spot a few minutes ago uneventfully.

Suddenly I felt the soil give and start to slip away.

I yelped and, in desperation, pulled myself back using every core muscle I'd ever toned. I bent my body uphill and to the right, struggling to forestall the downward pull of gravity—a futile fight, as it turned out.

My left leg dropped into a shifting hole in the soil, and would NOT budge. The heel of my boot became wedged between rocks and a deluge of muddy soil that moved swiftly to entomb it.

My arms flailed; my body twisted; I grabbed at anything I could.

My frenzied movements only propelled me up and over the fulcrum of my trapped leg. The snap and splintering of bone was the last thing that I heard.

TWENTY-FIVE

I lay face down in the cold, the wet, and the pain of my disastrous fall. Pressed into mud and rocks, I didn't dare move.

I summoned the strength to call shakily, "Jake? Rand? Anybody," but only menacing quiet enveloped me.

Seconds passed and then, from a distance, I heard panting and a softly spoken reassurance, "We're coming."

Whose voice was that?

It seemed so far away. Unrecognizable.

I realized neither Rand nor Jake could rush quickly to my side. They had to move, to crawl, to slowly and cautiously transport themselves to where I lay grotesquely splayed.

Anything else and they risked injury to themselves.

My body started to shiver. The sound of my friends' indistinct scrambling was extraneous to my suffering. I put out a hand to try and signal them, "Take your time," but that movement of a few millimeters telegraphed breathtaking pain up my leg, right to the center of me.

I don't how long it was, a moment, an eternity, before I heard a voice whispering, "We're here, Parry. We're here."

Was that Rand?

"We need to get the backpack off," I heard the same voice say. "She's carrying the emergency kit and all the meds."

Was Rand giving the orders now?

Leaning close, he asked with infinite gentleness, "Are you allergic to anything?"

I thought for a moment. Waded through the mental murk. "Penicillin."

"What about narcotics?"

Lost in the vagaries of pain, I struggled to remember. "Don't think I ever took any," I slobbered into dirt . "Could use them now."

"You wait just a second," Rand said kindly. "We're going to get some painkiller on board." He squeezed my arm in encouragement.

Who was this new Rand, I asked myself. Who was he channeling?

"Vicodin!" I suddenly cried. "Don't give me Vicodin." I'd taken a single dose a couple of years ago after a wisdom tooth extraction, and it'd made me sorry I was born.

"Demerol?" he suggested.

"'kay."

I felt someone cutting at the straps of the backpack, the slight jarring sending me into paroxysms of pain. "Please . . . stop."

A hand clasped mine, but the cutting continued. Was complete. I drifted off to the sound of someone rummaging through the pack.

When I stirred awake, I felt a hand somewhere between my hips and knees, pulling away the heavy blanket of Agnes' old coat.

The minor motion spawned reverberations through my every living cell. "Nooooo!" I moaned. "Don't do that!"

"It's just for a second Parry. We need to get to your thigh. To give you a shot." Jake was my comforter now. I imagined Rand, shakily drawing up meds.

My backside was exposed now to the cold afternoon air, but I couldn't have cared less. "Moon over Austria," I mumbled, and both men laughed.

"Pipe down," Jake ordered. "You don't always have to be the funny one."

I did have a pathological need to find the humor in every situation. I thought it lent perspective to life. Given my current predicament, maybe it wasn't the best time to indulge the decidedly warped St. Amand perspective.

A prick to my upper thigh, and within moments I was falling into a velvet cloud. I still felt pain, but it was far-removed, separated from the part of my brain where, with great difficulty, I was trying hard to form coherent thoughts.

I heard and felt digging somewhere near my feet, and there followed a heated exchange, the men apparently disagreeing on what to do next. Time passed, and my companions quieted. I felt hands lifting and clumsily turning me, loosing from ankle to hip pain so overpowering, I instantly faded to black.

When I became aware again of my surroundings, I was covered knee to neck with a grimy, smelly sleeping bag, and some fiend was moving my leg. I wanted to scream my objection, but the filter of opiates through which I saw sky, snow, and faces allowed for little verbal expression.

Hurt me, I thought. I don't give a flying fig.

I slept.

I opened my eyes at one point and saw Jake kneeling next to me. Felt the reassurance of his hand against my cheek as he leaned over, silly man, his full body covering mine hip to shoulder.

Strong hands pressed me into place.

In my head, I said "Not now, big boy," but my lips could only spread themselves into a smile.

My left leg and foot were naked in the cold. I felt a pair of hands, Rand's presumably, palpating. Feeling for pulses. Evaluating the damage which, I knew intuitively, was considerable.

Rand was asking, "Can you feel this?"

"Big toe," I softly responded.

"Third toe.

"Piggie going wee-wee all the way home!" I was blubbering now.

The fact I could feel as much as I did told me my fractures probably weren't impinging on major nerves.

Good.

I knew what came next and, despite the numbing meds, my muscles tensed.

Rand positioned his hands and with little warning, applied the varus pressure needed to realign the bones of my lower leg laterally. Pain and the accompanying sound of bone snapping into place were dwarfed by a voice screaming "Merciful GOD!!"

My voice.

I murmured an apology to my Maker, "Sorry 'bout that."

Wait. I hadn't taken the Lord's name in vain; there was a definite point to my supplication.

Cancel the breast beating.

I rallied and asked Rand, "Any crepitus?" The distinctive crunching sound that the tissue around an injury made when compressed. Its presence meant I'd probably managed to splinter, not just fracture the bone.

"A little," Rand admitted.

I surmised that surgery and pins were in my future.

He lifted my leg, again without warning, and I yelled at the devil torturing me, "STOP!"

Jake was unbuttoning my coat. Taking my scarf. Hey!

I slipped in and out of awareness.

I heard grunting, groaning noises (my own) and felt myself rocking back and forth. There was cussing at both my head and my feet, and then the tremendous and overwhelming stress of my body moving through space!

I must have fainted again or sunk deeper into a chemically-induced haze, because when my eyes finally opened fully to daylight, the sun had slipped much closer to the western horizon. I was no longer moving, but the hurt earlier dulled was back with a vengeance. It was piercing and prolonged, coming in waves from my lower leg and radiating all the way through my pelvis.

Could I be having a baby, I asked in my confusion.

I laughed. The oldest living virgin in the continental United States—by choice, thank you—that woman would've remembered getting pregnant!

"Parry?" A concerned Jake asked. "Are you laughing?"

Amazingly, "Yes." Pause. "Where . . . are . . .we?"

"We're in Austria."

""Safe?"

"Yes. We're safe. Almost two miles inside the border. We couldn't go any farther."

"You're sure we're safe?"

"No question."

I didn't know how or when we had made it, but thank goodness we'd arrived. "Rand?" I asked monosyllabically.

"He's resting."

"More . . . pain medication," I requested. It hurt so much getting out the words, I didn't bother saying more.

"We've used up our only ampoule of Demerol, Parry. There isn't anything more to give you. But help's on the way. A helo. You have to hang on a little longer."

A helicopter? "Hate them." Too many—medivacs; traffic helicopters; whirlybirds ferrying tourists on panoramic flyovers for fun—were prone to crashing and killing everyone on board.

The previous summer, in a suburban county north of D.C., a young woman had survived a serious car accident with her best friend only to be killed together with the pilot and paramedics airlifting her to Maryland Shock Trauma. It had been an especially senseless tragedy given that a regular ambulance ride could easily have gotten her to timely treatment.

"No. . . other . . . way?" I managed to ask. Snow machines maybe? They were more practical, cheaper, and stuck reassuringly close to the earth.

"There's not enough snow cover left," Jake assured me. "You're going to have to put your trust in technology one last time."

Perish the thought.

TWENTY-SIX

The loud, blustery machine touched down on the snowfield two hundred feet away, and a small army of attendants fanned out from the opening doors. Reaching us, they worked with calm and with competence, quickly assessing my injury and, on the basis of what Jake told them, administering more of the pain medication whose efficacy had long since faded.

"I'm all right," I insisted to the young corpsman tending to me. "Rand's the one who needs you."

Our friend lay collapsed a few feet away, completely unresponsive. Despite the roar of the helicopter blades and people shouting back and forth to one other at the top of their lungs, he couldn't be roused. From the pallid look of him, I was terrified that even the most aggressive and immediate care might not be enough to revive him.

Jake hovered in the background of all the activity, able to do little but gather what was left of our things and douse the massive bonfire he'd built to warm us. Every few minutes, he leaned in close, monitoring the caregivers as they took vital signs and started IVs. Later, aboard the bird, he huddled close, holding my hand and grilling the technicians for updates, his concern both for me and for Rand alive in his eyes and in the features of his wind-burned face.

We flew into a rising wind and a low-lying sun, landing in what seemed like very little time. We were enveloped by the chaos of arrival, surrounded by doctors, nurses, and a squad of health care personnel who rushed our damaged bodies into separate treatment bays and the welcomed warmth of indoors.

Inside my chemical cocoon, the commotion was a blur. I heard polite requests and questions from nurses and aides, spoken to me in English and followed up with asides (over my head) in the guttural unknown I assumed to be German.

An officious nurse issued frequent, if vague, updates on my companions' condition. "Your friend Mr. Spangler is stable, and we are tending to his injuries."

Jake? Hurt?

"Dr. Szabo has gone directly to the ward where a specialized team will meet him."

At last!

Hands cut away my clothes, and warm blankets were laid over me in their place. I apologized for the smell and the look of us, cryptically prattling, "We haven't brushed our teeth in four days.

"Just trying to fit in."

At the strange admission, eyebrows peaked, but sleepy in my pharmaceutical haze I felt no compunction to elaborate.

Over the next few hours, I was moved here and there. Strangers took over the private and personal functions that were usually my responsibility alone. They lifted me cautiously onto a fracture pan and when I was finished, wiped me clean. A nurse discovered that I'd started my period, and before I could request a tampon from the stash in my back-pack, she wedged a pad not all that comfortably between my thighs. I felt a heaviness and cramping low in my belly that meant this was going to be a tough one.

Nothing mattered except that I was safe. Jake was safe. And somewhere in the vast hospital innards, people were working overtime trying to save Rand.

Amid the activity and din, I started to feel better. Then a trifle ornery. I grew resentful having people look down at me, helpless and inert as they rolled me from one location to the next. From my vantage point I saw little but hallway lights, mold-ings, and high corners that were home to the occa-sional cobweb. "Hardly . . . sanitary," I disparaged at one point, but no one seemed interested in the observation.

In their busyness tearing open supplies, drawing up injections, and transferring my broken body, caregivers forgot that the exhausted person before them was more than a specimen. I was someone who still wanted her dignity preserved. "Pull that blanket up over my breast," I wanted to say to a young, no-nonsense nurse. "And this sheet, tuck it down over my naked backside.

"Pretend I'm your mother, or your sister, or your best friend," I wanted to lecture an especially pre-occupied aide. "Do the small, thoughtful things you would do for them.

"CLOSE THE DAMNED CURTAIN!"

After what seemed a veritable lifetime of x-rays and shots and prepping, I signed a few forms and was wheeled off to surgery, the rest of that day and the night that followed, a vague miasma of medical sights and smells.

Later I would recall flashes of myself sliding from stretcher to OR table, an entourage supporting my leg and naked rump; tubes and lines and monitors trailing behind like a life-saving tail. I would remember strangers' faces peering into my vacuous gaze and assuring me things were, "Very goote."

In the recovery room, I woke feeling nauseated and light-headed, and suffering the agony of a very sore throat. Someone explained, maybe in response to my complaints, that I had been difficult to intubate. "A very narrow bite and a short neck," he announced, as though such characteristics were my personal failure.

I slept off and on and woke the next morning feeling achy and hung over. I was in a private room. My injured leg was elevated and connected to a vein in my arm was a new intravenous line. A nurse greeted me with a brisk, "I am Leisel. Good morning."

I concurred with her automatic appraisal of the day, despite all evidence to the contrary.

How could it not be a good day? I was dry. From the smell of things, I was clean. Best of all, I was in a room, in a BED, and warm after days of penetrating winter cold.

"My friends?" I croaked softly.

"They are being cared for," she assured me noncommittally, the American standard of confidentiality evidently having found its way to Austria.

"When can I see them?"

"Soon. But first I will bring your breakfast."

The simple offer brought tears to my eyes. I didn't care if the place served gruel and grubs, I was going to lick the plate clean.

Leisel left, and as she did, I noticed a newspaper on the tray table nearby. I scooted painfully several inches to the edge of the bed, and I leaned over, movements that loosed a flood of darns, yikes and a single, "Lord in heaven!" before I was able to reach the thing.

The headlines were written in German, and while I had little idea what they said, a glimpse at the photo over the fold gave a me clue. The action shot showed the open door of a familiar military helicopter, and framed in the center of it stood a man who looked remarkably like Jake. The features of the people being rushed away on stretchers were impossible to distinguish, but I was pretty sure Rand and I were the patients whose privacy had been breached.

Great.

Our escape and rescue as media fodder.

Drama-hungry correspondents were going to be all over this, dogging us in the rabid way that was typical now of news reporting. It wouldn't matter that full disclosure could jeopardize the lives of those who'd helped us to escape, major news operations would make it their business to dig and poke and pester us for the facts, spouting the same old same old about the public's right to know.

"Calm down," I lectured. There were only three people who knew what happened. Rand was in no shape to talk; I would refuse to say a word. Jake would draw the proverbial line in the sand and be the stalwart presence he'd been all through this.

I forced myself to relax and waited for Leisel to return carrying a tray heaped with food. She helped me eat; tenderly bathed me; and she made me as presentable as I could be in a hospital gown with my hair permanently (and unattractively) matted.

A little after nine, Jake appeared wearing similar hospital garb and a smile.

"What happened to you?" I asked. He was limping and his face looked bruised.

"A little frostbite, they tell me. But I'm fine."

"So the IV's just for show?" I challenged.

He grinned. "Okay. I was dehydrated.

"May I?" he asked.

"Of course. Sit."

He pulled his IV pole close and settled into the chair next to my bed. "How're you feeling?"

"I won't be doing any extreme skiing anytime soon, but other than that, I think my parts all work.

"How's Rand?" I needed to know. My thoughts were consumed with the sight of him unresponsive and ghoulishly pale.

"They haven't let me see him," he revealed. "And they're not telling me much. From the little I've been able to surmise, he's critical."

My heart sank, and I felt a shiver of fear. Never had I been so disappointed at being proved right.

"His folks are on their way," Jake told me.

"Oh, no!"

Our families! In the tension and the struggle and the pain of the last few days, and in the utter joy of rescue that'd followed, I'd completely forgotten my parents. They must be frantic.

"You don't think his parents should come?" Jake asked in puzzlement.

"Of course they should come. But my parents. Yours." I had a horrible thought. "Are they seeing these pictures and headlines at home?" I demanded, thrusting the purloined newspaper at Jake.

"The staff wasn't supposed to leave this stuff lying around," he commented hotly.

"They didn't. I almost fell out of bed stealing it."

"Still."

"I need to call home!"

"I'll see about getting a line," he promised. "But for now, you shouldn't worry. The Embassy has been handling things."

"Yeah. I see how well they've 'handled things'," I said, again indicating the photograph. "We're spread across the front page."

"The press has been pretty aggressive," he explained.

"What a surprise."

"They're blaming the President and his failed foreign policy. More proof of his ineptitude."

Naturally.

Dwelling on the man's every perceived short-coming would only help the candidate that the press had crowned and anointed winner from the day he first announced his candidacy.

That no longer mattered much to me; the election had passed. I took solace from the fact that we truly got the leaders we deserved.

"Have you talked to your family?" I asked Jake.

"Yes." He didn't seem happy.

"Are they all right?" I probed. "Are you?"

"Things are fine with me. Them."

So what was wrong? He looked like he'd lost his last friend. I had a sudden, terrible thought. "Rand IS going to make it, isn't he?"

"The doctors are hopeful," he said, "but realistic. He had high levels of toxins in his blood when he came in, and they've done some damage.

"They're worried about his kidneys."

Dear God. Was he going to die after all this?

"Parry. There's something else."

"Matthias?" I asked immediately. Had his role in our escape been discovered? Had he been jailed? Worse?

"No. It's not Matthias," he interjected before I could have the man tried and condemned. "He and the nuns and the children are safe, as far as I've been able to determine."

"Adam and Judit?"

He shook his head. "I haven't heard a word."

His assurances were weak.

"Something is wrong," I challenged sharply. I saw it in his face and his defeated posture. In his lingering hesitancy.

Leisel came back in with a syringe. "What's that for," I asked.

"It is to help with your pain."

"I'm handling it," I told her. Then, "If you must, make it a light dose. I may need to stay sober."

She smiled and inserted the needle into my line, slowly administering the drug. Mindful of my request, she gave me only half the dose.

"Thanks."

"I will note the change in your chart and contact your doctor," she said efficiently.

"Please do."

When the door to my room had closed again, I turned my gaze back to a dejected Jake. "Tell me what's wrong."

There was no more room for equivocating, he saw that. Taking my hand, he looked at me levelly and sighed. "Parry. Things didn't go well for the others."

"Which others?"

"Ken, Bev, and Ted," he answered specifically. "Linda and Rich."

Those others.

He confided, "The news isn't good."

I was beginning to feel foggy from the painkiller slowly bathing the cells of my brain, but I fought to concentrate. "'What do you mean?"

He drew a cleansing breath before revealing, "The border guards used some kind of heat-sensing device on the load of oats."

Adam had been right; the new government was moving fast to secure its borders.

"They found Ken and the others?"

"Quickly."

We'd really underestimated the regime's preparedness.

I swallowed hard. "And the other team?" Crossing into Hungary.

I saw Jake's hesitancy.

"Tell me."

"The load had already been waved through," he explained. "The driver was told he needed to sign a few papers, a technicality rarely enforced before now."

"What happened?"

"Someone in the load sneezed. The guards heard. The rest you can imagine."

I had a sudden image of Linda, the previous Saturday, on her way to the nursery. She had been incubating a cold and thinking twice about spending time with the littles.

I could hardly breathe.

I remembered how jealous I'd been of my friends, imagining them safe and well and taking the easy way home, while Jake and Rand and I were plowing through snow and ice for days.

"What about Paul?" I managed. "Tell me at least he made it out!"

"He did. The guards let him use the facilities before taking him to a holding cell. He pulled a Bundy and somehow pried a window open. He jumped the two floors down into snow.

"He's made it to Budapest."

I could tell by his expression, there was more. Something I did not want to hear.

"What else?" I asked.

"All of them," Jake began, his voice cracking. "Our friends. The drivers. They were executed this morning at dawn.

"The State Department has just confirmed it."

"Noooo," I keened softly. "How could this happen?"

This was the twenty-first century! This was Europe, the self-proclaimed bastion of civility and enlightenment. From all its capitals, there had been long and loud demonstrations against the United States for the abuses at Abu Ghraib, and now this? In what universe did making violent POWs parade naked with underwear on their heads compete with the outright slaughter of innocent humanitarian volunteers?

Where was the European Union's outrage now? If I opened the window next to my bed, would I hear demonstrators' shouts and wild harangues in the face of this atrocity, or would there be only silence and the unspoken opinion that the United States was merely getting its due?

Pain and despair welled up inside me, and I helplessly started to sob. I had a hundred questions to ask of Jake, a thousand, but I didn't want to hear the answers. I just wanted the diabolical reason for my utter sadness and devastation not to BE.

Jake rose and positioned himself cautiously on the edge of the bed. He clumsily wrapped me in his arms and slowly, sadly, let me succumb both to grief and to the narcotic numbness spreading through me.

In my last few moments of full lucidity, I posed a question to myself and to my God. How did it happen that I was alive and so blessed, when five of the finest people I knew lay dead?

TWENTY-SEVEN

I'd realized by the end of my sophomore year in college that a degree in microbiology was likely to mean a professional life lived in a laboratory or, assuming success, years of paperwork and personnel issues tackled from behind a desk.

I'd just finished organic chemistry and calculus—and all the torture those courses entailed—and the prospect of standing bent to the eyepiece of a microscope or solving impossible equations did not appeal. I needed daily human contact and the immediacy of knowing that the work I did was somehow helpful if I were going to be professionally fulfilled.

Over summer months spent waitressing in Old Orchard Beach and earning fistfuls of Canadian dollars as tips, I researched alternative careers. I visited the library at the University of Southern Maine and there devoured shelves of catalogs, and by the end of July, I'd discovered that the world of medicine offered several very viable career paths.

The fact that I didn't gross out easily qualified me for several, and given the jobs I'd already held, I knew I could get along with a wide variety of personalities. I could handle pressure. Finally, I was doing well, if not brilliantly, in school, my grade point average within a whisker of a 3.7 at last check. Some really great program out there would want me.

My research had also taught me that I didn't want to become a doctor. Finishing college; going to medical school; completing an internship and surviving a three to five year residency—all that was far too great a commitment of time and money for me.

The brutal years of internship and residency, in particular, would consume my life at a time when I hoped to be settling down. (Yes. I was forced to admit it. My mother had rubbed off on me.) While I admired those who could and would want to pursue medical degrees, in my heart of hearts I was absolutely convinced I wasn't one of them.

Of all the careers I seriously investigated that summer, becoming a physician's assistant seemed the best fit. The job title didn't sound like much, but the work involved seemed a good fit. It would make full use of my hard science background and allow me to interact closely with patients. The profession was portable, state licensing laws notwithstanding, and the range of salaries quoted would allow me to support myself quite nicely if the "unimaginable" happened, and I wound up living single indefinitely.

The one stumbling block to the plan I started hatching in the USM stacks?

The best p.a. programs liked to see applicants with hospital experience, preferably a year or two of it, before starting coursework. By my calculation, that meant I would be at least twenty-six before actually beginning my career, and therein lay the problem.

I didn't want to wait that long

I wanted my formal education done and over with, another four years total being my absolute limit. Toward that end, I made inquiries and grilled a succession of admissions counselors. Based on their advice, I left Maine two weeks early that summer, and the very moment I hit Boston again, started pouring over *Globe* Classifieds for a job that would give me a leg up on the rest of the applicant pool. Following the recommendation of a pre-med friend, I looked into getting work as a phlebotomist, and sure enough, three of Boston's world class hospitals were hiring.

I applied, was interviewed, and got a job drawing blood at Mass. General. For the next two years, I kept a full course load by day and haunted hospital hallways evenings and weekends. Over twenty-four months, I raised my average by two tenths of a grade point—not an easy feat—and worked my way from phlebotomist to technician to full-fledged med. tech. By the time I was accepted into the program at Wake, I had no doubt at all that I'd found my life's work.

I thought I found my life's love at Mass. General as well.

I was a first semester junior, ambitious and fun-loving, when I met Blue-Eyed Joe, a fourth year medical student just beginning his required rotations through the services. Where his peers ran the gamut from painfully insecure to abhorrently egotistical, Joe was poised and eager to do anything that his supervising interns, residents, or attendings required of him. He weathered the hokey practical jokes inflicted on him, even saying good-naturedly, "You got it!" when his chief resident ordered, "Hey. Joe. Run down to the lab and get us a dozen fallopian tubes!"

Joe Franklin was cute, rather than handsome, and he was incredibly farm-boy fit. He biked everywhere he could, had a vicious tennis serve, and he never encountered a piano whose keys he could resist. Given his affability and good manners, he quickly endeared himself to co-workers and patients. Pretty much everyone loved seeing him show up on the ward, especially the little old ladies in wheelchairs who called after him, "Doctor Franklin," though by all rights he had almost a year to go before earning the title legitimately.

In the early days, neither Joe nor I had much time or money, so dating was sporadic and cheap. Stolen Saturday nights out for pizza or a late movie; Sunday afternoons picnicking on the grassy hillsides above the Charles. We spent hours in conversation at his place or mine, the time together punctuated with great kisses and handholding and the hopes for our happy lives.

In fairness, I don't think either one of us actually ever mentioned the "L" word, but for all intents and purposes, we were in it up to our eyes.

By the time I packed up my rented room, leaving for North Carolina, Joe was in the throes of his residency at New Hampshire's Dartmouth-Hitchcock. Our goodbyes came in a telephone conversation, quickly and with restraint, the two of us aware that we had years of hard work ahead and a thousand miles of highway to keep us apart.

We made no promises, and over the years that followed responsibilities and lack of time off eroded what remained of our feelings. We gradually drifted away from the couple we had been, toward something else.

In Joe's case, I suspected, someone else.

My first spring in Washington, we reconnected. Joe was close to finishing his residency and was planning to go home again to Kansas that July. "Twelve years away," he said tiredly. "I'm ready."

"I know I've had enough of winter." Which in the granite state wasn't officially over until May. "I called in the hundred and one favors I've done for all these ingrates the last four years," his classmates. "And I've strung together a whopping five days off.

"Mind if I come down your way for Easter?"

"Nothing would make me happier." The words, spoken wistfully, were true. It would be good to see Joseph Frederick Franklin again.

Search his eyes.

Confirm the suspicions roused in me by the occasional and inadvertent slip that somewhere back in Kansas, the sweet and pretty girl he'd loved in high school was living for his return.

Hanging up the phone, I had known I still had feelings for Joe. I loved his gentle humor; his perpetually lopsided smile; the twinkle in his blue eyes when he was caught being mischievous. I mourned the fact that those qualities and others would be filling another woman's life soon.

Another family's life.

Still, I threw open my front door to him on a sunny April day, saying "Get in here, you hot dog!" And after hugs and mutual exclamations of, "Hey, you look great," he stood on the threshold of my Alexandria garden apartment and handed me his wish list.

"Arlington National Cemetery," I read.

"The Vietnam Memorial.

"The Holocaust Museum.

"If you want a death tour of the nation's capital," I said impishly, "I believe you missed Ford's Theater."

"The list's not as macabre as it looks," he laughed. "I just want to pay my respects."

His great Uncle Jeb had been a World War II pilot shot down over Germany toward the end of the war. "Family lore has it that he spent time in the concentration camps, but he never talked about it.

"He was buried at Arlington a few years ago," Joe continued. "My folks couldn't come for the ceremony, so I want to visit for them."

That was Joe.

We made Arlington our first stop, then, and afterward drove into the city to visit the Vietnam Memorial where he made a rubbing for the father of a friend. The next day, Good Friday, we toured the Holocaust Museum together, and while the timing might've seemed strange, I came away feeling the timing couldn't have been more appropriate.

We rode the elevator to the top floor, as required by the museum staff, and joined the crowd of visitors exploring the maze of somber and poignant exhibits. We stood silent in the semi-darkness of rooms recreated in ghastly detail. We saw a railway car that once had transported the doomed and wooden bunks where innocents had slept and cried and wondered if the cruelty of their earthly trials would ever end. We listened to recordings of Hitler's maniacal rants. In no other single place before (or since) had I ever seen greater proof of man's total and undeniable turning from God.

While contemporary thought proposed the basic and fundamental goodness of man, seeing the artifacts of Nazi malevolence, I was convinced that the human race had an indisputable propensity for evil and was in many ways recalcitrant.

In the diaries of Jews long since dead; in hair cut from the heads of death camp residents and sold by the Nazis to felt factories; in the faces and bodies of mentally handicapped youngsters stripped naked for Nazi cameras before being led to tortures and deaths devoid of all decency, there existed incontrovertible evidence of man's capacity for sin and proof to me of the crying and eternal need for God's intervention in human affairs.

Conversely, if I'd ever doubted the existence of redemptive good in the world, my reaction to the museum assured me, I never would again.

Joe and I spent more than an hour listening to Holocaust survivors' stories preserved on film and featured as part of the tour's final stop. We saw how, in the midst of evil, good had blossomed and heard described the rare and courageous acts performed by both Jews and Gentiles who risked their lives saving others'. The accounts were the face of God in the bleakest moral times.

On the subway ride back to Virginia, Joe and I marveled at the spirit of forgiveness that had permeated the testimonials. These people, these survivors, would've had the complete right to exact revenge, yet most exhibited palpable joy at having lived. At having gone on to create beautiful families. At having loved.

Over dinner, Joe and I had resurrected the habit we had of praying together, thanking God that "somehow" a madman had been stopped. Years later, lying in my Austrian hospital bed, I remembered my time with Joe and wondered what it would take to stop the madman wreaking havoc a hundred miles away?

Who would stop him?

Maybe it would be men like Matthias and Akos and Adam, people who loved God and their country more than their narrow, quotidian interests; individuals who knew what it meant to put others' well being above their own and lived that generosity every day.

Practically speaking, the duty was theirs; the liberty being threatened, theirs. Stopping Bacenko was an endeavor they alone could rightfully lead and struggle through, though we—as their friends and comrades—could encourage, support and pray for them at a distance.

I closed my eyes. Tiredly, I wept for those three fine men and for all the others who would probably have to sacrifice their lives in setting things right. I felt my utter human powerlessness and prayed for a world where people could both recognize and own up to the power of decency and good.

I prayed for contemporaries turning their backs not only to religion but to faith, and I hoped one day they would understand the wisdom of a life lived in God's authentic righteousness. That they would understand what that concept even meant.

It wasn't the end of fun or enjoyment or competition. Legitimate goodness just meant remembering the source of our bounty and our responsibilities to those less fortunate. That failing, I asked they might see the value of using the Commandments as a foundation for decency, for lives made infinitely more bearable by genuine kindness.

My mind drifted back to the stories of survival I'd heard at the Holocaust Museum and to the faces of those who'd shared them. Those speakers had moved beyond the cruelty visited upon them by the Nazis and had gone on to build good lives.

Recent studies showed that those who made the deliberate decision to abandon vengefulness lived the happiest and most fulfilled of lives, while those who'd dwelled on the worst in life, who played painful events over and over again in their minds and couldn't seem to accept the beauty of a new day and new possibilities, they were the ones who reported the least satisfaction with life, often contemplating putting an end to it themselves.

Evidently there was value in truisms. "Don't cry over spilled milk." "Where there's a will, there's a way." "Today is the first day of the rest of your life." The thematic thread running through the expressions was the same: you had to MOVE on to fully LIVE on.

Which was precisely what Jake and Rand and I would have to do.

I would weep and mourn my lost friends, I knew that. But I wouldn't let myself drift into acrimony or bitterness because of their senseless deaths. When I got home, I'd seek out their husbands and wives and children. I'd introduce myself to the friends who'd loved them and make sure they knew how hard our colleagues had worked. How they'd thrown them- selves body, soul, and laughter, into the commit- ment they'd made.

Just as surely, I wouldn't let myself be drawn into the call—and I strongly suspected it would come—to attack a nation and its rogue leadership, the more pugilistic among Americans believing we should nuke innocent and guilty alike into the next century.

That kind of action would be the greatest sadness of all.

TWENTY-EIGHT

The State Department did its due diligence notifying my parents and assuring my worry-mad mother that all was well. A polite young man supplied a Washington number through which she could be connected to my hospital room, and he wisely reminded her of the time difference. "Call when it's midday there, ma'am. About five a.m. your time."

Predictably Mom did so much more. She shared the number with my siblings, so it was my brothers and their sleepy wives with whom I spoke first. The women were soft-spoken and sympathetic, while the males, my flesh and blood, expressed words of incredulity and admiration followed by a (predictable) *soupçon* of their abuse. Brad's was the most egregious comment, "Anything for a little attention, eh squirt!"

I doubted he'd heard yet of my colleagues' deaths.

Nephews and my one niece Annabelle, roused from sleep, whispered shy hellos on portable extensions, and they closed their short conversations with me by saying, "Miss you, *Tante* Parry. Love you."

The words, though likely coerced, warmed my heart.

They reminded me I hadn't seen the little urchins enough.

Played with them enough.

Loved them enough.

I echoed their sentiments, saying softly, "Love you guys, too."

My mother and father called well past my dinner hour. Mom started out by expressing her relief that I'd escaped that "crazy country" with just a broken leg. She quickly degenerated into subtle demands that I verify details of news reports coming out on MSNBC.

I couldn't bring myself to corroborate them, and pretty soon she realized she might've gone too far. "Sorry, Parry," she said. "I guess this must be hard."

I sighed and said truthfully, "I hope you never have to know," the sorrow in my voice convincing her it might be best to stop the inquisition.

We spoke about how I was feeling and when I thought I might come home. "You gonna need help?" she asked, and in that moment I thought how wonderful it was she was offering.

"I will. We can talk when I know, when they tell me I can go."

Signing off, Mom gave me what she believed were words of encouragement. "CNN says the President may send in troops."

My heart fell.

More lives on the line. Potentially, many more young people lost.

I told both my parents goodbye and heard Dad, quiet so far, getting out words I had never heard cross his lips. "Love you, *fille*."

In the face of his candor, I confessed, "I can't wait to come home."

I realized only after I hung up, that my parents and I had different ideas of where that was for me now. For sure, it wasn't northern Virginia, with its affluence and ambition and perpetual gridlock; I had never once felt connected to the area filled with transplants and transients. And, while Maine was the place I would always be from, I knew intuitively I might never set down roots there again.

The valley of my forbearers, two hundred miles from the nearest small city, was too far removed from the things, the places, and the people among whom I felt most comfortable now, though the state's southern reaches held promise. I loved the sea, there, and the sky. The wind blowing cold out of Canada. A small summer place there sounded good, but I had outgrown the habit of "doing" New England winters.

My mind strayed to Winston-Salem, to the easy cadences of genteel Southern speech and the colors of the region's early and spectacular spring. Delicate redbud. The piercing hot pinks of prized azaleas. The frothy whitecaps of dogwood and flowering pears whose appearance transformed neighborhoods into fairylands.

I'd loved my life in North Carolina; my work. Friends still called and e-mailed me regularly from Raleigh or Charlotte or Wilmington, urging me to come back to the Tar Heel state.

Could I make a move happen in the face of this debacle?

Would I want to?

Would there be any way to sell my condo with the northern Virginia real estate market still in free fall?

Before I could answer the questions plaguing me, my evening nurse bustled in. "Time for sleep," she announced, and I agreed.

I needed respite from the endless voices demanding to know.

At my nurse's behest, I brushed and flossed, and secretly reveled in the underappreciated glories of mint. She helped me to the bathroom and afterward settled me into bed. As she got ready to hit me with my sleep meds, I told her, "Go ahead. Give me the full deal." I wanted to slumber. To dream. To wake up tomorrow to find that the events of the last few days had just been a frightening dream.

On the floor above mine, Rand struggled. He showed signs of recovery one moment and the next, was in trouble again. His kidneys. His lungs. The effects of sepsis subsided one day and made frightening inroads the next.

I still wasn't traveling all that well, and the doctors were hesitant to allow Rand too many visitors, so I relied on Jake for progress reports.

"It's bad," he told me the morning after Rand's parents arrived. "His skin's mottled red and white. A couple of his fingers are swollen and black . . ."

Rand was delusional half the time.

Classic septicemia, I thought. Very scary.

Jake was discharged from the hospital our third full day in Vienna, but my doctors decided I should remain another few days to build up my strength. My appetite hadn't returned, and I wasn't eating nearly enough to recoup.

"I'd be fine in a hotel," I assured them.

"We need to watch for infection," my surgeon told me flatly. "And we are in charge."

On our fifth day in hospital, Rand began to show small but incontrovertible signs of improvement. No amputations would be necessary, his doctors told us warily, but he wasn't out of danger yet.

They transferred him to the equivalent of an American step-down unit and very closely watched his vitals, most especially his erratic kidney function. Jake took me to visit Rand's first morning on the ward.

He smiled weakly at the sight of us. "Parise St. Amand. Jake Spangler," he acknowledged. "These are my parents, Richard and Elizabethe Szabo."

His parents rose from their vigil and welcomed us like family, hugging and profusely thanking us for all we'd done. "If there is anything at all you need," Rand's mother said. "Do not hesitate to ask."

"Thank you," Jake said for both of us. "All we really need is for this lug to get well."

"Yes, yes, you're right," Elizabeth Szabo said tearfully. "We wish the same thing."

Rand's parents excused themselves after we settled, saying, "We must have our morning tea." In fact, they were allowing us a few private moments alone with their son.

Jake and I had discussed the wisdom of telling Rand the full truth of what had happened, and while we agreed we should at some point, my preference had been to wait before revealing the worst of it.

Seeing him so frail and gaunt against the blinding white of the hospital sheets, I was more convinced than ever that we should hold off. Tubes snaked from Rand's arm, his abdomen, and from an orifice better left unnamed. He was in no shape to hear information there was no easy or kind way to impart.

Jake had conferenced with Rand's parents and with his doctors by telephone that morning, and together they'd reached the determination, in spite of many reservations, that it might be best to affect full disclosure. "It's too difficult, now that he's fully conscious," Jake told me, "for staff to monitor all the possible avenues of news and information that could reveal the information too abruptly."

So it was that as the elder Szabos closed the door on our forlorn little trio, Jake quietly took on the role of spokesman. Laid out what we knew of the story.

"All of them?" Rand asked when Jake had finished. "They're all gone?"

"Paul made it out," Jake repeated. "His blood sugar was dangerously low by the time he got to help, and it took a couple of days to get him stabilized, but he's recovered."

"He flew home two days ago from Budapest," I added.

"The others? Their bodies were identified?"

"Through an international aid agency," Jake told him. "Copies of their passports were faxed to the State Department."

"When will they be returned?"

"State is negotiating, but nothing so far."

I thought of Linda's family and Bev's childless widower. Of other spouses and children and elderly parents for whom the loss had to be incomprehensible.

"How could Bacenko be so crazy?" Rand asked in an echo of my earlier thoughts. "And so cruel. We were only there to help."

"We've heard he paints all his enemies with the same broad strokes of hate," Jake told him. "There's no real logic to what he's doing."

"What will I say to their families?" Rand asked. "What is there to say?"

I took his hand. "You can work on that later," I told him. "For now, you need to concentrate on getting well." Advice I was sure he'd already heard many times, in many forms. As a word of comfort, if there was one, I added, "We all knew the dangers, Rand."

"I downplayed them."

"Maybe. But we were all adults."

I consciously used the past tense.

"We knew there was a chance that something like this could happen. . ." Jake insisted, and he was right. No matter that Rand would try to take the responsibility on himself for this gross miscarriage, he had to know we'd all been worldly enough to understand that the United States had enemies.

Some outspoken.

Others hidden.

This had become a world in which anyone with a grudge or a devotion to fanaticism could maim and kill at will. It behooved any and everyone to travel with care, no matter the destination.

"I'll do everything I can to make this right," Rand said with determination.

"We all will," I told him. This wasn't a burden fit for a dangerously sick man. I leaned in to hug him and was shocked at how little of Rand remained. "You need to eat," I said, pulling away.

This wasn't the robust man I loved to hate.

"Got any of that jerky left?" he joked.

"Fresh out. Some ingrate ate the last of our stock."

A current of forgiveness and affection passed between us. "If that's what you want, though, Jake here could probably find some."

He smiled. "Hospital food will do."

After a round of hugs, we left him. I went back to my room and Jake to his nearby hotel.

I bugged my surgeon again the following day to let me go home. "I won't have anything to carry except what I'm wearing," I cajoled.

Well, that and my passport. Jake had had the presence of mind, on our arrival in Vienna, to ask for our boots and a pair of scissors. He'd excised our documents, saving us the hurdle of getting new ones.

"See my new outfit!" I asked, holding up my good leg and the new, roomy exercise pants Rand's mother had graciously purchased for me. She bought shirts, workout clothes and underwear. All size medium. "I want you to be comfortable," she'd explained. "I hope I guessed right."

Everything was roomy, but better that than tight.

"I promise to ask for a wheel chair as soon as we get to the airport. And I won't overdo. Jake will do all the heavy lifting."

And pushing.

"I don't know, Mademoiselle St. Amand. It is a risk."

"I'll get excellent follow-up care at home," I assured him. "I work for a group of orthopedic surgeons."

"Do you?"

Hadn't anyone told him?

"You will promise to take every precaution?"

"I promise."

"You must be careful not to remain stationary for long periods. You are young but not immune to emboli."

"I understand. I'll get up from my seat at least once an hour."

"Drink fluids. Sit with your leg elevated as much as you can."

"Done and done."

Reluctantly, he agreed that I could go home.

Jake and I had to wait two interminable days to be able to get seats together on a non-stop flight. We stopped in to visit Rand on the way to the airport.

"I walked this morning," he told us proudly.

"With help," his mother reminded him.

Still an achievement. He was also down to two IVs.

"You'll call when you get back," I said, extracting a vow.

"I wouldn't think not to," Rand said with genuine warmth.

He and Jake shook hands, and I embraced him. Felt his ribs and bony shoulders.

"Good luck getting through the hordes," he said as we headed for the hall, and immediately we understood the reference.

There had to be over a hundred reporters camped out at the entrance to the hospital — all trying for the first exclusive photos of us. Statements. They'd been pestering staff and checking all visitors against unrecognizable DMV mug shots, for days demanding information.

So far they'd only gotten the occasional bone from a spokesman, and nothing he said led anywhere.

"They won't be a problem," Jake informed Rand. "The Embassy has a car waiting for us in the physicians' underground lot, and the driver's trained in evasive maneuvers.

"I bet they never get a peek."

The dam of privacy would hold.

"Thank you both for everything," Rand said again. "I'm forever indebted."

This new humility was remarkable.

"We owe you, too," Jake answered honestly. Rand had pushed himself beyond endurance helping Jake save me. There was valor and gratitude enough to go around.

We easily slipped from the hospital grounds and at the airport, were treated to a first class upgrade. "Rand insisted. He felt it was the least he could provide since we never got those deluxe accommodations in Budapest."

"I'll have to thank him when he gets home."

I was one of a few passengers allowed to board first. I settled into bulkhead seating, and when he arrived, Jake helped prop my leg before dropping into the seat next to mine. It wasn't long before attendants were offering appetizers and a selection of wines; giving us fragrant, heated towels to use freshening up.

After dinner had been served and the lights of the plane dimmed to make movie viewing more enjoyable, Jake leaned in close. At my request, he revealed what had happened to us in our last few hours on the trail. We hadn't talked about that yet.

"Do you remember Rand setting your leg?"

"I'll always remember Rand setting my leg. That and how much pain the two of you caused flipping me over." There weren't enough apologies in the world to make that memory recede.

He waited for my accusation to subside. He continued, admitting, "I don't know how Rand managed to do everything he did, Maybe explaining every move to me as he performed it helped his concentration. Helped him ignore his own pain.

"He was practically out of it minutes before you fell."

I knew that. I'd seen him.

"Seeing you down on the ground like that. All contorted. He snapped to."

He paused before adding, "I really underestimated the man."

"We both did."

Jake started up again. "Somehow, he got himself back up the hill to you. We rolled you over, which you know. He checked your pulses and the feeling in your toes. He realigned 'them bones.'"

"I was too busy screaming to thank him."

"You did fine," Jake reassured me. "Considering."

"What did you use as a splint?" I asked, just then realizing I didn't know.

"We broke apart your snowshoes and used the shafts and a couple of scarves to stabilize the leg."

I did have a vague memory of that.

"After your leg was set, Rand and I improvised on the idea you'd suggested earlier."

"What idea was that?" I had so many.

"We got you on the toboggan, then sat right down on the rock slide and inched our way down on our rumps."

I did remember, both the idea and later the excruciating pain I'd suffered when Rand and Jake implemented it.

The incremental movements.

My protracted cries as I called assorted saints down from heaven.

It was a miracle we hadn't been detected and arrested on the spot.

Jake confessed, "It was a real juggling act.

"We sat the toboggan between us and used our hands to keep it steady. I sat at the foot end, and Rand got up by your head. We used our feet for braking power."

"That couldn't have felt very good for Rand."

"I don't imagine it did."

It had taken them over an hour to reach the bottom of the slide. "The toboggan was scratched all to hell," Jake told me. "Our clothes were soaked and muddy and ripped in a hundred places."

He explained that once on flat terrain they'd slowly started walking again.

"It took relatively little time getting to the border, but we didn't know that going in. Every second we were on the move, we were expecting soldiers to rise up out of the ground.

"I kept that gun of Matthias' handy the whole, entire time."

"I hope you had the safety on."

"You got that right."

"So what was it like? How long did it take you??"

"We didn't see any low-flying aircraft, and not a single soldier. There wasn't even a fence to climb getting into Austria."

Borders were quite permeable in this new age of peace.

"After all we'd gone through, the crossing was completely uneventful.

"Rand gave you a second shot of Demerol somewhere on the trail, and you didn't come to until well after the call."

"The call?"

"For help."

I wondered how we'd come to be rescued but had neglected to ask.

"We had almost no charge left in the phone by the time we were safely inside Austria, and we had to get somebody on the horn. With Rand in the shape he was in, there was no way we were gonna make it to the train.

"We spent about twenty minutes in a pissing contest over what next move should be. I lobbied to call the American Embassy or the Consulate in Vienna. I had those numbers with me.

"Rand dismissed both ideas out of hand.

"'Don't be naïve,' he said. 'It'll take a half dozen transfers before we get to the right person. We don't have that much battery time left.'"

"I practically threw the thing at him. 'You're so smart,' I yelled. 'Do your thing!'"

Rand had programmed a long list of useful numbers into the phone, and it took a single call to the Chairman of the Senate Foreign Relations

Committee, a family friend, to make the wheels of rescue turn.

"I couldn't believe it," Jake said with newfound admiration for Rand. "He gave some guy our GPS coordinates and within three minutes, I swear, we got confirmation that help was on its way.

"They said it was gonna take a couple of hours to get a team together and to fly from the nearest base, but 'the cavalry' was coming."

"Or maybe the Air Force," I suggested.

"Same difference."

Hunkered down, Jake had gathered wood, and Rand had given me the last few drops of Demerol by injection. "There couldn't a been much left in the bottle, and I told him maybe he should give himself that last dose.

"He was hurting bad.

"Wouldn't hear of it. Gave it to you before I could say another word, and the two of us wrapped you up tight in a sleeping bag. You'd lost blood. He was worried you'd go into shock if we didn't keep you warm.

"Once he was sure you were set, he climbed into the one ratty sleeping bag that was left and asked me to wake him up in a half hour, forty-five minutes so he could check on you. Then he laid right down on the snow and passed out cold."

Jake had gotten more wood and built a fire. "A huge roaring thing," he explained. "I knew I had to keep the two of you from freezing. There was another cold front moving in.

"I figured it'd give the helo a visual fix, too, if for some reason the coordinates had gotten messed up. The rest you pretty much know."

I hesitated before asking the question that had been bothering me for a while. "Do you think the worst of this is over?"

He looked at me and said with candor, "Probably not.

"Between the media and angry relatives, this nightmare could drag on a while."

TWENTY-NINE

On the matter of newspapers, television, and assorted magazines, Jake was both right and wrong.

During our first few days back, the press was perpetually encamped on the sidewalk along my complex's property line and at the opening to his *cul-de-sac*. They kept vigil 24/7 waiting for us to appear and face the cameras.

Fortunately, Jake was practiced in outsmarting pursuers. He donned different jackets and hats and sunglasses as he came to and from my building. He parked blocks away and ran into the complex like a man training for a marathon one day, parked a rental car in a guest space under the building and used my SUV going out again on errands other days.

He shopped for groceries, collected my accumulated mail from the building concierge and later, sorting through it, gently lectured me on the merits of online bill payment. To that end, he helped me negotiate utility and credit card websites, all the while lauding the savings in time and energy that using them would mean.

"You know, Parry, you're an old soul," he observed one morning as I resisted another foray into technology.

"No," I corrected. "I'm a slightly cynical soul. Reliance on computers and electronics is going to bite us."

He grinned. "It already has, my dear. And whole new industries have emerged to deal with it."

"I know. I know."

"You do understand that if people are determined to steal, it doesn't matter much what technology you use. They find a way."

"It's a matter of scale," I volleyed back.

"And preparedness."

Ultimately, we agreed to disagree, and then did things Jake's way— a pattern that was beginning to concern me.

The day before my mother was due to arrive, Jake offered to clean the condo to my precise specifications. I'd mentioned a time, or twenty, that Patricia Ann St. Amand loved and lived for a spotless home. "She's not going to care that I've been out of the country or out of commission for over two weeks.

"Her dust and dirt radar will be up and running the minute she walks through that door." But there was good news. "As soon as she finishes the white glove inspection, she'll get back to being human again.

"She just has this thing about first impressions."

"No problem," he told me. "You just sit back and relax."

I was happy my mother was coming to see me through my first couple of weeks back, her high housekeeping standards notwithstanding. But I was disappointed that my father had chosen not to make the trip. While being fed and fussed over by Mom would be a treat after years of being on my own, what I yearned for, if just for a minute or two, were Dad's strong arms hugging me and his voice reassuring me, the same way it had when I fell off my bike or tore open my knee as a kid, "Everything's going to be all right."

Wasn't gonna happen.

Dad had long deferred to Mom in things child-related. It was a tactic that made his life easier and helped avoid disruptions to his sacrosanct evening routine of dinner, drinks, and sack time in front of the television.

My father loved us, and we, his children, had always known it. We were also aware that he gave the best of his time and talents to the job, and that if we wanted anything more from him than room, board, and the occasional show of affection, it had better be achievable from the living room sofa or we were out of luck.

He was the same way with his grandchildren.

When they visited, he lay back in his recliner issuing orders, and they did his bidding. Combed his hair, rubbed his feet, gladly fetched cookies and ice cream for a bedtime snack. They adored him, and he, them.

So, yes. Mom had been the practical choice to serve as my right hand, or more precisely, my left leg, during recovery. She was the one who would jump in, do the cooking, the cleaning, and the carting of my handicapped bod to the doctor's office, all the while decrying northern Virginia traffic and the drivers who made it infinitely worse indulging their sick addiction to cell phones.

Jake took cleaning a little too far. At least five times the day before Mom flew in, I told him to cease and desist, but he wouldn't quit. He washed the floors, the windows, and all the kitchen appliances, inside and out. He straightened the books in my library and beyond what I'd asked of him, found a hundred small ways to make the place look less lived in.

Frankly I was a little irked by his persistence. "I don't like all the toxicity," I said when I saw the cleaning products he'd purchased. "Really. A little Murphy's oil soap for the floors. A little Comet in the sinks. Vinegar and water for the windows."

I wanted to live the month to my thirtieth birthday.

"You go to your room, open a window, and take a nap," he advised. "I'll get the job done."

Gimpy and grumpy, I hobbled away.

Jake went out to Dulles to pick up my mother the next day, and it didn't surprise me, based on their mutual fondness for fastidiousness, that they bonded on the short drive from the airport. Mom's first words, as Jake left that night after dinner, were, "Where DID you find that boy?"

The need to be needed helped my mother adapt quickly to her new environment and responsibilities. Where once she'd hated visiting me, she seemed completely at ease running the gauntlet of reporters and negotiating the city streets she'd once feared. Her second day in Virginia, she picked up the dry cleaning, hit the library for reading supplies, and bravely chauffeured me the twenty-nine miles, one way, to the office where Geoff and Sam briefly skirmished over the issue of who would provide follow-up care for my injured leg.

"Why don't I alternate seeing each of you," I suggested as I boosted myself onto the examining table.

They looked at each other and shrugged.

Geoff declared, "Patient knows best," and watched as Sam showed himself the door.

Standing at his office view box, Geoff reviewed my records and latest films. He checked my knee then my ankle. Put the leg through a few maneuvers.

"You're doing pretty well," he announced. "But maybe you shouldn't plan on coming back to work until after the holidays. This is a serious injury."

Was he kidding? I'd go nuts.

I sat up and swung both legs off the table. "If I could be out that long, I would," I told him. "But I don't have enough sick time accumulated. Why don't I come in, say, next Monday, and start seeing patients here in the clinic."

"Not necessary," Geoff answered. "You take the time off. We'll spot you."

My eyes opened wide. "Do the accountants know you're playing Santa? Does the staff?"

Geoff was infamous for blaming the firm of Anderson and Mills every time he instituted a change aimed at improving the partners' bottom line. I doubted they'd agreed to this ill-advised outlay of cash. Anything that smacked of favoritism, moreover, would disrupt the office's fragile social equilibrium.

"Everyone's fine with it. You just go home and get some rest," he ordered a second time. "Your films look great. Your man in Vienna did a superb job. If you stay on track, we'll be able to take out your hardware ahead of schedule."

It was Rand who'd done the great job, I thought, and under daunting conditions. The doctors in Vienna had just built on his expertise. I didn't argue the point.

"Guess I'll have to find a way to stay busy," I said, zipping up the side of my warm-up pants. I got down from the table without help but stumbled as I started toward the door.

Geoff reached out a hand to steady me. "Here, sit down a sec. It's all right to take a breather."

"No thanks. I'm good to go." I knew when I wasn't wanted.

Jake came over that night at my mother's invitation. He was handsome dressed in a crisp white shirt, tailored slacks, and a tie that my mother fawned over.

"Jerry Garcia," he said when I asked about the brand. "I've had it forever."

Must have. The Grateful Dead singer had been, well, dead, for quite some time.

Hearing about Geoff's offer of protracted time off, Jake asked, "You are going to use the time for R&R, right?"

"Not really," Mom said, betraying me. "I caught her cleaning out her walk-in closet this afternoon."

In fact, I'd just been messing with the meticulous job Jake had done on it the day before. The order in there had me spooked.

"I need to get some activity going," I fibbed. "I feel atrophy setting in."

I was getting claustrophobic having Jake over so often, not a good sign. I was the kind of person who chafed when people imposed themselves on me. I liked my time alone.

I had too little time to think. To read. To ponder matters of great import which, for the last few days, meant I kept asking myself if there had been something more we could've done to prevent our friends' tragic end. Some legitimate avenue that, in our rush, we hadn't explored.

I also played over in my mind what I might say when I met the people who'd loved my friends. What I'd do to console them.

I hated that there'd been no contact among us.

Initially, I'd agreed with Jake that it might be best to wait until Rand was home and on the mend before we made overtures, and that it would probably be best to reach out as a group, together with Paul. Now I was beginning to feel that our hesitation was ill-advised and inadequate.

I revisited the decision with Jake that night while Mom was cleaning up. "I want to call them," I said simply.

"Call who?"

"The families."

"It's really not up to us," Jake insisted. "The bodies haven't been returned. We aren't in charge. Matthias and Rand made the call. It's appropriate they answer for it."

Ah, a chain of command guy.

"I know there isn't much we can do," I said. "But as a human being, I know I would want to meet the people who'd last been with the person I loved. To hear how they'd been. What they'd done."

Jake didn't respond. Instead, he suggested, "What do you say we grab some lunch in Middleburg tomorrow. Get some fresh air. I think I like the idea of spending my last day off miles from the Fourth Estate." Reporters were still hounding both our landlines and our cells.

"You're going back to work?"

"Yep. My boss tried to keep me away for my 'own good,' but I prevailed."

Somehow that didn't surprise me.

"So what do you say? We could do a little driving through horse country. Maybe figure out where the celebrities live."

Cissy Spacek. Kate Jackson. Duvall in The Plains. They were mostly actors whose heyday had come and gone, but I remembered them. Or remembered my parents mentioning them.

"You know, I don't think I'm in the mood," I told him honestly.

"We could stay in the downtown. Have lunch. Buy you something nice."

"Something overpriced . . ." I responded. The first pair of Spanx I'd ever bought had cost me almost $40 in a shop there. They were nineteen at my favorite discount clothing store.

Mom weighed in from the kitchen. "It would be good for you, Parise. Go with the man!"

I equivocated, "We'll see."

She appeared with a gooey dessert a few minutes later, even though Jake and I insisted we were full. After overindulging, the three of us beached ourselves on the living room furniture to watch a movie.

Seeing Jake out later, I laid it on the line. "You know, Jake, I don't think Middleburg's what I need. Maybe another time."

"You sure?"

"I'm sure. I'm not really ready to get out there." Not ready for the F-U-N that had seemed a good idea not long ago.

He hugged me goodbye and kissed my cheek. He searched my face as though expecting to find some revelation there. "Anything I can do to help lift you out of this funk you seem to be in?"

I hesitated. "Get me a few phone numbers?"

"For?"

"The families."

"I thought we'd let that go."

He had.

"I haven't."

"Parry, it's not our place." Spoken with finality.

"Fine. Not OUR place. But maybe it's mine. I'll accept responsibility for overstepping, if it comes to that."

He didn't respond.

"There are only a few numbers I couldn't get from 411 or the Internet white pages. But I've decided I don't want to call anyone if I can't call everyone."

"You're stubborn," he observed.

Was that a smile I saw playing at the corners of his mouth?

He thought I was completely off base putting myself in the middle of other people's pain, and still he was considering helping me.

For my part, I was counting on him to relent, but that really wasn't fair. I was using the feelings he had for me. Feelings I didn't share.

Shame, too. He was exactly the kind of man to whom I should have been attracted. He was strong. For the most part thoughtful. And I had seen firsthand that he was good at what he did—exemplary—and he knew who he was and what he believed.

Alas, I had dated the type before, and while I was comfortable with it, I had invariably moved on. There was something claustrophobia-inducing about them. Something that made me feel at the same time safe but really, really smothered.

"I'd really appreciate your help."

"I'll see what I can do."

I gave his cheek a soft kiss and leaned out the door, watching as he walked to the elevator. I waved goodbye as the doors slid shut.

"What a nice young man," my mother opined as I came back inside. She winked and said, "You could do worse."

"That's an underwhelming endorsement."

"You know what I mean," she sing-songed as she headed for bed. "Tick-tock."

"Good night to you, too," I said, pitching my latest *Atlantic Monthly* in her direction.

She ducked and disappeared.

I turned off lights and bolted the door.

Alone in my room, I fed CDs into the player. Turned down the lights and stared out the wall of windows into a foggy night. When my cell phone purred on the bedside table, I hoped it wasn't Jake calling from the car to revisit his Middleburg invitation. I flipped open the phone and seeing a D.C. number, I thought maybe it was a friend working third shift calling to check in. Despite the late hour, I answered. "Parry St. Amand."

"Hello."

The voice was familiar but fainter than I remembered. "Rand?"

"The one and only."

"How are you feeling?" I asked. "When did you get back?"

"Still weak," he replied to my first question. "But they tell me I'm getting better. Well enough to fly home I guess.

"We got in a little while ago; I'm staying with the folks." His breathlessness was pronounced as he finished speaking.

"You should be resting," I advised. "With the time change, you must be exhausted . . ." In Vienna, it was the middle of the night. I glanced at the clock. No, almost morning. "How was your flight?"

"Long."

"We thought so, too."

"I wanted to find out how you and Jake were doing."

"I'm lurching around the condo, and my mother's here." I told him. "You know how that goes."

"Nothing like a Mom to soothe our hurts."

Spoken like a true and only son.

There was quiet on both ends of the connection, then Rand said, "Look, Parry. I wanted to apologize again for being such a pain, you know, those few days on the trail."

"Only then?"

"Hey," he said mildly. "I'm trying to show a little contrition here."

"Sorry," I said. "Apology accepted. But you have to know, helping save my leg, maybe even my life, you more than made up for the annoying things you said and did."

"Are you sure? Because I'm sensing a little hostility."

Who knew? He'd grown a tiny sense of humor.

I took a moment to reflect and remember. "Wait. There were a couple of comments I could've lived without at the airport. And several times on the ward, I believe you came off as snippy.

"Oh, and at the orphanage that time . . ."

"I get the picture, Ms. St. Amand. *Mea culpa. A thousand mea culpas.*"

"But is that enough?"

Now came the laugh. Not quite hearty but definitely more than a chuckle.

"Actually, your question, while not especially gracious, helps me segue into the second reason for my call. I wanted to remind you that I'm going to reimburse you and Jake for the gear you lost on the trip and the expenses you incurred getting back."

"And for your sick time."

"Now you're talkin'," I teased, like the mercenary I was.

"Showing your true colors," he mocked. "I should've known."

"All right. Truce. Seriously Rand, you don't have to do any of that."

"I want to. In fact, I already called and talked to Geoff about your time off."

"And?"

"I'm covering you until after New Year's. It's the least I can do to help you fully recover."

Soooo. Good old Geoff had shaded the truth to make himself look good. Now that was a shock.

"That's too generous . . ." I started to protest.

"There's no negotiating this, Parry. I've made arrangements. I'll still need you to send me a list of the things you lost and a rough estimate of the replacement costs."

Sparks of the old, bossy Rand.

"And don't underestimate. I want to see current market value for clothes, shoes. toiletries. Those handsome carry-ons of yours . . ."

"You don't have enough money to compensate me for those suitcases."

"Try me."

"All right," I allowed. "I just might."

The business side of things settled, Rand offered new information. "Paul and Matthias supplied a few details when I was finally able to get in touch," he told me. "But I won't go into it unless . . ."

"No," I said. "Tell me. I want to know."

He sighed deeply, and I thought I heard him shift. "Well, after they were taken into custody," he still couldn't say their names, "they were hand-cuffed and taken to local jails. I guess security was pretty lax, the overthrow and the government still so new. That's probably why Paul was able to get away.

"As soon as that happened, though, new orders came through. Guards were assigned to the Americans around the clock and followed them everywhere. As soon as transportation could be arranged they were transferred to the capital."

He cleared his throat. "Sorry. A little tired."

"Rand, you don't have to finish this now. Why don't you get to bed? We can talk tomorrow."

"No," he said resolutely. "I just need to pace myself."

"Take your time, then. I'll wait."

He resumed the description of events. "Our friends came to be housed in a central jail, apart from the general population of accused thieves and rapists, thank goodness, but still under conditions that were pretty severe.

"They were given very little to eat or drink."

"Were they together?"

"According to Matthias' friend Akos, who made inquiries, we believe they were segregated for a time, the women from the men. Toward the end, though, they occupied the same cell."

Once in the city, they had undergone brutal cavity searches, Rand divulged, and the women were hurt. "Akos' contact, a friend, was ashamed of what transpired, but the abuse occurred while he was away.

"He wouldn't provide details, but he assured Akos that those responsible had been punished."

Small comfort.

"The friend also claimed to have argued against execution, and Matthias has corroboration of that claim. Unfortunately, Bacenko wouldn't back down. He assigned a squad of his most trusted sycophants to carry out his orders. They have killed at least five prisoners a day for over two weeks."

I had given up watching the news, avoiding just such information, but listening to Rand I took solace from the fact that our friends had had an advocate trying to save them, no matter his impotence. I couldn't imagine the terror they would've felt in the hours leading up to their deaths. "Have you spoken with their families?" I asked finally.

"I have."

"How much have you told them?"

"All I know," he confessed softly. "They've been nothing but kind."

A brief silence ensued, and Rand changed the subject entirely. "Have the media been bothering you?"

"They're here, but they aren't able to get at me. They have to stay off private property, and since I haven't been leaving the condo all that much, they haven't really had a chance.

"I don't have anything to say to them, Rand."

The families yes; the voyeurs, no.

Reporters were about ratings and the sale of advertising time, which by definition meant they lived and died by the bottom line. I wouldn't trivialize our friends' misfortune and suffering by turning them into profits for communications conglomerates.

"We're frustrating them," Rand told me. "The hospital in Vienna didn't give an inch. UMC's put a tight lid on things at this end as well.

"Like you, I think there's nothing about this tragedy that makes me want to see my reaction to it trumpeted in a headline."

His voice was no more than a whisper, and I finally had to say, "Rand, you need to rest."

"I do," he said. "But my busy mind resists."

So did mine. Especially now. There was something about the tone and the content of my conversation with Rand that was comforting, and I didn't want it to end.

"Would you mind if I called you again?" Rand asked. "No one else seems to quite understand."

The old Parry would've had a wiseacre come-back. Something like, "Gee. That makes me feel special." But I was a changed Parry, someone who had figured out that there were things in the world that defied a comic spin, and the senseless, violent death of good people was one.

"Sure," I answered. "Call.

"This number," I added. "Not my landline." Which I'd taken to ignoring. "This time of evening is good."

"Thanks," he said before hanging up. "I will call."

"Goodnight."

"Goodnight."

Two days later, Jake returned to his regular life.

He drove to his Crystal City office from Falls Church and worked a full eight hours that first day. That evening, he battled traffic stalled on I-66 West and the Toll Road after that, just to have dinner at my place.

He repeated the process several nights in a row.

At the table, he sat; he ate; and he refused to let Mom or me clean up when we were done. "It's the only exercise I get now," he claimed. "Let me do this."

Every night, Mom followed him into the kitchen on the pretext of drying the dishes, but while she had him trapped, boldly asked him a hundred questions about his Texas childhood, his family, and his plans for the future. I overheard it all.

For his part, Jake seemed eager to respond.

"A little heavy, Mom," I warned her one night after he left.

"What do you mean?"

"I MEAN the man's not a moron. He can see you're trying to marry me off."

"And you think he has a problem with that?" she asked. *"Mon Dieu, Parise. Ouvre tes yeux."* Open your eyes.

In the bathroom that same night, after Jake had left, I swathed my cast in dry cleaning bags, showered, and dried hair long overdue for a cut. In the privacy of my room, I smoothed on flowery and fresh body lotion, turned back the sheets, then went out to the living room to indulge Mom a final fifteen minutes with Larry King while I steeped a pot of decaf Earl Grey. When the program was over, she carried the tea to my room on a tray and set it by my bed. "You're turning in awfully early," she commented.

"It's that time of year," I explained. "The cold and dark make me want to hibernate."

"That wouldn't happen if you didn't keep it as cold as a tomb in here."

We'd had words on that topic when she first arrived, and I'd boosted the thermostat to sixty-eight. I limped over and reset the thing to seventy. "Any higher and I won't be able to breathe."

She grinned and left believing she'd won.

I switched on the television and created a wall of white noise, waiting for my cell to vibrate.

In that in-between time, I had to admit to myself that I couldn't go on seeing Jake. Couldn't allow him to court me, with my mother's obvious encouragement, the whole time being drawn to another man. A complicated and brilliant man whose attention and need to control, not that long ago, I would've deemed romantic anathema.

In the quiet of late night, Rand was opening his heart to me, describing the loneliness of his childhood and the ways in which his parents had pressed and pushed and demanded, all his life, that he live up to their idea of success.

There had been expensive private schools and tutors and music lessons—piano, violin, and cello—but only the most superficial signs of affection. A pat of congratulations for perfect report cards. Obligatory forehead kisses on birthdays. "I remember an awkward hug once from my father when I was less than successful at something."

"What was that?"

"Something sports-related I think. I put it quickly out of my mind."

Rand's confidences strayed to the subject of college life, and the times at Harvard when he'd only occasionally made a friend. He discussed his decision, at twenty, to go down the path toward a medical career, saying, "It was the place I finally fit in."

The secrets he shared, while they built on the pain that Rand and I had already shared, also allowed me to know a man who for too long had only been a caricature to me. They gave me insights into a complex and troubled soul. Better, they allowed me to see how our time in Europe had fundamentally changed this man, had tempered the intellect and striving to reveal a searcher.

To our supreme relief, the execution of Americans finally stopped, and officials from the U.S. side and from General Bacenko's began to meet in undisclosed locations to negotiate. There was still no word of what had become of our friends' bodies, but Rand, his parents, and their influential friends were tenacious in exerting pressure on the State Department behind the scenes.

We all prayed for the horrific episode to be fully resolved.

On a Friday afternoon in December the telephone rang, and it was Rand. "They're coming home," was all he said.

No hello.

No, "Are you sitting down?"

Just the blunt honesty reasserting itself as his trademark.

"When?" I asked.

"Next Wednesday." He paused before asking, "Do you want to come out to Andrews to meet them?"

"Nothing could keep me away." In the next breath I asked, "How did it happen?"

"A high level military officer defected. He 'borrowed' some kind of truck, had subordinates load it with as many caskets as it could carry, then just drove away.

"Our five were among those bodies he rescued."

"Pretty brave," I commented.

"Quite. He ran a border crossing and was shot at in the bargain."

"Do you think it was Akos' informant friend from the prison?" The one who'd been sympathetic.

"I doubt it. I'm told this fellow was a close friend of President Novak's son, a contemporary of his at the national military academy. He had nothing to do with prisons.

"He issued a statement saying he had done this to prove allegiance to the old regime."

One man, alone and determined, had succeeded where the U.S. diplomatic corps had not. "I'd say he put the professionals to shame."

"I'd say you're right," Rand agreed.

"Do we know anything about him?"

"Nothing except what I've just told you. After dropping the truck at the American Embassy in Vienna, he seems to have disappeared."

"Smart. He's a marked man."

Days later, I rode the northern half of the Beltway toward Andrews Air Force Base in the same white limo Rand had rented weeks before, my eyes filled with tears at the silly, sweet gesture. Jake, Paul, and Rand were somber as well.

The four of us walked out on the tarmac just after three o'clock, watching as a military transport touched down.

No press.

No military.

No crowds.

Not even our colleagues' immediate families were there. They waited in a hanger for an even more private homecoming, having graciously allowed us a moment with our fallen friends.

The belly of the plane opened, and the five coffins slowly emerged. We approached them, and Rand offered a surprisingly eloquent prayer. When he finished, Jake and I spontaneously sang the last verse of the Ortega song that had come to represent our foreign tragedy, Rand and Paul joining in the simple lyric a little off-key.

Five separate funerals followed, and we attended them all. We heard the kind words of pastors and friends and the people who'd loved Ted. Rich. Linda, Beverly, and Ken. At the families' request, Rand walked to the front of five different congregations and looked out into crowds of tear-streaked faces. He honored those who'd been taken from life in the moment of their greatest charity, and he reminded us that the word was Scripture's synonym for love.

He talked humorously of Linda, his right hand for the last seven years, and more formally of Bev, a respected colleague. He spoke words of admiration for Ken, a man for whom he had great affection, and after admitting he hadn't known Rich or Ted all that well, read the words of condolence sent from the community at St. Maria's, a place where their work and their sacrifice would be long remembered.

Next to our escape, it was the longest week of my life.

My mother left for home on the morning of December16th, whispering as Jake circled around to the back of the car for her bags, "Don't let this one get away."

"Right."

"You're still coming home for Christmas, aren't you?"

"One week from today," I verified. "In time for the thirtieth anniversary of my birth."

"Why don't you bring Jake?" she suggested. "I'm sure everyone will want to meet him."

Great, I thought. She'd been talking.

"I'll see," I answered. But inside, I knew it would never happen. I had plans for Jake, plans that involved only a heart-to-heart. That night I prepared dishes I knew, from my mother's constant grilling, were among his favorites. Pot roast. Spinach salad. A delicious caramel mousse.

When we finished eating, I insisted on cleaning up. "I can do that now. It's time I get back into the swing."

"How about I change the bulbs in the guest bathroom, then. I noticed a couple of the halogens are out."

I hesitated, then said, "Sure."

One last favor for us both.

When the last dish was dried and put away; when Jake had strolled back to the kitchen with the burned out bulbs, carefully wrapping them in news-paper to keep them from shattering in the trash, I started the tough conversation. "Here. Why don't you sit down here so we can talk."

"Sure. Shoot."

I was clumsy expressing myself. A little more tentative than I would've liked. Still, I got the message across. Circumstance had drawn me to Jake. The grueling days; the cold nights; the days spent worrying almost every minute of what might become of us. While I was grateful to have had him as a protector and friend, gratitude wasn't the surest foundation for love.

"I see that now. I think you might see it, too."

He was disappointed, but it was true. "I've had the feeling that something had changed, but your Mom seemed so encouraging. I thought maybe she knew something I didn't."

"Forgive her for that. She's just the tiniest bit panicked that her baby's turning thirty in a week and has no prospects."

"She doesn't have to worry," he said. "You'll be fine."

"And you?"

He looked at me wearing a bittersweet smile. "I'll be fine, too."

"No broken heart?"

He grinned. "Only if it'll make you feel better."

We both smiled at his largesse.

Rising to go, Jake had a question, succinctly expressed. "Is it Rand?"

Was it?

"Honestly, I don't know."

Upon reconsideration, I tendered a more honest opinion. "It might be."

We stood at the door, silent together for several moments. We shared a sweet and soft kiss. Then a hug.

As dignified as always, Jake Spangler put on his coat, opened the door, and walked out of my life.

I only felt relief at seeing him go.

THIRTY

I hadn't always been honest with myself on the subject of men. While objectively I did like, admire, and enjoy being around them, likewise working with, and learning from them, I often thought they weren't worth the trouble.

Correction: that dating wasn't worth the trouble.

Men came with expectations and complications and huge commitments of time, and with my record for not always letting relationships evolve, I'd pretty much given up on the idea of ever finding a man with whom I could build a life.

The short path to my epiphany had begun three weeks before Christmas a year ago.

Alana and Trent had decided they were going to host a holiday party (no one called them Christmas parties anymore; who would come?), and although I'd begged off attending when I called to R.S.V.P, Alana phoned me a few days before the big event to urge me to come.

"You have to be there," she whimpered pathetically on the phone. "Trent's boring accountant friends are going to be here, and I'm worried they're going to ruin the night."

"Poor you."

"Boo-hoo," she said, feigning upset.

"I'm sure there'll be people in your vastly more interesting medical crowd who can dilute the monotony of tax talk," I reassured her. "You Duke folks don't lack for fascinating misadventures."

That drew a laugh. A few of her colleagues WERE certifiable.

"Look, you know I'd love to come," I exaggerated. "But ten hours of driving just to hold your hand at a party that'll last two, three hours tops? Not gonna happen, schweetie.

"I don't even like parties."

I didn't.

Along with drudgery of travel, they were the most overrated of human activities. All the work involved dressing up. Holding a drink in one hand and a plate of high-calorie, low-flavor appetizers in the other. Trying to think of something scintillating to say, ask, or observe as you struggled to keep a conversation from falling flat.

Give me a sledding or skating party; a few days at the beach boogie boarding. I'd even drive a distance to attend a lecture by someone who had something new and worthwhile to say.

But a party? Not even.

"Come on," Alana droned on. "There'll be a bunch of unmarried guys . . ."

"Are they gay?" At least then I could count on a few laughs.

"No, they're not gay."

Darn.

"Well, maybe a couple of them are."

Okay then; there was hope.

"It's my first time having so many people over . . ." she lied.

"I was in school with you, remember?" Her apartment had been a mob scene almost every weekend. Party central.

"It's my first real party here," she corrected. "For grown ups. Come on, Parry. I'm desperate for help."

And therein lay the crux of the matter.

While enhancing MY social life might have been the stated benefit having me drive the 250 miles to Raleigh, the real point of Alana's invitation was getting me to help her cook. The woman was helpless in her designer kitchen.

"All right," I capitulated. "I'll come if I can get Friday off; I don't do weekend traffic on I-95. If I can't get away, you're on your own."

"You can talk Geoff into it. LOVE YOU!!" she shrieked. Alana was never happier than when she got her way.

I gave my boss every out the next day at work, but the traitor only shrugged, "The schedule's light. Yeah. Go ahead."

I left home the next morning at six—any later and I'd have been caught in the Toll Road mess— and got to suburban Raleigh by eleven-thirty. Alana was at home and frantic. She hadn't cleaned. She hadn't cooked. She didn't have the slightest idea what she was going to wear.

I sat her down, told her to suck it up, and together the two of us spent that day and the next getting ready for the fifty people who'd promised to show. She'd invited eighty; I guess things could've been worse.

Fortunately, I carried my recipe book in my head and was good at improvisation. While Alana decorated and cleaned, something at which she was truly expert, and Trent picked out music for the night, something at which he excelled, I laid out a spread people still talked about a year after the fact.

There was something for everyone: vegetarian, carnivore, and *gourmand*. I made puff pastry empanadas and miniature tortierre, the Acadian meat pie that was a standard at my family's Christmas celebrations. I whipped up a chicken and mushroom pate´ for the health conscious; fruit, vegetables, and bruscetta for the nibblers. I baked cheesecake, hummingbird cake, and flan. I simmered a huge pot of peppery cauliflower soup that we served in espresso cups—a last minute inspiration—and a dozen people later demanded I hand over the recipe, or they'd make it so I couldn't drive home.

At my urging, Alana blew her budget and hired a trio of Meredith College seniors to serve. That way, while we canoodled with her friends, there was always someone pouring drinks or refilling trays of food. "I didn't come here to work all day and all night," was the way I'd made the suggestion. "Get us help."

After finishing the party preparations, Alana and I went to our separate corners to affect our transformations. I decided to wear deep burgundy: a formfitting cashmere sweater; nicely tailored slacks; an uncomfortable pair of high-heeled boots in matching calfskin that I'd purchased on a whim. A black leather belt cinched my waist to nothing and emphasized the twin gifts God had bestowed.

After checking myself out in the bathroom mirror, I turned up the volume on my make-up. Usually, I went low key, but that night I opted for the works. Thick mascara. Eye shadow to set off my indecisively blue-grey eyes. Delicate cream blush and lipstick that was a striking blood red. "There," I said, adding shine enhancer to my hair. Success. I barely recognized the wanna-be Cosmo girl who stared back at me in the mirror.

Pleased with my work, I lifted a glass and instructed my reflection: "Par-tay."

After going through a few bowls of Sangria and lots of designer beer, Trent's friends turned out to be a pretty fun-loving bunch. Ditto the Duke crowd. I found myself talking to a colorful cross-section of them and wondering if maybe it was time for me to move back to the Tar Heel state.

What was holding me back? There had to be a practice somewhere in the general Winston-Raleigh-Wilmington region that needed a p.a. with my skills. Maybe it was time I look around.

The party continued with no sign of abating, so around nine, I stole into the kitchen to check the food inventory. "Girls. Girls. Get some more of this finger food out there!" I prompted. "We do not want leftovers."

They hustled buns (theirs) back out to the crowd.

I was trying to open a jar of olives when a man's voice startled me, saying, "Here, let me help."

I turned, holding a butter knife, and said, "I was just gonna give it a slam."

"This might be safer," the newcomer insisted. He took the jar, popped it open, and handed it back to me.

"Thanks . . .?"

"Tom. Tom Torgerson."

"Thanks Tom Torgerson. Nice alliteration by the way."

"I'll compliment my parents the next time I see them. And you're . . .?"

"Parry St. Amand."

We shook hands.

"Perry? I thought that was a man's name."

"Well, this IS the south.," I explained. "Where women with traditionally male names abound. But I'm P-A," I emphasized. "Not P-E. Parry's short for Parise."

"Well, Parry-with-an-a, I've seen you making your way around the room tonight, and this is the first chance I've had to catch up with you. Would you like to dance?"

Trent had moved aside the furniture in their expansive family room and dimmed the lights. Four or five couples were slow dancing to oldies, at the moment an old Clapton song in which the singer was telling his significant other that she looked wonderful tonight.

"I think they're playing your song . . ." Tom said, oozing charm.

In spite of the corny reference, he seemed like a decent guy. Attractive. Polite.

Breathing.

"Why not?" I asked.

He guided me to the island of gleaming hardwood and recessed lighting where gas fireplace logs provided twenty-first century ambience. He held me as a practiced dancer might, right hand to my waist, left hand upraised, and led me smoothly around the floor in a subtly executed waltz.

His breath was warm against the side of my neck as threw out the occasional question.

How did I know Trent and Alana?"

Did I live in the area?

Did I realize I had the most refreshingly wholesome look of any girl in the room?

Wholesome, I wanted to shout. With all the work I'd put in trying for sexy? I guess I was to the manner born.

Tom and I spent the rest of the night dancing. Talking. Sampling the food every now and again, with Tom declaring after each indulgence, "Man. This is the best party food I've ever tasted."

I couldn't decide if he was flattering me or really had no clue I'd made it all.

Either way, I guess, I won.

After the last of the stragglers went home, we spent a long time saying goodnight out by his car, agreeing to meet the next day in Durham for an early lunch.

I was packed and set to head north on I-85, the more lightly traveled road to Petersburg, VA, and the juncture there with I-95. He arrived looking scrubbed and smelling of something deliciously clean.

We lingered over Shoney's omelets until I could no longer delay the inevitable. "Traffic will be wicked by time I get back to D.C." It was that way every Sunday night.

At my car, he opened the driver's side door and as I turned to say goodbye, inquired with genuine shyness, "Are you going to give a guy your home phone number?"

I ignored the conventional wisdom against long distance romances and gave it up. What did I have to lose? Here was a man bypassing the modern impersonality of e-mail and texting, actually eager to hear the sound of my voice!

In short order, he did.

And I heard his.

We burned up the lines (or satellite beams) between D.C. and Raleigh, talking at night after work. In the morning. We even chatted in our cars going to and from our jobs, hands free, a practice I to that point deplored. Slowly we drifted into texting each other mid-day. Between my cases and his meetings with clients, we spirited quick bursts of abbreviated words. We couldn't know enough about each other and quick finger-tapping exchanges accelerated the process.

Tom came up to D.C. the weekend after we met, and I offered him my guest room. He was fine with that and especially impressed by my collection of three hundred or so favorite books, a dozen of them first editions.

We ate dinner on the Alexandria waterfront that night and spent Saturday exploring the Mall. We started at the Colder mobile in the East Wing of the National Gallery and after ending our visit at the gift shop, strolled toward the windswept architecture of the new Native American Museum. Indulging Tom's romance with flight, we spent late afternoon at Air and Space.

The holidays arrived, and we didn't see much of one another. I was on call Christmas, and he had longstanding plans to stand up for an old college friend at a New Year's eve wedding in Florida. Early January was filled with commitments for us both.

Missing me, he paid for my flight to Raleigh the weekend of Super Bowl Sunday, and we had a wonderful time with Alana and Trent. After the game ended with the Giants eking it out against the Pats, Tom got ready to drive me to RDU.

His cell rang and at the other end was a-none-too-happy boss. Trouble with a client in Atlanta, I heard him yelling over the phone. Tom needed to get himself to a computer and take part in a teleconference due to begin any minute now.

"I'll take her to the airport," Alana offered as Tom hung up. "It's no big deal."

"I'll make it up to you," he promised as he kissed me goodbye running out the door. "I had a really great time."

I called as the door closed, "So did I!"

The airport seemed dead as we approached it. I had a forty-minute wait, so I suggested to Alana she come in. "We can catch up."

I'd been too busy to share many details of this new relationship with her, and I could tell she saw this as her chance to pump me for information. "Sure," she said. "Why not?"

We parked, walked inside, and after I got my boarding pass, we popped into an airport lounge where I ordered a shot of Amaretto in my coffee to calm pre-flight jitters, and Alana opted for ginger ale. As we were being served our drinks, a nearby loudspeaker announced a half hour delay in my flight. "Now we have plenty of time," she said. "Spill."

I filled her in on those things I considered public domain and kept the more intimate aspects of my blossoming relationship to myself. It would've been childish to say more.

When I felt like I'd hit all the highlights, I leaned back to let her talk. Or rather, to interrogate.

"You know," she said, popping a handful of tiny pretzels into her mouth, "it's really surprised me, you and Tom."

"Really? He's a great guy."

"No argument there." She chewed and then continued, "I don't know Tom all that well, but Trent says he's well respected. Always does great work. Clients love him.

"Probably because he'll talk to them on Sunday nights."

She grinned. "Couldn't hurt."

"How did Trent meet Tom?

"They coach in a basketball league for under-privileged kids downtown together. And he goes to our church."

Tom hadn't mentioned the basketball, but he didn't strike me as the kind who was into self-promotion.

"Still," Alana ruminated "I just remember you telling me how you felt about divorce."

"Divorce?"

"Yeah. We've discussed it a few times."

I remembered.

"You remember that guy Ken I dated just before I met Trent. He was divorced, and we talked about how complicated things got sometimes, seeing someone with an -ex. Marrying him. You told me you could understand people making mistakes and all, but that growing up Catholic, you believed what you'd been taught about the sanctity of marriage."

"I do."

"You said you didn't think you could marry someone who'd taken vows with someone else, out of respect for the permanence of the bond."

"And for my eternal soul," I quipped.

Alana was right. I had very strong ideas about marriage. They were an integral part of who I was. "So why are you bringing up divorce and Tom in the same conversation?" I asked.

She picked through the pretzels in the bowl looking for peanuts and answered matter-of-factly. "You know why. Tom's divorced."

When she looked up, Alana knew instantly that something was wrong. "He hasn't told you." Spoken as a statement, not a question.

"No." He hadn't said a word; and it was that, more than anything, that took my breath away.

Alana reached for my hand. "Hey. I'm sorry. I thought with all the talking you guys have done, he'd have mentioned it."

"He hasn't," I managed, disillusionment sliding over me like a late afternoon shadow. I was drained of any warmth I'd earlier felt for Tom.

"Look, Parry. It doesn't matter. Times have changed. Things have changed."

"How long?" I asked, practically choking on the question. "How long was he married?"

"I don't know exactly. Maybe three years. I think it was just after he passed the last of his CPA exams."

"Any children?"

"One. A girl."

I felt like I'd been sucker punched a second time.

Tom hadn't thought to mention a marriage OR a child?

I pushed my coffee away and felt sick at the completely unexpected news.

This wasn't Parry being judgmental or self-righteous. It was me being who I was, someone who believed with all that was in her, that marriage should last a lifetime. That her marriage would last a lifetime.

That was the standard that had been breathed into me by my parents, my church, and my God for twenty-nine years; and having seen the emotional havoc created in society by a turning away from it, I quietly and sincerely embraced it.

Alana apologized. At the table. Walking me to the security gate. As she hugged me goodbye. "I really thought you knew."

"It's okay," I assured her. "It would've come out."

"He's a great guy . . ." she said again on Tom's behalf.

"He is," I agreed. "He's just not the great guy for me."

"Parry, please don't rush to judgment."

Not that old tune.

"It's not about judgment," I told her earnestly. "Trust me there are times I wish I didn't think the way I do; it would make life easier.

"There are just some compromises I can't make. And this is one."

Turning to leave, thinking sadly of Tom and what we might have been to one another, that was the first time in my life I wondered if there would ever be anyone for me.

It wouldn't be the last.

THIRTY-ONE

I had a quiet and beautiful Christmas in Maine and, quite honestly, the best birthday I'd had in years. My three brothers, their wives, and all their children invaded Mom and Dad's house, and together we spent our time together stepping over clothes and toys and handheld video games, our mother in a state of near-apoplexy, trying to clean up.

One especially cold and clear night, I snuck up to the lake with my old high school best friend, Trish, home for the holidays from California. Wrapped in old blankets and cozy in front of a blazing fire, we drank hot chocolate and discovered, delightedly, that twelve years of living thousands of miles apart hadn't broken our bond.

The week after New Year's, I went back into work.

In my first few weeks on the job, I put in short days and didn't take call. I negotiated a new agreement with the practice, the partners making a few concessions in terms of salary, benefits, and responsibilities. I agreed to take on more of the teaching duties associated with the interns and residents.

"You drive a hard bargain," Geoff told me when we finally shook on things.

"So they tell me."

"You want us to put this in writing right away?"

"How about we try it out, month to month for a while?"

I could tell from the grin on his face, he thought he'd gotten a deal. Maybe he had. But I'd won the freedom to look around.

With fewer weekends of call and more breathing space on weeknights, I started attending Mass at a Redemptorist parish a few miles from where I lived. A close friend had described the men of that order as, "Jesuits with a heart," and so, I decided one Sunday to put her opinion to the test.

I started by sitting quietly at Mass, listening more with my spirit than my head. I sang. I prayed. I took communion, more aware than ever of my undeserving heart.

I asked for clarity in making better decisions for my life. Taking a more purposeful direction. In February, when the pastor issued a challenge to the congregation at large, I joined a group of parish adults committed to living, not just playing, at Christian community.

To my relief, the people I met on my first evening weren't fanatics or holy rollers. They were a hodgepodge of young professionals and experienced parents and singles who, like me, had known a few of life's bumps and bruises, and who considered themselves flawed and imperfect.

At that first meeting, several in the group refreshingly proclaimed themselves hypocrites. "We're people who espouse one thing and live another," a man named Ray Keegan acknowledged. "The very reason every one of us needs redemption."

The pastor, Father Bill, reinforced this theme on a Sunday morning in early March. "It is impossible for human beings not to fall short of the Christian ideal," he said. "We have good intentions and then stray. We struggle against our shortcomings, and yet fall into them again and again. We yearn for the full forgiveness that only a life in Christ can provide and yet do all we can to avoid the requirements of that life.

"What sets us apart as believers," he continued, "is that we never give up on the existence of the Ideal made real in God and in the Son sent to redeem, guide, and teach us.

"We are a weary band of sinners, but we are His weary band of sinners." He leaned in close to the microphone, speaking directly to me. "Redemption is the only true antidote to our gross imperfections and perpetual waywardness."

Father Bill's common-sense approach and words stayed with me. The latter echoed in my heart and helped me get beyond all that had happened. To finally and freely move on.

In nightly conversations with Rand, I kept him apprised of what was happening at St. Al's, and more important, what was happening to me at St. Al's.

I shared but didn't lecture.

It wasn't God's way with me, and I wouldn't let it be mine with Rand.

He asked questions, despite my reticence sharing, and made thoughtful comments. He didn't dismiss, out of hand, the value of a life spent leaning into God.

"My parents were Catholic at one time," he told me "But they haven't practiced in decades. They didn't raise me to believe."

"But do you?"

"Do I . . ."

"Believe?"

"I didn't before."

"And now?"

"Now, I think I'm getting a new perspective."

It was a start.

Rand came back to work two weeks after I did, and in addition to talking at night, the two of us started meeting for lunch some days, almost always his treat. He was still pale and still dealing with problems created by the rigors of our escape, but he felt as though he was on the way to recovery. "I have to pace myself," he confided. "Not something I've ever had a lot of success doing."

"Maybe you need help," I told him.

He smiled and agreed, "Maybe I do."

Officially, we left it at that, but we started spending more free time together. An occa-sional evening movie. A professional meeting at

Georgetown or GW. Sometimes we ventured into the Virginia countryside on weekends just to eat lunch.

He called me on a Saturday afternoon a couple of weeks before Easter, an unusual time of day for me to hear from him. "You okay?" I asked.

"I guess. I'm just a little at loose ends."

He had planned to move back into his apartment that day. "Are you alone?"

"I am."

"Would you prefer not to be?"

"Are you psychic?"

"Not really. I had the same kind of restlessness for a while after Mom left. It'll pass."

"Hmmm."

"Would you like to come over for dinner?"

I'd never once invited him over, but a meal seemed an easy first step. "I've had lots of time to indulge my penchant for cooking the last couple of months. You won't be sorry."

"I'll come," he said. "But I have a favor to ask."

"In return for your delightful companionship?"

He laughed. "I guess I did sound a little pompous."

"Just a smidge."

"Sorry."

"Never mind," I said charitably. "What's the favor?"

He hesitated before asking, "Do you think I could go to church with you tomorrow?"

"That isn't a favor," I told him honestly. "It would be a privilege."

"Are you sure? Because if it's an imposition, we could make it another time."

I responded tenderly and truthfully, "Randall Atticus Szabo, you are not going to get out of it that easily."

And so it began.

We went to St. Al's together the next morning, and I introduced him. "Rand Szabo, this is Father William Dennis. Bill, Dr. Randall Szabo."

Rand was aware, through our conversations, that Bill was both a scholar and a man of the cloth. He had taught for over twenty years at the Academia Alfonso in Rome and had published a small library of serious theological tomes. He still taught courses from time to time at Catholic in northeast D.C.

I'd confided to Rand that it was Bill's spirit, as much as his mind, that drew people to him as a priest. He spoke truth and made God's love, His forgiveness, and His will accessible in ways that less gifted clergy could not.

For his part, Bill knew Rand was searching and had promised that when they met, he would not take undue advantage. "I won't have to. It'll all be God's doing."

So it was that through the spring and summer, Rand kept coming to Mass with me on Sundays and started attending my weekly home group as well. He made plans with Bill, regularly meeting for coffee, and he began to realize through these new experiences that intellect and faith didn't have to be mutually exclusive.

In those same months, Rand and I discovered love, or more realistically, gave in to it.

He shyly kissed me. He held me. He accepted the boundaries I put on us both, insisting we explore one another in ways other than the physical, and understood me when I said (and really meant it), "Premature intimacy muddies the waters."

I took an occasional late night phone call from Rand on the subject of faith. "How do you know?" he asked. "How are you always so sure?"

"I'm not."

"You seem to be."

"I think it's just that I don't freak out at the first inkling of doubt."

"How do you handle it ?"

"I look around. At the order in the world. At the miracle of birth. At the very smallest kindnesses I've been the beneficiary of. And I surrender to belief."

"And the evil? The sickness? The really, really bad luck."

"None of it endures, Rand. The equilibrium in the world leans toward goodness. And that is God."

I knew it to my core and slowly I could see Rand coming to a similar understanding, if not yet to belief.

"Is it hard, handing over that control?" A reasonable and expected question from a surgeon.

"It really isn't. Not for me anyway. I figure if I put God in the center of my universe, instead of me, the pressure's off."

He laughed and said, 'St. Amand. There's really no one else like you."

Over the next several weeks, nearly non-stop, the two of us talked career, family, and the plans we had for the rest of our lives—with increasing specificity. We talked about Matthias and St. Maria's and the ways in which we could help them, for now at a distance, expressing disappointment that U.S. and European embargos were adding to our friends' woes, both to ourselves and to our Congressional delegation. We prayed hard for our friends' safety as rumors of an imminent contra-*coup* began to emerge.

Dominik Novak, son of the deceased prime minister, had moved from London to Vienna, and he was forming a provisional government there. He was promising to come home to hold elections as soon as the public will made itself known.

There was a picture of Novak in the Sunday Washington Post, in early June, and it was Rand who pointed out a familiar face in the background. "Isn't that Adam?" he asked.

I studied the photograph closely. "It could be."

He looked at me thoughtfully. "Maybe it wasn't an accident he knew so much about the particulars of the bridge. Or that somehow we were able to make it across undiscovered.

"Maybe he had plans to use it himself, so he reassigned some work."

I read the accompanying article and was smiling by the time I reached the end of it. "He didn't use the bridge," I told Rand. "But I'll bet any money it was his back-up."

"What do you mean? How did he get out?"

"It says here he commandeered a troop transport . . ."

Rand's head spun, and he finished the sentence for me, ". . . and he drove our friends out!"

He had waited until Judit recovered. Bided his time. Then he had done for us what our own government hadn't been able to do. "It's official," Rand declared. "Any debt he might've felt toward us for delivering his baby is officially and permanently settled."

"And how. It says here he named his son Randall Jacob." A lasting memorial to his gratitude and his regard for us.

Letters from *Soeur St. Helena* held equally wonderful news, coming to us through the mother house in Montreal. The missives spoke of the children's steady performance despite the political upheaval, and of their work expanding the orphanage garden that summer. "The teenagers are taking on the extra burden because they want to feed those in the community who have less."

Another lesson in charity from an unlikely source.

Inspired we found additional ways to help. We spoke to friends and members of our home group and urged them to contribute to a fund. We collected used children's clothing and shoes, funneling both the goods and money to St. Maria's through the

Canadian foundation still headed by *Monsieur* Miroslav.

By late summer, my leg had fully recovered. Only an occasional ache on rainy days reminded me of our still-haunting loss. I saw Rand on the job every day, sometimes by accident, sometimes by design, and we spent evenings together at his place or mine.

Despite some silly backsliding—an argument here; a disagreement there; an occasional knock down-drag out when he relied more on his brilliance than his decency—it became obvious to both of us that the trajectory of our lives was beginning to track a single, conjoined course.

I was drawn to Rand's stamina, his brilliance, and his occasional unpredictability. I think he saw in me the kind of faith he envied as well as the kind of irreverence he could never bring himself to express. My weirdness let him laugh at his own. My quietly intense desire to do good and to be good, traits that might have been off-putting in anyone else, he found strangely appealing. Almost every day, I teased him about his demanding and unreasonable nature, and he held me unapologetically to the same standard of excellence he used evaluating everything and everyone, including himself.

I refused to go to work for him whenever he had the bad judgment to offer a job.

Over a rushed lunch one August afternoon, Rand confided that he was getting a lot of pressure from UMC administrators. "I still can't do a full day's surgery or carry the kind of patient load I used to.

"They want me to make the move upstairs."

"It's not the place for you."

I knew it.

He knew it.

"What am I going to do?"

Having reached the point in our relationship where I felt I could, I said simply, "You could pray."

The thought hadn't occurred to him, I could tell. He was a man accustomed to doing for himself. Achieving for himself. But he'd been going with me to home group for a while, and he'd seen a different way. He might be ready to implement this change — if I helped.

Instead of resisting, he asked, "What do I have to lose?"

Not a ringing endorsement of the approach, but it would do.

To his well-concealed mortification, we gave it a try right there at a small cafeteria table. Quietly; on my part at least, fervently. We said a few words. We prayed again on the phone before saying goodnight, which admittedly felt a little strange.

A week went by. Two. I was spotty, though sincere, in beseeching the heavens on Rand's behalf, my uneven devotion a recurring and regrettable life theme.

Rand grew a little more anxious dealing with the UMC administration, he disclosed, and a little bolder in his demands of God.

The weekend before Labor Day, he met me at church. We sat where we always did, about three quarters of the way toward the back. He was restless beside me, distracted and distracting from the opening hymn to the recessional.

"Do you have worms?" I asked on our way out. "You wiggled like a six year-old."

"Sorry," he said, and I could see he meant it.

"Is something wrong?"

"Not wrong exactly."

"What exactly?"

"I'm not sure I should say anything."

"Because?"

"Because I'm not sure how you'll react."

"Well that's progress," I deadpanned.

"Meaning?"

"Meaning I thought we were at a place that we could say what was on our minds. Haven't you learned yet that even if you hold bad things in as tightly as you can, they have a way of working their way out."

We'd had a couple of episodes of that kind, and it hadn't been pretty.

He looked down at his feet. He raised his gaze to meet mine.

"I know you like your job," he stated cryptically.

"What does my job have to do with your restlessness?"

He hesitated. "I got a call last night."

"And?"

"It was a job offer. A very tempting job offer."

"Great."

"A former professor of mine recommended me for a faculty appointment; a joint appointment, actually, teaching orthopedics and biomedical engineering."

"Are you kidding? That's an absolutely perfect fit." I hugged him and said, "I guess our prayers helped."

"It would seem," he grudgingly admitted.

"So what's wrong?"

"The timing's a bit off . . ."

"Well, it is a little late to be hiring for this academic year; classes are starting soon, aren't they?"

"They are. I guess funding hit a few snags, which is why the offer wasn't made sooner."

"So. Where's the job?"

"Well . . ."

"It's not in Boston is it?" While I'd lived there for four years, frankly, I hadn't liked it all that much.

"No, not Boston. But the job would involve a move."

"Okay."

He peered into my eyes. "WE would have to move."

I read between the lines.

I had to.

The words weren't all I'd ever hoped for in a proposal, but given Rand's social ineptitude, they weren't all that bad. "I might be persuaded," I hinted.

"I want this to be our decision," Rand said, trying to sound like a true modern man. "I want your input . . ."

"All right then, for the record, there are places I won't go. The Deep South, for example. And California."

He had a worried look on his face as he asked, "What do you consider the 'Deep South'?"

"Florida. Texas. Louisiana. The heat and humidity there would kill me."

He relaxed a little and smiled. He pulled me close. "I want you to tell me how you really feel about this, Parise St. Amand, and don't hold back."

"Do I ever?"

"Point taken. So you'll tell me if this is a deal breaker?"

"Cross my heart and hope to die."

Bad choice of words.

"I'll tell you."

He cleared his throat and looked me in the eye. "Parise Marie St. Amand. How would you feel about a life in Winston-Salem, North Carolina?"

I was stunned. He could see it. I saw him want to take back those last few words.

"No. No," I said, trying to clear up the misunderstanding. I could see he had no idea what my reaction meant.

"I'm sorry . . ." he apologized.

"Don't be sorry, you crazy man. Ask me again."

Now he was completely flummoxed, convinced this was a trap.

I put my hands on his shoulders and stared him down. "Ask . . . me . . . again," I ordered firmly.

For once in his life he obeyed and swallowed hard. "Parry, how would you feel about a life with me in Winston-Salem, North Carolina?"

Rand Szabo's question would forever resonate in my heart.